"A suspense   with gal-
lantly passio   the deadly
machinations of a traitor. A promising debut from a talented new author."

—*New York Times* bestselling author Nicole Jordan

"A riveting read. Samantha Saxon writes a marvelously poignant story full of whimsy and charm. Once you start reading, you won't be able to put it down."

—*New York Times* bestselling author Karen Hawkins

"A riveting must-read, brimming with vibrant characters. Saxon's talent is amazing!"

—*New York Times* bestselling author Virginia Henley

Berkley Sensation books by Samantha Saxon

THE LADY LIES
THE LADY KILLER

The
Lady Killer

Samantha Saxon

B

BERKLEY SENSATION, NEW YORK

THE BERKLEY PUBLISHING GROUP
Published by the Penguin Group
Penguin Group (USA) Inc.
375 Hudson Street, New York, New York 10014, USA
Penguin Group (Canada), 90 Eglinton Avenue East, Suite 700, Toronto, Ontario M4P 2Y3, Canada
(a division of Pearson Penguin Canada Inc.)
Penguin Books Ltd., 80 Strand, London WC2R 0RL, England
Penguin Group Ireland, 25 St. Stephen's Green, Dublin 2, Ireland (a division of Penguin Books Ltd.)
Penguin Group (Australia), 250 Camberwell Road, Camberwell, Victoria 3124, Australia
(a division of Pearson Australia Group Pty. Ltd.)
Penguin Books India Pvt. Ltd., 11 Community Centre, Panchsheel Park, New Delhi—110 017, India
Penguin Group (NZ), Cnr. Airborne and Rosedale Roads, Albany, Auckland 1310, New Zealand
(a division of Pearson New Zealand Ltd.)
Penguin Books (South Africa) (Pty.) Ltd., 24 Sturdee Avenue, Rosebank, Johannesburg 2196, South
Africa

Penguin Books Ltd., Registered Offices: 80 Strand, London WC2R 0RL, England

THE LADY KILLER

A Berkley Sensation Book / published by arrangement with the author

PRINTING HISTORY
Berkley Sensation edition / December 2005

ISBN: 0-425-20732-3

BERKLEY® SENSATION
Berkley Sensation Books are published by The Berkley Publishing Group,
a division of Penguin Group (USA) Inc.,
375 Hudson Street, New York, New York 10014.
BERKLEY SENSATION and the "B" design are trademarks belonging to Penguin Group (USA) Inc.

PRINTED IN THE UNITED STATES OF AMERICA

10 9 8 7 6 5 4 3 2 1

To my children,
Sierra and Tristan.
God gave you to me so that
I might glimpse His divinity.
I love you both so very much.

ACKNOWLEDGMENTS

My eternal gratitude to Professor Wood
for breathing life into Napoleon's Paris.

One

Nicole closed her eyes, but she could still see the image of General Capette sprawled across the mahogany desk with blood pouring from the ragged wound in the back of his head. She could still smell the gunpowder drifting through the luxurious fifth-floor suite she had just been given admittance to clean.

Her eyes snapped open as she turned toward the fearsome crack that splintered the gilded doors nearest the ornate brass locks. Nicole froze, astonished by the transformation of the amiable French soldiers who had searched her moments ago.

They entered the cavernous room with their pistols drawn, but it was not their weapons that made them lethal. It was the coiled muscles, the hard set of their features, and the cold that had settled in their eyes.

"What has happened here?" the lieutenant bellowed as

he ran toward her, the sound of his black polished boots bouncing off the carved panel walls.

Nicole opened her mouth to explain, but she had no words to describe the horrific scene she had just witnessed. Blood trickled onto the inlaid wooden floor and she dropped to her knees, scrubbing at the sticky liquid before it was absorbed into the tiny crevasses.

The tall man lifted her from shock with a firm grip on her upper arms. *"Mademoiselle!"*

Nicole jumped, startled into answering by his shouting.

"I . . . I was airing the general's room when a man . . ." She pointed to an elongated window and the second soldier rushed toward it, leaning out.

"There is a rope hanging from the roof," he reported to his superior.

Nicole felt a callused finger lifting her chin, and she was forced to look into the hard eyes of the young lieutenant.

"Describe this man," he said, the muscles in his jaw throbbing.

"Fair hair." A tear streamed down her face as she forced herself to continue. "Tall, handsome. He . . . He shot the general and climbed onto the balcony."

"Gaston." He glanced at the other man. "Search the roof. I'll take to the street. *Mademoiselle.*" His eyes darted back to her the instant that they were alone. "You must remain here until I return."

"No!" she protested, desperate to get out of the room. "Do not leave me here. What if—"

"Do not fear, *mademoiselle,*" the lieutenant said, patting her hand as if she were a child awoken by some gruesome dream. "This man will want to get away from the hotel as quickly as is possible."

He turned to go but Nicole grabbed his arm. "Please, don't leave me," she whispered, sounding terrified.

The lieutenant looked down and sighed with frustration, then propelled her out the damaged doors and toward the servants' staircase. They had descended two flights of stairs when they rounded a corner on the third floor and very nearly collided with an elderly butler holding a laden dinner tray.

The lieutenant scarcely stopped, leaving her with the bewildered servant and saying, "I must go if I am to capture the general's murderer."

But she knew he would never capture the assassin.

General Capette had been so reviled by the French themselves that Napoleon had assigned bodyguards to protect his most victorious commander. The objection to the general, it was commonly agreed, was the barbaric manner in which he had obtained those many victories.

There had even been rumors that the general had raped a chambermaid at the hotel, which undoubtedly was the reason Nicole had so easily obtained the position a mere eight days ago.

"General Capette has been murdered?" The old man stared at her blood-spattered apron in disbelief.

"Yes," Nicole nodded. "A man climbed from the roof onto the balcony."

"Are you injured?"

Nicole's chin began to quiver. "No." She was not injured, but she would never be the same.

The old man turned to escort her to the kitchens, but needing to be alone, she stopped him. "Your supper is becoming cold. I am unharmed, I assure you."

Nicole could sense the butler's apprehension so she descended the stairs before he could protest further. She continued her brisk pace until a mixture of aromas wafted up the stairwell from the direction of the noisy kitchen.

Slowing, she stepped onto the landing and cautiously pushed the door inward. The deafening sound of metal pots, determined chopping, and shouting greeted her as she walked in. Colorful fruits were piled everywhere as pastry cooks agonized over the finishing touches to their evening's creations.

She continued walking, trying not to disturb the kitchen

staff during the most-chaotic portion of their day. They would learn of General Capette's murder soon enough; she envied them their last moments of ignorance.

The back door of the hotel came into view, and Nicole felt the anxiety ease from her shoulders. She had no intention of sobbing like a child in front of the entire kitchen, but feared if she did not leave soon, she would.

Exhausted, she opened the white door and lifted her face to greet the cool autumn breeze before stepping onto the uneven cobblestone street that ran the length of the fashionable hotel. The door closed behind her and she walked toward the Seine as she did every night, stopping only once.

She removed her shapeless lace cap and bloody apron, tossing them both into the river. Even in the dark, she could see the powerful current carrying them away. Nicole watched from the embankment until the white cloth was swallowed by the dark waters beneath the Pont Neuf.

Nicole turned north toward her apartment, reaching into the pocket of her black muslin dress. Engraved silver glinted in the moonlight as she removed her pistol and absently reloaded the exquisite weapon.

The streets of Paris could be very dangerous at night.

Two

~~❧~~

Nicole stripped the chambermaid costume from her body and placed it in the small fire of the boardinghouse washroom. She watched as the flames flared, causing little puffs of smoke to mingle with the steam already rising from her bath.

Once the garment had been consumed, she turned to the task of cleaning herself by sinking into the small copper tub. She winced at the intense heat of the water and tried to absorb the pain as she lifted a small square of coarse cloth. She scrubbed, as she always did, starting with the tips of her left fingers and continuing up her arm.

Her teeth clamped shut and she ignored the red streaks she was creating on her delicate white skin. She scrubbed harder, faster, avoiding the deep gash on her forearm made by a protruding piece of metal roofing when she had reached up to untie the pistol from the rope just before . . . before . . .

She swallowed her guilt and scrubbed. Nicole had no idea how long she had been cleansing herself, but the water was getting cold. She leaned over and pulled the worn silk cord hanging to the right of the narrow door.

The beleaguered maid entered the bathing room and her eyes narrowed in confusion on the full tub when Nicole snapped, "I need more water."

But when the girl continued to stare, Nicole cursed herself for not having sat facing the opposite direction. She tensed, knowing that the maid was counting the scars on her back, and knowing also that she had not had time to count them all.

"Are you finished?" The girl's eyes grew wide in contrast to Nicole's violet slits. "Get . . . me . . . more . . . water." Nicole enunciated each word as if the maid were a complete simpleton.

The girl bobbed a curtsy and fled the room, and Nicole returned to her cleansing, starting by roughly swiping at eyes that seemed never to stop crying.

She scoured the back of her neck, telling herself, as she always did, that she was necessary, that these men would continue to commit violence against the innocent if they were not stopped. And who better to protect the innocent than a person as equally wicked and depraved as the men she killed?

Nicole stared at the water, its calming reflection calling to her. Her eyelids drifted closed as she slid down until her back lay flat against the bottom of the tub. Black hair swirled around her and she brushed it aside. Her eyes stung as she opened them to stare through the water at the contorted features of the small room. The glow of the fire as it danced on the ceiling, the ancient wooden beams of the ramshackle boardinghouse.

Her lungs were burning now, and she told herself that if she had the courage, the will to hold herself down, it would all be over. She would not have to kill again and it would all be over for her. She exhaled beneath the surface.

But not for the next man. It would all begin for the next man sent to carry out the assassinations.

Nicole bolted upright, sucking in a breath mingled with

water. She coughed violently, hanging her head over the rounded metal sides of the battered tub.

Nicole smoothed long hair away from her face. She was already condemned. Her last act of contrition would be to save another from being sent into this perpetual hell.

She rose, rivers of water streaming down her body as she reached for a white bath sheet. Nicole ignored them, wrapping herself in the numbness of indifference as the maid entered the room and poured steaming water into the vacated tub.

"Merci," she said with utmost sincerity.

The girl left and Nicole crossed the hall to the small bedchamber that had been her home for the last two months. She sat on the edge of her uncomfortable mattress and stared at the missive her English contact had given her three days earlier.

André Tuchelles's distinctive seal was still intact. Nicole had not been able to bring herself to read the name of the next man she was to kill before completing her previous assignment. But General Capette was dead, and soon the man beneath the blue paraffin would be, too.

Both by her hands.

She ran a finger beneath the wax, creating light blue flakes that fell to the dusty vermillion carpet. Her heart was racing and she paused, not wanting to read the name, knowing that the man would be safe if she did not.

Her right hand was trembling when she summoned the courage to lift the top third of the parchment and then the bottom. She took a calming breath then focused her eyes on Andre's bold handwriting. Nicole stared, her heart seizing as she read the name and location of her next assassination.

"He can't be serious," she mumbled.

Dazed, Nicole hid the missive and dropped her bath sheet to the floor. She climbed, nude, into the minuscule bed and stared out the window, praying that God would grant his nightly reprieve.

But knowing, also, that the wicked never rest and the condemned . . . the condemned never sleep.

Three

❧

The minister of police sat at his enormous desk, as he always did, with his back to the brick wall while facing the solitary door to his illustrious office. These were, perhaps, extreme safeguards, but Joseph LeCoeur had learned early on in his career that a careless man was a dead man.

And he was not a careless man.

He stared at the proof of his precaution in the form of a black wax seal that he had not seen in a very long time. Three years, to be precise. Apprehension rolled in his stomach as he broke the wax arrows and read the brief communiqué.

"Merde," he muttered, his fist clenched. "Rousseau!"

His handsome young assistant entered the office and stood before him, ready to be of service. And while the man was excellent at keeping schedules and making appointments, few knew his true value.

"I have a job for you." Major Rousseau stared at him with eyes so dark no man could glean his thoughts. "One of our agents has been captured." Joseph cursed again, bemoaning the capture of an informant who had, for a price, been able to identify British agents working throughout France. "Lord Cunningham is being held at the Foreign Office in London."

"When do I leave?" The austere man did not even blink before accepting the assassination of the informant whom he himself had trained when the Englishman turned traitor.

"Have you finished the other business?"

"I call on him tonight."

"*Bon,* after that matter has been resolved, you will leave for London." Joseph reached into a drawer and pulled out a stack of English pounds, handing it to the smaller man. "You know where to go for assistance," he continued, holding up the fractured seal.

"*Oui,*" Major Rousseau said, his lips twitching ever so slightly at the corner. It was as close to a smile as his associate had ever come.

"But remember, I need you here in two weeks' time."

They stared at one another and the younger man nodded, saying, "Nothing would keep me from making my introduction to Scorpion."

The minister laughed, thinking Major Rousseau the only man in all of Paris who hated defeat more than he. This British assassin, Scorpion, had not only eluded them, but was becoming a blemish to Minister LeCoeur's impressive career. He had paid the English traitor, Cunningham, handsomely for setting a trap for their elusive adversary and had even used himself as bait.

"No, I don't imagine that anything would keep you from Empress Bonaparte's Feast, but do remember that I want Scorpion kept alive."

Joseph relished the thought of staring into the eyes of

Scorpion as Major Rousseau introduced the English assassin to his darker talents. The minister vowed to himself that Scorpion would not die until he begged for the pain to stop, until the assassin begged for his own death.

"You would be amazed at what a man can survive." The major's shoulders lifted and a noise escaped his lips in what Joseph assumed was laughter. "Just ask our friend being held in London."

"*Oui,* Lord Cunningham endured several months of your company, if I recall." He stared at the man, remembering the meticulous medical attention Major Rousseau had given Lord Cunningham after inflicting equally meticulous torture. "But this time I want Cunningham killed and quickly. A proven traitor has no allegiance to anyone. He will sell any secrets the British are willing to buy."

His assistant pointed to the black seal. "Does he know about—"

"No. I never spoke of Enigma."

"I shall report to you when I return." The agile man walked toward the door and then stopped, turning. "Did you require anything from my journey?"

"*Oui, merci,*" Joseph said, appreciative of the major's thoughtfulness. "I want his tongue."

Major Rousseau's lips twitched again, revealing crooked teeth. "May I do it before I kill him?"

Joseph LeCoeur raised his left brow and stared at the cold, dark eyes of his most accomplished assassin. "I would prefer it."

The man bowed then left the room as the minister returned to weaving the net that would snare Major Rousseau's talented English counterpart, Scorpion.

Four

$\mathcal{A}$ soft tapping at her bedchamber door pulled Nicole from peaceful oblivion back into the depths of her despair. Irritated, she ordered her heavy limbs to function as she lit a candle and stared at the small clock sitting atop her armoire. The gold hands glistened, reading three forty-eight, and she knew only one person who would venture out to a ladies' boardinghouse so early in the morning.

Her British contact, Andre Tuchelles.

Trepidation engulfed her, bringing her fully awake. She grabbed the damp bathing cloth and wrapped it around her body, tucking the corner between her full breasts. Improper, she knew, but Andre had seen her in far more revealing brothel costumes and she needed to get him inside her bedchamber before he was seen.

Barefooted, she strode across the carpet, her left hand holding a candle while her right opened the simple wooden door.

"What . . ." But her words dissolved when she saw that it was not Andre who stood at her threshold.

The hair at the base of her neck bristled and her breath was extracted by the force standing before her in the deceptive form of a man—a very handsome man with auburn hair and impossibly wide shoulders covered by an ill-fitting russet jacket. His square jaw was set in a determined line, and she made the mistake of looking up to meet his penetrating gaze.

"My apologies, *mademoiselle,*" he whispered in French, his expressive brows drawing together in confusion as he glanced about the bedchamber and found that she was alone. "I was told that an acquaintance of mine was in residence at this location."

"I . . ." Nicole blinked, lost in the sky blue of his eyes. "Am afraid that your information was incorrect, *monsieur.* I have been living at this location for well over two months."

The man nodded as if he understood, but clearly he did not. "Well, thank you very much. I'm sorry to have disturbed you," he said, bowing with a refined elegance that came only to a man with full command of his body.

A beautiful body she could not stop herself from envisioning.

Flushed, Nicole lifted the towel, suddenly very aware that she was nude beneath the thin, white cloth. She smoothed down her black curls, which had dried to a tangled mess about her shoulders.

"Do not concern yourself," she said, smiling pleasantly and trying to ignore the disappointment she felt as he turned away from her.

She watched the immense man take two steps down the hall, and then he stopped, removing something from the breast pocket of his jacket. Nicole tensed with a rush of anticipation when he walked back, saying, more to himself than to her, "You spoke English."

Damn!

"Pardon?" Nicole feigned ignorance, her eyes innocent and wide.

"When you opened the door a moment ago . . . " He

stared, reassessing this new information . . . and her. "You said 'what' in English."

Nicole swallowed, then considered her options and found that she had none. She stood before him completely vulnerable, her only weapon . . . herself.

"Did I?" she asked in French.

His sensuous chuckle made her toes curl, but it was the accompanying smile that slayed her. "*Oui,* you did."

"I don't think—" she began, still recovering.

"*Oui,*" he said, his voice dropping to a baritone murmur. He stepped into her bedchamber, forcing her back as he closed the door behind him. "You did."

Nicole stood, listening to her heart pounding in her ear as her visitor lifted his right hand toward her chest. She was about to pay for her sins, but had no desire to see the instrument of her destruction. She willed herself to stare into the soul of the man who would exact her punishment.

However, when no punishment came, she glanced down, her brows drawing together when she saw not a weapon in his large hand, but a missive displaying Andre's familiar seal.

"My friend wished for me to deliver this to . . ." He caught her eye. "Scorpion."

Nicole's jaw dropped. *Why had Andre not come himself?*

But the enormous man confused her further by asking, "Where might I find him?"

Him?

Her head was spinning and she tried desperately to sort things out in her mind.

This man had Andre Tuchelles's seal. Yet Andre had not identified her as Scorpion. *Why?*

"Andre is well, I trust?" she asked, stalling.

Trust.

Andre was protecting her. He did not trust this man and was warning her to be cautious.

"Very well, when last I saw him." Her visitor grinned, fully aware that she had avoided answering his question.

"Then why is he not delivering this message to Scorpion himself?"

"Andre Tuchelles is leaving Paris."

"What?" Nicole gasped, feeling completely abandoned.

"I have been commissioned to warn Scorpion that British agents working in France have been compromised.

"The Foreign Office sent me to deliver the warning, as the French may already be watching Monsieur Tuchelles. Andre Tuchelles is returning to London for his own protection and Scorpion has been ordered to do the same."

Return to England!

Nicole was having difficulty breathing, so she sat on the faded duvet and attempted to think. She could not go back to England. They would arrest her the moment she arrived.

Misinterpreting her distress, the large man sank to his haunches, saying, "I'm quite sure our government would welcome Scorpion's . . . collaborators."

Confused, Nicole looked up, meeting his eyes. As she stared into the clear, blue depths, realization dawned. He believed her to be Scorpion's lover. Yes, that would be this man's first conclusion, and she could use that to her advantage.

"Let me read the missive." She reached out to grasp the thick paper but the man rose, indecision etched on his all-too-masculine features.

"You will forgive me if I deny your request, *mademoiselle*. This communiqué is to be given to Scorpion, and Scorpion alone."

They seemed to have reached a stalemate and Nicole was losing her patience. She stood, looking up at the enormous messenger and vaguely wondering if she could retrieve her pistol before he could stop her.

"What did Andre Tuchelles say when he gave you the letter?"

The man lifted his left eyebrow in what she was discovering to be condescension. "What makes you believe I will divulge that to anyone but Scorpion?"

Nicole swallowed her sarcasm, choosing rather to

become the flirt. "I promise you, Scorpion and I have no secrets from one another."

The man's gaze slowly descended, taking in every detail of her scantily clad figure and causing her to blush.

"Yes, I'm quite sure that is true," the messenger said, his eyes returning to hers. "Therefore, you should have no difficulty in informing me of his direction."

Discomfited, Nicole rolled her eyes in a manner she hoped conveyed frustration.

"I don't know where Scorpion resides. He insisted I remain ignorant for my own protection."

"And his," the man added with a note of disapproval.

Nicole stared at the acerbic messenger. Infusing her tone with sugar, she said, "Perhaps if I read the missive, I would be able to help you locate Scorpion. Andre Tuchelles undoubtedly sent you to me for a reason."

The man blinked, his sculpted jaw setting as he evidently concluded that he had no other option.

"Very well." He lifted the missive over the expanse that separated them and Nicole was once again struck by how large a man he was. She pulled the communiqué from between two long fingers, but her progress was stopped as he tightened his hold on the folded parchment. "But I shall read it when you've finished."

Nicole agreed, breaking the seal and praying that Andre's art for ambiguity was displayed to full effect within the one-page document.

Scorpion,
   You are in grave danger and must abandon all
previous orders. The French are closing on your
location. Trust no one and return to England
immediately. This man has been sent to arrange for
your transportation.

                                                    Andre

Nicole stared at the untidy scrawl of Andre's typically fluid hand.

"This was written in haste?" she asked, returning the innocuous missive to her formidable guest.

"Yes." His forehead furrowed, a spark of surprised admiration growing in his turquoise eyes. "Monsieur Tuchelles wrote the communiqué while packing his belongings in hopes of boarding a ship that was scheduled to set sail . . ." The handsome man pulled a gold watch from his shoddy waistcoat, causing Nicole to pause at the incongruity. "Not twenty minutes past."

"And Scorpion's ship?"

"*Les Helios* sails in three hours for Honfleur, where we will board a Dutch merchant vessel willing to transport us back to England."

Nicole let the information settle in her mind before choosing a course of action.

"*Bon.*" She walked to the armoire and removed a modest blue dress, tossing it on the bed. "If you would be so kind as to turn your back." The man opened his mouth to protest, but as the cloth was already sliding down her nude body, he quickly turned with suspicion still lingering in his astute eyes. "I shall locate Scorpion while you pack my possessions and we will rendezvous at *Les Helios* in approximately one hour."

The courier gave an incredulous grunt, saying over his left shoulder, "I thought you had no idea how to contact the man. 'For your own protection,' I believe were your exact words."

She stared at his broad back, hoping for divine guidance in formulating a credible lie. "I believe I said I had no idea where Scorpion resides. I do, however, know of an establishment he frequents."

Nicole finished dressing then spun to face the armoire and retrieve her pistol from beneath a threadbare chemise. But before she could slip the weapon into her skirt pocket, she heard the unmistakable click of a firearm being cocked behind her head. She stilled, her mind reeling.

"What are your intentions with that pistol, *mademoiselle*?" he whispered in her ear as he peered over her left shoulder, carefully watching any movement of her right hand.

Nicole licked her lips, suddenly very articulate. "The streets of Paris are dangerous. I always carry a weapon when I venture out at night."

There was a long pause and then she felt the powerful man step back.

"You don't need a weapon." Confused, she turned to look up at him. "I will be with you," the courier added with such arrogance that she almost believed him.

"No." She shook her head adamantly. "You will draw far too much attention. Scorpion is a very jealous man. One look at you and he will very likely shoot you before you have the opportunity to explain your commission."

"Will he?" The messenger's sensual gaze made her immediately regret voicing the backhanded compliment.

"Oui," she mumbled, distracted as she peered more closely at his striking features. A thought tickled the back of her mind, presenting itself in the form of a question. "You're a Scot?"

He looked like a big, handsome, altogether too tempting Scot.

"Aye," he whispered, uttering the first English word she had heard in two years. *Well, almost English.* "But how did ya know? My French is perfect."

Nicole raised a haughty brow and walked toward her bedchamber door. "Yes, it is. It was your Scottish bravado that gave you away."

"A man is what he is, *mademoiselle*." The courier's amused words caressed her back like a fire in winter and she could not help feeling the touch of heat.

Nicole turned to look at him as she reached the door, saying, "Until he is not, *monsieur*," dousing them both with a splash of cold reality. "I suggest we hurry as I fear you would not survive long in Paris."

Her escort bowed gracefully, adding to her growing suspicion that he was gently bred. "I believe I shall manage for three hours."

"Perhaps," she mused, inbuing the word with a considerable amount of doubt. "Scorpion will want to know your name."

"A careful man, this Scorpion."

"Very." She held his eyes.

"Daniel Damont at your service, Mademoiselle . . . ?" He inclined his noble head toward her.

"Beauvoire, Nicole Beauvoire," she offered, not hesitating to give the name she had assumed that terrible day two years ago.

Five

❧

Daniel McCurren was numb and had been for a year.

He scratched his chest where his heart should have been and stared through the countless ships floating on the Seine, wondering how the bloody hell he had come to be in Paris.

Damnation, he was not even the Foreign Office's first choice!

Of course, he had been foxed when Falcon proposed this little excursion, but that was no excuse for poor judgment. No, he had known precisely the danger he was getting himself into, and if he were truthful, he knew why he had volunteered.

"Monsieur Damont?"

Daniel nodded, his attention drawn toward the approaching captain of the ship that would carry them to Honfleur. The sturdy man trudged down the gangplank, his large hand curled around a whalebone pipe as he removed it from between lips obscured by a dense gray beard.

"*Oui.*"

"Welcome to *Les Helios.* I believe you have secured

passage for three?" the captain asked, scouring the docks for his wayward travelers.

"Your remaining guests will be joining us shortly."

"Bon." The captain of the ship snapped his thick fingers and a boy of no more than fifteen appeared at his side. "Please, allow me to stow your luggage in your cabin?"

The boy made a move toward the trunks and Daniel stilled his progress with a slight lifting of his right hand. "I prefer to await my companions."

"As you wish, Monsieur Damont." The captain inclined his head then turned his mind to the harried activity on deck, leaving Daniel alone with his thoughts.

Curious thoughts about this strange British assassin, Scorpion.

It was quite ingenious of the man to lodge in a women's boardinghouse. The establishment would never be searched, never be watched by the French army. The only danger lay in being seen by one of the female lodgers, and that could easily be explained away with one seductive smile, one wink from a healthy young buck visiting his beautiful mistress in the dead of the night.

Daniel shifted his weight, uncomfortable with the vision of Nicole Beauvoire forming in his mind. He crossed his arms over his chest and his eyes narrowed as he considered her small burgundy trunk to the right of his brown Hessian boot. It was not so much the chipped paint or dented hinges that piqued his interest, but rather the size of the trunk itself.

In all of Daniel's twenty-seven years, he had never met a woman with a wardrobe so small. It had taken him no more than ten minutes to pack all the girl's earthly possessions and place them in the shoddy trunk. She had no jewelry, no hair combs, not even a miniature portrait of her family to take back to England with her.

He shook his head in disgust, wondering what sort of man would provide his lover so few comforts. The woman was obviously educated, beautiful . . .

Stunning, really.

His mind returned to the moment when she had opened the door in nothing more than a tattered bath sheet. Those unusual violet eyes widening with surprise, her black hair falling around her shoulders as if she had just made love.

The thought made his mouth go dry, and Daniel realized that it was the first time he had been enticed by a woman in well over a year.

He felt the familiar burn of envy for men with a woman to welcome them home. A woman to greet them wearing nothing more than a damp bath towel that clung to every exquisite curve of her luxurious body.

Men like Scorpion, men like . . . Glenbroke.

Censuring himself, Daniel closed his eyes and filled his murky mind with thoughts of seducing the tantalizing girl. She would respond, he knew. He had seen the spark of attraction in her lovely eyes, had felt the pull of the hunt coursing through his veins.

However, that would hardly endear him to Scorpion, the Crown's most effectual assassin. An assassin, it would appear, unable to satisfy his beautiful paramour. Daniel chuckled at the irony and tried to put the alluring Mademoiselle Beauvoire out of his overheated mind while he waited for her deadly lover to arrive.

Nicole took one last look at the unmistakable figure of Daniel Damont before slipping from the shadows of the noisy dockside tavern, Le Grotto.

She had followed him from her apartment and then on to his lodging, but not once had her escort veered from their arrangements. There were no French soldiers, no ruffians waiting to carry Scorpion off to the famed Parisian prison, the Conciergerie. He had, in fact, done precisely what he told her he would do, and for some incomprehensible reason, she was pleased.

Surely, it was her accurate assessment of his honorable character that gave her pleasure, not the thought of spending several days alone on a ship with such an attractive emissary of the British government.

A man so brave he endangered his life to deliver a warning to an English assassin operating deep within enemy territory, a man so captivatingly handsome he was undoubtedly a rake and a rogue who would try to seduce her at every opportunity.

The thought was not unappealing.

Hell's teeth!

This was not the time to be distracted by a pretty man. Lord knows, he could have come to her apartment to kill her and all she could do was stand there gawking at how magnificently constructed he was, like some addle-brained schoolgirl attending her first ball.

Nicole lengthened her strides as she traveled toward Andre's apartment, irritation punctuating every step. No, this was the time to weigh her options, to decide if she was going to board *Les Helios* and face her fate in England.

Andre Tuchelles was the only person in France who knew her true identity, the only person who knew what she risked by going home. As she approached his apartment building, Nicole prayed that he had had the opportunity to leave a communiqué advising her of the threat the French posed. Andre would know if this recalling of British agents was merely precautionary or if there was indeed a credible danger.

A danger strong enough to risk going home.

Glancing up, Nicole saw that Andre had left a candle burning in the loft of his third-floor apartment. A smile pulled at her heart when she thought of her dear, sweet Andre.

She knew that was not his name. She did not know his real name.

However, she did know that he was the son of an English vicar, who, unlike her, had enlisted in this war from his deep, moral conviction that it was his duty as a Christian to fight the tyranny that the French government inflicted upon the people of Europe. It was his conviction that standing by and watching the atrocities take place, yet doing nothing, was a mortal sin, an affront to God and to all of humanity.

Andre Tuchelles was light and knew nothing of the darkness of man. He assumed that, given the choice, man would choose to do good, would choose light over darkness.

She knew better.

Nicole scanned the third-floor corridor of Andre's building and then slipped, unseen, into his apartment. She leaned her back against the door, waiting for her eyes to adjust to the dim light that fell from the bedchamber loft.

She walked to the first step leading to the modest room and bent down, hoping that he had affixed a note beneath it, some small good-bye so that she did not feel so completely alone.

However, when her fingers caressed the bottom of the step, she felt nothing but a sinking disappointment. Her eyes swept over the empty room and she wondered if she would ever see her dear friend again. The candlelight flickered in Andre's loft, beckoning her up the wooden stairs.

Nicole smiled, wondering if he had left a farewell note atop his desk. She envisioned what he would say, wondered if he would confess, in parting, the *tendre* she knew he felt for her but had never had the courage to express.

She climbed the steps, not truly expecting to find anything because Andre Tuchelles was the sort of man to take his heart's desire to his grave, never daring to presume that a lady would return his all-too-worthy affections.

She looked down, lifting her skirts as she neared the top of the steep staircase. The heel of her black ankle boots sounded on the wooden floor, and she raised her head then gasped at the sight of Andre Tuchelles asleep at his desk.

He has missed his ship.

"Andre," Nicole whispered, glancing at the trunk to the right of his tidy bed. "Andre."

But he did not move.

Her breath became short and she felt suddenly lightheaded, causing the room to dim and then brighten beyond bearing.

"Andre?"

She crept over and placed her gloved hand on his right

shoulder, shaking him. But rather than awaken, he fell limp to the floor.

It was then that she saw his face. The bruising, the broken nose, his eyes swollen shut . . . the blood oozing from the left side of his olive-colored jacket.

"No!" Nicole dropped to the carpet, stripping her gloves so she could caress his cheek with the back of her bare hand. She took care to move gently over his horrifying injuries. "Not Andre."

Her anguished words turned to whispered tears as Nicole searched in vain for a portion of his face that she recognized. She looked down and suppressed a surge of nausea the moment she saw that his beautiful, long fingers had all been broken.

"Not Andre," she breathed, knowing it was her fault, knowing that Andre Tuchelles had been tortured to get to her.

To get to Scorpion.

She glanced at his desk and saw his brass seal, then remembered the hasty scrawl of his communiqué. The French are closing on your location. Trust no one . . .

Her mind leapt to the enormous Scot, a man perfectly capable of overpowering Andre, of coercing him into writing the short missive.

Just before . . .

She closed her eyes, praying that his death had been swift, but knowing that it had not. Even in death Andre had protected her. The Scot had come to her apartment thinking Scorpion a man. It was undoubtedly the reason that she was still alive. He needed her, needed her to deliver Scorpion to the French before "he" was able to perform "his" next assignment.

She rose and stared at the man who had given his life so that she could perform that commission. And she would, killing Joseph LeCoeur at the empress's Toussaint Feast in three weeks' time.

And then . . . she would kill the Scot.

Six

"*I* am sorry, Monsieur Damont, but we must depart."

Daniel glanced up at the captain of *Les Helios,* saying, "I'm grateful to you for delaying your journey as long as you have, and offer my most sincere apologies for the tardiness of my companions."

"These things are often out of one's control." The older man gave a sympathetic shrug before dismissing the matter and boarding his frenzied vessel.

"Bloody hell," Daniel muttered as he watched the mooring being cast toward the ancient Parisian docks.

Young sailors scurried to retrieve the heavy lines and he stared at the ship, knowing this was his last chance to board her, knowing that he had no other means of getting home.

But he could not leave without Scorpion.

Falcon's instructions had been dead simple: Warn Scorpion's contact, Andre Tuchelles, that they were in danger and being called back to England. Then deliver Tuchelles's missive verifying those orders and escort Scorpion back to London.

"A simple errand," Falcon had said.

Daniel smirked. *Simple.* He had been standing on this bloody dock for the past three hours awaiting an English assassin and his lover. Had no idea where the lass had gone, nor how to contact Scorpion, and he now had no transportation back to England even if he did.

He should have gone with her, but something in those large, violet eyes had seemed so incapable of deception. To be fair to himself, there was no logical reason to doubt her word. Both Scorpion and Nicole Beauvoire were in danger, and he was providing a means of escape. Why then would they not have met him at the appointed time? There was only one explanation.

Something had delayed them.

Daniel curled his lower lip over his bottom teeth and whistled to one of the dock workers, who ran over, eager to earn a bit of extra blunt.

"Keep an eye on these trunks," he said, handing the man a generous amount of coin, adding, "I'll double your fee when I return to claim my possessions," with a menacing tone that made clear the consequences of absconding.

"Merci, monsieur." The man bowed, removing a black woolen cap.

But Daniel did not hear him. He was already running in the direction of Mademoiselle Beauvoire's apartment, hoping to find anything to indicate where she had gone. Apprehension pressed on his chest when he considered that if the French military was already watching Scorpion, he may very well have just pushed the unsuspecting girl into the enemy's proverbial lap.

He had to find her.

Daniel glanced up at the lightening sky, an unwanted confirmation that he would have very little time in which to conduct his search. He slipped into the boardinghouse through a back window then quietly made his way to Mademoiselle Beauvoire's room.

The bedchamber was just as he had left it, cold, dark, and empty. He lit the single candle and held it up, illuminating the only items remaining in the room: a chair, a bed, the armoire, and a small side table.

Starting with the simplest objects, Daniel lifted the chair with his left hand and peered under it, studying the legs and seeing that they were indeed solid. He then moved on to the side table and bed, mattress and armoire.

Nothing.

He stared at the floor boards and knew that he would only have time for a cursory examination, determining that the best course of action would be to interview the other residents of the boardinghouse.

A women's boardinghouse, where a concerned brother . . .

He paused, his thoughts returning to Scotland and his eccentric Uncle William. Daniel stared at the armoire's simple ornamentation, remembering that his Uncle William had taken to hiding his jewels from the thieving British in a hollowed-out compartment beneath a decorative finial.

This armoire had four.

He tugged at the first two finials, thinking himself as mad as his Uncle William, then reached for the third and the finial gave, not much, but it moved nonetheless. Daniel stepped toward the wall and gently lifted up, careful not to pull too hard lest the dowel break, sealing the contents within the secret recess.

His heart was pounding as the soft scraping of wood continued until, with a sudden jerk, the finial was in his hand. He tossed it on the bed and stared at the floorboards as his fingers probed the small compartment, closing on a bit of curled parchment.

He pulled and the document unwound like a paper spring, recoiling into its scrolled form the moment it broke the confines of its hiding place. Daniel grinned at his success and sat on the bed, reaching for the thin candle.

He unfurled the parchment with his left hand and anchored it with the base of the wooden candleholder in his right. He stared down, wondering what secrets the lovely

Mademoiselle Beauvoire held as the candlelight danced across the blackened words. Words, he could see, that had been written by Andre Tuchelles's hand.

Words that irrefutably pronounced that Daniel had just been played for a fool.

Seven

Falcon was seated in the study of his London townhome enjoying a plate of kippers and parsnips when he felt a sudden breeze sweeping up his back.

He lifted his glass and took a sip of thirty-year-old scotch before saying to his uninvited guest, "Good evening . . . Mister McCurren, was it?" without even looking toward the closing door.

There was a pause and then a young man in his mid-twenties walked silently across his Aubusson carpet and took the seat opposite him in front of the small fire.

"That's right. Seamus McCurren—as my card has indicated for the past four days."

The young man was exceptionally handsome, as all the McCurrens were. However, Seamus McCurren was darker than his brother Daniel, less striking in his coloring but more ominous in his carriage.

Falcon waited, intrigued.

"Yes, Smith mentioned that you had been so kind as to drop by. I apologize for not having been available before this evening." He smiled, the model of civility. "How may I assist you, Mister McCurren?"

The man leaned forward and handed Falcon his own card. "You can tell me where my brother has gone."

Falcon glanced at the card as if seeing it for the first time then raised his gray eyebrows along with his sloping shoulders. "I'm sorry, and your brother might be?"

The young lord gritted his teeth. "Viscount DunDonell, Daniel *McCurren*. You see, I believe you might know his whereabouts as I found that card . . ." The gentleman pointed toward Falcon's hand. "In his home."

"Oh, yes." He wiped his mouth with a napkin and nodded as he stared at the black and white card baring his own name and title. "Viscount DunDonell. I do recall visiting the viscount Monday last. Oh dear, has the viscount gone missing?"

"Yes, my lord, the viscount has gone missing." Falcon could see the Scot's anger in the set of his jaw, but nowhere else. "And as you were the last man to see him, I thought you would be so kind as to point me in his direction."

Falcon shrugged. "I'm sorry, but I've no idea where the viscount has gone. Have you checked the hospitals?" the old man offered, helpfully. "Footpads are—"

"Yes. My father, the Earl of DunDonell," he pointedly reminded him, "has made inquiries." The gentleman leaned back and crossed his legs in one elegant motion that declared his intention of staying as surely as if he had drawn a pistol. "But I thought you a more likely source of information."

"Well, I am sorry to have disappointed you."

"Oh, but you haven't, my lord." The young lord shook his dark head. "You are everything I imagined you to be."

"Odd that you have imagined me at all."

"Is it?" The man held his eyes.

"Yes." The old man laughed. "Now, if you will forgive

me, my dinner is getting cold." Falcon picked up his sterling silver fork and looked at the young gentleman, dismissing him.

"Then you will not object if I contact the newspapers?"

Falcon was finding it very difficult not to flinch. "And why would you do that?"

Seamus McCurren leaned forward, an acute intelligence flaring in his hazel eyes. "My brother has disappeared, and if you have no idea of his whereabouts, I see no other alternative than to alert the local authorities and newspapers of Viscount DunDonell's disappearance in hopes of his safe return."

A smile spread across the old man's features and he chuckled with approval, saying, "The duke has underestimated you, my boy."

"Glenbroke?"

"Yes, Glenbroke." The old man mimicked the man's brogue, which had suddenly thickened. "You have outplayed me, just as your brother did."

"Where is he?"

"Paris."

The gentleman paled. "Why?" he asked.

"I needed a courier we could trust to issue a warning to agents working in France. Glenbroke recommended you." The young man's dark brows pulled together in surprise and Falcon continued. "I went to Viscount DunDonell's home to inquire as to your direction and he volunteered for the assignment."

"Why would Daniel—"

"A woman? That is the only reasonable explanation for a gentleman to deteriorate so markedly and so rapidly." Seamus McCurren stared, not giving a flicker of confirmation, so Falcon continued. "Frankly, I believe the viscount does not care if he survives."

The gentleman inhaled and the tension returned to his jaw. "And why would you say that?"

"The viscount commented that he had six brothers to succeed him."

"Aye, but none willingly."

Falcon saw the distress in the young man's eyes and he decided to ease his fears. "Your brother is simply delivering a message, Mister McCurren, and will return in one week's time. It is really a very simple assignment."

" 'The best-laid plans of mice and men . . .' " The gentleman's complex gaze met his, neither needing him to finish the famous words of the Scots poet Robert Burns, for they hung in the air like a black cloud.

"Leaves us nought but grieve an' pain."

Eight

Nicole walked through the expensive apartment in the most exclusive section of Paris with disappointment pulling at her refined features. She adjusted her four-carat diamond ear bobs and stared at the enormous canopy bed of the master suite as if it were a cot.

"And this is all you have available at present?" she asked the young man responsible for leasing the ten-room apartment.

The fair-haired clerk had not only groveled at her financial feet, but was making it increasingly clear that he was desirous of her feminine favors as well.

He seized her upper arm and laughed indulgently as he guided her toward the bedchamber window.

"This is the only furnished apartment in all of Paris with five bedchambers, two salons, a music room, a morning room, and a library." She turned her head and stared out at the magnificent square as he intended her to do. "So beautiful," he whispered so close to her ear that she could feel the heat of him against her back.

Fighting down a surge of panic, Nicole turned to face him. She looked into his gray eyes and gave a coquettish smile, saying, "You're correct, it is a spectacular view." Her delicately arched brows rose. "When can I have it?"

The man blinked, still staring at her breasts. *"Pardon?"*

"The apartment." She glanced about the room, her black curls bouncing prettily. "When might I take possession of the apartment?"

The man shook his head as if to dislodge his carnal thoughts.

"Uh, let me see," the clerk said, breathing awkwardly as he retreated across the room to reference his superfluous legal documents. "You may move in today if you wish, Mademoiselle Beauvoire."

Nicole turned to stare out the window again, but this time she was not looking at the stunning view of Place Vendôme. Her eyes were firmly fixed on the enormous apartment across the square, owned by the man she had been ordered by Andre Tuchelles to kill.

"Excellent. Where do I sign?"

Daniel waited until she had walked away from the window before stepping out from beneath the canopy of trees. He had been searching for Nicole Beauvoire for three days, and now that he had found her, he had no intention of alerting her to his presence.

Striding across the square, he made for the apartment while straightening his quality, if a bit fussy, waistcoat. The damn tailor had added to his already exorbitant fee, claiming that his height and broad shoulders would require additional yards of brocaded blue silk.

But he had paid, knowing that a new wardrobe would be required if he were to follow Mademoiselle Beauvoire into the upper echelons of Parisian society. She, of course, had already made the transformation.

He could scarcely believe her metamorphosis when she had stepped from her carriage not half an hour ago. Her ebony coiffure and lilac silk gown were designed to impress and the immodest neckline meant to draw attention to the web of diamonds shimmering above the plump curves of her breasts.

The missive he had discovered in her bedchamber revealed that she was luring a very large fish who would only be baited by the most tantalizing of morsels. And after seeing her as she was, as she should be adorned, Daniel had no doubt that Joseph LeCoeur would be hooked.

Nicole paced impatiently as the young clerk sat in the carved wooden chair of the gaudy desk extracting the documents that would require her fictitious signature.

"May I inquire as to how long you intend—"

A knock at the entrance to her newly acquired apartment disrupted their conversation, drawing both their curiosity and their attention. With a quill in one hand and a fistful of papers in the other, the clerk began to rise.

"I'll see to the door," Nicole said with impatience, wanting nothing more than to be rid of the tedious man as soon as was possible.

She strolled through the apartment and opened the door, ready to dismiss the intruder. But when she looked up to see Daniel Damont staring at her with a knowing grin, her mouth fell open from searing shock.

She reached for her pistol, but before she could withdraw the weapon from the pocket of her gown, Damont seized her in a kiss that took her breath away.

He pressed her against the entryway wall, his tongue slipping into the heat of her mouth and extracting a soft sigh which gave him grounds to band his left arm more tightly around her waist. His right hand burned its way down her spine before grasping her backside and fitting her firmly against his powerful body.

And, God, how well they fit.

She could feel the hard muscles of his thighs shifting as

he bent her backward, kissing her more deeply, more thoroughly, the moist heat of his mouth an alluring balm to her lips. His capable hands continued their carnal exploration and then, with jarring ease, he lifted her upright.

His reluctance to break their embrace was palpable as he stared down into her eyes and whispered, "Hello, Scorpion."

Fear and shame shot through her and she was incapable of speech, incapable of turning away from his incisive gaze.

"Mademoiselle Beauvoire," the clerk's voice echoed nervously. "Is this gentleman . . . known to you?"

Nicole blushed, her eyes turning to icy shards when she realized he had kissed her merely for the benefit of the clerk, who stood gaping at them from down the expansive hall.

Anger located her tongue, sharpening it. "As a matter of fact—"

"Careful," Damont whispered, raising her own pistol between them, his back to the clerk.

Nicole sucked in a breath, unable to believe that his kiss had so disarmed her that he had literally rifled through her pockets and disarmed her.

Incensed, she looked up to meet his satisfied gaze and was humiliated further when he arrogantly said, in English no less, "I believe that's the second time I've made you gasp. Now tell your amorous companion that you are indeed well . . ." He winked. "Acquainted with me, and then get rid of the lad."

"Why are you here, Monsieur Damont?" she spat.

"To see you, *ma chérie.* Why else would I have come all this way?" Nicole could hear the amusement in his perfectly accented French and she wanted nothing more than to slap him.

So, she did. Hard.

Before turning to the astounded clerk and demanding, "Where do I sign?"

Nicole snatched the quill from the clerk's hand and he hesitantly pointed to the bottom of several papers. She was busily signing the legal documents when she saw the clerk shrink in the ornate desk chair. Not that she needed to witness the cowardly display to know that Daniel Damont was towering over her, watching every dot, every loop that she made.

"Are you purchasing this apartment, darling?" the impudent man inquired, rubbing his crimson cheek. "It appears a trifle small for you, don't you think?"

Darling!

Tired of playing games, Nicole turned to the clerk with a dismissive smile. "Is that all?"

"*Oui. Merci,* Mademoiselle Beauvoire," the clerk said, rising, stuffing the remaining papers into a leather satchel and leaving the apartment almost at a run.

"Why are you here, Monsieur Damont?" Nicole inquired, seating herself in the chair left vacant by the discomfited clerk.

The man's lips parted and Nicole could not help remembering how they tasted. She was still caught in the memory when he breathed, "You're Scorpion."

She lifted her gaze to meet his eye and was surprised to see uncertainty contorting his handsome features. And then the truth hit her with absolute certainty.

He was not sure.

She remained silent, gathering information as she let him talk.

"Why did you not meet me at the docks?"

Nicole scoffed, saying "Well," as she tilted her head to one side. "After discovering that you had killed Scorpion's contact, meeting you seemed ill advised."

"Andre Tuchelles is dead?"

He was staring at her with such astonishment that she blinked, saying with a tad less conviction, "You know very well that Monsieur Tuchelles is dead."

"You think *I* killed him?" he all but yelled.

"How else would you have extorted that missive?"

Bewildered, he opened his mouth to defend himself and then his sky blue eyes cleared.

"Andre Tuchelles struck me as the sort of man who would die rather than write a communiqué that would surely endanger Scorpion's life."

The Scot was right. Damn him.

Andre had to have known that he was a dead man either way. He never would have sent an assassin to her doorstep. Never. Andre had sent the missive implying that Scorpion was a man merely to give Nicole time to decide if she wished to return to England with her adamant escort.

It would seem that the Scot was telling the truth, and someone else had killed Andre Tuchelles after Daniel Damont had left the apartment. A man she had every intention of meeting.

Just before she killed him.

But Damont did not need to know why she was going to stay in Paris. Nor did he need to know why she would never return to England.

"You are Scorpion, aren't you?"

"Yes." She nodded, suddenly cold.

"You're a woman?" He was shaking his head, but his eyes never left hers.

"Yes, thank you for pointing that out to me," she snapped, gathering her copy of the lease. "I can see why Falcon hired you."

"My apologies, I've just never met a woman capable of—"

"Of killing a man?" she scoffed, wishing she were not capable of such a thing. "Do you have siblings?" She threw the documents in the desk drawer and looked up at him, slamming it closed.

"What?" He blinked. "Yes, six." He was still staring at her, and Nicole felt the sting of his shock.

"And if a man tried to harm the youngest, what would your mother do?"

"She would rip the man apart."

Nicole lifted her chin. "Then consider me the mother of England." She hid her sorrow and forced herself to meet his beautiful eyes. "If that helps ease your conscience."

"It was not my intention to offend." His eyes remained on hers. "I can see why you have been so . . . successful. No one would suspect—"

"A woman?"

"Aye."

Nicole looked away from the pity pulling at his striking features and knew that London would be no different now than it had been two years ago. She had seen the same expression for an entire year as she was paraded from Newgate to the Old Bailey.

She could not live through that again.

"I'm not leaving Paris." Daniel Damont was so stunned he could not even speak, so she continued to confuse him, saying, "You hand me a missive from Andre Tuchelles, informing me that the French have infiltrated our ranks, further ordering me to disregard his previous commission of assassination?"

The Scot nodded slowly.

"So, pray tell, which communiqué should I disregard? The first missive ordering the assassination and written by Andre Tuchelles, whom I have known for two very long years? Or the second missive rescinding that order and delivered by Daniel Damont, who I have never laid eyes on before the night Andre is murdered and who may very well be a French agent himself?"

The man rocked back on his heels, and she could see his astute mind spinning.

"I see your difficulty, truly, but this assassination is a trap orchestrated by the French to capture Scor . . . you."

"Most likely, but better to err on the side of caution and complete the mission." She rose, smoothing out her expensive gown. "Don't you agree?"

"No, I don't." He exhaled, interpreting her intention to leave the apartment correctly. "You'll be killed if you go through with this assassination."

"And so will Joseph LeCoeur."

She took one step toward the door and he blocked her path with one long stride.

Daniel's heart was pounding in his chest and he had no notion what to do. His patriotic act of distraction had just turned into a nightmare. He licked his lips, trying to think of a way to convince the lass that he was telling the truth.

"How could I be a French agent if I brought you a missive bearing Monsieur Tuchelles's seal?"

She shrugged, the motion echoed by her plentiful breasts as they bounced in the bodice of her gown. "Which you could have forced Andre to write before you killed him."

Daniel speared his fingers through his thick hair and said, "Damn it, woman, I'm trying to protect you," with all the frustration he was feeling. "Is there nothing I can say to convince you that I was sent by the Foreign Office?"

The girl said nothing but he could see a powerful mind at work behind those bewitching eyes.

"No," she finally said. "I am afraid we are at yet another impasse. You are either telling the truth and Andre Tuchelles sent you, or you are lying and are a representative of France sent to capture Scorpion. I have no way of knowing."

Daniel smiled fully as he found an answer that he was sure would convince her. "If I am an agent of France, then why have I not arrested you?"

She did not even hesitate before saying, "Because you hope I will lead you to Scorpion and other British agents working in Paris."

Daniel held out his arms, defeated. "You're Scorpion!"

"But you don't truly believe that I'm Scorpion."

A shadow of doubt passed over his face as he looked down at the petite woman, and she saw it.

"There you are," she said in triumph. "Good evening, Monsieur Damont."

But before she could make it out the door, Daniel had grasped her upper arm.

"Prior to giving me the missive which warned you of the danger you are in, Andre Tuchelles made me swear that I would do anything in my power to get Scorpion out of France. I gave my word of honor."

Daniel glanced at the woman who was hell-bent on remaining in Paris and decided that he had until the assassination of Joseph LeCoeur to persuade her.

A flash of heat bloomed in his chest as he remembered the way she had responded to his touch, the way she had thawed in his arms. She might be Falcon's most valuable assassin, but she was also a woman.

And for as long as Daniel could remember, women had been throwing themselves in his path. He was powerfully built and well formed of face, a gift given him by his parents. He took no pride in that fact, but neither did he shy away from the truth of it.

The only time he had refrained from using his sexual appeal, it had cost him. Daniel had wanted, needed, Sarah Duhearst to fall in love with the man and not his exterior. But he had waited too long to introduce her to his more sensual self, and the Duke of Glenbroke had awakened that part of her.

Daniel shook off his regret and turned his attention to the woman he had sworn to protect. She was not immune to him, and he intended to use his appeal to lure her back to England.

But she did not need to know that. All Mademoiselle Beauvoire needed to know was that she would not be rid of him.

"And at the moment, the only way I see of protecting you is to aid you in your commission," he lied. "I'm moving in with you."

The lass wrenched her arm free and stared at him as if he were mad. "You most certainly are not."

"And just how do you intend to stop me?" he asked seductively as he stared at her lips.

He had her flustered. He could see it in her quickened breathing.

"I could kill you."

Daniel chuckled, truly amused. "But you have no way of knowing if I was sent by Andre Tuchelles, and killing a British agent would not be very patriotic." He leaned down and whispered in her ear, making sure to send the heat of his breath down her neck. "Let me help you."

She shuddered and he knew it was not from the cold. Then she resisted him.

"I work alone," she snapped, yanking the door of the apartment open and stepping into the dim hall.

Daniel followed and wrapped his fingers around her upper arm. "Not anymore."

Nine

❧

Nicole tried to pull free from her would-be rescuer, but his hold was like a warm vise tightening to steel when she struggled against him.

"Where are you taking me?" she asked, her breath becoming short.

The enormous man said nothing.

She glanced up to look at his face, his eyes, knowing she was totally under his control. His set features gave no indication of his intention, and as they descended the first flight of stairs, she could feel her anxiety rising.

"Let go of me." Nicole stopped, yanking her body to one side. But he was so large, so muscular, her slight weight scarcely moved him.

He continued to ignore her, propelling her down the stairs and moving her where he wanted her to go, forcing her to do as he willed.

Memories engulfed her, and as they reached the landing between the first and second floors, her fear won out.

"Let me go!" Nicole said, hitting his arm with every

ounce of strength she had, but the man did not budge an inch.

A wave of panic crashed over her, and she kicked and clawed her way to the surface, striking out at anything in her path. She kept flailing until her fists stopped making contact with the solid wall of his body.

Her sight slowly returned, and before she realized that he had released her, Nicole found herself pressed into the corner of the stairwell. Her arms were outstretched, bracing her body against the wall as she struggled to breathe. Disoriented, she remembered the Scot and glanced at him beneath dark lashes.

He stood with both hands raised as if calming a mare that had just bolted, but it was the look in his turquoise eyes that made her stomach seize with humiliation. His eyes were fixed on her as if she were a madwoman, and his auburn brows were drawn together so tightly that his handsome features were marred by lines of miscomprehension.

"I don't like to be handled," Nicole said, offering a weak explanation for her unwarranted behavior.

The Scot took a moment to respond as he continued to stare, his mouth hanging open.

"I can see that." He nodded, his left hand remaining raised as his right swept toward the staircase. "After you, *mademoiselle.*"

Glancing down, Nicole gathered as much dignity as she could muster and then licked her dry lips, saying, *"Merci,"* before gliding down the stairs as if nothing had occurred.

She stepped beneath the open arcade of Place Vendôme and stopped, breathing deeply as she stared at the setting sun disappearing below the brick buildings.

"I'm going to call for a carriage," Damont said slowly, gauging her reaction as if to ensure that she had no objection to carriage rides.

Nicole nodded, mortified, as she tucked an errant piece of black hair behind her right ear.

The Scot returned moments later, offering her his arm. She took his peace offering, but could sense the tension in the muscles beneath his cobalt jacket.

He handed her up into the conveyance, making sure to give her plenty of room, then followed cautiously after her. Monsieur Damont took a moment to settle into the seat opposite her, and the carriage suddenly became very small.

Uncomfortable, Nicole stared at his broad chest, wondering when he had purchased the quintessential French attire. The high lapels and fitted waistcoat were exquisite, and while she knew that Daniel Damont flattered even the shoddiest of garments, these clothes he wore with ease.

The man leaned back, placing his right ankle on his left knee, his arms outstretched as he rested them atop the golden squabs. Unlike a member of the lower classes, Daniel Damont was totally unconcerned with soiling the expensive garments. He inhabited his clothing, and indeed the carriage, as if he had been thusly clad and conveyed his entire life.

She glanced at his profile as he stared out the window, strong handsome features, striking coloring, and the unmistakable air of aristocracy that swirled thickly about him. He was of the *haute ton,* she was certain, and would unquestionably be popular with the gentlemen, but even more popular with the ladies of polite society. All of which begged the question: Why was he here? Was it simply out of boredom?

He looked the sort of man that needed excitement, craved adventure. No doubt conquering women and wagering on horses would become tiresome for a man of his age and obvious intelligence.

How old was he? Thirty? No, not quite so old.

He was a man in his physical and mental prime, and Nicole found herself drawn to him. Not so much to his physical beauty, although God knew he had that in spades, but his confidence, his acceptance of who and what he was.

"How did you find me?" Nicole asked in English, hoping to distract herself from his overpowering presence.

Her efforts failed when he smiled, pleased with himself, then he spoke in a deliciously thick brogue, saying, "I followed yer target," as he tossed a rolled parchment in her lap.

Damn!

Nicole stared down, not having to read the parchment to know that it was the missive ordering LeCoeur's assassination. But she could not believe that he had found it, could not believe that she had been so careless as to have left it in her armoire. Yet his giving her the communiqué was further proof that Daniel Damont had indeed been sent by the English to extract her from Paris.

Damont?

That was not his name, of course, and she wondered if she had known him in London, if her father had introduced her to his family when she was a child.

No, she would have remembered him. However, he was older than she, and as Nicole had never made her debut, it was highly unlikely that their paths had ever crossed.

"Where are you taking me?"

Nicole again swept her hair behind her right ear, trying to appear at ease as she asked the question that would inevitably draw his mind back to her fit of panic. The man met her eyes and proceeded with such caution that she wanted nothing more than to be enveloped by the velvet cushions on which she sat.

"We must retrieve our belongings and transfer them to the apartment. I assume"—his eyes swept over her extravagant gown—"that you are no longer in need of the items in your burgundy trunk?"

"As a matter of fact, I am." Nicole looked out the window, feeling his amused condescension to the core. "One never knows when those gowns might become useful."

Monsieur Damont shrugged. "Very well. And after that, I thought we could dine. I have not eaten a bite since Minister LeCoeur arrived at his office."

Appalled, Nicole turned from the window and stared at him in surprise. "That was at eight o'clock this morning!"

"Aye, I'm starved." He chuckled. "But I dared not miss you merely because I was peckish."

Daniel's fork paused on the way to his mouth as he sat staring at the beautiful woman opposite him in a private dining room of an exclusive café located at the Palace Royal.

It was not her breathtaking appearance that had impeded his progress, but the manner in which she was separating the breast meat from the bone of her duck à l'orange. She worked with the precision of a skilled surgeon, and Daniel felt a chill dance down his spine as he contemplated how she had acquired such deadly proficiency.

"How old are you?" he asked baldly, breaking every gentlemanly decree ever made.

The woman blinked several times as if she had not heard him correctly.

"Why do you wish to know?"

He could hardly tell her the truth; tell her that he wondered how old she was and how long she had been executing men for money.

"Just curious." Daniel looked down at his sumptuous meal. "I thought as we are going to be spending the next three weeks—"

"Two and a half."

"Pardon?"

"We will be spending two and one half weeks together, after which you can return to London with your conscience clear."

"I would prefer to go now."

"I'm not stopping you."

"Aye, you are." He nodded, his anger causing him to revert to English. "I cannot leave you alone in Paris, knowing that you are placing yourself in danger."

"If I choose to do so, then what difference could it possibly make to you?"

Daniel grinned, incredulous. "No gentleman can leave a lady unprotected."

"Is that a passage from some sort of tonnish pamphlet given you when you enter polite society? 'No gentleman shall leave a lady unprotected'—which no doubt follows 'No gentleman shall rut with a whore unless wearing protection.'"

Daniel could not believe the coarse words spewing from

such a pretty little mouth. "A gentleman would rather forfeit his own life than see a lady harmed."

At this noble avowal, the peculiar woman threw her head back and laughed.

"Oh, Monsieur Damont, you are so utterly naive. I can see now how they convinced you to leave the comforts of London. 'Damsel in distress' was it?"

Her hilarity was so caustic, so jaded, that Daniel could not help feeling its bite. But she wasn't finished feeding.

"And while I do appreciate the gesture, I can assure you that I have no need of rescuing, so allow me to do it for you." She met his eye. "Go home, Monsieur Damont, before you are arrested and hanged for espionage."

"I have been commissioned to deliver you a warning—"

"Consider me warned."

"And"—Daniel spoke over her interruption—"bring you home to London."

"I won't go back."

"Why?" he asked in an airy rush.

She placed her fork down and smiled. "London is far too oppressive."

How could one possibly argue with such a bizarre declaration? He could not, so he simply reiterated, "I will assist you until the assassination is complete and then we will revisit the subject of returning to England."

The woman ignored this pronouncement, saying only, "You may assist, provided that you do exactly as I instruct." She took a sip of wine, her authority absolute. "You must trust my judgment and remember that I have done this successfully many times."

Daniel's heart bumped in his chest but curiosity got the better of him.

"How many times?"

Mademoiselle Beauvoire looked up, intentionally holding his gaze so that she could watch him flinch when she said, "Nine."

Ten

❧❧

Daniel towered over the petite woman as she fumbled with a ring of keys just outside the apartment door. She was so small, so beautiful, that he could not imagine her harming anything, much less killing nine men.

Nine!

"You're staring at me again," she snapped in French, pushing the gilded door open before stepping inside the darkened apartment.

"My apologies," he whispered in English, following her in with his trunk biting into his right shoulder.

He watched as she set her keys on a small marble table then lit a candelabra that illuminated her face, emphasizing a profile that any artist would long to paint. She was a study in contrasts, black eyebrows and crimson lips against a canvas of creamy white skin.

Soft, feminine . . . deadly.

Nine men!

"But I cannot seem to help myself."

The woman ignored him and walked along the inlaid wooden entry and opened the first door to their right.

"This is the dining room, and the kitchen is through that door," she said, clinging to her patrician French as she pointed down the corridor. "I never hire staff. So, if you are determined to stay, you will have to prepare your own meals."

"No problem." Daniel grinned and picked up the gauntlet. "My mother insisted that we all know our way round a kitchen."

The woman stopped walking, her violet eyes wide with surprise. "The males as well?" Mademoiselle Beauvoire asked in English, giving ground.

Daniel leaned forward as if he were confiding some great secret. "We're all male."

"Seven boys?" She stared, remembering their previous conversation.

Daniel nodded, amused.

"Your poor mother." She continued down the hall. "You must be Catholic."

Her pronouncement was said with that touch of superiority that every Protestant injected into observations on the Catholic faith. But at seven and twenty and a longtime resident of Protestant London, Daniel was impervious to insults.

"Aye," he said, deliberately thickening his brogue. " 'Tis my favorite doctrine of the Holy Catholic Church."

He waited and curiosity eventually caused the woman to stop in her tracks.

"What doctrine is that?" She turned to look up at him.

"That a wife cannot deny her husband his marital rights," he teased, lying through his teeth and thinking it more likely that his mother had demanded hers.

But rather than lightening the mood, his jesting had pulled her eyes into angry slits.

"Yet another reason I am not Catholic." She paused. "Nor Protestant, for that matter, as they are equally barbaric to their women."

Bloody hell. Perhaps he could see her killing nine men after all.

"We shall allocate this as your parlor." Daniel glanced about the room lined with numerous books and dominated by an enormous marble fireplace. She pointed across the hall. "And you may sleep in the front bedchamber." She opened the door and placed the candelabra on the table next to a large bed surrounded by yards of chartreuse velvet that hung from a walnut canopy. "Good night."

"Wait," he requested, his fingers overlapping as they wrapped gently around her wrist. "Aren't you going to show me the remainder of the apartment? I'm afraid I did not see much when I was divesting you of your pistol."

Even in the dim light he could see her cheeks turn an enticing shade of pink.

"In the morning I shall take you on a tour," she said with a considerable amount of irritation. "As for now, it is well past midnight, and I'm very tired."

Daniel looked at her lovely face and saw fatigue clinging to her delicate features. He nodded and, with a rakish grin, agreed. "All right, a tour first thing tomorrow morning."

She closed the door to his bedchamber and Daniel sighed, kicking off his absurd French shoes. His tightly fitted jacket came next, followed by his exorbitant silk waistcoat. He began to unbutton his linen shirt when a disturbing thought struck.

What if she left the apartment? It had taken him three days to track her and he did not relish repeating the exercise.

He picked up the candelabra and silently walked to the front door, which was, as far as he could tell, the only way into the fourth-floor apartment. He lifted the candles over the marble table and sighed with relief the moment he saw the set of brass keys.

Daniel lifted the ring, wondering why she had so many and hoping it would not take long to find the key that fit the front door. But his eyes narrowed when he saw that the hoop held not keys but an impressive array of brass picks.

His mind spun as he twisted the picks around the ring

until he held the apartment key in his right hand. He locked the front door and returned to his room, hiding the keys in the one place a woman of her height would never think to look—atop the velvet canopy.

Daniel sat on the duvet, the mattress sinking under his weight as he stripped off his stockings. But the more he thought of the picks and the dangerous woman that used them, the more he thought it prudent to sleep in a different bedchamber.

He cautiously stepped into the corridor, half expecting the lethal woman to fall from the ceiling and slit his throat. It was disconcerting, to say the least, and he kept a sharp eye, walking slowly as he proceeded into the depths of the luxurious apartment.

Daniel had just entered the back salon lined with windows that overlooked the square when he heard, "Blow them out!" nearly stopping his heart.

"Bloody hell, you startled me."

Nicole refrained from cursing as she ran toward the Scot and blew out his candles, which had lit up the apartment like a tree at Yuletide.

"I said I would give you a tour of the apartment in the morning!"

She ran back to her window and lifted her mother-of-pearl opera glasses, pointing them in the direction of the residence across the square. The apartment remained dark and she sighed with relief, saying, "Get down, will you?"

His brows furrowed, but not being a complete idiot, he sank to his rather impressive haunches. "Is this some kind of bizarre foreplay, or is there a purpose to us skulking around your apartment in the dark?"

"Go to bed, Monsieur Damont." Nicole lowered the glasses and squinted as she jotted down the time in a small journal.

"Not until you tell me what you're doing," he said.

"I am monitoring the nocturnal changes of the moon."

"And has the moon suddenly taken up residence in the apartment across the way?" Damont asked, staring at her with eyes so clear they appeared to glow in the dim light.

She blinked, disconcerted by the alluring shadows the moonlight was casting over the masculine line of his jaw, the hollow of his cheeks, the curve of his delicious lips . . .

"Don't be ridiculous."

"Then who's there?"

"No one." But then a light bloomed in the apartment across the way, proving her a liar.

Nicole ducked and pulled on the Scot's left forearm until his massive frame sank below the windowsill. She lifted the opera glasses and watched as the minister of police returned to his home after spending the evening with his current mistress.

"So that's Minister LeCoeur's apartment." The Scot jerked his head toward the window.

Nicole ignored him. "What time is it?" she asked, trying not to compare the stunning agent seated next to her with the man disrobing across the square.

"Twelve forty-seven."

Nicole swallowed her lecherous thoughts, placing the opera glasses on the floor and noting the time her objective had returned to his apartment. "Thank you."

"No problem, lass," he said in a Scot's brogue that made Nicole wonder why any woman thought French romantic.

She turned her head and saw Daniel Damont leaning against the wall with his right arm draped over one knee and the other long, powerful leg stretched out in front of him. Her eyes scanned his torso and she stopped breathing entirely when she saw that his cravat was gone and the first three buttons of his shirt were undone.

For most men, this state of dishabille would have elicited nothing more than a raised brow, a reproachful glance. However, with Daniel Damont, she had felt what lay beneath his shirt as he held her in his arms. She had felt the heavy muscles shifting against her breasts as he sank expertly into her mouth, and if he would just release one more button, she would be able to view the chest that had felt so . . .

"Is there anything else I can do for you?" he all but purred, the deep words laced with so much sensual suggestion that Nicole had to stop herself from shuddering at the carnal possibilities gallivanting through her head.

"No," she denied herself before turning back to the window, her face burning as she added, "Assassins *usually* work alone."

The comment was meant to be sarcastic but Nicole knew that she was reminding herself of who she was, of what she had become.

"You don't have to work alone. You don't have to do this at all," he whispered, more persuasive than Lucifer. "Come to London with me."

He touched her hand, and the ensuing jolt brought Nicole back to her senses.

"I have a job to finish." She rose, saying, "Good night, Monsieur Damont," before walking to her bedchamber and shutting the white double doors.

Daniel stared at the doors, his breathing heavy. He had meant to seduce the woman and lure her to England, but the thing that was causing his heart to thunder in his chest was not her reaction to his proposition, but his.

He wanted the woman, badly, and that had not happened since the day Sarah Duhearst had married the Duke of Glenbroke.

Confused, Daniel stared into the darkness and after many minutes of contemplation decided that his gentlemanly desire to protect the woman had manifested itself as a less than chivalrous desire to claim her. It was a primal need of every male, he knew, to protect and possess. However, in this instance, the line between the two masculine instincts had simply blurred.

Satisfied with his convoluted reasoning, Daniel stood and retrieved the candelabra, vowing not to confuse the two impulses again.

Eleven

❦

Evariste Rousseau sat, staring at the English dandies in disgust as they groped the whores at Dante's Inferno with all the finesse of a pig given a bucket of slop.

God, how he hated the English.

He hated their filthy city, their ugly women, their condescending arrogance that made them think themselves superior to the liberated citizens of France. Made them believe that their blue blood was somehow more precious than his own.

Evariste smiled to himself as he looked about the room remembering all of the Englishmen he had shown the true color of their aristocratic blood as it poured from their bodies, remembering the look of surprise on their idiotic faces when they realized that they were not, in fact, invincible, and were going to die.

Wincing as he wrapped his hand around a glass of ale,

Major Rousseau begrudgingly remembered that there had been the occasional exception.

He glanced down, flexing knuckles that were still raw from the beating he had given Andre Tuchelles.

That one had been different.

Monsieur Tuchelles had looked at him with understanding in his eyes, comprehending not only that he was going to die, but that he would die slowly, painfully.

Evariste had enjoyed, as he always did, beating the man. But when his hands were as swollen as the Englishman's face, and with each finger he took his time in breaking, Andre Tuchelles's eyes had shown only resolve. Had reflected his knowledge of Scorpion's identity and a mocking silence that had held until shock had comforted Tuchelles's body. Leaving Evariste with the threat of death as his only means of coercion, his only hope of extracting the name he so desperately desired.

He had allowed Tuchelles a moment to contemplate, to decide if Scorpion was worth dying for. He asked him one last time for the name and location of the elusive English assassin, and then with a respect he had never felt for any other man, Evariste had stabbed Andre Tuchelles in the heart.

No, Monsieur Tuchelles had been different.

Not like these men. These men were concerned only with their clothes and their cocks, their estates and standing within Britain's *haute ton* while people starved on the dirty streets of London.

The English deserved what Napoleon was planning, and Evariste could not wait to witness the destruction of the antiquated Empire.

"You look absolutely murderous, and I suggest you alter your countinence before you get us both killed." His companion's voice was light, jovial, but Major Rousseau could hear the familiar steel that cut beneath it.

Evariste laughed, his dark eyes turning to meet the steady gray gaze of Enigma. "I hardly think—"

"And that would be your first mistake. You are not paid

to think. When in London, you will do as I bid, when I bid you. Is that clear?"

Hackles raised, Evariste forced himself to bow his head to indicate submission, knowing that Enigma was the one French collaborator with the power, the intelligence, to sweep him aside before he knew that danger was approaching.

"What would you have me do?"

Enigma chuckled, enjoying his subjugation. "Lord Cunningham is being transported in two days' time from the Foreign Office at Whitehall to Newgate prison. He will be guarded by five men, two of whom will ride in the carriage, two at the rear and a coachman."

"Five men?"

Enigma lifted a brow. "Is the task too much for you? I could hire a few of these whores, if you are not up for the job."

"I meant only to verify the information." Their eyes held until Major Rousseau looked down, saying, "Forgive the interruption."

"He will be transported at night, so you will have no difficulty in making your way to the docks, where you will board *The Siren* bound for Sweden. Before reaching shore, however, you will be rowed to a second vessel anchored in the harbor which leaves for France the following morning. Do you have any questions?"

"And if something goes awry, and I fail to board *The Siren*. Is there an alternate plan in place?"

"Yes." Enigma stared and Evariste could feel his pulse steadily increase. He heard the scraping of metal and looked down to see a small dagger that lay on the wooden bench between them. "Cut your own throat or I will find you and do it for you."

Evariste pushed the dagger back and said with all the arrogance he was known for, "Five men will present no problems, and I expect to have bathed, imbibed, and fornicated before the English even know that Lord Cunningham has been killed."

"Excellent," Enigma said, sounding unimpressed.

"And as for fornicating, does Chloe still entertain here?"

"Ah, Chloe! She is quite accomplished with the whip, is she not?"

They both smiled, knowing that Chloe had mastered many more sensual torments than just the whip.

"Very." Evariste felt his blood begin to stir, felt the need to walk the thin line between pain and pleasure.

"Then I shall leave you to your amusements—or rather Chloe's." His superior rose, and then with a friendly smile said, "Do not contact me again," before blending into the crush of London's most exclusive gaming hell.

Twelve

"*What* have you done with my keys?" Nicole demanded, throwing open the door of the bedchamber she had given the Scot.

But when he did not immediately respond, a flicker of uneasiness replaced her irritation—only to return when she saw the near empty decanter of brandy.

"Damont!"

His head jerked off the crushed pillows, his auburn hair streaked with gold as he ran his fingers through the thick mane with one eye completely closed and the other blinking against the morning light.

"Christ almighty!" He licked his parched lips. "What time is it?"

Nicole glanced at the silver watch she had pinned to the bodice of her morning gown.

"Half past . . ." But her words trailed off and she bit her

bottom lip when she saw the Scot sitting up in bed. "Seven."

The silk sheet was sliding down an abdomen so muscled that she wondered if he had an ounce of fat on his exquisite body. His shoulders were square, padded with hard muscles that were balanced by thoroughly male curves. His chest was thick, solid, the heavy weight of muscle evident just below the dark disks of his nipples.

He was breathtakingly, mouthwateringly male and she had to grab hold of her muslin skirts or risk walking to his bed and running her hands up and down him as if he were made entirely of mink.

"The sun is scarcely up!" The Scot planted his hands on the mattress and finished pushing himself upright. However, it was not his flexing arms that made her jaw fall open but the glimpse of bare thigh that revealed unequivocally that he was nude beneath the golden silk. "What is so damn urgent that necessitates waking me at this ungodly hour?"

"Walking." Fortunately, he was still half foxed and oblivious to her lustful perusal. "I want to take a stroll around the square."

"Why?" Damont asked, lifting his bulky arm to rub the back of his tousled head.

"Why what?" Nicole had totally lost the thread of conversation, wanting nothing more than to take over the task for him.

The man clicked his tongue, apparently frustrated by something, but she had no idea what.

"Why would you want to go strolling so early in the mornin'?"

"Oh, damn!" She remembered why. "Just give me the keys!"

"They're atop the canopy. If you would just step outside for a minute, I—"

But Nicole was already dragging a wing-backed chair from the corner of the room to the side of his unkempt bed. She lifted her skirts and stood atop the vermilion chair cushion, feeling around the canopy for the heavy key ring.

"They're not up here!"

"Yes, they are."

Nicole stretched her arm out as far as she could reach and found them, curling her middle finger inside the brass ring.

"If you would just let me get my clothes on—"

At that moment, her precarious position and the unstable cushion on which she stood combined to overset her weight. She began to fall but caught herself on the velvet canopy only to have the chair slide backward, leaving her sprawled across the Scot's muscular abdomen. His breath gave with a whoosh, but fortunately Nicole had managed to retain hold of the brass ring.

"Sorry," she said, scrambling off him and then running down the corridor, the delicious heat of his body still clinging to her breasts.

Nicole unlocked the front door and flew down the stairs, only to emerge into the square just in time to see Joseph LeCoeur's carriage rumbling out of sight.

Damn!

Nicole's heavy breathing had slowed to a silent pant by the time she returned to the fourth-floor apartment. She opened the door and was greeted by Daniel Damont standing in the hall with the silk sheet wrapped about his lean waist.

Lord, he was handsome.

"Oh, well. I'm glad to see that your elbows broke your fall," Monsieur Damont chided her as she walked toward the back of the apartment and, unfortunately, him. "I, for one, was delighted that my stomach could be of service."

Nicole stopped and looked up, knowing that she should have been intimidated by a man who stood at least a foot taller than she. But when she was angry, the size of a man made no difference to her at all.

She lifted her index finger and poked him in his massive chest, saying, "Do not interfere with my work again. Joseph LeCoeur was walking in the square this morning and now I shall have to wait, along with half of the ladies in Paris, to make my introduction at the masquerade ball hosted by the Marquis La Roche."

"You hope to introduce yourself to Minister LeCoeur before you kill him?"

Nicole shook her head with the patience of Job. "No, Monsieur Damont, I want to seduce the minister before I kill him."

"Why?"

"Well, I am sure that the idea is quite foreign to you, but a man is often alone with a woman when he beds her, thus giving me the opportunity to kill him."

The Scot nodded, acquiescing to her experience, his expressive brows drawing together over those luminous eyes.

"What did he do?"

That stopped her cold, forcing Nicole to slow her breathing so that she could think. "Who? Minister LeCoeur?"

"Aye. What did Minister LeCoeur do to deserve his execution?"

Nicole shrugged then looked down to avoid meeting his eyes as her mind cataloged Minister LeCoeur's many sins. "He has murdered three men to reach the position of minister of police for Paris. He has imprisoned countless others— men, women, and their children who oppose the French government's policies. He has ordered the suppression of protests within Paris and even aided in the capture of Andreas Hofer following the Tyrolian Insurrection."

"Forgive me, Mademoiselle Beauvoire, but what business is it of yours if Minister LeCoeur kills his own people?"

"Surely you jest," Nicole sputtered, unable to comprehend such thinking. "The man has murdered lord knows how many innocent people, and you say this is none of Britain's affair? Would you object to Minister LeCoeur's methods if he turned his sadistic eye on England?"

"The minister will not turn his attention to England." The arrogant man smiled, the sight muddling her brain further.

"And how, pray tell, do you know that he will not?" she asked, trying to concentrate.

"Because you're going to kill him before the bastard gets the chance."

"Then you approve of the assassination?"

"Aye." Daniel Damont nodded as if he were the most reasonable gentleman in all of France. "He sounds a right bastard who deserves to be killed."

"Your support astounds me, Monsieur Damont."

The Scot held up one hand, his bright eyes going wide as he laughed.

"Not that I could do it, mind you. I would need a man looking me in the eye when I killed him." He turned and walked into his bedchamber. "But it sounds as though you've plenty of justification for killing the minister."

Nicole followed, feeling the need to argue even though Monsieur Damont had just agreed with her. "The British government has justified this assassination, not I." She glared at him while he sat on the edge of his bed, pulling on brown pantaloons beneath the silk bed sheet.

"Perhaps, but it'll be you who answers for your sins, not the Foreign Office."

The Scot tossed the sheet on the rumpled bed then stamped on his frilly shoes, distaste curling his upper lip.

"He's a murderer!"

"As are you, nine times over if I recall."

Nicole felt the back of her throat constrict, the back of her eyes sting.

"Assassination is not murder. I kill to protect the innocent and helpless people of this country; people that have no one to champion them, people that are beaten, raped, and robbed every day that this war continues. How can I, how can anyone, watch men like Joseph LeCoeur abuse their power and just walk away?"

Nicole lifted her chin, staring at Monsieur Damont while she braced herself against his condemnation.

"You haven't walked away." He smiled, not with amusement, but not quite with admiration either.

No, she had not walked away. She had not walked away at Newgate. She had not walked away at Honfleur, nor

Versailles, nor the fifth-floor suite of the Palace Royal. She had not walked away and it had cost her dearly and was costing her still.

Unable to endure another moment of his penetrating gaze, Nicole spun, saying over her shoulder, "Get dressed."

"Where are we going?" the man asked with his enchanting brogue.

"Shopping."

Thirteen

Daniel watched Nicole Beauvoire from the corner of his eye as they strolled along the rue Saint-Honoré, trying to decide if the woman was mad, or merely a patriot.

Her impassioned speech pertaining to the assassinations had certainly sounded reasonable, sane. She was protecting the innocent, defending her country against the tyranny of the corrupt. Yet, as he tried to envision executing a man in cold blood, without provocation . . . No image came.

But that was the point of contention, was it not . . . provocation.

She was a woman, and perhaps her understanding of provocation was entirely different from his own. Nicole Beauvoire believed that she was protecting the innocents of this war, believed that she was justified in performing the assassinations.

He was undecided as to whether her position was defensible, the philosophical question being murky at best.

If a man was in the process of murdering a woman, Daniel would not only be justified in stopping the man with any force needed, but condemned if he allowed the crime to happen. Yet if that same man were simply *intending* to murder the woman, would he then be justified in precluding the violent act by any means necessary?

And the more pertinent question that had been bothering him, eating away at his conscience all night—Was Daniel himself then culpable for the assassination of Joseph LeCoeur if he did nothing to stop it from taking place?

Again, he could not say.

"Here we are."

Daniel was pulled from his deliberation and into the agreeable surroundings of the unusual shop they had just entered. To his surprise, the shop was not that of a modiste, or a milliner, but a shop that sold children's play things.

Colorful silk butterflies hung from the ceiling, and Daniel smiled as a towheaded boy barreled out the door, aiming a wooden pistol that popped a cork when the child pulled the trigger. Tiny toy soldiers lined the shelves of one wall with exquisitely detailed rocking horses sitting beneath them.

Strolling over, Daniel fingered the black mane of one of the horses, confirming that it was indeed made from coarse horse hair. He looked up, staring at the back of the woman who had brought him here as she bent forward to speak in whispered tones with the elderly owner of the colorful shop.

Curious as to what an assassin could possibly want in a toy shop, Daniel circled a display of dolls and slowly made his way toward the counter so that he might hear their conversation.

"Three years, if my memory serves?" the proprietor of the shop was asking.

The petite woman nodded and the shopkeeper disappeared behind a curtain, only to return a minute later. The merchant smiled, holding up a brightly painted wooden top.

"If you will note, *mademoiselle,* the circular pattern adds interest for the child when the top is spun." The older man twisted his fingers, sending the top spinning on the surface of the counter. *"Voilà."*

Nicole Beauvoire stood on her tiptoes so that she might peer down directly over the rotating toy.

"Oh." She laughed, taking Daniel by surprise. The sound was so light, so genuine, so divested of the dark deeds which she now contemplated that he found himself walking to the counter to have a look. "How wonderful."

She was still grinning when Daniel approached and the sight caused him to miscalculate the distance and he bumped the counter with the tip of his atrocious shoe. The top began to wobble and she scooped it up and stared at him, her violet eyes lit with pleasure.

"Observe what happens to the blue and red lines when the top begins to rotate," she said, excited to share her new discovery.

Crossing his forearms on the polished counter, Daniel hunched over, prepared to be amazed. But at the moment it was her smile, the contrast between white teeth and raspberry red lips, that tempted him to lick the juice from every recess of her luscious little mouth.

"Uh, spin away," Daniel said, a bit strained.

She mimicked the shopkeeper's quick movements, but it took several attempts before she could set the top to spinning.

"Look," the lady said, delighted, forcing him to quell his baser instincts.

Daniel dutifully bent his head and smiled genuinely as the colorful swirls appeared to expand then contract to the outer edges of the top, only to do it all over again.

"Brilliant," he chuckled, joined by the shopkeeper and the beautiful woman to his left.

Still smiling, Daniel glanced up, but as he bent his head to view the top once more, he noticed that the striking woman had also placed her forearms on the oak counter. This had the delightful effect of pushing her rather large breasts to the point of bursting from the bodice of her extravagant gown. And while he preferred a woman's rounded backside to her rounded bosom, no man could help admiring the lady's all too feminine curves.

Including, he realized, the elderly shopkeeper.

With a menacing glare at the lecherous old man, Daniel snatched up the top, causing Mademoiselle Beauvoire to scowl prettily as she uncoiled from her provocative position.

"I'll take it, Monsieur Gaulet, and if you would please be so kind as to wrap the top with this." She passed the shopkeeper a sealed correspondence, her canary yellow reticule dangling from her delicate wrist. "I would be most appreciative."

"Of course, Mademoiselle Beauvoire. I assume you would like this gift sent to Honfleur?"

"Oui."

The man bowed and then went off to wrap the top, leaving Daniel to wonder as to who would be the recipient of the interesting toy, but more importantly, the letter.

"Mademoiselle Beauvoire?" Daniel raised his brows. "You must come here often."

He watched her stiffen slightly and confirm with a nod. *"Oui,* quite often."

The woman turned away and examined the toy soldiers with such scrutiny that Daniel was sure her lovely violet eyes would cross. She obviously had no intention of revealing the information he had been fishing for, so he reached into his pocket and pulled out enough blunt to pay for the inexpensive toy.

"How much do we owe you?" he asked as the shopkeeper emerged from the back.

The man glanced at Nicole Beauvoire, who smiled graciously, saying, "Just add the purchase to my account, Monsieur Gaulet. *Au revoir.*"

Stepping onto the street, the alluring spy yanked at her gloves and turned on him in anger.

"We!" she snarled through a charming smile. "Unless you intend all of Paris to think you my protector, I would prefer that you not toss money about as if we were somehow aligned."

"My apologies. I suppose it was merely a matter of habit."

The lady swept a speculative gaze over the length of him and apparently found him wanting. "I suppose paying for a woman would be habitual with you. However, it is difficult enough working with you tagging along at my heels. I could do without your attracting unnecessary attention."

Mademoiselle Beauvoire turned her head to the right, her black hair glistening in the morning sun. Her eyes fixed in the distance and he could see from her pristine profile that she was thinking.

"As a matter of fact . . ." She loosened the strings of her reticule and removed a small piece of paper. "Go to this address and collect the items on the list. I shall meet you back at the apartment later this evening. Here is my key."

Daniel shook his head and, with a crooked grin, said, "No chance I'm leaving your side, lass."

Sighing, the woman looked up and spoke to him as if he were an idiot. "Monsieur Damont, I am going to the apothecary, where I plan to discuss, in great detail, remedies for feminine ailments. And while I am sure the topic would prove most fascinating for you, the fact remains that you know my objective, leaving me very little choice but to return to the apartment or risk your exposing this mission to every citizen of France!"

Unaccustomed to being spoken to in such a manner by anyone, much less a woman, Daniel swallowed his pride and nodded, looking down at the elegant scrawl.

"Oh, you can't be serious," he groaned, reading the list.

"Deadly," she sang, her lips curving to betray her amusement.

A thought struck and Daniel straightened himself, saying with his most charming of smiles, "As you wish, Mademoiselle Beauvoire. I shall happily retrieve the items on your list and anxiously await your return to the apartment."

Her brows drew together with suspicion, but when he lifted her hand to his lips and kissed it, whispering, *"Au revoir."* She out and out glowered.

Daniel turned and walked down the wide boulevard, feeling her eyes on his back every step of the way. He slowed his pace, enjoying her discomfiture, knowing that she was wondering, speculating as to his newfound amicability.

But the lady had no notion of how amiable he intended to get.

He had come to Paris to forget, to be distracted from his hurt, but his pain had followed him and all he wanted to do now was go home to Scotland, to drink himself into a peaceful stupor and forget about the ethical quagmire in which he was now sinking.

Assist in Joseph LeCoeur's execution, or abandon the woman who intended to kill the man?

Both alternatives were grim, but he knew himself too well. Minister LeCoeur damn well deserved the wrath of the British government, and he could not leave Nicole Beauvoire to perform the task alone, knowing she was in peril. He had considered it, prodded by her humiliating barbs and supported by the knowledge that she was indeed choosing to remain in Paris.

The troublesome question still remained. Why?

What had happened to this lovely woman to turn her heart so cold, to make her capable of such a thing? Was she equally deserving of her punishment should she be captured by the French? Daniel was not sure that he wanted to know.

He was much more inclined to avoid the situation altogether. Seduce the woman; lure her to Honfleur before he had the killing of Joseph LeCoeur forever on his conscience and a black mark against his soul.

Fourteen

Lady Juliet Pervill walked toward the Duchess of Glen-broke's townhome on Grosvenor Square, bemoaning the fact that they were indeed walking.

"Why in heaven's name did we stroll today?"

Her cousin, Lady Felicity Appleton, closed her fawn-colored eyes and lifted her perfectly sculpted face toward the sun.

"Mmm. How can we not walk on such a glorious day?" Her lids fluttered open and she searched the blue expanse. "There's not a single cloud in the sky."

Truth be told, Juliet was pleased to see her cousin take such pleasure in their afternoon outing. It was the first time since the murder of her dear friend, Lord Elkin, that Felic-ity had truly enjoyed herself.

But at present her cheerfulness was damned annoying.

"Yes, yes, beautiful, beautiful." Juliet winced. "Nevertheless, these new boots are making mincemeat of my feet."

Felicity stopped and Juliet sighed with relief, thankful to her considerate cousin for giving her a moment to rest.

"We can't dally too long, dearest. Sarah was quite adamant that we arrive punctually."

This time.

Felicity had not said the words but she knew her cousin was thinking them. Juliet blushed, remembering the kisses she had exchanged with Robert Barksdale that had led her to utterly forget the hour the last time she was invited to tea by the Duchess of Glenbroke.

Juliet resumed walking, relegating the delicious Lord Barksdale to the back of her mind. "Yes, Sarah was quite insistent in her invitation. I gathered that she wanted to speak with us about a matter in particular."

"Yes, I felt similarly when I spoke with her at Hyde Park." Juliet stared at the enormous façade of the Duchess of Glenbroke's home, trying to decide what might be going on in Sarah's pretty little head. "Do you think she is increasing?"

"Oh," Felicity gasped as she always did when discussing babies. "Wouldn't that be delightful?"

Juliet gave a mental shrug, not a woman who particularly liked infants. Children she adored, but the moment she took a babe in her arms, it never failed to spit up its breakfast all over her favorite gown.

"Yes," she muttered, but her eyes narrowed as a man came out of Sarah's front door. "That would be lovely."

Juliet watched, eliminating their acquaintances as the man walked toward them; too broad to be Aidan Duhearst, too dark to be Christian St. John. She focused all of her attention on the man's face while trying to appear as though she were not.

She could see his features now. High cheekbones, full lips for a man, a square jaw that was echoed by closely trimmed sideburns. He was ten paces away and her forehead creased as she out and out stared, trying desperately to understand why the man seemed so familiar.

The gentleman tipped his hat as he passed them, and Juliet all but gasped when she met his gaze. His severe eyes burrowed into her as though he understood every thought that she ever had or ever would have.

Her head snapped round as they continued walking and she stared at his back and then his backside in open, appreciative assessment. He must have felt her evaluation because he, too, looked back, meeting her eyes just before his dark brows furrowed in what appeared to be confusion. Thinking he also felt some familiarity, she was enlightened as to his bewilderment the moment she walked headlong into a lamppost.

"Oh, dear, Juliet! Are you all right?" Felicity fussed.

Mortified, Juliet rubbed her head and glanced at the man from beneath her hand, praying that he had not noticed her inelegance. But he had, and she knew it with the slight quirking of his lips as the handsome gentleman turned around and continued on his way.

"I'm fine," she said irritably. "But who was that man? He seemed so familiar."

Felicity shrugged her lovely shoulders. "I've never seen him before."

"He came out of Sarah's house."

"Really?"

Juliet rolled her eyes, amazed at Felicity's lack of observation. "Perhaps he was the man Glenbroke hired to locate Daniel?"

"Do you suppose he could have brought news of Viscount DunDonell's whereabouts?" Felicity said, her hand at her chest. "Oh, I do hope so. Sarah has been making herself sick with worry."

"We are all concerned, Felicity."

"Yes, I know, but it is different for Sarah. We have known Daniel McCurren for three years while Sarah and Aidàn Duhearst have know him a lifetime."

The compassion in her cousin's voice caused Juliet to

soften her words. "Shall we inquire with Sarah? Come on," she prodded, her aching feet completely forgotten.

Mr. Seamus McCurren had just stopped laughing at the silly chit who had so flatteringly crashed into the lamppost while giving him a second, infinitely more thorough look, when his mind returned to the task at hand.

He continued down the road with disquiet echoing each step that took him that much closer to his parents' townhome.

Oh, his commission was simple enough. Inform his parents that his brother had been found, that Daniel's never-ending state of drunkenness had, no doubt, been instrumental in his offering his service to the Crown . . . in Paris.

"Bugger me," he muttered, already picturing his father's reaction. Seamus felt he could cheerfully throttle Daniel for making him be the one to feel it.

Seamus had gone to his brother's townhome to confront Daniel about his drinking, but instead of his impulsive elder brother, he had found only a white calling card. The gentleman on the card had been surprisingly difficult to trace. Their ensuing conversation, combined with the additional information just provided by the Duke of Glenbroke, would be enough to convey to his parents the events of Daniel's departure with some semblance of accuracy.

He could not, however, explain the why of it.

His parents would demand to know why the heir apparent to the earldom of DunDonell would do something so stupid, so careless, as to run off to war.

But Seamus was unsure if he wished to divulge his suspicions.

Daniel had been shocked, as everyone had, by Sarah Duhearst's sudden marriage to the Duke of Glenbroke. But Seamus was beginning to believe that Daniel's shock had been more in the line of desolation.

His brother's decline had begun shortly after Lady Duhearst's unexpected nuptials, and as they had been lifelong friends without even the hint of interest on Daniel's part, no one had connected the two events.

But Seamus knew his brother, knew that the things closest to his boisterous brother's heart were held that much tighter to Daniel's chest. Seamus knew that what Daniel needed to get over the girl was to face Sarah herself, to see the contented duchess in her home with the Duke of Glenbroke at her side. But his brother could not do that while in Paris—which was, no doubt, why Daniel had volunteered for this little excursion.

"Bloody idiot," Seamus muttered, not looking forward to witnessing his mother's fear.

He took a deep breath, then blew out his tension with one quick puff as he banged twice against the ornate oak door.

The door to the Earl of DunDonell's townhouse was opened by his parents' diminutive butler, and Seamus stepped inside. "Afternoon, Hopkins. Are my parents available?" he asked, hoping they were not.

"The earl and countess are taking tea in the small drawing room, my lord."

Damn.

"Thank you, Hopkins. I'll announce myself."

"Very good, my lord."

Seamus walked silently to the small drawing room, all the while reviewing his stratagem for dealing with his volatile parents. He knocked on the door and heard his father's deep voice.

"Come."

Seamus walked into the room and glanced from his father to his mother. The countess placed her embroidery on the small mahogany table in front of her and smiled brilliantly, saying, "Seamus!" with such enthusiasm that he felt a right bastard for not visiting more often.

"Mother," Seamus said, kissing her on the cheek and trying to avoid his father's disapproving stare as the earl folded his newspaper and placed it on his lap.

"Father." Seamus bowed, his mother's hand still on his

shoulder as they turned to look at the enormous man as he rose from his chair.

"Father, is it?" The earl's bushy brown brows arched and Seamus felt his spine go rigid. "Tara, is this one of our offspring? For I do not recognize the lad."

"Malcolm, do stop teasing him." His mother indicated a chair, her strawberry blond hair and pale blue eyes shining as she offered, "Have a seat, Seamus, dear."

Seamus met his father's amber eyes and knew that the man was far from jesting.

"Yes." His father resumed his seat. "Tell us what you have been up to for the past nine months."

Seamus gave a polite smile, not about to tell his father that he had been living with his mistress, that he had been happily researching ancient manuscripts in the quieter corners of the West End. He hated the obligations of polite society and, as the second son, had been allowed to pursue his interests unencumbered by the responsibilities of position.

And if something were to happen to Daniel, he would have to endure the responsibilities . . . but he would never get over the pain.

"I've discovered Daniel's location." His parents stared at him expectantly, far too practical to waste words on questions they knew would be answered. "He's in Paris."

His mother sat back, her subtle intake of breath more devastating a reaction than another lady's fainting dead away.

"He has volunteered for a mission that I am assured will take no more than two weeks."

"Mission?" His father spoke for both his parents.

"Daniel is merely delivering a message and will return on the next available ship."

"Bloody hell!" his father roared as he shot out of his seat. "Has the lad no sense? 'Tis not enough that he gallivants around town two sheets to the wind. No." His father's bulky arm thrust forward. "That is not entertaining enough for the boy."

"Calm down, Malcolm."

"Now," his father bellowed with a snort. "The lad, my heir . . ." He thumbed his burly chest twice with the palm of his large hand. "Runs off to Paris, where he might very well get himself killed!"

His mother raised a handkerchief to cover her mouth and then walked toward the fireplace. His father looked in her direction and blinked away his remorse for upsetting his wife as he said in a more subdued tone, "You've let your brother run wild, Seamus."

"This is not his fault, Malcolm."

"Aye, it is, in part." His father nodded then pointed his thick finger at him. "You've been in London for so long, Seamus, that you've no notion what your brothers are about." Seamus lifted his chin, straining against the weight of his guilt. "And you damn sure were in town when Daniel started to imbibe."

"God, you're an ass at times, Malcolm!" His mother's pretty forehead pulled together in an all-too-familiar and totally uncontrollable anger. "Daniel has always done what he damn well pleased, and I'll not have you blaming the other lads for it."

But Seamus did not need his father's censure. He already blamed himself.

Daniel had never been one to drink in excess, and the moment Seamus heard the rumors of his brother's drunken escapades, he should have been there to ascertain their cause.

But he hadn't been there for Daniel, and he realized that he had not been there for his family for quite some time. He was the black sheep of his enormous clan, totally opposite from his brothers in appearance and demeanor.

"He'll be home in two weeks' time, Mother."

And if he was not . . . Seamus would be forced to go and get him.

Fifteen

✦◈✦

Nicole returned to the apartment at seven o'clock that evening after having endured her final fitting with her modiste and consulted with the apothecary.

She was mentally tired and drained of emotions, using all of her energy to spin a web that would end in yet another man's death. She opened the front door and was immediately engulfed by an array of appetizing aromas.

Nicole scanned the entry as she pulled her reticule from her wrist, setting it next to the keys atop the useful marble table. She walked to the dining room and stopped, trepidation filling her as she saw the polished mahogany table set for two.

The fine bone china was edged with gold, and the hand-painted flowers were echoed by the enormous bouquet that sprang from a stunning baroque vase sitting in the middle of the table. Claret had been allowed to breathe in an exquisitely cut crystal decanter, which was matched in design by the glasses placed to the right of their gold spoons.

A clatter from the kitchen drew her attention, and Nicole continued on, stopping when she saw Daniel Damont busily preparing their dinner. He stood before the stove wearing neither jacket nor waistcoat, only buckskins and a thin linen shirt. The white shirt was untucked with the sleeves rolled up to his elbows, the voluminous fabric drawn to his narrow hips by the ties of an inadequate apron that she knew would swallow any woman.

She smiled at the sight of him, and when he began to whistle, Nicole almost forgot why he was here, picturing instead the boy who had been forced into a Scottish kitchen. *A very large boy.* She stared at his broad back, his firm backside, as he faced the stove.

She really should make him aware of her presence.

Her lips parted with the best of intentions but no sound escaped them. He was so tall, so male, that she was finding it difficult to look away, to give up the pure pleasure of watching him move.

He glanced to the right, reaching for a plate, and Nicole blurted out, "What are you doing?" before he had a chance to catch her staring.

Startled, he turned and looked directly at her. "I'm cooking dinner. You dinna eat while you were out?"

"No," Nicole admitted, her stomach responding to the enticing smells with a low growl.

"Good." Daniel Damont smiled, so open and friendly that she immediately became suspicious. "Have a seat. I'm just serving up our meal now. Oh," he said over his solid shoulder as she walked into the dining room, "I've left the parcels from the list atop your bed."

"Thank you." Nicole sat down on the cushioned chair, not entirely sure that she liked his entering her bedchamber. Or perhaps she liked the vision of Daniel Damont lying, nude, on her bed far too much. Her cheeks flushed as the focus of her fantasy walked into the room carrying three ceramic bowls.

"Here we are. Quail." The Scot placed a bowl with braised quail topped with sautéed mushrooms on the table. "Roasted potatoes and buttered carrots." He set the remaining dishes in front of her and then took the seat at the head of the table that she had left vacant. "I apologize if 'tis a bit rustic."

"No, it . . ." She met his striking eyes. "It smells wonderful, thank you."

He pulled his chair forward then reached for the decanter, pouring them both a glass of claret. Nicole reached for the quail but he stopped her saying, "Allow me," before serving her a delectable breast.

She watched, starving, as he served her the potatoes and carrots, but a niggling cautiousness caused her to pause before eating the marvelously prepared meal.

Monsieur Damont met her eye, confused by her hesitation. "Did you want me to pray before—"

"No." The man continued to stare and she dropped her eyes the moment he groaned with understanding.

"My God, you really are an assassin." His gold fork struck out, spearing a mushroom, a carrot, and a wedge of potato from her plate. "Poisoned a few people, have you?" he asked, not needing an answer.

Nicole blushed, ashamed that he had interpreted her hesitancy correctly.

"One or two," she admitted with painful honesty, banishing the faces of those men to the darkest recess of her memory.

Her *cuisinier* placed the food in his mouth, chewing as he reached for her claret, not his. Sipping the burgundy liquid, Damont smiled and then declared, "There, you're safe."

Nicole glanced at his masculine features. She could not remember feeling less safe.

"Thank you. I appreciate your efforts and apologize—"

"No apologies necessary." The man lifted his glass, inviting her to join him.

She sampled the claret and was surprised by how much she enjoyed the crispness of the brandy mingled with the sweetness of the wine.

"This is very good," Nicole said, understanding for the first time the popularity of the imported drink among the gentlemen of the British aristocracy.

Damont chuckled, saying, "Yes, it is," making her feel decidedly uneasy.

Why she was so discomfited, she was not sure. She had never worked with anyone but Andre Tuchelles, and that was primarily to receive her orders. This, however, was different. Daniel Damont intended to stay by her side and watch while she constructed and sprung her deadly snare.

But that was not what was causing her discomfort.

Nicole took her first mouthful of quail and moaned, "Mmmm," in appreciation of the simple flavors.

Daniel Damont beamed, and as she looked at him, Nicole understood that her anxiety came from wanting him here. She had trusted Andre, but she had never been attracted to him. Nicole placed her lips on the glass where his lips had been and then swallowed a large portion of claret and continued to eat.

The food filled her stomach while the claret warmed her mind, and Nicole felt her fear disappearing along with the sumptuous meal.

"Thank you, again," she said when she had finished eating. "The meal was quite delicious."

"You sound surprised." Damont grinned, making her warmer still.

"Let us say, impressed." Their eyes held until Nicole forced herself to push back her chair, lifting her plate and his from the table. "I'm afraid I must return to my observation of Minister LeCoeur. The masquerade ball is tomorrow evening and any piece of information I can learn about the minister might prove useful."

Monsieur Damont rose, his fingertips brushing hers as he took the plates from her hands. "Then please allow me to tidy up," he offered, looking down at her with those stunning eyes that made her chest collapse with breathtaking desire.

She acquiesced, withdrawing to the large salon facing the picturesque square. Removing her slippers, she sat on the floor and absently stared at Minister LeCoeur's empty apartment. The sun was descending, leaving a soft yellow glow that illuminated the perfectly manicured grounds below. She scanned the fashionable couples that meandered through the awning of trees, confirming that the minister was not among them.

Nicole noted the time in her journal and then lifted her opera glasses to peer into the open windows of Joseph LeCoeur's apartment.

The minister collected Roman antiquities and he seemed uncommonly fond of Julius Caesar. An interesting hero for the minister of police, a public servant, a man purportedly devoted to the liberated people of France.

"May I join you?"

Nicole gave a start and turned to see Daniel Damont standing five feet behind her, holding the half-empty decanter and two clean glasses in his elegantly shaped hands.

"If you wish," she said, amazed that he had asked.

Damont poured claret for them both and handed her the heavy crystal, but before sitting on the floor, he walked across the room and brought back a small wooden table.

"Do you play chess?"

She did, of course, but Nicole waited to answer until she had considered his reasons for asking.

"Yes, but I think perhaps—"

"Mademoiselle Beauvoire, you will be sitting here until well past midnight, as we both know Joseph LeCoeur spends the evenings with his mistress. I am simply trying to occupy our minds while we wait for the illustrious minister to return to his own bed."

Nicole took a sip of claret as she thought, but before she could answer, the man was bending over the minuscule table and lifting the lid.

Her eyes opened in surprise and he eliminated her confusion, saying, "The table detaches so that chess may be played in bed or on a carpeted saloon floor." The man set the painted board between them, retrieving the many chess pieces.

"Now, what color would you like to—No, wait." He stopped himself, a broad smile brightening his already dazzling features. "You, of course, will be black. And I, rescuer of 'damsels in distress,' will naturally . . ." He lifted the white knight. "Be white."

White knight, indeed.

"But then you shall go first," Nicole teased, the claret releasing her mind from its carefully constructed confines. "Not very gentlemanly for such a white knight."

"Oh, but I am the most chivalrous of knights." His eyes sparkled in the dissolving sunlight and she was captivated by the sight. "We both know that you prefer for your opponent to make the first move."

Nicole stiffened, tearing her mind from the pleasing form of his face to gaze into the man's perceptive soul.

"The pretty knight has a brain."

"And the skillful Scorpion is full of venom." But it was Nicole who felt the sting.

Daniel looked down at the board, stunned by the wounded look in her beautiful violet eyes. He had meant to tease, to play and enjoy each other's company. Positioning his knight, he sat back and considered the implications of his little discovery.

Scorpion was indeed human.

The fact that she waited to assess a situation before choosing a plan of action had been evident from the moment he arrived at the boardinghouse. From the first, she had gathered information by letting him talk, providing only what was required to further her inquiry and establish his credibility as courier for the Crown.

But this pained reaction to her deadly vocation needed further examination. Surely, he had merely misconstrued the subtle changes in her facial features.

"How do you intend to kill Minister LeCoeur?" She flinched, her hand hovering over a pawn for the briefest of moments.

"I think it best if you do not know."

"But you've decided?" Daniel looked at her, making sure to keep his face blank, his eyes vacant but watchful.

"Yes." The lady nodded irritably as she positioned her queen within striking distance of his knight.

Interesting.

Perhaps Scorpion was not as keen on killing as her namesake would imply—perhaps the task of enticing her away from her assignment would not be as difficult as he had anticipated.

"Well, lass, you might know how to play chess, but I'm afraid you're not very good at it."

The white knight took the black queen.

The lass blushed, clearly embarrassed by her ill-considered move. She had left her queen, her most powerful weapon, open and vulnerable to his attack.

"I'm sorry. I don't think I shall be able to concentrate on the match. I really must watch for Minister LeCoeur."

Mademoiselle Beauvoire turned her regal head and stared out the saloon window.

Daniel sat for a moment, thinking as he slid the chess pieces about the board.

"I've killed a man," he offered. The woman's head snapped around so quickly that Daniel was sure she had injured her neck. But now that he had her attention, Daniel continued, "Two, actually."

"Did you forget the other man?" she asked sardonically.

"No." He would never forget the second man. "They attacked me together, so I think of it as one event."

Mademoiselle Beauvoire looked at him, studied him, her surveillance of Joseph LeCoeur utterly forgotten. "Why did you kill them?"

"I was traveling to my estates in Scotland when they ambushed me." Daniel thought back, feeling no remorse, only the bitter taste of an objectionable occurrence. "I shot the first man as he pulled me from my horse. The second highwayman had a knife. I didn't, so I broke his neck."

"And yet you object to *my* role in this war?"

Daniel paused, astounded that she had so misinterpreted their previous discussion.

"Not at all. You and your counterparts are a necessary component of war. I merely said that I would have difficulty fulfilling that roll."

"But you have killed before!"

"Aye, but that was in defense of my life."

"Oh, I see." The woman nodded, angry. "You will save yourself, but not others."

"Now, that's a bit harsh, as I am in Paris trying to save you."

"I don't want saving."

Daniel's forehead furrowed and he glanced into the depths of her striking eyes. But whatever meaning had been infused in those words vanished when she went on the offensive, asking, "Why have you not gone to war, Monsieur Damont? Why have you let other men die for your country?"

Guilt overcame him as Daniel thought of the injuries, the hardships that Aidan Duhearst had endured defending Britain.

"It wasn't possible."

"Why? Are you afraid of battle?" Her voice was diamond hard, making him wonder what had happened to this woman, this girl, who should be thinking of nothing more than marriage and the latest London fashions.

"No. I've often . . . *ached* . . . wanted to fight on the Peninsula, but . . ." He closed his mouth, already giving her more information than he had intended. "What about you, Mademoiselle Beauvoire?" She blinked and he smiled. "How did you come to be in Paris?"

The angry light drained from her eyes, leaving them blank and lifeless.

"My husband."

It was a kick in the gut and Daniel felt a bastard.

There were many wartime widows, many women grieving the loss of their husbands. But no woman of his acquaintance loved so much, so deeply, that she would avenge her husband's death by killing those she considered to be responsible.

Daniel felt a twinge of envy, yearning to be loved so well. But Sarah Duhearst had chosen another man and he had been left with an emptiness that was reflected in the beautiful eyes of a grieving widow.

"I'm sorry, lass," he whispered.

Tears welled in her eyes and Daniel knew he had pulled them from her. He reached out and dried her cheek with the back of his fingers.

"I'm so sorry for your loss."

"You've nothing to be sorry for." She stared at him and he wanted only to put the life back in her beautiful eyes.

"Aye, I do. I've caused you pain, and for that I'm sorry." Daniel reached out and pulled the girl to his chest, letting her quiet tears soak the front of his shirt.

He stroked her back and her dark hair, soothing her with soft Scottish words whispered in her ear; words of comfort, words of consolation for this woman so deprived of nourishment, so starved for the tenderness of a loving husband that the lass clung to his tenderness as if she were drowning.

"I'm so sorry." Daniel lifted her chin so that she could see the sincerity in his eyes, the understanding in his heart.

His fingers disappeared into the soft curls of her ebony hair, and he could feel himself warming with desire for this courageous woman. His eyes remained fixed on her lovely face as he continued his rhythmic strokes, his sympathetic caresses at the back of her head.

Their eyes held, and Mademoiselle Beauvoire leaned ever so slightly toward his hand.

The gesture was all the encouragement he needed. Daniel guided her toward him as he bent to taste her alluring lips. She was so soft, so sweet, and she met his kiss with the longing of a woman deprived of a man's touch for far too long.

He parted her lips and delved into the heat of her

mouth, where he was greeted by the bold strokes of an experienced woman determined to extract every drop of pleasure from the embrace.

She reached up, cradling the back of his head, and when her tongue swirled its way down his own, Daniel's lust went spiraling with it. He wallowed there in the rushing current of mutual attraction as she darted deeper into his mouth, tasting, exploring, enjoying. Until, suddenly, she pulled her head back, suckling his bottom lip as she reluctantly released the sensual sensation.

Her eyes drifted open and he stared down at her, his blood pumping down his neck as it drained from his light head.

"I think you missed a spot, lass." He grinned, his voice as rigid as his erection. "You best go back and get it."

Daniel bent his head, looking forward to the second tantalizing round, but the girl placed her fingers over his lips.

"No." She shook her pretty little head. "I think that is enough practice for one day."

"Practice?" Daniel's stomach tightened as if in preparation for a blow.

"Yes, for the masquerade ball tomorrow night. Minister LeCoeur is very experienced, and it has been quite some time since I have seduced a man of his . . . caliber." Mademoiselle Beauvoire stared at him, showing no signs of the heat that still surged through his body. "But apparently it is rather like riding a horse—one never quite forgets."

The girl rose, taking his temper with her. "No, lass, I'd say you stayed your mount quite nicely."

"How kind." She smiled politely then started toward her bedchamber. "I think I shall have a bath before Minister LeCoeur returns. Would you mind keeping watch in the interim?"

"I live to serve, *Madame* Beauvoire," Daniel said with a searing sarcasm that apparently missed its mark.

"Thank you," the vixen replied sweetly before disappearing behind the double doors of her bedchamber, leaving him a frustrated heap on the sitting room floor.

* * *

Nicole sat, shaking, in the chair nearest her bedchamber doors.

Why had he touched her? But she already knew.

She pulled a handkerchief from her pocket and covered her mouth, smothering a sob. Nicole pressed harder, clamping down on her self-control as she forced herself to swallow her distress, her hurt.

Daniel Damont had kissed her because he wanted to go home. He had been sent to bring her back to London, and his misguided chivalry was keeping him here.

She was keeping him here.

But if he could lure her, get her to accompany him willingly, then his task would be complete and he could, with a clear conscience, return safely, triumphantly, to the bosom of Britain's *haute ton*.

And, God, she had been willing. She had allowed the claret to lower her defenses and he had capitalized on her weakness, swooping down to exploit her vulnerabilities, her need to be loved.

Well, not all women were so weak, so foolish, as to believe a man's lust was anything more than that. A base need to spill his seed as often as the opportunity presented itself.

But the manipulation was not entirely his fault. Nicole had allowed him to detect her weakness, her attraction to him, and he had used his sensuality against her. No, she was not angry with him but rather with herself. She had not guarded herself against his sensory attack.

She should be thankful, she supposed, that he had not simply drugged her and thrown her on the next ship to Honfleur. No doubt that would be his next tactic once she realized that his seduction had failed.

Damont would try again, she was sure, after her wanton response to his caress. It was inevitable. Nicole took a deep breath and mentally girded her loins, preparing herself for his further advances. She had played him well, had confessed to a carnal curiosity as pertaining to her work, her assignment.

Minister LeCoeur was indeed a worldly man, not such a young buck that any lure would entice. No, the minister was of an age to know what he preferred, to know what type of bed sport would arouse him. She would have to spend the evening in thoughtful consideration of the best means of breaching the minister's sensual defenses, of embodying Joseph LeCoeur's sexual fantasies.

All the while, avoiding Daniel Damont and her own.

Sixteen

An invitation to the masquerade ball hosted by the Marquis La Roche was very difficult to procure, but Nicole had managed, as she always did. She had to. Prudent Parisian ministers rarely ventured out in public, and when they did, they were surrounded by highly trained guards.

However, for the powerful marquis, exceptions were made. Her target had become a minister by knowing with whom to align himself and by knowing which men to appease. He was cautious, clever, and never made a move without considering every possible outcome of that decision.

But the minister did have a weakness.

He enjoyed competing.

A virgin was no match for his prowess, while forcing a woman to his bed would be equally disappointing. No, she suspected after hours of discreet observation that a woman equally matched in sexual sophistication would arouse Minister LeCoeur's interest far more than any virtuous lady.

Competition was fuel to his fire and Nicole dressed accordingly. She had ordered a black lace mask cut in the shape of a butterfly and edged all the way around with small yellow diamonds. But she had chosen not to line the mask with satin so as to leave the pliable lace to reveal provocative glimpses of the woman beneath.

Her eyes had been decorated with the kohl she had asked Monsieur Damont to purchase, and the black cosmetic had the effect of intensifying the violet color.

Anxious, Nicole reached into the bodice of her gown and adjusted her breasts, lifting them to give a more titillating view than was provided by the low-slung neckline of her distinctive costume.

She sat back as the carriage churned steadily toward the masquerade ball, where she would make her first contact with Joseph LeCoeur. She closed her eyes, rehearsing what she would say, what he might say in return, as she rolled her head from side to side, trying to lessen the tension pulling at her neck.

However, her anxiety returned the moment the carriage came to a stop. Nicole reached down and gathered her capacious skirts then stepped down from the luxurious carriage. The crisp autumn air stung her cheeks as she looked up at the enormous château, which was artfully lit by hundreds of flickering torches.

Glancing at the arriving guests, Nicole adjusted the yards of black tulle that her modiste had painstakingly sewn in confusing swirls to the black silk of the skirt beneath. Satisfied with the effect, she tugged at her long black gloves, taking care not to dislodge the ring of diamonds capping the heavy satin well past her elbows.

Her carriage clattered away down the drive and Nicole swallowed her distaste of the task before her, then walked up the pretentious staircase into the enormous home of the

Marquis La Roche. Nicole smiled contentedly as she looked down at the dancing couples, noting that she was the only woman in view dressed entirely in black.

Heads turned with curious interest, and Nicole took a deep breath as she descended the marble stairs to the ballroom below. She smiled politely at the gentlemen, who behind the shield of their required masks stared at her décolletage in open appreciation before lifting their eyes to meet her disinterested gaze.

A brave young buck approached, wearing a black domino and mask and she was too busy trying to divine his identity to note the blond Zeus approaching from her right. The gentleman opened his mouth to speak, but his eyes darted to his left and he promptly shut it, bowing to the fair man now standing at her side.

Nicole turned her head to the right and smiled at the tall gentleman clad in a white silk robe and a golden mask fashioned in the shape of a lightning bolt.

He smiled and small wrinkles appeared at the corners of his brown eyes when he said, "Good evening, *mademoiselle,* and welcome to my home."

"Marquis La Roche," Nicole surmised as she curtsied, making sure to leave her head up so that the marquis would be able to view her breasts, which were threatening to burst from her intricately embroidered gown. "Thank you for inviting me."

"Did I?" The marquis quirked a fair brow.

"Did you what?"

"Did I invite you?"

Nicole laughed at the bluntness of his question. "Well, I must confess that I am newly arrived in Paris, but when I received this invitation . . ." She withdrew an invitation from a pocket hidden in the folds of her gown. "I assumed that you wanted me here."

The marquis could not help glancing her over, saying, "I very much want you here, *mademoiselle,* as I feel resourcefulness should be rewarded."

Nicole grinned, knowing that her forged invitation had

been identified and appreciative that the man had not thrown her out on her ear. "How very progressive of you, Marquis La Roche."

Her host bent his head in acceptance of her compliment. "If there is anything you require, *mademoiselle,* please do not hesitate to seek me out."

"You are quite generous."

The marquis laughed, saying, "Generosity has nothing to do with it, my dear. Enjoy your evening." He kissed her gloved hand, but before he had released her, a small murmur drew their attention to the head of the elaborate staircase.

Nicole's mouth fell open and her eyebrows rose. She stared, along with everyone else in the room, at the unmasked figure of Daniel Damont dressed as a Roman general. The Scot wore a golden breast plate stamped with the Eagled Crest of the Holy Roman Empire, and while that was wildly impressive, it was the shocking amount of flesh not covered by the costume that held the guests in thrall.

Strips of leather cut to points hung around his narrow hips and upper arms, leaving every woman in the ballroom with a clear view of the man's beautifully muscled arms and thighs.

And view him they did.

No woman could help gawking, as Daniel Damont was a Roman sculpture come to life. And just to emphasize his mortality, the stunning man surveyed the ballroom and then grinned as if he approved of what he was undoubtedly about to conquer.

He sauntered down the white marble staircase. The brown leather strips flared, drawing all feminine eyes to his flexing thighs.

"I am quite certain I did not invite *him,*" the marquis muttered, bringing Nicole's mind up to pace with her racing heart. "Excuse me."

Marquis La Roche made for the base of the stairs, and Nicole grabbed the arm of the young buck who had approached her when she first arrived.

"I do so enjoy a waltz," she said, not giving the boy time

to think as she led him through the crush and away from Daniel Damont.

She needed time, needed a moment to wrap her mind around Damont's reasons for following her to the masquerade ball. He was compromising her mission by distracting her at the very moment when she needed all of her faculties to seduce Minister LeCoeur.

She glanced over her partner's shoulder as they spun the length of the room. Daniel Damont's handsome face was clearly visible over the heads of the other guests, and he was looking for something.

Her.

And then Nicole smiled to herself, remembering that she had gone to the modiste to receive assistance in dressing. Damont had not seen her gown and would have no way to identify her. She was wearing a mask, and although he could see her black hair, there were many women present at the ball with ebony coiffures. Nicole sighed with relief and ducked behind her partner just to be sure.

If she hurried, she would be able to contact Minister LeCoeur and leave the ball before . . .

"Good evening." Nicole's heart stopped and apprehension bled into her chest. "Might I have the pleasure of cutting in on this set."

The boy she danced with was clearly taken aback. He stared at Daniel Damont, who stood in the middle of the ballroom floor waiting for the upstart to relinquish his partner as if it were inevitable.

"Keep dancing," Nicole whispered to the buck.

They turned away from Damont, but her eyes met his before she spun to the far side of the wooden floor. Damont watched, a Roman warrior waiting for the perfect moment to attack. He crossed sculpted arms over his chest and smiled, oblivious to the disapproving stares of the couples forced to dodge him as they danced.

They continued to twirl, but as the waltz swept them back toward Monsieur Damont, her young partner tensed, spinning them a shade too early in hopes of avoiding the unavoidable.

Daniel Damont anticipated them, stepping to his right and blocking their progress. The Scot stared down and informed her partner, "I'm stepping in."

To his credit Nicole's partner paused, thinking to defend her. The buck's eyes slid to hers and his mouth opened, but she cut him off, saying, "Don't bother, you won't win and I shall be perfectly all right. He's not dangerous." Nicole met Damont's eye. "Just unbearable."

The wretch chuckled and then bowed as the boy skulked away, embarrassed, to the edge of the ballroom's exquisite maple floor.

"My dance, I believe," he said, just as the opening chords of a second, much slower, waltz began.

Nicole went into Damont's arms, her lips pinched as she glanced at the aghast guests.

"You have drawn the attention of everyone in attendance."

Monsieur Damont's large hand slid farther around her waist and he smiled suggestively, saying, "You had done that already, *mademoiselle.*"

His gaze slipped to her low-cut gown and Nicole felt the ache of disillusionment blossom in her chest, tightening the back of her throat. Men had always been obscenely drawn by her abundant breasts, and why she expected Daniel Damont to be any different she could not fathom.

"You look stunning, Mademoiselle Beauvoire."

Nicole snorted in disgust and stopped dead on the dance floor, causing the unsuspecting couple behind them to crash into Monsieur Damont's massive back. She yanked her hand from his and stormed off the dance floor toward the balcony on a cloud of indignant black silk.

She stood on the balcony, needing to be alone, needing to remember that she was alone, and more importantly, needing to remember the reason she had come to this sad state in the middle of a Parisian ballroom.

"What did you do that for?"

Nicole turned, her eyes darting about the balcony to verify that they were indeed alone.

"How dare you follow me?" she hissed. "Have you any idea of the position you have just placed me in?"

Monsieur Damont's masculine lips pulled into a seductive grin and he walked toward her, placing one hand on the balustrade and the other on her right cheek.

"I can only envision the position I've put you in."

Nicole swallowed, asking, "Who are you supposed to resemble?" as she pulled away from his scorching touch.

"Marc Antony. Who better to compete with Caesar?" Daniel Damont tossed his auburn head toward the ballroom. "Do you see him?" he whispered down at her. "The minister is wearing a red velvet robe."

Nicole slid her eyes to the right and saw Joseph LeCoeur standing at the edge of the ballroom nearest the open glass doors.

"He has been watching you the entire time that I've been here."

"You've only been here ten minutes," Nicole said with utmost sarcasm.

"Aye." Damont took a step closer. "But I, like Caesar, know which women are worth seducing."

Before she had time to react, Daniel Damont had grasped the back of her neck and bent his head, seizing her in a carnal kiss meant to conquer and claim.

Stunned by the Scot's very public display, Nicole jerked her head back and voiced her incredulity in the form of an offended exhalation.

"Are you mad?"

Damont smiled, unrepentant and sure of his sensual appeal. But what was even more irritating than the man's arrogance was the fact that his confidence was warranted, as evidenced by her less than stable knees.

"Competition should hasten the minister's pursuit of you." Monsieur Damont was correct. *Damn the man.* "Now, all you need do is slap—"

The Scot's head snapped to the right with the force of

her enthusiastic blow to his left cheek. His jaw clenched and Nicole could see the anger burning in his bright eyes as Damont struggled to regain his amiable façade.

"You needn't have struck me quite so hard, lass," he growled, his compressed lips scarcely moving.

Guilt flooded her. Nicole stared at his perfect profile, knowing that it was her inability to control her desire for Daniel Damont that had caused her fit of frustration.

"Is Antony disturbing you, *mademoiselle*?"

Nicole drained the remorse from her features, forcing her face to harden with contempt before turning toward Minister LeCoeur and saying with utmost disappointment, "No, I'm afraid that is the difficulty. Marc Antony disturbs me not at all."

The minister of police chuckled and Daniel Damont threw him the most menacing of glares before turning his cold eyes on her.

"May tonight's ball provide you precisely what you deserve," the Scot growled in aristocratic French before spinning on his Roman sandals and marching inside, the crowd parting as if he were indeed Marc Antony and they, his compliant troops.

Nicole smiled as she watched him leave, knowing that her target was observing her carefully when she added to Daniel Damont's impressive back, "Thank you for your concern, *monsieur*, as the evening is proving rather disappointing."

"Is it?" Nicole heard to her right.

She turned her head and smiled playfully at Joseph LeCoeur as the minister walked toward her with two champagne glasses in hand.

"Is it what?" Nicole asked, making him work for the pleasure of her company.

The minister stopped, handing her a glass, his dark eyes peering into hers. "Disappointing?"

She turned toward the ballroom and sipped the lively liquid, scanning the twirling couples as if assessing the evening's prospects, and then her eyes returned to meet his.

"It was," she said.

"And now?"

They stared at each other and Nicole raised a brow, circling him as she took in every detail of his solid form until she stood before him once again, pronouncing, "Yes, still disappointing."

At this outrageous decree, Minister LeCoeur laughed aloud, drawing several speculative glares from eligible young ladies.

"What is your name, *mademoiselle*?"

Stepping back, Nicole held out both of her arms theatrically. "I am Eris."

"Ah, Goddess of Discord." The minister nodded, raising an amused brow. "It suits you."

Nicole curtsied. "Yes, I thought it rather did."

Joseph LeCoeur stepped closer, echoing his increasing interest. "Why not Aphrodite?"

"Aphrodite? It's a bit presumptuous, don't you think, declaring one's self Goddess of Desire?" Nicole inhaled, drawing attention to her breasts. "And besides, there are at least five Aphrodites present . . . but only one Eris."

"*Oui,* you are causing quite the stir and I am certain that many men will leave the masquerade ball very discontent."

"As will you," she informed him.

"You think so?" Joseph LeCoeur smiled, accepting her challenge. "I've been told by a very reliable lady that there are no less than five 'Goddesses of Desire' present at the ball this evening. How about that one?" the minister asked, pointing to a blond Aphrodite spinning on the dance floor.

"Oh, no!" Nicole shook her head, appalled. "Far too domesticated for the likes of Julius Caesar. The poor girl looks as though she would lie on her back with her eyes closed throughout the entire interlude."

"And what of Eris?" LeCoeur whispered, wondering aloud if Nicole would watch as he made love to her.

"Absolutely not!" Nicole tilted her head to one side just in time to see the minister's disappointment before adding, "I never lie on my back."

The man laughed, but it was more a lustful rush of air.

Joseph LeCoeur turned to look at her, his gaze immediately dropping to her lips as they pulled into a seductive smile of anticipation.

"Now if you will excuse me," Nicole said, disrupting his fantasy. "I have an apple to drop. 'For the fairest' of the ball." She repeated the myth.

"I suggest you keep it for yourself, Madmosielle . . . ?"

"Eris, Goddess of Discord," she reminded him. "And how you do flatter me, Julius."

Nicole turned away but she felt his fingers curl around her upper arm, halting her progress. Nicole glanced down at his presumption, and her left brow rose before meeting his eye.

The minister released her arm, a flash of respect pulling at the corners of his mouth. "LeCoeur. Minister of police, Joseph LeCoeur."

The man waited for his title to sink in, waited for her to see what a powerful protector he could be.

"Good night, Joseph LeCoeur," Nicole purred, unimpressed, before leaving him alone in a sea full of people.

Seventeen

Daniel sat, waiting in Nicole Beauvoire's darkened apartment while he contemplated the wisdom of having attended the masquerade ball. He had aggressively and publicly courted Nicole in order to hasten Minister LeCoeur's pursuit. But had he been thinking clearly, had he not been so damn compelled to protect her, he would have realized the limitations he had now placed upon them both.

He had cast them in far too confining roles; she, the wanton seductress, and he, the unwanted suitor. Gone in one impulsive act of protectiveness was his ability to escort the lady about Paris; gone was his ability to offer her a secure ride home from events in his conveyance.

Daniel sipped his brandy and repositioned the breast plate of his elaborate costume away from the edge of the elevated settee. He had given his word to the manager of the theater that he would return the uniform unscathed. In the end, however, it had been the money and not his word that had persuaded the man to temporarily part with the outrageous garment.

It had taken Daniel half the evening to find a costume that not only fit him, but was suitable for a masquerade ball. He had hoped for something a bit more dignified than walking into a crowded ballroom in scarcely more than his drawers, but . . .

Daniel had cringed as the faces of the ladies in attendance at the ball flashed through his brandy-soaked head. The women had worn masks, but if anything, that had made their gawking all the worse. As if he could not see their eyes as big as saucers behind specks of flimsy silk. Daniel had felt the wave of censure as it crashed over him, but there was nothing to be done but lift his head and wade into the water.

Because of her.

Nicole Beauvoire had been down there in that ocean of rakes and libertines, and all he could think was to get her out of the water as quickly as possible, to help her make contact with Minister LeCoeur and then drag her out the damn door. But then he'd mucked things up and been forced to leave her with him. With a clever man whom Nicole Beauvoire knew to be a murderer and a powerful member of the governing body of France.

Yet, she had remained in harm's way, was there still, dancing toe to toe with the lethal LeCoeur, armed, because of Daniel's stupidity, with nothing more than her bravery and an exquisitely conceived gown.

A gown designed to fit her as tightly as her sensual gloves, accentuated by a mask that dared a man to glimpse her face. A mask that hinted at the lovely skin that lay beneath the black silk gown, flesh that would taste as good as her lips, her throat . . .

Bloody hell!

Daniel shot out of his chair, the leather strips of his tunic slapping together then swinging downward to create a solid, yet fluid, skirt of protection. He took a step toward the decanter, and the garment flew out of the way of his right thigh. It reminded him of a kilt, and Daniel enjoyed the freedom of movement as well as the small reminder of home.

He was tired of the French and this bloody game of cloaks and daggers. If the woman had killed nine men, then she was perfectly capable of seeing after herself. His misguided, and unwanted for that matter, chivalry was not needed. He could do more good for the war effort at home.

He would just have to avoid the Duke and Duchess of Glenbroke until he had time to heal from his pain . . . and his guilt.

"Oh," Nicole said, startled upon her return to the apartment to see Daniel Damont sitting in the salon chair nearest the window, his bare legs and an outstretched arm illuminated to a pale violet by the moonlight streaming through the half-drawn curtain. "You're awake."

"Aye," Damont grunted as a flash of light glinted near his chest and Nicole heard him swallow the contents of the crystal tumbler. "I'm awake."

His thigh muscles flexed and his knee bent, causing his right shin to disappear into the shadows clinging to the base of the wing-backed chair, shadows that still hid his handsome face from view.

Damont said nothing, and Nicole felt the need to fill the awkward emptiness.

"I wanted to apologize, and to thank you for your help this evening. You were correct in your assessment of Minister LeCoeur's character. The minister did indeed respond to your . . ."

His leather chair squeaked and light from a match flooded the room, saving her from trying to explain the effects of his kiss. Nicole blinked several times, having just become accustomed to the dark, before Damont finally came into view as he touched the match to a candlewick.

"Mind my breast plate." Monsieur Damont pointed to the settee where the golden metal pieces lay cradled between two cushions. "I have to take the damn thing back tomorrow morning." The man leaned forward and lifted himself from the chair, which, with his excessive height, seemed to take an eternity.

"I'm not sure"—Nicole had to concentrate on her words, not him—"that you should take it back, Monsieur Damont. You had several admirers amongst the ladies at the ball, and I had no fewer than three women ask if I could give them your direction."

Daniel Damont bent down, his boyish grin holding the tiniest hint of embarrassment as he lifted the breast plate off the settee then set it carefully against the outer wall.

"And what did you tell them?" he asked, standing before her with his glass still cradled in hand.

"I . . ." Nicole hesitated and he raised a brow. "I told them that I'd no idea of your direction and that my tastes ran more toward men of subtle refinement."

"'Subtle refinement'?" Damont tossed back the remainder of his brandy then grinned and her heart bumped so markedly that it startled her. "Aye, I've never been described as a man of 'subtle refinement,' but I'd lay six to one at White's that Joseph LeCoeur has."

White's? He was a member of White's?

Nicole looked at her gloves, away from him, and tugged at the black fingertips. The tips elongated slightly, but the heat of the ballroom had caused the satin to adhere to her skin.

She sighed, taking firm hold of the index finger of her left hand and wiggling the tip of the glove to no avail. It was then that Nicole heard Monsieur Damont set down his glass on the wooden floor. His beautiful legs came into view as he stopped before her with his weight supported by the hardened muscles of his left leg.

His right foot thrust forward, splitting the leather strips that hung about his hips to give her an even more tantalizing glimpse of the man's power.

"Here, let me help ya, lass." The Scot grabbed her right wrist with his left hand, but rather than pull on the fingers as Nicole expected him to do, he reached for her upper arm.

She watched helplessly as one long finger slipped beneath the diamond-studded fabric, caressing her arm. Remembered sensations from the previous night rekindled beneath her skin. Nicole held her breath to contain the fire as his thumb and finger met before he flipped the satin over on itself. Monsieur Damont pulled downward and they both watched the satin sliding ever so slowly down her upper arm.

"Are you determined to go through with this assassination?"

"Yes," Nicole breathed, as the glove peeled its way past her elbow.

"Right," Damont whispered, his mind split by two tasks. "Then I've made a decision."

"Yes?" she asked, but when he did not answer, Nicole looked at his distracted face.

His striking eyes were staring at her arm the way that she stared at his, and when the glove finally gave, his breath caught. She could see his back tense as Damont fought with the need to touch her. But unlike other men she had known, Nicole knew that Daniel Damont would not touch her unless invited to do so.

An invitation her body begged Nicole to make.

"You've made a decision?" she repeated, helping him— and herself—regain some semblance of self-control.

The Scot cleared his throat and reached for her other arm, both of them pretending that Nicole needed his continued assistance.

"Aye, while I've hastened your association with Minister LeCoeur, my continued presence in your apartment would do nothing but lead to speculation as to the true nature of our relationship."

"Yes," Nicole said, her left glove slowing its descent the closer it came to her wrist.

"Therefore," Damont continued as she watched his large hands slowly work the silk from her fingers. "Therefore, I think if you have any chance of survival, it would be best if I were to acquiesce to your demands."

"Yes." She watched, mesmerized as he tossed the second glove on top of the first.

"And return to England on the next available ship."

"Yes." Nicole blinked, shaking her head. "Wait. What?" She looked up to meet his turquoise eyes.

Damont's forehead furrowed and he reached around her head, saying, "Take off that bloody mask so I can speak with you."

Nicole closed her eyes, knowing that if she leaned forward a mere few inches, she would be cradled by the tempting muscles of his chest. His arms were surrounding her, he was surrounding her as Damont picked at the ties at the back of her head, and all Nicole wanted to do was reach up and hold on to his strength.

"Damn," he muttered, and her heart warmed at his gentleness as he reached for her mask. Daniel Damont had not so much as pulled a single strand of her hair. "I canna protect you, lass. It pains me to admit it, but I've never been one to view things as pretty pictures."

He leaned closer, and Nicole was overwhelmed by the heat of him, the masculine scent of Daniel Damont as he peered over her head to view the obstinate knot. The ties gave and Nicole felt the mask fall from her face, but the man surrounding her did not move.

Their desire mingled and Nicole watched his broad chest take several unsteady breaths before he whispered in her ear, "I'll go down to the docks tomorrow and book my passage home." Daniel Damont lifted his head and took a step back, staring down at her with the black lace mask dangling from his elegant fingers. "You're free."

Nicole glanced at the mask, not entirely sure she wanted her freedom, but heard herself say, "Thank you."

"Just answer me this, lass."

Nicole looked up, feeling flushed, heated. "Yes?"

"What would you do if you knew you had but two weeks to live?"

They stared at one another for the beat of one heart and then Nicole wrapped her arms around his neck, saying, "I have one week," just before kissing him like a woman condemned.

His tongue fit her mouth like a missing puzzle piece and

she groaned, willingly succumbing to his sensual siege. Damont grabbed her backside, lifting her with his right hand as Nicole rose on her tiptoes.

Daniel leaned her backward, but rather than kiss her breasts as men always did, he kissed her on the neck just behind her left ear.

"You're so soft, so beautiful, lass," he breathed, the brandy covering his words with honesty. "I've wanted to taste you since the moment you opened that door in nothing more than a damp bath towel. Your beautiful hair . . ."

His light eyes followed the movement of his fingers as they combed out the pins holding her coiffure, causing her hair to fall into his hands, causing her to fall more deeply into his arms.

"Your hair tumbling about yer shoulders as if you had just made love." One long finger traced over her left shoulder, taking her sleeve down with it. "God, how I envied Scorpion when I saw you."

Her right sleeve was next, and then Daniel was lifting her, kissing her as he carried her to the burgundy settee. He tugged insistently on her black gown, and her bodice gave, exposing her breasts to him. Nicole inhaled sharply, aching to be touched. And he obliged her, lowering his head and taking her nipple in his mouth, suckling gently, rhythmically.

The heat of his mouth continued up her neck, and he persuaded her with his lips, whispering, "Make love to me, Nicole." His large hand supported the back of her neck. "Grant me the pleasure of having you before we die."

No, that's wrong.

Her mind began to clear as his hand descended on her back. She did not want him to die at all. She was the one who would die. She was the one—his hand!

"Stop!" Nicole gasped, lifting her elbow to knock his heavy arm away from the scars that he had been precariously close to feeling. Daniel Damont stared at his muscular forearm as if he had no idea how it had gotten there and then he turned to meet her eye.

Nicole stood, her right hand yanking up her left sleeve as she sought a reason for her outburst. "I don't want your help with this assassination, Monsieur Damont."

If this were, and it most likely was, a trap set by the French, she could not bear to be the cause of another innocent death.

Not again, not him.

"Right then." She could hear the frustration, the anger in his voice. "I shall return to Falcon and tell him that you have things well in—"

"Excellent!" Nicole nodded vigorously. "Yes, you should go back to England." *Where you'll be safe.* "And tell Falcon that I have been warned of the danger and will plan accordingly."

"Right." He stared at her.

"Right." She stared at his chest.

"I could seduce you." Daniel bent his head so that he could look at her stunning features, feel her heat drifting up to him on a lavender tide.

"I know," she whispered.

But he would not seduce her.

Nicole Beauvoire wanted him, he knew it, had tasted it in her mouth, on her skin. But Daniel wanted her willing, wanted her to come to him, give herself to him so that he might give himself to her. Daniel knew all too well the pain of wanting a woman, but not being wanted in return, and he was not eager to feel the sting of it again.

Eighteen

❧❧❧

"*Would* you like to guess how I have spent my morning, Lord Falcon?"

The elderly lord glanced up from the stacks of correspondence on his desk, irritated that the Duke of Glenbroke had breached his discreet sanctuary at the Foreign Office.

He did not welcome the interruption, not now.

Not today.

"I never 'guess,' Your Grace," he said, looking down. "And please refrain from calling me by that ridiculous title. You know I find it tiresome, not to mention unwise."

"Fearful a French collaborator might overhear us?" the duke asked, determined to get a rise from him.

"That is not amusing, Your Grace, and frankly quite beneath you."

"It was not meant to be amusing, my lord." Gilbert de

Clare sat in the chair opposite his desk, his silver eyes set aglow with anger. "As I have just received a tongue-lashing from the gentleman we had both agreed to send to Paris. So, picture my surprise when Seamus McCurren informed me that you had sent his brother instead, that you had sent a gentleman who, if you will recall, is a very dear friend of mine."

Falcon looked down at the paper in his hand, choosing to ignore the young duke's impertinence. "I did not send Viscount DunDonell to Paris, Your Grace."

"You didn't?"

"No." Falcon looked up, forced to deal with the situation before him. "He volunteered."

"Why?" It was a disbelieving demand, backed by the authority of aristocratic position. "And don't fob me off with heartwarming tales of patriotism. Viscount Dun-Donell has done more than his share for the war effort by securing ammunition and financial support from the northern gentry."

Falcon sat back, hardly able to tell the duke that the viscount's altruism was a direct result of his being in love with another man's wife.

The duke's wife, to be precise.

"Time was of the essence, Your Grace. We needed a new man to warn Scorpion of the danger, a man whom Cunningham could not have identified as a British agent to the French. Seamus McCurren was ideally suited to the task, and I simply called on his brother to ascertain his direction.

"Unfortunately, the viscount refused to divulge his brother's location without explanation, and when it was given, Viscount DunDonell promptly volunteered for the assignment."

"Are you saying, Lord Falcon, that you sent a viscount of the British Realm, a man as handsome as the devil and as subtle as a peacock, you sent *this* man behind enemy lines to issue your warning?" The duke expelled his disbelief in one airy grunt. "Have you any idea of what the French will do to Viscount DunDonell if he is captured?"

"Don't be so bloody condescending, Gilbert. It is my job to know, but I had no choice in the matter. Scorpion's value to the Crown is immeasurable."

"Of course it is, my lord," the duke said through clenched teeth. "You just declared it worth more than Daniel Mc-Curren's life."

They stared at one another, allowing tempers to cool.

"And his." Falcon broke the silence, leaning forward to hand the missive to Glenbroke, adding, "Andre Tuchelles is dead."

"The vicar's son?" the duke asked, resigned regret coloring his silver eyes.

"Yes, and *he* was a dear friend of *mine,* a young patriot who was mercilessly tortured by the French in order to capture the far more troublesome Scorpion."

"Then Viscount DunDonell is in more danger than you anticipated."

Falcon picked up a bit of smooth wood, clutching it in his hand as he tried to remember a time when he did not expect the death of his agents. He prayed for the men under his command, prayed that they would survive and prayed that, if they did not, their last moments were quickly delivered.

Neither prayer had been answered in the case of Andre Tuchelles.

"As is Scorpion."

They stared at one another, both realistic men, both knowing nothing further could be done to save either agent.

The duke looked down, his dark brows furrowing as he glanced at the colorful wooden toy. "What do you have there?"

"A top, Your Grace."

"Scorpion sends you gifts?"

"Scorpion sends my grandson gifts."

"Forgive me, my lord, but I was under the impression that your grandson died at Vimeiro."

"He did." Falcon sat forward to dislodge the pain in

his chest. "My daughter has since adopted a child, a foundling."

"Very noble of her," the duke said with all sincerity.

"More than you know, Your Grace."

Gilbert de Clare quirked a brow, inviting further explanation, an explanation that Falcon would never be willing to provide.

Unaccustomed to rising at such an early hour, Nicole yawned as she walked the pristine arcades of the Place Vendôme, wishing she had taken the time to eat before strolling the square.

She placed the back of her gloved hand over her mouth and was just about to return to the apartment and declare the entire morning a failure when she heard, *"Mademoiselle,"* from a liveried footman racing across the square.

Nicole turned her head with consternation in her eyes as if she did not approve of being hailed by a servant like a hired hackney. She looked the man over from head to toe, examining every detail of his quality uniform from blue silk waistcoat to the silver buckles of his garish shoes.

"Oui," Nicole said, finding him minimally acceptable.

"Pardon, mademoiselle, but my employer begs that you stroll a moment longer."

Nicole turned to face the footman, making sure that Minister LeCoeur had an excellent view of the exchange from his apartment window.

"Your employer?"

"Oui, mademoiselle." The footman bowed. "Joseph LeCoeur, Minister"—Nicole rolled her eyes and let her head fall back with an exaggerated tisk of exasperation—"of Police for the city of Paris, resides in the apartments behind me."

Nicole's attention shifted to the building in question, her left brow lifting as if she were reluctantly impressed. "That is very kind, however—"

A second servant came barreling out of Joseph LeCoeur's home holding a heavy mahogany tray on which lay an assortment of pastries and a pot of what she assumed to be coffee.

"Minister LeCoeur offers his compliments and hopes that you will join him for morning refreshment."

Nicole laughed despite her best efforts. The whole scene was ridiculous and would have been romantic if she were ignorant of the deadly man with whom she was dealing.

"You may tell your employer that he has five minutes in which to join me before I retire to my own apartment across the square."

The first footman ran toward Minister LeCoeur's front door, while the second servant led her toward a wooden bench beneath the trees before pouring her a cup of coffee then withdrawing to a discreet distance of twenty feet.

Nicole prepared her coffee with cream and sugar and had just taken a sip when she heard, "I was not sure you would wait."

"I wasn't going to until you bribed me with coffee." She looked up and to her left as an amused Joseph LeCoeur rounded the bench and sat down beside her, waving the second footman inside.

"I rather thought not."

"It's very good coffee, by the way." Nicole took another appreciative sip and met his astute eyes, allowing hers to linger.

"I must apologize. I was indisposed when first I saw you strolling the square."

"I'm quite sure that you were, Minister LeCoeur, but won't she be angry that you've abandoned her?" Nicole teased, knowing full well that Joseph LeCoeur's paramour had spent the entire evening in his apartment.

The minister chuckled, saying, "You've a sharp tongue, *mademoiselle*."

"You have only felt the dull edge thus far."

"Might I feel the other?"

"If you are very good." She grinned, lowering her chin and exposing the nape of her neck.

His eye traveled the line of her neck and continued

down her back, only to meander up the front of her tight bodice. He paused at her full breasts before once again meeting her self-assured eye.

"For you, *mademoiselle,* I vow my behavior would rival the saints."

"Let us not go overboard, Minister LeCoeur," she quipped. "A saint is of no use to me."

Joseph LeCoeur threw his head back and laughed at her audacity. "A devil then?"

"Oui." Nicole eyed him speculatively. "A handsome devil is far more accurate, I should think, and a much better match for Eris."

"And will the 'Goddess of Discord' leave me unsatisfied, or will *Eris* grace me with her worldly name?"

"Nicole Beauvoire, and before you become overconfident," she said, rising and continuing to hold his gaze, "keep in mind that I tell you this because even the minister of police could not miss my walking across the square to my own apartment." His gray eyes flicked toward the stone building and then back to hers with a triumphant glint. "Furthermore, I have not decided if I even like you, much less whether I intend to bed you."

He tried very hard not to smile upon hearing her frank declaration, but the corners of his mouth pulled up even as his full lips remained firmly shut.

"Then you have not ruled out the possibility?"

"Of course not." Nicole shrugged. "I've only been in Paris a short amount of time. However, I suspect the more gentlemen I meet, the less likely your prospects."

LeCoeur drew his brows together in a great show of concern. "Then you advise a hasty seduction?"

"I should think it your only chance."

Nicole realized her mistake the moment the man stood and she saw that the square was deserted, with trees shielding them from view of the surrounding apartments.

Minister LeCoeur reached out with his right hand and grasped her upper arm, pulling her toward him. His left hand settled on her neck and jaw, and Nicole had to stop herself from shivering with revulsion . . . and a touch of fear.

His lips pressed to hers, and she fought an overwhelming wave of nausea. Nicole closed her eyes and told herself that she was playing the seductress, but her tension remained. Any moment the minister would sense her aversion, and her interest would become suspect.

She would become suspect.

Nicole opened her mouth and her mind, letting him sweep in as she conjured a picture of Daniel Damont. She envisioned that it was him kissing her, holding her as he had last night.

Leaning into the kiss, Nicole took the lead, brushing her breasts against the man's chest, giving Joseph LeCoeur a taste of her fabricated fervor. And just when she felt him becoming aroused, Nicole stepped back and slapped him, with very little conviction, across the left cheek.

The minister smiled, expecting her censure, saying, "Mmm, very good coffee," whilst rubbing the side of his face.

Nicole turned in a seductive swish and lifted her white-gloved hand, waving as she said, "Good-bye, Minister LeCoeur."

"Would you care to attend the theater with me this evening, Mademoiselle Beauvoire?" the minister countered, full of amusement and confidence.

Nicole stopped and turned to look at him over her left shoulder. "How close is your box?"

"How close do you want it?"

"Very." She grinned.

"Eight."

"The curtain rises at ten. What do you intend to do with me for two full hours, Minister LeCoeur?"

His eyes slid down her body and up again, in one slow, anticipatory assessment.

"Show you the city."

"I've seen the city," Nicole said, lifting her shoulders in

a regretful shrug. "Then I suppose you shall have to retrieve me at nine. *Au revoir.*"

Joseph LeCoeur chuckled and tilted his head to one side in appreciative observation of the lady's swaying backside. He watched her walk all the way across the square and noted with keen interest which door she disappeared behind.

He looked up at the many windows of the south façade, trying to deduce which was her bedchamber.

A rush of heat came to life as Joseph remembered the feel of those exquisite breasts, pressing against his chest. He wanted to feel them pressed naked against him, to grasp them in his hands, all the while knowing it would be too much for him, any man to hold.

Joseph was becoming visibly erect and he glanced about the square before turning toward his home. The heavy door was opened by his servants, and he called to the guard on his right.

"Captain Turgeon."

The man clicked his polished heels and saluted, saying, "*Oui,* Minister LeCoeur?"

"Mademoiselle Nicole Beauvoire. I want to know everything about her. From where she hails, how she acquired her fortune, ex-lovers." The captain nodded his understanding. "Find something that I can wield over her. Political affiliations, indiscreet affairs, anything."

"*Oui,* but it will take time."

"How long?"

"Preliminary information . . ." The captain looked at the ceiling. "A day. A complete history of the woman . . . it could take as much as a month, dependent upon which province her family hails."

"You have a week."

It was a daunting task, but his men knew better than to show even a glimmer of displeasure.

"As you wish," Captain Turgeon said with a respectful inclination of his head.

Joseph turned, satisfaction pulling at the left corner of his mouth as he bounded up the stairs, opening the door to his expansive bedroom suite.

His mistress stood on thé far side of the velvet settee, staring out the window, clad in nothing more than a purple silk sheet. Her golden hair spilled down her back as she turned toward the large four-poster bed.

"Who was that?" the woman spat as if she had a right to an answer.

Joseph smiled, stepping around a three-footed side table, a bouquet of flowers brushing his chartreuse jacket as he walked toward his paramour.

"That," he announced, "was my future mistress," before grasping the sheet above her breasts and stripping the girl of her last shred of dignity.

"But as I have yet to seduce her . . ." Joseph raised his left eyebrow, meeting his lover's green eyes as he removed his jacket. "You will have to do."

"You bastard!" She drew her hand back to strike him, and his jaw set with anger as he caught her wrist.

He twisted her arm behind her back, causing her to cry out in pain.

"Don't ever try to strike me again." Joseph stared down at his paramour until the girl felt his threat. "Now get on the bed."

"You don't expect me to make love to you after—"

His cold chuckle froze the words of protest in her skilled mouth. He had forgotten how pampered the rich women of this city had become, and the general's wife was more pampered than most.

"I expect you"—Joseph continued to strip—"to do what you are told. Get . . . on . . . the bed!" he ordered.

His mistress flinched, never having seen his violent nature, choosing to assume that the men who ruled France had acquired their prominent positions by performing noble deeds. And while the general performed his duty in southern France, his whore of a wife sought to bed the men who ruled the city.

Joseph had been the third to receive such intimate attention, and he was sure he would not be the last.

He watched the girl climb on the bed, and as he stared down at her blond hair and adequate breasts, he pictured instead the stunning Nicole Beauvoire.

"Spread your thighs," Joseph ordered, hardening with need. He climbed over her, his weight crushing her into the luxurious mattress. "Wider," he ordered, and when she obeyed, he drove into her.

Joseph closed his eyes and rolled his hips, thrusting harder, deeper as his vision urged him toward ecstasy. He had to concentrate to maintain the picture of Nicole Beauvoire in his mind, prolonging his state of excitement.

He shifted the girl's hips as he plunged deeper. He was becoming light-headed and Joseph could feel the coiling of heat that he frantically kindled with long, deep strokes.

The woman beneath him moaned and he ignored her, his breath caught in the web of his own fantasy as he thrust again, causing the kindling to ignite in a mind-altering climax that shook him to the core.

Joseph withdrew only to throw himself toward the reverberations of his carnal detonation, reaching desperately for its elusive source.

But he knew its source.

Her name was Nicole Beauvoire, and she lived just across the square. Joseph smiled as he lay inside his ex-mistress, vowing that within a fortnight, Nicole Beauvoire would be the woman warming his bed.

Nineteen

Lady Juliet Pervill sat embroidering with her cousin in the lovely drawing room of Lady Felicity Appleton's townhome. Or rather, Felicity was embroidering while Juliet stabbed herself, staining her entire handkerchief with little crimson dots of blood.

"Ow! Why on earth do we not have the servants do this for us? Are we not paying them to do the domestic chores the *ton* finds beneath them? Why is embroidering not considered one of those tedious tasks?"

Felicity's fawn eyes concentrated on an intricate stitch as she said in a voice that made it clear she was only half listening, "Embroidery is not a chore, Juliet, it is an art."

"According to whom?"

"Society, and as you have no objection to performing 'chores' within your own home, I fail to see why you are so reluctant to do this one."

"I'm not reluctant to embroider, Felicity." Juliet stared at the ugly flowers that would have been prettier had she wadded up the colorful silk threads and tossed them on the linen. "I just . . . I can't do it properly!"

Her artistic cousin looked up, startled by the amount of frustration in Juliet's voice.

"Oh, I see," Felicity said, smiling. "It is not the embroidery that offends you so. It is the fact that you, the brilliant Juliet, cannot 'do' something."

Juliet's freckled nose wrinkled, and her eyes turned to slits. "Everyone thinks that you, the fair Felicity, are so sweet and kind. Little does the *ton* know that you are really the mean cousin."

"True," Felicity agreed, laughing. "I've often wondered why no one has noticed that you are by far the superior person."

Though the comment was lightly made, the conviction in Felicity's voice made Juliet look up to try and catch her gaze. But her cousin had already bent her head and returned to her elaborate embroidery when the drawing room doors burst open to admit, unannounced of course, Lord Christian St. John.

"Morning," he said far too cheerfully before placing his left hand on the back of the chaise and jumping over the fine velvet back.

Christian landed hard with legs outstretched, causing the air to rush from the cushions of the expensive chaise in one groaning gush.

Juliet giggled and Christian St. John flashed a look of unrepentant remorse toward his hostess.

"Morning, Felicity. Sorry about the chaise, but I had recalled that I was a bit lighter."

Choosing to ignore her visitor's lack of decorum, Felicity asked, "What might we do for you, Lord St. John?"

Christian sat up and raised fair brows over Nordic blue eyes as he looked toward Juliet.

"Lord St. John? Oh, she is angry." He leaned forward and grabbed Juliet's embroidery hoop. "Let's see what you're working on, Lady Pervill."

"Give that back!" Juliet protested, embarrassed.

"I just want to have a look." Christian stared down at the handkerchief, turning his head from side to side like a child trying to comprehend some mathematical equation, but not quite grasping it. "My God, you're awful at embroidery, Juliet."

"Thank you, Lord St. John," Juliet spat, yanking her hoop away from him.

"Now yours, Lady Appleton," Christian demanded with great humor.

Felicity voluntarily gave Lord St. John her larger hoop and he whistled in admiration.

"The detail is incredible. Did you design this?"

"Yes." Her cousin smiled prettily as she took the hoop back. "What can we do for you, Christian?"

"Well," he said to them both, forgetting the embroidery altogether. "I have been commissioned by my illustrious brother to invite you ladies to the opera Saturday next. Ian is keen on seeing this new production, and you are the only females in all of London that will not expect him to make an offer at intermission."

"True," Felicity laughed. "Tell the marquis that we would be delighted—"

"I can't," Juliet interrupted. "Lord Barksdale has already invited me to the opera tomorrow evening."

Christian leaned both elbows on his muscular thighs and waggled his brows at Juliet.

"Seeing a lot of Lord Barksdale, are we?" Juliet rolled her eyes, and Christian turned a rakish smile on Felicity. "Are you available Saturday evening, Lady Appleton?"

"Yes, I believe so."

"Excellent." Christian slapped his knees, signifying the matter settled. "Ian will pick you up at seven, and I will meet you at our box."

"Why meet them?" Juliet asked, confused.

Christian grinned like the rogue that he was and said, "Because, I intend to invite that loveliest of widows, Lady

Graves. Met her outside Tattersall's last week. She was buying a prime piece of horseflesh, and I could not help but notice that she was a bit of prime flesh herself."

Juliet's eyes were scarcely visible beneath her irritation. "Perhaps you should have purchased a donkey at Tattersall's." Christian stared, confused. "As you are such an ass!"

"Juliet!" Felicity admonished.

Lord St. John flushed and made light of his indelicate remark. "My apologies, but I often think of you as younger sisters, and siblings share . . . things."

"Male siblings perhaps, and not always then, Christian. You have only to look at the McCurrens. Daniel has disappeared with nary a word to his brothers."

Christian nodded his blond head, conceding her point. "They were devastated by Daniel's lack of confidence in them."

"And his parents?" her empathetic cousin interjected. "Countess DunDonell appeared quite concerned about the viscount when last I saw her."

"The countess is very troubled and the earl was determined to locate him." Christian shrugged exquisitely tailored shoulders. "But if Daniel does not want to be found . . . he won't be."

Felicity nodded and met Juliet's eye. "We should call on Lady DunDonell. Perhaps they have had word of where the viscount has gone."

Juliet agreed, wondering how one went about locating a man who did not want to be found.

Daniel arose well past noon after having spent the night imbibing and trying to understand what in God's name was wrong with him.

Mademoiselle Beauvoire was quickly becoming a fascination and he did not know how to stop it, did not understand why he continued to want women who had no want of him.

Not sexually. Nicole Beauvoire desired him sexually. But that was a fleeting want, easily satisfied by one night of physical passion.

No, the desire he longed for was the need of one person for another, the need to join together, body and soul. The union that, throughout his numerous physical encounters, had remained painfully elusive.

Why then, of all the society women who continually chased after him, had he set his sights on Sarah Duhearst? Set his sights on the one woman who had shown no interest in attaining his affection or his fortune.

Why now was he becoming increasingly fixated upon Nicole Beauvoire? A woman similarly disinterested.

He had no notion.

All he knew was that the moment he laid hands on Nicole Beauvoire, returning to England was no longer an option. And the idea of her spending the evening with Joseph LeCoeur was altogether intolerable.

Protect, possess.

The two-headed beast of masculine instinct reared its head, stronger and more resolute than it had been before. And God help him, but he had no idea how to send it back to the primitive recesses from whence it came.

"Minister LeCoeur is dangerous." Daniel stared, helpless, at Nicole's reflection as she put the finishing touches on an already captivating evening gown.

"Of course he's dangerous. All the men I kill are dangerous; that is why I kill them."

"You do not understand, lass." The woman tilted her head, fastening her left ear bob and giving him a provocative glimpse of the neck he had been kissing just last night. "You did not see the way the man was looking at you."

"I didn't need to see the way he was looking at me, Monsieur Damont." She glanced in the mirror to verify that her appearance was acceptable. "Men have been looking at me in such a manner since I grew these." She cupped her full breasts, and Daniel wondered how any man could look beyond her stunning violet eyes. "At the age of fourteen."

"Fourteen?" Distaste wrinkled his nose. "That's unconscionable."

"I thought so." The woman grasped her reticule and examined the contents as she continued to speak. "So you see, Monsieur Damont, I am well accustomed to dealing with lecherous men." Daniel felt as if the comment was directed toward him, and he replayed in his mind the brandy-filtered events of last night. "Now, if you will excuse me."

"I should go with you."

Nicole stopped and stared at him as if he were stark-raving mad.

"I don't think Monsieur LeCoeur would appreciate a third wheel twisting about his little seduction. And furthermore, I thought you were leaving." She bent over to smell a red rose from the pretentious bouquet that Minister LeCoeur had sent earlier that afternoon.

"I was, but now that I am a bit more—"

"Sober?"

"Clear-headed." Daniel glared at the caustic woman. "I think it would be best if I were to remain in Paris."

The lady stiffened, her eyes growing wide with . . . suspicion?

"Why?" she asked.

"The presence of a spurned lover is easily explained, and you must admit, proved quite useful. But the disappearance of a man such as myself—"

"A man such as yourself?" Her stunning eyes widened and she tilted her head, causing the sapphire necklace around her neck to come alive.

"Well, lass." Daniel gave a self-deprecating grin. "You must admit, a man of my ilk would be unlikely to give up quite so easily."

"Then our only alternative, Monsieur Damont, is for you to pretend that I am the first woman to disappoint you." Daniel tensed as the image of Sarah Duhearst flashed in his mind, pulling his thoughts a thousand miles away, but the lady continued to talk. "Forcing you to sulk all the way back to wherever it is you came from. Don't wait up for me."

Daniel realized that she was gone with the click of the closing door. He moved to the window and watched Nicole being assisted into Minister LeCoeur's expensive carriage. The clock in the parlor chimed, punctuating how little time Daniel had before the opening curtain.

He walked toward his bedchamber and yanked open the drawer to his side table, pulling out the five cards slipped to him at the masquerade ball. Daniel read the names quickly, placing one behind the other as he mentally reviewed the streets of Paris in proximity to the theater.

When he had settled on a name, Daniel tossed the other cards on his bed then walked back into the parlor and, with a malicious grin, snatched the enormous bouquet of flowers from the sturdy Grecian vase.

Twenty

꧁꧂

"*I* must admit that I'm rather impressed. These are quite good seats." Nicole smiled up at Joseph LeCoeur, both of them knowing that their boxed seats were the best in the theater house.

Her escort seated Nicole closest to the stage and then sat on her left, saying, "Yes, they're not at all bad."

"And what production will we be seeing this evening, Minister LeCocur?"

The man shrugged, his slashing lips pulling into a subtle grin. "I have no idea."

Nicole laughed, staring into his gray eyes as she said, "Not an aficionado of the theater, I take it?"

Minister LeCoeur leaned forward. "*Au contraire, ma chérie.* I very much enjoy the theater, but at the moment I am more interested in you."

A bell sounded three times, indicating that theatergoers should find their seats. Nicole turned her head and watched the crème de la crème of Parisian society sit in the beautiful theater as if they had not a care in the world.

As if there were not a war raging throughout Europe.

The candlelight began to dim, but just before it faded completely, movement from the box across the theater drew Nicole's attention. Her eyes widened in disbelief as she watched Daniel Damont lead a beautiful brunette to one of the four gilded chairs in the very private box.

Damont's smile was devastating, and she could see that the woman with him was completely charmed. He sat in his angled chair and turned toward his lady. Damont bent his head and whispered in the woman's ear, and just before the last of the lights was extinguished, his striking eyes met Nicole's.

She leaned heavily against her chair for support and then felt the heat of Joseph LeCoeur's thumb as it made a sensual arc on her bare shoulder.

"Would you care for a glass of champagne, *ma chérie?*"

Nicole turned toward him, but allowed the minister's hand to remain resting on the back of her chair. "That would all depend upon the quality of the champagne."

Joseph LeCoeur smiled, his hollow cheeks filling with amusement as he turned to pour from a bottle that had been left to chill by one of the minister's many footmen.

"My men have been ordered to supply champagne equal to the quality of the woman who drinks it," the minister explained, handing her a glass. "And for you, *ma chérie,* they have been asked to supply the best France has to offer."

"Merci," she replied, thanking him more for the compliment than the exceptional champagne. Nicole held the man's eyes as she tipped back her head, swallowing the airy alcohol as if it were him. "Mmm, a very high quality."

Joseph LeCoeur threw back some champagne to quench his thirst, and Nicole turned her attention to the actor who had just entered stage left. But from their prime position, Nicole was able to discreetly observe Daniel Damont, yet look as though she were engrossed entirely in the production and not the alluring man in the box to her right.

Nicole watched Daniel bend over and whisper in the worldly woman's ear before his lips pulled back into that contagious smile. Her stomach flipped as she remembered the feel of those beautiful lips on her own neck, her breast as if they were on her still.

Her eyes flickered back to the stage and Nicole breathed deeply, knowing that last night Daniel had wanted her, that he had followed her to the theater because he was concerned for her safety.

She smiled, realizing that Daniel had acquired a companion in less than an hour all because he feared Britain's most successful assassin incapable of ensuring her own safety.

"You are enjoying the play?"

Nicole felt the heat of Joseph LeCoeur's question down her neck, and she turned to look up at him with a genuine grin, saying truthfully, "*Oui,* I am enjoying the evening very much," before glancing back toward the stage.

She spent the remainder of the first act engrossed in the production and ignoring the periodic stares from both men. Daniel was easier to disregard from sheer lack of proximity, so when the lights blazed at intermission, Nicole turned her back on him entirely, giving her full attention to Minister LeCoeur and her mission.

"So, what did you think?" Nicole asked playfully when the curtain swung closed.

The elegant man raised his left brow, and Nicole could see why women found his confidence so alluring.

"Of the play?"

Nicole leaned toward him, her eyes aglow. "Oh, you were not thinking of the production? Now, you must tell me what you are thinking or I shall expire from curiosity."

Minister LeCoeur bent his head and whispered, "This is neither the place nor the time to tell you what I have been thinking, indeed, envisioning, since the moment I laid eyes on you, Mademoiselle Beauvoire."

Nicole sucked in a breath, wondering what this dangerous man would "envision" if he had the slightest indication that she and Scorpion were one and the same.

"I can only imagine," Nicole said, looking at him from the corner of her eye.

"I very much doubt that, *ma chérie*." However, his lust faded, replaced by irritation as his dark brows pulled together. "Who is the man who follows you with such determination?" He indicated Damont with a slight toss of his head.

She glanced at Daniel as he flirted outrageously with the brunette in his box, while keeping his turquoise eyes fixed firmly on Nicole.

"That"—she rolled her eyes and lied nimbly—"is my stepbrother. My stepfather's heir, to be precise."

"You were lovers?"

"*Oui.*" Nicole nodded, knowing better than to lie about the obvious. "A long time ago, and before I understood."

"Before you understood what?"

Nicole shifted under the minister's intense scrutiny, laughing as she answered, "Men."

Joseph LeCoeur gave an elegant exhalation of laughter. "And what did this stepbrother teach you of men?"

Nicole turned and held his eyes, making sure that the minister understood her meaning. "My stepbrother taught me that a gentleman who appears quite capable might very well be a fumbling fool."

"And how do I appear to you, Mademoiselle Beauvoire?" LeCoeur grinned, delighted that a man as handsome as Daniel Damont had been maligned as an incompetent lover.

"You, Minister LeCoeur, strike me as a man who savors the subtle nuances of lovemaking, a man who savors the curve of a woman's breast." His gaze dropped to her décolletage as Nicole leaned increasingly closer to his ear.

"A man who savors the heat of a woman's mouth, the silky flesh of a woman's inner thigh, the heady taste . . ." Nicole ran her tongue, ever so slowly, ever so lightly, around the outer edge of the minister's right ear. "Of a woman's desire."

The tip of her nose nuzzled his temple as her heated words penetrated his mind. "The sound of a woman's voice as she begs 'yes' just before trembling with ecstasy while you plunge, headlong, to find your own."

The lights of the theater dimmed and Nicole caressed his thigh with the white satin glove that insulated her, to some degree, from the intimacy of touching him.

"That is the sort of man, the type of lover, I envision you to be, Minister LeCoeur."

The minister's left hand stilled hers on his upper thigh, his gloveless fingers curling between her own.

"If we were not seated in this theater, *ma chérie*"—his eyes met hers—"you would not have to envision at all, as I would already have you pressed against the wall."

Minister LeCoeur had meant to shock—she could see it in his eyes—but Nicole knew also that he had rarely himself been so surprised by a woman.

"Promises, promises, Minister LeCoeur," she whispered, sliding her hand from beneath his but not before feeling the lean muscles of his thigh go instantly rigid.

The remainder of the production went by in one continuous blur of color and sound. Nicole attempted to concentrate on the play, but it was difficult to be attentive when under such scrutiny.

Daniel continued to watch her progress with Minister LeCoeur while she witnessed his obvious success with the brunette, a countess if Nicole remembered correctly.

The tawdry woman was taking every opportunity to touch Daniel. Not that Nicole could blame her, or any woman, for wanting to touch such male perfection.

Just once.

But must the countess be so obvious and must Damont be so responsive? They were making a spectacle of themselves, and no doubt distracting other patrons from the production as much as they were disturbing her.

Thankfully, the production finally ended, and she and her escort rose to exit their front box. Nicole felt a hand at the small of her back as Minister LeCoeur guided her out.

"Oh, my reticule." She bent down to retrieve the silk

bag, and when Nicole looked up, her mouth fell open as she glimpsed the countess leaving their box with her hand on Damont's backside.

Her jaw set and Nicole said, "Found it," convinced that Daniel would take his time in returning to the apartment while she risked her life for Crown and country.

"Are you all right?" Joseph LeCoeur glanced back at the empty box across the theater and then to her face, speculation dancing in his eyes.

"I'm a touch heated, I'm afraid."

"Ah," the minister said, reassured. "Then let us get you outside so that you might become more comfortable."

Joseph LeCoeur smiled to himself as they descended the front steps of Le Royale.

The woman on his arm had proven to be as stimulating as he had hoped, and Joseph was enjoying the overwhelming anticipation before he took her to his home and his bed.

His most extravagant carriage was waiting, as ordered, directly outside the entrance to the prestigious theater. Joseph grasped Mademoiselle Beauvoire firmly by the upper arm and guided them toward his conveyance, but ten feet from their goal, the provocative woman stopped cold.

Nicole Beauvoire turned to face him and then curtsied saying, "Thank you for a most enjoyable evening, Minister LeCoeur."

"Surely," he chuckled, "our farewells can wait until I escort you home, Mademoiselle Beauvoire?"

"Ah, but to whose home?" The girl smiled broadly, knowingly, her enticing lips pulled up provocatively at one corner. "Furthermore, Minister LeCoeur, I never tolerate an audience unless I have invited them to watch."

"I'm afraid you have completely lost me, *ma chérie*."

"Have I?" The lady walked away and Joseph felt unbalanced, confused, until Mademoiselle Beauvoire stopped in front of his bodyguards, saying, *"Au revoir."*

His eyes narrowed and his interest peaked. The girl

was not only stunning, but intelligent. Joseph's pride had required that his guards remain on the periphery of any function he attended. They were to remain in the shadows, unseen.

But she had seen them.

Mademoiselle Beauvoire had looked past the footmen and servants and identified the two most dangerous men in the theater. Surmising, correctly, that his guards would also be close when he made love to her in his own home.

No, Nicole Beauvoire was no simple conquest. The woman was beautiful, intelligent, and rich, a lethal combination to any man, a combination that could prove quite useful to a minister's wife.

Joseph chuckled, thinking how ironic it was to consider the one woman in Paris who would surely turn down his proposal of marriage. But of course, that was the allure. At this moment, he was not entirely sure that the lady would even bed him, but Joseph had the distinct feeling that once she did, he would want her again and again.

Flesh to flesh, mind to mind.

He buttoned up his lust behind his black silk jacket then looked at the more senior of his guards.

Captain Turgeon walked discreetly to his side and the minister whispered, "I would like the preliminary report on Mademoiselle Beauvoire," as he watched her carriage meander down the congested cobblestone street in front of the theater.

"Now?" The captain's blue eyes widened with alarm, and Joseph turned his attention away from the enticing subject being discussed.

"*Oui.*"

Captain Turgeon inclined his flaxen head, making no further protest. "Mademoiselle Beauvoire has been in Paris for two weeks only. She acquired her apartment through a leasing agent by name of . . ." The captain reached into his breast pocket, referencing a small tablet of paper. "Monsieur Pinoche. After considering three other apartments of comparable value, Mademoiselle Beauvoire settled upon her current residence because she enjoyed 'the view of Place Vendôme.' "

"She is wealthy?" Joseph asked, his mind relegating the woman to mistress if she were not.

Captain Turgeon looked down at his notes. "Mademoiselle Beauvoire paid cash for the first three months of her lease and her clothing and—"

"You tell me nothing." The minister dismissed the captain's answer with a wave of his hand. "Her family? I wish to know of Mademoiselle Beauvoire's holdings."

The captain paled and Joseph reminded himself that the man had gathered a great deal of information in a short amount of time.

"The leasing agent did say that he thought her from a large city in northern France."

"What made him believe this?"

"A gentleman arrived as she was signing the lease. Tall, auburn hair, and from his clothing, equally affluent."

"*Oui,* I know this man. Daniel Damont," Minister LeCoeur said coolly.

"The gentleman kissed Mademoiselle Beauvoire intimately, calling her *'cherie'* and speaking to her as though they were longtime . . . acquaintances."

Joseph bristled, his spine stretched by masculine competition. "And how did the lady respond?"

Captain Turgeon smirked, saying, "Mademoiselle Beauvoire slapped the gentleman, asking why he was in Paris." Joseph smiled to himself but his satisfaction faded when the captain added, "The leasing agent was then asked to leave, but said it was quite apparent that the two had been lovers."

"*Merci.*" Joseph nodded when the captain had finished. "Now go round to this leasing agent's home and dissuade the man from publicly speculating about Mademoiselle Beauvoire's personal affairs."

"Right or left hand?"

"Left," Joseph said, feeling magnanimous.

Captain Turgeon bowed, but before he had turned away, the minister had a second thought. "And investigate Monsieur Damont. I want to know what brings this man to Paris."

But he was fairly certain that he had an idea.

Daniel Damont had traveled from northern France to find his erstwhile lover. A woman, Joseph thought hungrily, who must be well worth the trip.

Twenty-one

❦

It was now midnight and Daniel sat, cornered in his carriage by the beautiful Countess Constantine. Her hands roamed over his waistcoat as the lady looked longingly into his eyes.

"I thought that we could retire to your apartment, Monsieur Damont. You can don that Marc Antony costume and I can become your Cleopatra." Her hand descended, skimming Daniel's shaft as she continued down his thigh. "You can conquer me all night," the countess whispered, kissing him.

Daniel lifted his head to dislodge himself from her mouth. "Well, Countess, have we really known one another long enough to be 'conquering' each oth—"

The sophisticated woman laughed, removing his cravat. "I do not believe Marc Antony asked Cleopatra if she desired to be 'conquered.'"

"Now, that is where you're mistaken. Cleopatra . . ." Daniel groaned as the woman expertly caressed his length.

He pulled her hand away and concentrated on their inane conversation.

"It is believed that Cleopatra seduced Antony to force . . . Oh, bloody hell!" The countess was unbuttoning his trousers, ready to service him then and there, when the carriage stopped in front of her home as per his previous instructions. "Here we are," Daniel announced, hastily buttoning his garments and retying his cravat.

"Surely you jest?" the woman asked on an incredulous huff.

"I very much enjoyed our evening, Countess Constantine." Daniel smiled politely and opened the carriage door, holding his hand out to her. The countess stared at his hand as if she had no idea what it was and then slowly, reluctantly accepted his assistance.

"You arrive at my home less than an hour before opening curtain and abandon me at my door less than an hour afterward. I have no idea what you are about, Monsieur Damont." Her dark eyes met his. "But I do know that I detest being used."

"The feeling is entirely mutual."

They stared at one another until the countess conceded his point. "Most men dream of being my bed fodder."

"Feed on someone else, Countess, as I prefer to entertain women of whom I am genuinely fond. Good evening."

Daniel bowed, pausing at the truth of his pronouncement.

He had always enjoyed women more in bed if he first enjoyed them outside of it, if he had experienced an affable affiliation prior to carnal knowledge.

In short, if he gave a damn about them.

"Sod me," he said, climbing into his darkened carriage a bit shaken.

Daniel closed his eyes and leaned his head against the squabs, trying to comprehend this new epiphany. It would seem that he cared more for a woman's mind than her body.

The idea was indeed disturbing, for if one were to chase

such circular logic, it would then follow that his happiness was dependent upon the incomprehensible mind of a woman.

He was surely doomed to a life of miserable solitude.

Yet Daniel understood now why he had developed such an affinity for Sarah Duhearst. He had known the lass since he was ten years of age, had danced with her, gone to birthday celebrations, gone riding with her and her brother more times than he could remember. Daniel cared for Sarah and knew that she would have made an excellent wife and companion, an excellent mother to their children.

And she was. Sarah was an excellent wife to the Duke of Glenbroke and exemplary mother to his children.

Daniel felt the familiar ache of loss in his chest, but he was beginning to wonder if it was the loss of the friendship, the loss of the caring he wanted so desperately to give her.

He would simply have to be more guarded with his affections. More careful to shield himself from women he could never have.

Unattainable women such as Nicole Beauvoire.

But why these women? His father had instilled a deep protectiveness of the fairer sex in all seven of the McCurren men. This tendency would undoubtedly need to be overcome, but Mademoiselle Beauvoire was more than capable of taking care of herself.

She had killed nine men, perhaps even more, and had no need of a bodyguard. The woman had endured the loss of her beloved husband and had volunteered to travel to France in service to the Crown. No, if any woman did not need his caring, his affection, it was Nicole Beauvoire.

All Daniel needed to do was to harden himself against the lass. He would aid her in the assassination and then be on his way home to London where, with his new insight, he could find a woman with whom he could share his life.

He would take his time in selecting a woman capable of

returning his affection, a simple woman who would gladly bear his many children and build their happy home.

Daniel took the stairs to the apartment two at a time, invigorated by the idyllic image of his home in the highlands overrun by his bairns. Contentment washed over him, and Daniel wanted nothing more than to soak in the soothing waters of a steaming hot bath.

He opened the door and kicked off his impractical shoes before peeling off his jacket and waistcoat and tossing them on his bed. Daniel wrestled with his cravat, and his mind drifted down from the highlands of Scotland to the darkened homes on Place Vendôme.

Nicole would be across the street by now, and when he finished with his bath, Daniel planned to resume his impartial observations. He would note the activities taking place at Minister LeCoeur's home with detachment, hoping only to aid Scorpion in her self-appointed mission.

After all, the woman was a widow, and well acquainted with the ways of the world. If Nicole chose to compromise herself in order to gain the minister's trust, then that was her decision. She had most likely done it before, and would again once Daniel left her alone in Paris.

Daniel hardened himself against his chivalrous tendencies and yanked his shirt over his head, mussing further his unruly hair. He combed it back with his fingers as he made his way to the washroom off the master suite, trying not to think about the assassination.

The entire manner of this killing went against everything that Daniel believed, if not human nature. A woman should be protected, should not be someone any man would need protection from. Nicole needed a guardian, not a man who sat by while she willingly compromised herself to achieve her goal and Britian's.

There was an answer, of course, but he did not know—

Daniel stilled the moment he heard a splash of water coming from the washroom. He crept forward, his bare feet stepping lightly on the cold wood of the threshold floor. He turned the brass knob and slowly opened the tall door, then stopped, stunned by the sight of Nicole Beauvoire sitting in the decorative copper tub.

Her hair hung free in chaotic black ropes, cascading down her nude body like twists of licorice. Her pink nipples were peaking above the water as she held out her left arm to scrub it with her right. Daniel stared, frozen by the sight of her milky skin, until he heard a feminine gasp.

He lifted his gaze to meet those violet eyes, and for the first time in his life, Daniel was rendered speechless. His words were stolen away by neither embarrassment nor remorse, but by the power of a beautiful woman to pull the air from a man's lungs. He understood suddenly why men painted and wrote maudlin poetry in the vain hope of capturing this elusive allure that women wielded over men.

"What are you doing?" Nicole Beauvoire sat back with a splash and covered herself with her arms, but her delicate forearms scarcely hid the rosebuds of her nipples. The feminine curve of her waist, the outline of her hips, was clearly visible from his elevated height.

"I . . ." Daniel lowered his eyes, speaking to the talon feet of the tub as he said, "My apologies. I thought to have a bath as I believed you to be . . ." His eyes darted back and forth as he sought for the appropriate word on the oak floor. "Out."

"Well, I am here." Irritation, and something harder to interpret, colored her voice. "As you can clearly see."

"Yes." He had seen quite clearly. "Right, I'll just go then." Daniel spun on his heels and reached for the door, but his hand stilled, warming the cold brass knob.

Why he paused, Daniel could not say, but something in their exchange was not right. Had not been right since the moment he entered the washroom. Daniel turned round and the lady gasped, covering herself as his eyes scanned the small room.

Candles blazed in the far corner and thick velvet drapes were drawn across the window to keep out the cold or, Daniel glanced at the woman in the tub, to keep in the heat.

He walked across the lush green carpet and lifted the white towel and neatly folded garments.

Nothing.

He tilted his head and peered at the base of the metal tub. Nothing seemed amiss, so his eyes traveled once again to the lady in it. Daniel stared at Nicole, at her hair. Something was not right about the woman herself.

"What are you doing?" she asked as he continued to stare and ponder. "Leave this instant!"

Daniel's eyes squinted as his concentration sharpened.

"What do you have behind your back?"

Nicole froze in the hot waters of her bath.

"Nothing," she said forcefully.

"Aye, you have something behind your back." Daniel nodded, convinced. "A woman would lean forward to cover herself. Unless"—Daniel's eyes met the violet of hers—"she was hiding something behind her. Then . . . then a woman would lean back and cover herself as best she could. As you've just done. Twice."

"Don't be ridiculous. Remove yourself immediately!" Nicole felt fear twisting her muscles, but as the man planted his feet, she realized that she had no place to run.

"I will." Daniel crossed his arms over his naked chest to punctuate his resolve. "As soon as you show me what you're hiding."

"I have nothing behind my back," she said truthfully.

He did not even blink. "Then you won't mind if I have a look."

Her heart seized and Nicole held his turquoise eyes as he stood unrelenting at the foot of the tub. Then, slowly, reluctantly she leaned forward. Her breasts brushed the tops of her thighs and she wrapped her arms around herself, forming a sphere of protection.

A smirk lifted the right side of his mouth and then he made his way behind her. Nicole rested her forehead on her knees and closed her eyes, shivering in the warm water as she waited an eternity for Daniel Damont to view her imperfection.

Water dripped from the dangling strings of her hair and she could feel herself holding her breath, ready to absorb the impact of his revulsion. Daniel had wanted her last night, but after he saw her marred back, no amount of washing would make her appealing.

"Oh, lass." She heard his low voice above her. "What have they done to you?" A tear escaped her and Nicole hugged herself tighter, her scars answering for her.

And then she felt the featherlight caress of his fingertips as they sought their way around her waist, his other hand darting beneath her knees. He lifted her from the safety of the tub gently, softly, as if her wounds had never healed.

Nicole leaned against the taut muscles of his bare chest, soaking him, but Daniel did not seem to notice as he walked toward her bedchamber. She reached up with her left hand and covered herself with the towel he had so thoughtfully placed across his shoulder. Nicole covered her face, not wanting to be seen, and not wanting to see the pity in his beautiful eyes.

Unobserved, her tears came steadily and she nuzzled deeper into the crook of his neck. Nicole hated that the raised flesh of her scars rested against his forearm as he effortlessly carried her. She thought to lift herself, but then he was setting her on the duvet of the master suite bed.

Daniel Damont said nothing as he worked the velvet duvet beneath her as if she weighed nothing more than a sick child. He bent over, his right hand grasping the heavy cloth as he pulled it toward her head. But rather than release the duvet, the man lifted his left leg and crawled in next to her, tucking the layers of blankets behind him to keep them both warm.

He pulled her back against his chest as if to absorb the wounds, her wet head resting on his bulky left arm. Nicole felt his muscle flex as his elbow bent before his hand came across to rest on her right shoulder. His right hand smoothed the hair from her face before circling Nicole's waist, the towel still bunched between them.

She lay surrounded, shielded by his strength before his

baritone voice rumbled in her ear. "How long did they hold you captive?"

They?

"Over a year," Nicole said to her pillow.

The arm around her waist tightened, almost painfully so. "Was there no attempt to rescue you?"

Nicole sifted through the pain of her memories, the faces of the people she had considered friends, people who just stood by and allowed her torment to continue.

"No," she managed.

He took in one long breath as if to speak, but it took several moments of careful consideration before Daniel asked, "And this is why you became an assassin?"

"Yes." That was why she murdered Frenchmen, because she had murdered, because she had finally defended herself and killed her captor.

"To kill the French who did this to you," Damont said to himself. Her brows furrowed as Nicole sought the words to tell him the truth.

"I'm so sorry, lass," he whispered, and all her anguished thoughts were overcome by his kindness, and her own tears.

Daniel eased his hold on her waist, and Nicole felt his right hand splay across her disfigured back.

"How could any man harm . . . I'm so sorry." He rubbed the pain of the scars away in small soothing circles. "I'm so sorry," he whispered again, then kissed her where her shoulder and neck came together.

His hand dipped down to her waist and slowly traveled up her bare hip. Nicole could feel his callused fingertips curling as he gently cupped her backside, more insistent in their explorations as his hand lingered then reluctantly dragged his fingers up the softness of her skin.

"You're so beautiful, lass." Daniel reached in front of her and tugged at the towel, causing her to roll on her back as he intended her to do.

She stared up at him as he braced himself on his left elbow. The heat of his muscular chest warmed her right breast, and Nicole could scarcely breathe. She flinched when the heavy towel dropped to the floor, and she waited for the panic to take hold of her, but it did not. Daniel was caressing the left side of her face with the backs of his fingers, and Nicole closed her eyes, feeling . . . secure.

"You're so beautiful." Her eyes opened to view his sincerity. "How could any man flaw such beauty?"

But she was flawed, not by the marks on her back but by the manner in which they had gnawed away at her soul, shredding it until Nicole was capable of killing a man, of killing nine men, in cold blood. But as she stared at the masculine symmetry of Daniel's features, the clear, warm blue of his eyes, she did not feel defective.

He let his chest settle against her breasts, the warmth of him eliciting a soft, satisfied moan. Nicole watched as his eyes closed momentarily, then opened more determined, more focused.

"I want to make love to you, lass," Daniel Damont breathed, sexual desire thickening his Scots brogue. "But I will not." He met her eyes, imploring her to understand. "I *can't* . . . touch you further if you will not have me."

Daniel's heavy jaw set and he waited for Nicole to answer, but she could not speak. No man had ever asked for permission to bed her, and she was not sure how to respond to his request.

The silence grew and the anticipation drained from his stunning eyes, filling them with disappointment as he pushed himself away from her, severing their bodily bond. Nicole felt the loss, and her hands darted out to counter his retreat, settling on the tense muscles of his broad back.

"Make love to me, Monsieur Damont."

His brows furrowed, confusion plainly written on his features. "Daniel," he said with force. "My name is Daniel."

The stunning man dipped his head, his succulent lips skillfully parting hers. His tongue swept into her mouth leisurely, seeming to savor the taste, the heat, the pliant texture of her lips as she savored his. Each stroke of his tongue was built upon the last until finally their explorations were complete.

He dragged his lips from her mouth and ministered to her neck, pressing his lips just above her collarbone. Nicole turned her head to give him more room to roam as she breathed in the man who was making love to her. Daniel Damont smelled of distant soap and leather, overlaid with the potency of a man in his sexual prime.

She was awash in his scent, claimed by it, and Nicole felt herself responding, felt her nipples hardening and her back arching as she offered herself to him. He took her lure, his head lifting to view one breast and then the other, unable to decide where his loyalties lay.

The searing heat of his mouth descended on her right nipple as his hand covered her left breast. Daniel voiced his pleasure in the back of his throat as he laved and suckled, his long fingers kneading her sensitive flesh. He nipped at the hardened peak of her nipple and Nicole gasped at the pleasure Daniel induced.

His right hand rolled her nipple between his fingers as his tongue and teeth continued to incite her lust. She was aching and could feel herself opening to him, preparing for him. His left hand skimmed her hip, using it as a map to find the globes of her backside.

He gave a primal grunt of approval and then relinquished her breast, his large hands holding her hips down as he tasted his way down her belly. His mouth descended further, but when Nicole realized his intention, she protested before he reached his goal.

"Stop!"

He lifted his head, his chest heaving, his masculine features pulled together in frustration.

"Why?" Daniel met her wide eyes and he gave a disbelieving chuckle. "Did your husband never . . . ?"

Nicole shook her head and he grinned, his eyes lighting with anticipation. "I'll be your first then."

"Don't," she whispered, embarrassed.

The man smiled again, but this time it held none of the triumphant glint of before, only the gentleness of compassion.

"Trust me, lass." Daniel crawled over her and kissed her on the lips, rubbing his thumb across her left cheek as he stared into her eyes. "Trust me."

Nicole fought her fear and he waited, obviously unaware of what he was asking. She looked into his eyes and nodded her assent, and Daniel smiled, kissing her again, then allowing his head to drop down to her breasts. His fingers roamed over her, working to rekindle the heat between them, and then his hands were on her hips. He lowered his head between her thighs and she closed her eyes, trusting him.

The heat of his mouth pressed against her moist petals, stealing her breath. He ran his tongue ever so lightly over her sex until the tip danced over the protruding crux of her sensuality.

Her hips came off the bed, but he held her down, probing deeply, laving longer. Daniel groaned with pleasure, and the masculine reverberation added to her desire, driving it to new and undiscovered heights. Nicole stilled, sure she would burst, and she wanted him, needed him, to contain her.

"Please, Daniel." She did not know how to tell him, but he understood.

He stripped off his trousers and she had but a moment to glimpse the beautiful man who would have her. Sharp lines and masculine angles were softened by the heavy padding of lean muscles. All of which complemented his thick and unrepentant sex, which thrust forward from his body as if seeking a home.

Nicole ached to accommodate him as he lay atop her, his flat stomach and muscled chest amazingly gentle as he pressed her farther into the comfortable bed. He kissed her again and then she felt him easing into her. Nicole sucked the air from his mouth and he pushed forward, stroking deeper, stretching her farther than she could have thought possible.

"My God," Daniel said above her, his jaw resting at her temple. She felt the small of his back arch as he withdrew, and then she was being pressed into the mattress as he surged into her once more.

It was sensual torture, and every time he left her, she held her breath until his return. Nicole reached for his powerful backside, entreating him to increase his tantalizing pace, his force.

He did and she moaned, closing her eyes to concentrate on the place where they were joined. Time was lost as he stroked deeper, faster. His right hand reached back, capturing her behind the left knee.

"Wrap your legs around my waist," he grated.

Nicole locked herself around his trim waist and they both gasped at his penetrating depth, the pleasure of the increased closeness, and then she was being consumed.

"Daniel," she said, panicked.

"I know, lass. We'll go together." He stroked faster and then he wasn't breathing, and with a blinding flash behind her eyes, neither was she.

Nicole was falling into the bed and Daniel was plunging after her, reaching to stay with her. He pulled her to him, and then she was safe, tucked away in the warmth of his arms as she fell back to the present.

Her eyelids fluttered open and she listened to his rhythmic panting, felt it in the gentle rising and falling of his abdomen. Nicole glanced from his corded neck, amazed that his muscular chest was wider than her shoulders. Daniel Damont was powerfully built, beautifully formed, and she could not help thinking that this was what God had intended between man and wife.

What she had missed, what she would never know.

Tears welled in her eyes and Nicole let her hands fall away from him. Daniel Damont no doubt elicited such passion from every woman he took to his bed. Silly notions of a loving husband, a home full of children born of that love. Ridiculous thoughts that should have died long ago. Her body was rocked by the idea and Nicole shook with it.

Her a mother? A wife? It was ridiculous.

"Well, that was—"

Daniel lifted himself, startled by the racking of her fragile frame. He stared into her violet eyes and verified that the lass was indeed crying.

But he could scarcely blame her. He, too, was having difficulty comprehending what had just happened. Daniel had poured himself into their lovemaking, driven by the desire to ease her many wounds. As he stared at her tears, he could only hope that he had not just added to them.

"I did not hurt you, did I?"

The woman shook her head and then snorted.

His head jerked back, and Daniel stared at her face as Nicole swiped at her eyes, realizing that she was laughing. His face contorted with confusion as the lass met his eyes, and she laughed harder still.

Daniel felt the sting of . . . embarrassment, perhaps, and then rose from where he had lain cradled between the warmth of her soft thighs. He sat on the edge of the bed and leaned forward to retrieve his garments. Daniel felt the slight dip of the mattress as the woman sat up and propped herself against the multitude of pillows as she struggled to control her laughter.

"It's not you, Monsieur Damont."

Daniel closed his eyes, sure that if ever there were words to shrivel a man's pride, it was those. He thrust his right foot into his prissy trousers and then rose, hauling them over his bare backside.

"Oh, then I suppose you're snickering at the other gent you just rogered?" he asked, looking down at her before stalking out of the enormous master suite.

"No. No, no, no, you misunderstand entirely." Daniel heard her scramble from the bed and he glanced over his right shoulder as she trailed after him wrapped only in a cerulean sheet. "It is not you I found amusing, Monsieur Damont."

"DunDonell," Daniel said. Any woman with whom he

had shared such profound intimacy could bloody well call him by his proper title.

"Pardon?"

Irritated, he stopped and looked into her lovely eyes framed by thick, black lashes that were splayed across her flushed cheeks like a decorative fan.

"My name is DunDonell."

"Monsieur Daniel DunDonell?" she asked, her nose crinkling with apparent distaste.

"Daniel McCurren. Ack, never mind." He shook his head and rolled his eyes more at himself than at her. "Forget I said anything." Daniel spun and continued walking toward the decanter of brandy in his bedchamber. "Call me what you bloody well like. What difference does it make?"

"It does indeed make a difference. I want to address you as you wish to be addressed." Nicole was running after him trying to keep up with his angry strides. "I'm just a bit confused. Monsieur McCurren?"

Daniel laughed. The entire subject was so painfully preposterous. "Oh, Christ Almighty, just drop the matter."

"No, I'm afraid I can't. Every time I look at you, I shall have names bouncing about my head. So, which is it? Monsieur Damont, McCurren, or DunDonell?"

Daniel clenched his jaw and spun around so quickly that Nicole was pressed to the wall by his ominous anger.

"Lord DunDonell." Daniel watched, satisfied by her shock. "Viscount DunDonell, if we're being accurate."

"You're a viscount."

"Aye." He grinned. "Lord DunDonell, heir to Malcolm McCurren, Earl of DunDonell."

The woman stared at the wooden floor as her right hand felt round for the chair she knew was there. Her fingers hit the padded wood and she sank into the brocaded cushion.

"You're to be an . . ." She blinked.

"Earl," he finished for her. "So, you may call me Monsieur Damont in public, Lord DunDonell in private . . ." He paused, waiting for the lass to look up to meet his gaze. "And Daniel in bed."

Nicole paled, her pretty mouth hanging open as her eyes dropped to search the floor. Her breathing became audible, labored, and Daniel's satisfaction turned quickly to concern.

"How could he do this?" Tears spilled on her alabaster cheeks, and her nostrils flared as the lady fought to take air into her clogged lungs. "How could he do this?"

"Who, lass?" Daniel dropped to his haunches, and she jumped to her feet.

"Falcon." Her brows pulled together and Nicole Beauvoire looked at Daniel as though he were mad. "You have to leave."

She darted to his bedchamber and threw open his armoire, reaching in and grabbing stacks of costly garments and tossing them on his bed.

"Calm down." Daniel gestured with his right hand, but the woman was not listening.

"You must leave Paris, tonight." She spoke to the armoire. "I know a man who can take you as far as—"

Daniel grabbed her gently from behind, whispering, "It's all right, lass." But Nicole tossed her right elbow back, refusing his embrace.

"No, it is not all right, Viscount DunDonell!" She turned to face him. "Have you *any* idea of what the French will do to you if they discover that you are a viscount? Because I do." The scores of scars on her back were raised to the forefront of his memory. "And I know exactly how long it will take them to do it."

His teeth clenched and his eyes shut as Daniel tried to obliterate the ugly pictures that flooded his mind, pictures of a woman forced to endure God only knew what.

"You're leaving. I'll not have another . . ." She paused. "You're leaving tonight."

Nicole dropped to the floor and dragged out a trunk from beneath his bed.

"No, I'm not." He could not. Daniel could not allow her to be captured, could not allow her to go through it all again.

"Yes, you are!"

"No. I'm not leaving Paris." Daniel lifted her from the carpet so that he could reason with her. "I'm in no more danger than I was five minutes ago. You're the only one who knows who I am, and I'm fairly confident that neither of us will be blabbering the circumstances of my birth to the French."

The lady's mind was turned inward as her eyes studied his chest.

"The safest course of action for us both is to finish this assignment and make our way back to England together," he argued. "Now, can you perform the assassination any sooner?"

Nicole was composed now, thinking clearly.

"No," she said, shaking her head. "Empress Bonaparte's Toussaint Feast is the perfect opportunity to perform the assassination."

"You realize the missive ordering that the assassination take place at the feast was most assuredly written by the French," Daniel reminded her, hoping that she would change her mind.

"I know."

"So why not just kill the minister now?"

She sighed as if explaining addition to a stupid child. "Ideally, an assassination would be performed in isolation. However, Minister LeCoeur is a very careful man who keeps his bodyguards very close at hand. If I were to attempt to kill the minister prior to the Toussaint Feast, their attention would be focused entirely upon me.

"However, the feast provides the perfect distraction for the assassination. His bodyguards will have their attention focused outward, waiting for the assassin 'Scorpion' to arrive rather than watching the woman standing beneath their noses. Minister LeCoeur will feel confident in the precautions taken and protected by the crush of guests."

"And how will you escape?"

Nicole turned away, clearly tired of their discussion. "Lord DunDonell, I have escaped from sanctions nine times over. Might I suggest that you worry about your own safety?"

In many ways Daniel admired this woman, the cold confidence of competence bolstered by previous successes. Nicole Beauvoire was intelligent, capable, and would forever be underestimated by the men she would kill.

Had killed.

But as Daniel looked at her beautiful profile, looked at her shimmering hair as it engulfed her silky shoulders, he could not help remembering the vulnerable woman he had just taken to bed. He could not help remembering the woman who had clung desperately to him as he made love to her, the woman who had given herself as she made love to him.

That was the woman he preferred; that woman . . . he would protect.

Twenty-two

⚜

They were ten minutes late, but that only helped to increase the anticipation Evariste Rousseau felt as he watched the carriage holding the traitorous Lord Cunningham inch down the dark alleyway directly toward him.

He stared around the corner, savoring this moment. The seconds just before the game began, when he was the only one who realized there was a game being played.

His eyes followed the wheel of the conveyance as it dipped into a puddle to the right of the heavy landau. Water splashed over the narrow cobblestone street that led to the back entrance of Newgate prison.

The rhythmic pounding of hooves spurred his excitement and Evariste took a deep, relaxing breath then stepped out from the shadows. He raised one of two pistols, shooting the guard seated to the right of the driver. The driver turned, gasping with surprise, but his breath caught, stuck there by one of Evariste's many daggers.

One of the horses reared as the driver fell to the street, taking the leather reins with him. The two guards at the back of the conveyance jumped off their perch and crouched down as they inched toward him from either side of the carriage. But Evariste had slipped back into the shadows and they were having a difficult time locating him through their panic.

"Where is he?" the larger man asked, his hand resting on the haunches of the horse as he attempted to calm the animal.

"I don't know, I don't know!" The guard closest to Evariste scanned the alley.

Evariste felt the rush of danger for one second more before spinning from his hiding place, his greatcoat flaring behind him.

The guard fired and an orange spark illuminated his face, giving the guard a glimpse of his murderer just before Rousseau slit the man's throat.

The corpse collapsed to the filthy street, and Evariste drew his second pistol as he rounded the carriage and approached the remaining guard from behind. The man was crouching beside the gelding, who seemed more spooked by the smell of blood than it had been by the gunfire.

The horse stomped and snorted, his harness jingling, making the guard's ears utterly useless. The man sensed his danger the instant before Evariste grabbed him from behind, placing the cocked pistol just below the guard's right ear.

Wisely, the man lay down his firearm and raised both hands, admitting defeat. Evariste smiled to himself in the darkness.

"Quiet," Evariste warned as he shoved the guard in the back and toward the darkened carriage. The guard was breathing heavily, but Evariste scarcely noticed as his eyes were fixed on the silver handle of the conveyance door.

He listened for sudden movement within the carriage, but between the agitated horse and the cowardly Englishman, Evariste could hear nothing. They reached the left side door and he released the guard, his pistol still trained on the man's head.

Evariste pressed his back against the black landau, his muscular legs stilling in readiness. He jerked his head toward the carriage door, indicating that the guard was to open it.

The man hesitated, his thoughts very nearly audible as he stared at Evariste. The guard licked his lips and threw open the door, shouting, "Colonel—"

But his words were cut off the moment the bullet entered his forehead, knocking him back against the alley wall. Evariste spun into the void where the guard had been, and before the colonel could regroup, Evariste fired, killing the man where he sat on the squabs opposite the primary target.

Evariste felt a swell of pride when Lord Cunningham's blue eyes widened with fear the instant the coward saw who had ambushed their transport. His shackled legs kicked out, but Evariste was on him, using his lesser weight to drive the Englishman against the squabs.

The traitor cried out, the shackles behind his back cutting into his wrists as Evariste grinned down at him in triumph, saying, "*Bonsoir,* Lord Cunningham. The emperor sends his regards."

Lord Barksdale had been late collecting her for their evening at the opera, and Juliet Pervill discreetly glanced at her watch, afraid that they would arrive after the opening curtain.

"I'm sorry, Juliet," Robert said, shaking his head in frustration.

Juliet smiled at her anxious escort, feeling guilty that she had added to his worry by looking at the hour.

"It's all right, Robert. Nothing you could do about a lame horse. The poor thing had to be changed out."

"My driver assures me that he can get us to the theater via these back alleys in plenty of time for the opening curtain."

"I'm sure that he will, and if we miss the opera," Juliet said, smiling, "we shall just have to find something else with which to occupy ourselves."

Lord Barksdale's head snapped round so fast that it made her giggle. "Like what?"

"Really, Robert." Juliet rolled her eyes, and then he was bending his head to kiss her.

"I knew you would be like this," Robert whispered, kissing her again.

"Like what?" Juliet leaned back and raised a brow, not sure she wanted to know.

The amorous young lord stared into her eyes, his arms banding around her waist. "Intoxicating."

"How?" Juliet wondered aloud, knowing full well that she was not a beauty like her cousin.

Felicity was far lovelier than she could ever hope to be, and Juliet could never quite comprehend Robert's preference for her over the gorgeous Lady Appleton.

"How, what?" He nibbled on her ear and Juliet pushed on his chest so that she might look into his midnight eyes.

"How did you know I would be 'intoxicating'?"

Robert let out an exasperated breath, saying, "Juliet, you are forcing me to be rather blunt."

"Do be blunt, Robert." Juliet nodded, looking at him as she impatiently awaited his response. "Why is it that when most men are enticed by a beautiful woman, you are enticed by . . . well, me?"

"Lady Pervill, you have been in your cousin's shadow for far too long." Robert placed the back of his fingers on her cheek, his eyes heating as he tried to explain. "I don't want a docile woman warming my bed, Juliet."

They stared at one another, both envisioning the marriage bed.

"Oh," Juliet whispered, finally grasping his meaning.

"Exactly," Robert chuckled, bending his head to kiss her deeply this time, and she could not help thinking how proficient he was at kissing.

Lord Barksdale must have liked it, too, because his right hand was rapidly traveling up her ribs and toward her breast.

"Perhaps we should just drive around the park a couple of hundred times?" he breathed hopefully.

"Why would I want to do that?" Juliet teased him,

stopping his ascent with the touch of her fingers to his right wrist. "I've heard *Fidelio* is quite moving."

Lord Barksdale grinned seductively, saying, "It could not possibly be as moving as what we are doing—"

Robert's words were cut off by a bloodcurdling scream that pierced their romantic thoughts and forced them to turn in the direction of the horrifying noise.

Juliet could not help shuddering, sure that a man would make such a desperate cry only while in the throes of death. She froze, listening intently while hoping fervently never to hear that sound again for the rest of her life.

"There is a carriage just down the alley, my lord," the driver shouted down. "But I see no one atop the landau."

Robert glanced at her, giving Juliet the option, she knew, of continuing on to the theater or stopping to aid the distressed conveyance. Juliet nodded and he squeezed her hand, saying to his driver, "Stop and ask the gentleman in the landau if he is in need of assistance."

Lord Barksdale's carriage stopped at the head of the alley and his driver descended with the footman at his heels. Juliet watched through Robert's window as his two men approached the quiet carriage with pistols drawn.

She squeezed Robert's hand and he squeezed back as they waited in silence.

Then Lord Barksdale's driver fell to one knee, shouting, "They're all dead."

"How many?"

"Four men. Guards they look to be, my lord."

"Guards?" Robert asked, his brow furrowed as he spoke in the direction of his driver.

"Could have been transporting a prisoner to Newgate. A dangerous fellow, if they were in need of four—"

"Jesus!" Juliet tensed at the sound of the young footman's voice. "It weren't no prisoner what did this. The man, or what's left of him, is still shackled inside the landau along with another gentleman."

Lord Barksdale turned to look at Juliet, and she knew that he remained in the carriage because of her.

"Go, Robert." She jerked her head in the direction of the alley. "There is no one loitering in the alley, or the villain would have confronted your men by now."

"Are you sure?" Juliet could see his indecision as Lord Barksdale was torn between his duty to her and his duty to those unfortunate men.

"Yes, the sooner you assess the situation, the sooner we can send for the night watch."

"Two minutes." Robert kissed her hurriedly and then stepped down from the conveyance.

Juliet sat in the darkened interior of Lord Barksdale's landau, trying to believe everything she had just told him. She stared down the alley on her left and watched the four men looking over the gruesome scene. So, her attention was on Robert when Juliet glimpsed something from the corner of her eye, a movement in the shadows to the right of her door.

The hairs on her neck stood on end and Juliet turned slowly toward the building nearest her side of the carriage just as a figure was born of the dark. But rather than the filthy footpad she might have expected, this was a handsome young man, meticulously dressed in a tailored gold waistcoat and black jacket.

Their gazes met and Juliet froze, staring into ebony eyes with no light in them. The gentleman glanced in Robert's direction and back toward her, a knife suddenly appearing in his right hand. He held it up and grinned, offering her a choice: Scream and he would kill Robert, or remain silent and let him disappear into the shadows of London.

The sinister apparition lifted a gloved finger to his full lips, but rather than being white, his gloves were dripping red with the blood of five men.

"Shhh," the specter whispered, making his surreal image all too real, all too threatening.

Juliet shivered then nodded once, knowing that a man who could kill six men would not hesitate to kill again.

Twenty-three

Nicole had spent the entire morning writing a letter with detailed instructions to her contact in Honfleur that would then be sent on to London.

Nicole shook her head in disbelief as she folded the completed missive. How could Falcon have been so careless as to send a viscount to extract her?

Particularly, this viscount!

Viscount DunDonell was unforgettable: enormous, handsome, with distinctive coloring and carriage. All it would take was one chance meeting with a person of minimal memory who had visited London prior to the start of the war to throw suspicion on the distinguished viscount, if not land him directly in prison.

Nor, for that matter, was the McCurren family one to be forgotten. Nicole herself had met the viscount's parents when she was a child. His father, Malcolm McCurren, Earl of DunDonell, was a mountain of a man with a thick, dark beard and a thundering voice that had frightened her no end.

His similarity in size and facial features to his handsome heir was clear to anyone who had met them. The earl was himself a handsome man, but it was his mother from whom the viscount had acquired his striking turquoise eyes and auburn hair.

Nicole recalled the countess very clearly. Lady DunDonell had been very kind when Nicole's mother had died. The Earl of DunDonell and his beautiful wife had stayed in Nicole's home on several occasions over the years, but it was that visit she remembered most.

Lady DunDonell had been the only guest present at the funeral to acknowledge Nicole's pain, acknowledge the loss a child felt for her mother.

The kindly countess had done what she could to be of assistance, had spoken to Nicole's tutor, excusing her from her lessons. Lady DunDonell had even played cards with her on the eve of her mother's burial. Yet the earl and countess were merely acquaintances, nothing more, and by the end of that horrible week, Nicole was once again alone.

Her decadent father had never spent much time with her, and why Nicole had expected him to comfort her after her mother's death she did not know. It just seemed to her, as a child of eleven, that it was something a father ought to do for his offspring.

Comfort, protect.

Her father had loved her, but he was a vain man incapable of showering affection on anyone but himself. Nicole resembled her father in appearance, and she suspected that his pride and vanity bonded her to him in some peculiar way. He was forever telling Nicole how pretty she was or how beautiful she appeared riding her mount.

But even his cursory interest in Nicole had waned when her father had met Lady Langston a mere three months after her mother's death.

Lady Langston was even prettier and appeared even more beautiful as she rode at Nicole's father's side.

Looking back with the eyes of a mature woman, Nicole could now see that they had become lovers almost immediately. But they had waited the requisite mourning period before announcing their engagement.

Her father had been so happy that evening. Nicole smiled as the picture of her father standing with champagne glass in hand bubbled through her more painful memories.

The earl was not a dreadful man; quite the contrary. Everyone liked her father. He had been kind to her, kind to the servants, and had been a great deal of fun for his friends.

No, he was not a dreadful man. Her father had just been lacking in depth and incapable of—

"What are you doing?"

Nicole flinched in her delicately carved chair. She turned and looked at the man who had consumed her thoughts all through the night. He was so perfect of face, and his form . . . Her eyes drifted down his exceptional body, and Nicole blushed, quickly turning to look at her letter lest the man realize her lecherous intentions.

"I'm writing my sister."

Not that the man was unacquainted with lustful looks. Undoubtedly, the handsome viscount had innumerable society ladies throwing themselves across his path. And the prowess with which he had made love to her indicated that he had picked up quite a few along the way.

She had not thought of that, had not wanted to think about the countless women he had taken to bed. For one sublime moment, Nicole had felt like the most precious woman in all the world, and she would forever be grateful for that illuminating instant.

Viscount DunDonell walked toward her, and Nicole leaned so close to her parchment that one might suspect that she required spectacles.

"And what will you tell your sister?" the viscount whispered, intentionally seductive, inviting.

His left palm pressed to the oak desk and Nicole stared at his hand, remembering the heat, the power of it as it explored her body.

"Nothing." She was inarticulate, slow of mind.

Daniel McCurren was leaning over her, peering at the letter over her right shoulder. "Will you tell your sister about last night?"

"No—" Her words stuck in her throat the moment his searing lips pressed to the right side of her neck. Nicole allowed him a second kiss. Perhaps, just once more and then she would stop him. "Tell her what?"

Oh, God yes, another. She could not breathe.

His soft laughter tickled her nape. "Tell her about us, tell her how we made love." The viscount kissed the sensitive skin at the base of her neck and her spine tingled with wanting.

Nicole leaned to the left, pulling back. "Why should I tell her about our . . . evening?"

"You're absolutely right, lass." The viscount looked down at her smiling. "Best your family—"

"It won't happen again." Lord DunDonell's brows furrowed as she continued to talk. "I'd no idea when we . . ."

"Made love." He nodded angrily, finishing for her.

"Yes." Nicole spoke to the desk. "I'd no idea when we made love that you were a viscount."

"What bloody difference does that make?"

She lit the sealing wax and watched the red liquid drip on the back of the veiled letter.

"It makes a great deal of difference." Nicole pressed her ring to the paraffin and then rose, careful not to meet his striking eyes. "Last night, I thought you a fellow patriot offering his services to the Crown."

"I am!"

"But I now know," she continued, ignoring him, "that you are a viscount with enormous wealth and responsibility."

"So?"

"Who came to Paris on a lark." Nicole picked up the communiqué, her reticule dangling from her left wrist.

"What business is it of yours why I came to Paris?"

"Ahh, I've so missed the aristocratic arrogance of

Britain's *haute ton*." Daniel McCurren was angry, defensive as she stared into his icy eyes. "Very well, why did you come to Paris, Viscount DunDonell?"

This viscount's jaw set. "My reasons are my own."

"I'm sure that they are, and I shall leave you to them as I have preparations to make."

Daniel watched Nicole walk toward the front door. He watched the way she held her head, her shoulders, and then he was sure of his suspicions.

"Well, lass, I may have my reasons for coming to Paris, but you're not exactly being truthful." Now that Daniel had her attention, he kept it, walking toward her. "Only ladies of the *haute ton* 'miss the aristocratic arrogance' of its gentlemen."

The woman saw her mistake and Daniel watched her lovely eyes as she began to spin a tidy lie. "I could have been a lady's maid, a governess—"

"With your education, your comportment? I think not Lady . . . Come now, lass, make the proper introductions. Lady . . ." Daniel smiled down at her, the idea of their equal status decidedly intriguing. "I'm sure we've never been introduced." He tilted his head, his eyes staring into hers as Daniel teased her with the possibility of a kiss. "I would have remembered," he breathed.

His lips fell to hers and Nicole tasted as sweet as she had last night. His fingers slid around the silky skin at the base of her neck, just below her bonnet. But the lass was as skittish as a fawn, ready to jump at the first opportunity, so he reassured her with gentle caresses. Daniel moved closer, deeper, and his right hand went round her waist as he slowly coaxed her against his body.

The heat of her flooded him with memories of last night, and he was hardening with renewed desire. Their lovemaking had been languid as Daniel took the time to explore her exquisite body and ease her fears. But it was that time, the delaying of pleasure, that had culminated in a climax that shook him body and soul.

And he wanted to feel the shake of it again.

"Oh, I would have remembered you," Daniel whispered to himself, but she had heard him.

The lass hit him in the chest with both palms, but it was their mouths that punctuated their disentanglement with a wet dislodging of lips.

"You could not have known me in London." Nicole stared at the floor then spun, deserting the apartment without a backward glance and leaving Daniel to wonder who the hell she was and what the hell had happened to her.

Twenty-four

❦

*L*ady Juliet Pervill sat in her parlor with her arms crossed over her chest as an annoying barrage of drivel washed over her.

"It is entirely too dangerous, Juliet." Lord Barksdale shook his chestnut head. "The blackguard in the alley saw your face. The assassin may even have recognized you. Identifying the man to the Foreign Office is ill-advised."

Juliet rolled her eyes and sighed with impatience. "Really, Robert, if I did not recognize the assassin, then it is highly probable that he did not recognize me."

The young Lord Barksdale continued stalking in front of the settee on which Juliet sat as if he were her omnipotent guardian. "The murderer could know *of* you, darling. You must admit that your father travels in rather seedy circles."

Juliet felt the heated flash of irritation. Lord Pervill was a scoundrel, to be sure, but she and her mother were the only persons allowed to label him as such.

"You're overwrought," Juliet said, rising. She walked to

the bell pull, sure that a cup of tea would do the agitated young lord some good.

"I am not overwrought, Juliet." Robert lifted his sculpted chin, saying in his most deeply masculine voice, "You are not to go to the Foreign Office. I absolutely forbid it."

Lady Pervill alighted from her carriage a quarter of an hour later, stepping onto the hallowed ground of Whitehall. Men in every shade of gray scurried past, and Juliet squinted against the sun to locate the front entrance of the Foreign Office. Finding it, she lifted her skirts and walked up the wide steps, a gallant gentleman holding the door open as she swept inside.

Juliet took a moment to look about the impressive foyer before making her way to an authoritative figure and asking, "I have some information that I wish to discuss with a representative of the Foreign Office. Would you be so kind as to direct me?"

The enormous man looked down and, with a thick cockney accent, sneered, "Do ya have an appointment?"

"No, I'm afraid I don't. You see, if I knew with whom to make the appointment, then I would not be speaking with you."

The man's unruly eyebrows pulled together as he tried to decide if he had just been insulted.

"You can't speak with a member of the Foreign Office without an appointment, ma'am," the impolite sentry said, evidently deciding that he had.

Juliet proceeded into the hall to find a gentleman with some modicum of intelligence, but the large guard blocked her progress.

"I'm afraid you will be needing an appointment," the man said, staring down at her like Cerberus guarding the entrance to Hades.

"Look here, sir," Juliet began reasonably. "I have information concerning several murders which took place two nights ago—"

"Well, miss, that would be a Home Office matter," the man smirked, condescension wafting off him.

Anger sharpened her mind as well as her tongue.

"You will address me as Lady Pervill." Juliet's displeasure was audible to every man in the front entrance as she brought the guard to heel. "Furthermore, you will *fetch*"—she paused, using the demeaning word intentionally—"your superior and tell him that I have information pertaining to the murder of a prisoner being transported to Newgate prison two nights past."

All heads were now turned in her direction, but Juliet paid the gentlemen in the foyer no mind.

"If you do not perform the task for which you have been hired, I shall make certain that your employer is aware of your insolence, as well as your disregard for the lives of the six men murdered."

A tidy gentleman, not much taller than herself, wandered on the unsightly scene. "It's all right, Mister Jones. I shall take Lady . . . ?"

"Pervill," Juliet said, by way of introduction.

"I shall escort Lady Pervill."

The guard nodded once, embarrassed by her dressing-down. "Very good, my lord."

The gentleman held out his arm and Juliet took it, resuming the order of things.

"You must forgive Mister Jones," the gentleman beseeched, smiling as they proceeded down the main corridor. "It is his job to . . . assess the significance of visitors to the Foreign Office."

Unconvinced, Juliet slipped him a sidelong look. "The man is large. I will give you that, but he is not very good at the assessing portion of his post."

"Perhaps not." The gentleman chuckled, ushering her through a myriad of doors. "Mister Jones is just returned from Portugal, and is unaccustomed to dealing with the fairer sex, much less a lady of your caliber."

Juliet knew damn well when she was being placated, but she liked it nonetheless.

"If you would be so kind as to wait here?"

"Certainly."

The tidy man knocked on a nondescript door and then entered. Juliet strained to listen but heard only muffled conversation before her amiable escort returned, saying, "This gentleman will be able to assist you, Lady Pervill."

Juliet entered the small room and glanced at the old man behind the desk, thoroughly disappointed. She had half hoped to be shown to some dashing officer, who would fall at her feet and thank her for the vital information needed to apprehend the villain who had murdered those poor men.

But this man was neither young nor dashing. He was not even an officer, for goodness' sake.

"Good afternoon."

"Good afternoon, Lady Pervill." Falcon nodded at his assistant to close his office door while trying not to laugh at the girl's obvious disillusionment. "I was told that you have information pertaining to the murders of six men?"

"Yes, that is correct."

He stared at her wholesome face and dusting of freckles, understanding why Mister Jones had stopped the young lady. She looked all of twelve.

"I am told that you made quite a scene in the foyer," Falcon said, adding disapproval then watching her reaction, noting not one twinge of embarrassment or remorse.

"I came to the Foreign Office because I have information pertaining to the murder of those men," the lady began. "What difference could my behavior possibly make to them? Indeed, my inaction would harm their families and the investigation of their murders a great deal more. Do you not agree?"

Falcon ignored her philosophical inquiry and looked down to hide his sharpening eyes.

"What is this information you believe that you have, Lady Pervill?"

"I saw the murderer."

Forced back in his chair by the woman's revelation,

Falcon very nearly knocked his coffee cup to the wooden floor.

"How do you know it was he?"

"It was the murderer." The girl's eyes held, burning with intelligence. "The man was covered in blood."

"Go on."

"He was rather short, young, twenty-five years or so. French in appearance, dark eyes and hair, olive skin, handsome. He was impeccably dressed with a golden waistcoat and white gloves that were covered red with blood."

"How did you happen upon him?"

The young lady paled, which from Falcon's cursory assessment of this woman's character, seemed to take a great deal to accomplish.

"He threatened my companion, Lord Barksdale."

"What did the man say?"

"Nothing, not a word, which further indicates that he was French. As to our ill-fated meeting, I was traveling to the opera when Lord Barksdale's driver happened upon the horrible scene. Seeing no signs of danger, Lord Barksdale went to assist and the murderer appeared from the shadows nearest my side of the conveyance. The man revealed a knife . . . I understood his meaning. He had, after all, just killed six men."

"Are you sure it was only one man?"

"Quite."

"How do you know?"

"I saw it in his eyes. He . . ." The young woman lifted her eyes to meet his. "He enjoyed it." She swallowed. "Killing, he enjoyed the killing of those men."

Falcon nodded, his thoughts flickering to his murdered friend, Colonel Lancaster. The colonel had insisted that he, as military liaison to the Foreign Office, be the one to accompany Lord Cunningham to Newgate, and Falcon was not sure that he would ever forgive himself for letting him do so.

"Thank you, Lady Pervill." Falcon rose to his feet. "You are very brave to come here and give us this information."

The young woman shrugged. "I am in no danger. If the murderer wished me harm, he had every opportunity that night. No, I suspect this Frenchman has long since fled London."

"Why do you say so?" Falcon asked, intrigued by her logic.

"He was very calm, and I believe had formulated an escape route prior to performing the murders. I would have."

"Would you?"

"Yes," the girl said with not a moment of hesitation. "Six armed men—I would have planned my attack very carefully, as well as my escape."

Falcon laughed, deliberately lightening the mood. "I fear for your Lord Barksdale."

Lady Pervill smiled, once again resembling a child of twelve. "As well you should."

"Thank you, Lady Pervill. I shall inform you if the murderer should be apprehended."

"He won't be, but it was kind of you to offer, my lord."

Falcon watched the girl leave, thinking her undoubtedly correct. He sat down, nevertheless, and dutifully pulled the files of known French collaborators working throughout England. However, none of the men presently being watched by his office matched the description of this bold assassin.

He wrote down this murderer's description and stared at his desk, wondering how to relay this information to Scorpion, wondering if Nicole was still in Paris. He prayed to God that she was not. Many of his agents had already returned to London safely, but Scorpion's situation was . . . complex.

Falcon had hoped to send Daniel McCurren to Paris not only with a warning, but also with a pardon. However, it was argued by certain members of the Foreign Office that the lady's extraordinary service to the Crown only further proved her capacity toward violence.

Idiots.

He spun the wooden top and stared as it twirled about his desk. The brightly painted circles moved across the toy and an idea took hold of him. Falcon snatched the top up and turned it over, smiling at the name scrawled in blue paint.

He called to his assistant and handed him the letter, ordering, "Have one of our new men deliver the communiqué to this shop in Paris," all the while praying that the missive would arrive before the man it described.

Twenty-five

❧

Evariste Rousseau closed his eyes and breathed in the scent of Paris as he was rowed out to the barge that anchored every Saturday evening in the center of the Seine. Music drifted to his ears as he walked up the guarded gangplank, using the thin strips of wood for leverage against the force of the swaying ship.

"Welcome home, Major Rousseau." The owner of the popular gambling hell bowed. "Minister LeCoeur is expecting you in the blue room."

Evariste looked through him and toward the short ladder that led to the more entertaining level of the exclusive club. He discreetly swept his black jacket to the side, making his pistols accessible if the need should arise.

Security upon *Neptune's Paradise* was exceptional and quite comforting to the Parisian elite. Yet it was this isolation, this total control of the surroundings by the club owner, that put Evariste on edge. He had learned long ago that places reputed to be safe were often the most dangerous of all.

Smoke and drink flowed freely on the open deck of the hell, and he descended the ladder, leaving temptation behind. The hull of the inspired ship had been transformed into ten luxurious rooms, five on either side of the debauched barge.

The favored blue room, he knew from experience, was the second on his left. Evariste knocked and the door was opened by one of the men he had hired to protect Minister LeCoeur.

"Rousseau!" the minister shouted, pleased to see him. Evariste's lips rose fractionally at one corner. It was pleasant to be needed. "Have a seat."

Evariste glanced at the round table where the five men sat. Cards and snifters of brandy littered the table with an empty wooden chair waiting to be occupied. Evariste glanced at the door and back to the empty chair, eliciting a laugh from his employer.

"Leave us, gentlemen, so that our wayward friend might sit facing the door." Major Rousseau stepped to the side, his back against the wall, while the four guards filed out, not quite meeting his eye. "And have our host send along his finest selection of women," Minister LeCoeur said to Captain Turgeon.

The captain bowed, closing the door, and Evariste walked to a corner chair opposite the illustrious minister of police.

"You're back." Minister LeCoeur met his eye. "Might I then assume that you have been successful in your commission?"

Evariste smirked then tossed atop the table a package wrapped in brown paper and secured in a wiry knot with thin, taupe twine.

The minister smiled fully, reaching for the package as he sat back, crossing his legs. He stripped the untidy twine and the many layers of paper fell open. Minister LeCoeur unrolled the package with great expectation, revealing the severed tongue of the English traitor Lord Cunningham.

But that was not all.

Evariste waited eagerly as the minister's brows furrowed and he continued to unroll the bulky package. A second tongue lay lifeless, a grayish brown against the moist brown paper.

"Who?" his employer asked, meeting his eye.

Evariste could not contain his smile. "Colonel Lancaster was himself escorting Lord Cunningham to Newgate."

Minister LeCoeur glanced at the second tongue in disbelief. "Lancaster? Falcon's own military advisor?" The minister laughed and Evariste felt the contentment of pride. "Oh, you are good to me, Major Rousseau."

A knock at the door interrupted his accolade and three whores were ushered into the small room. Evariste glanced at the women with disinterest but was surprised when Minister LeCoeur chose a black-haired girl over his typical preference for blondes.

"What has become of your mistress?" Evariste inquired.

"Ah, *oui,* I forget you have been in London." Minister LeCoeur smiled like a fiend entering an opium den. "I have met a lady, an ebony-haired goddess with whom I am becoming increasingly enamored."

Evariste did not like it. "What do you know of this woman?"

"The lady is being investigated," his employer said, the minister's tone a dismissive set-down, and Evariste knew the personal affair was to be dropped. "Would you like one of the other whores?"

"No," Evariste said, not even bothering to look at the amenable women. "I wish to access the Conciergerie."

"The prison is still standing, I can assure you, *mon ami.*" Evariste said nothing, his mind made up. "Visit if you must." The minister sighed. "I shall meet you tomorrow afternoon to discuss the details of your journey to London." Major Rousseau rose, bowing before stepping around the large table. "Take those two with you on your way out, will you?" Minister LeCoeur asked, his attention already drifting to the ebony-haired whore.

Evariste ushered the discarded women out of the blue

room and then pushed past them on his way up the ladder and toward the main deck. The rowboat was ready, as ordered, to take him the short distance to the *Ile de la Cité*.

They rowed in silence, and Evariste stared as they approached the dock that led to a staircase close to the prison entrance. Major Rousseau ascended to the street, where he was greeted first by the stench of the imprisoned citizens of Paris, and then by the prison sentry.

"Name?" Evariste looked up at the man, his gaze reflecting his reputation. "*Pardon,* Major Rousseau," the guard groveled. "I was told that you were away on business."

"Do I look 'away'?" The sentry swallowed. "Open the fucking gate."

The gate was opened without further comment, and Major Rousseau made his way to his prison office. It was located in the basement as he had requested, far away from the annoyance and scrutiny of the bureaucratic custodians of the Conciergerie.

Evariste opened the door to his office and smiled despite himself. He walked to his desk, sank into the leather chair, and just breathed. He felt at ease here, both comfortable and comforted, in charge and in control.

The major glanced at his tidy desk to verify that all was as he had left it, then leaned over and pulled out the bottom right-hand drawer of his enormous desk. He lifted the heavy wooden case and opened it, inspecting his tools one by one. The metal glinted and Evariste called to his assistant.

"Jean-Luc."

"Sir." The boy opened his office door, entering from the outer hall.

"You have done an excellent job in cleaning these tools. I commend you."

"Thank you, sir," the young guard said, trying to hide his pride.

"Now, bring in tonight's arrivals."

"Right away, Major Rousseau." The boy spun and ran down the hall, eager to please him further.

The soldier returned several minutes later with files in hand and four bedraggled young women following behind him. They ranged in age from sixteen to twenty-one, all of them charged with petty theft.

"Line them up." Evariste sat in his chair watching the women carefully as his guard arranged the prisoners shoulder to shoulder. The major lifted the files and found the name he had been seeking.

"Brigitte?" Evariste walked toward a small blonde with unkempt hair and a dirty capot sitting askew atop her head. "You are but sixteen, and already a thief. Surely your mother has taught you better than this?"

The girl was looking at her hands, tears streaming down her pale face. "My mother is dead, *monsieur*."

The tallest of the women sniggered with sympathetic contempt, drawing his attention. Evariste glanced at the woman and sorted the four files, estimating her to be the oldest.

"Angelique?" he asked, walking toward the disdainful woman as she stared straight ahead, refusing to answer him.

"*Oui*, Major Rousseau," his assistant interjected. "She is called Angelique."

Evariste placed the files on his desk and walked to stand toe to toe with the young woman. "You are a thief?"

"If your file says so, then it must be true." Defiance sparkled in her gray eyes, causing a swell of excitement in his chest.

"You must be very good with your hands to be a thief." They were the only two in the room, the others disregarded as weak competition. "I, too, am good with my hands," Evariste whispered, leaning forward and caressing her breast.

The woman slapped him and Evariste became aroused.

"Leave her."

His prisoner paled, realizing her fate as the other women were escorted from the room. Evariste locked the door and removed his jacket, carefully laying it over the back of his leather chair.

"I'll scream." The girl lifted her chin but he could still see her fear, respected her for fighting it.

Evariste removed his tools in the order in which they would be used, and smiled, saying, "*Oui,* you will."

Twenty-six

❦

Nicole entered the small doors of Saint Gervais at five o'clock in the afternoon, having completed the preparation for what was likely to be her final mission. She bowed her head, making the sign of the cross as she turned to climb the ancient steps to the floor above.

The final steps were the most difficult, as her soul longed to be in the presence of God. She emerged into the vaulted chamber and looked up at stained glass windows set aglow like a fine red wine by the afternoon sun.

She was alone in the chapel, and immensely thankful for it, as Nicole had many things to discuss, many burdens to bear. On the whole, Parisians seemed to prefer the majesty of Notre Dame, but it was here, in this intimate chapel, that Nicole found comfort. She knelt in front of the small altar, clutching Falcon's missive in her right hand.

It was clever of her "sister" to send a missive directly to Monsieur Gaulet's toy shop, but then Falcon had always been clever. It was easy enough to explain to the elderly shopkeeper that her "sister" had not yet received the location of her new apartment and that she must have taken the direction from the package sent Friday last.

An appreciative smile and an expensive purchase for her "nephew" had quelled any suspicion the old man might have had about the letter. Nicole had left the shop and read the missive as she strolled along the wide boulevards. However, it was not the autumn wind that had driven her to the sanctuary of Saint Gervais but rather the information contained within the brief communique.

A Frenchman was suspected of single-handedly killing six men, including the notorious traitor, Lord Cunningham. Falcon had written a description of the man, but to little effect, as Nicole had no idea who this deadly French assassin might be.

Minister LeCoeur was lethal, to be sure, but he had been with her at the time of Lord Cunningham's murder and was also far taller than the man described. No, Joseph LeCoeur was not the man for whom Falcon had risked exposing her location, her identity as Scorpion.

Predictably, the old man had rescinded the fabricated order of assassination, warning her of this unidentified adversary in the process. Yet as she knelt at the altar of this small chapel Nicole could not think of a single reason for abandoning the mission.

Both she and Falcon knew what awaited her if she returned to England. The old man had fought for her release two long years ago, and it had been granted by the Foreign Office.

Conditionally.

If Lady Nicole Stratton agreed to accept the Foreign Office's commission, then she was also consenting never again to set foot on British soil, or her sentence of execution would be carried out. At that moment, Nicole had become an orphan of England, an assassin with no home and no country. She had become Scorpion, a hollow instrument used by the Crown to further His Majesty's interests in France.

No, she would never go back to England. Better to die at

the hands of the French for a noble cause than to be executed by her countrymen for an unspeakable injustice.

Either way, her life was over.

The only question that remained was whether or not she would take another life with her. Nicole paused, never before having questioned the necessity of an assassination.

Initially, she had completed her missions out of fear and self-preservation. Kill or be killed. And then it did not seem to matter; nothing seemed to matter. The men chosen were as deserving of death as she. She had been ordered to kill them and they deserved to be killed. It was quite simple, black and white.

Until she met him.

Daniel McCurren had put ideas in her head, disturbing thoughts of justification and the right of one man to judge another.

It was all very disconcerting.

"You have been in prayer for quite some time, my child. Is there something of which you wish to speak?"

Nicole looked up at the elderly priest, his hands clasped in patient contemplation, his sagging face lifted by kindness. She sat on the wooden pew and opened her mouth, and then closed it, cordoning her thoughts.

"It is all right, *ma petite*. We are very much alone and all matters discussed shall remain between us and these four walls." He smiled, his teeth hidden by his thin lips. "You are very troubled."

It was not a question, and all Nicole could do was whisper, *"Oui."*

"You have a confession to make?" The priest leaned toward her with concern, his eyes holding hers.

"No. Not yet." Her eyes filled with shame and the kindly man nodded.

"Ah, you contemplate a sinful deed, no?"

"Oui," Nicole admitted, coerced by his gentleness.

"It is sometimes good to discuss these things." The priest waited patiently and the silence stretched as Nicole made her decision to confide.

"If a man has determined to steal from another . . ." She met the man's faded eyes. "And has confessed so to me, but I take no action. Am I then—"

"*Oui,* you also are guilty of the sin of theft."

Nicole's eyes filled with tears, knowing in her heart the truth of the priest's pronouncement.

"If you had attempted to dissuade this would-be 'thief' or had warned the man about to be robbed, then you would be absolved of this sinful crime. But to sit by complacently and watch this theft occur . . ." The priest shrugged. "This is wrong in the eyes of God."

Nicole cried harder, searching for any doctrinal ambiguity. "And if this thief cannot be dissuaded?"

"His victim must be warned."

"And if I am harmed as a result of this warning? Is this right with God?" Nicole could not keep the bitterness from her tone.

"Fear," the old priest said regretfully, "is not a satisfactory excuse for sin." He placed his gentle hand on hers. "If righteous men fail to protect the innocent of this world, then wickedness will have victory and dominion over us all."

Nicole thought of the countless men and women of Britain's *haute ton* who had done nothing to aid her, knowing her fate and knowing that it was going to happen again.

The innocent must be protected.

"I am not a righteous woman," she argued. *And never could be.*

"Righteousness is determined by righteous deeds."

"And if one sin is committed to prevent a greater evil?"

"Such sins are for God to determine. If a man feels justified in accordance with the laws of God . . . prayer and his own heart must guide his path."

"You have been of very little assistance, Father." Nicole smiled, disheartened.

The priest lifted his hands, conceding her point. "Men do not enter the house of God seeking easy answers, merely righteous ones."

"I would have preferred the answers I wished to hear." She met his eye in feigned annoyance.

"And I would have preferred to be taller." He shrugged again and Nicole could not help laughing as the elderly priest rose to his diminutive height, saying, "Take all of the time you wish, *ma petite*. God will listen to your prayers."

"But will he answer them?"

"*Oui,* he always answers prayer." The priest held up a bony finger. "Just not always in the way we would like."

Nicole sat for a moment longer, contemplating what the priest had said.

She had known what he would say, but perhaps that was why she had come to Saint Gervais. Nicole knew that the priest would never condone the assassination. But she knew also that God had given her such terrible trials so that she might understand the need to protect the powerless. She knew that God had made her strong enough to exact punishment, no matter what the personal cost.

In her heart, Nicole knew that the assassination of Joseph LeCoeur was not murder, but defense of the innocent in the midst of a wicked war devised by wicked men.

Nicole returned to the apartment sooner than Daniel had expected.

He tossed his leather-bound copy of *Atala* by Chateaubriand on his bed and stood in the doorway of his bedchamber, his fingertips grasping the doorframe just over his head.

"That did not take long."

"No, the market was quite empty today." She glanced in his direction, and for a moment Daniel regretted having removed his jacket. "I see you have given up your observations of Joseph LeCoeur."

God above, but those violet eyes were fetching when she was angry.

"Minister LeCoeur left his home several hours ago,"

Daniel offered, following her into the back parlor as he tucked the tails of his linen shirt beneath the soft buckskin of his breeches.

"And how do you know the minister has not returned to his apartment?"

Daniel ducked his head and glanced out the window nearest him. "Still gone." He grinned, winking.

The lass was not amused.

"Monsieur Damont, the empress's Toussaint Feast is in two days, and while I realize this assignment impinges upon your imbibing, please keep in mind that it is my life with which you are playing."

"You're the one playing games with your life, lass. We both know you could leave for London tonight. I have nothing to do with it."

The irritated woman sought a retort but found none. "Well, if you insist on staying, you might at least aid me in the observations."

"He's gone."

"I know he's gone!" she snapped, then closed her eyes and sighed with frustration for allowing him to successfully bait her. "I know Minister LeCoeur is gone at present." She looked at him calmly, more in control.

God, she was pretty, he thought.

"But you might at least have napped in front of the window."

Daniel stared at her angry expression and was unable to resist teasing her. "I tried, but there was far too much sunlight by the window," he lied.

Nicole rolled those beautiful eyes and he laughed, grabbing her arm as she walked away.

"Here." Daniel handed her the journal with detailed observations up to twenty minutes ago. "He's been gone for . . ." Daniel glanced at the mantle clock as she opened the small leather journal. "Two-and-a-half hours."

"Three-quarters." Her dark head was bent over the open journal, and her index finger pointed to the middle of the last page on which Daniel had written. "Minister LeCoeur has been gone for two-and-three-quarter hours."

Daniel nodded his head. "Oh, well, that's different then."

"There is no need to be rude, Monsieur Damont."

"Nor, apparently, is there a need for gratitude." The lady blushed and he added, "And my name is Daniel."

"You're correct." Nicole closed the journal, folding her hands over it and sighing as if he were some old woman to be coddled. "Please, accept my apologies."

"No." Daniel shook his head, and her fine black brows furrowed.

"No?"

"No, I don't accept your apology." Daniel leaned forward. "You did not mean it."

"What?"

"You did not mean a word of that apology and we both know it."

"I most certainly did!"

"No, you did not, but you can have another go if you wish to make it up to me."

"Oh, this is ridiculous, but if it will ease your sensibilities . . ." Nicole swallowed and looked into his eyes with exaggerated contrition. "Viscount DunDonell." Daniel nodded. "Please, accept my apologies for . . ." She blinked. "Please, accept my apologies for not . . ."

"See! You do not even know why you are apologizing."

"Of course I do," the lass said and he grinned. "I apologize, Viscount DunDonell, for being rude."

"There," Daniel cooed, full of sarcasm as he placed his hands on her delicate shoulders. "That was not so difficult, and if you like, I can sit here with you while you watch the empty apartment across the way."

"Shut up."

Daniel laughed, his arms dropping to his side. "My God, lass, but you've got no sense of humor." Her spine stiffened and he shook his head, reflecting, "If I knew I was going to die, I sure as hell would spend my last days differently than you have been spending yours."

"Oh, I see." Her eyes challenged. "Saving Britain is not a worthy enough task for you, Viscount DunDonell?"

"It is a grand goal, lass. I'm just suggesting that you enjoy yourself while you do it. But . . ." Daniel sighed, walking toward his bedchamber. "I can see that you're determined to squander the time remaining to you. So, I'll just go and retrieve my book so that we can stare at LeCoeur's apartment in morose silence."

Daniel opened the door to his bedchamber and reached across the bed, lifting the half-read copy of *Atala* from the velvet duvet. The door slammed shut and Daniel spun round only to see the deadly Mademoiselle Beauvoire staring up at him.

"Did you want to borrow my book?" He held the novel out, confused.

The lady snatched the book from his hand then tossed it on the bed as she continued to stare, making him decidedly uneasy.

"You suggested I find something with which to entertain myself."

"Aye," Daniel agreed with considerable trepidation.

"Well, I don't have time to read," the woman said, pushing him in the chest. Daniel sat hard on the bed, overbalanced as he looked up at the woman who was already unfastening the second button of his shirt. "You don't object, do you, Daniel?"

Daniel?

"Hell no, lass." He chuckled, anticipation widening his eyes the moment he took her sensual meaning. "I don't mind at all." Nicole Beauvoire was standing between his thighs and he kissed her elegant neck, whispering, "But I thought you vowed never to bed me again."

"True, but as you have chosen to stay in Paris and are in 'no more danger than you were five minutes ago'—"

"You thought to enjoy yourself?" he teased.

A feminine tisk of irritation sounded overhead and she tried to step away from him, but Daniel had placed a firm grasp on that lovely backside. "I'm only jesting,

Nicole," he said, as he kissed her neck just below the ear.
Nicole.

He liked the sound of her name on his lips, the taste of
her as he made his way down her neck. She pealed his shirt
over his shoulders and the lass liked what she found; he
could see it in her eyes, her touch. He was forced to let go
of her delightful derrière as she impatiently yanked the voluminous sleeves from his arms.

His desire swelled, bolstered by her eagerness, as her
eyes fell to the contours of his arms like a foundling at a
Christmas feast. She was a woman starved, and he was determined to let the lass have her fill. He looked down at her
feminine hands as they slid round the muscles of his chest
and the sight, the feel, of her impatient touch all but drove
him wild.

Daniel leaned back slowly and she liked that, too, following him as if joined by threads of mutual attraction. Her
palms descended to the flexing muscles of his abdomen as
they rolled out before her.

Nicole straddled his thighs, her left hand planted on the
mattress as her right index finger traced the delineation of
his belly as if he were fashioned from costly crystal.

"You like that?" Daniel's eyes darted to hers, anxious to
capture the foundations of her lust so that he might build
on his own.

Her eyes roamed over his chest and stomach, accessing
every dip and curve with her lovely hands.

"Yes." She nodded imperceptibly, annoyed to be distracted from her primal assessment of his form.

Daniel grinned, the airy word winding him tight.

"I'll not break, lass. Have a good, long feel."

Her hands splayed on his stomach and Daniel closed his
eyes, awash with pleasure and unable to keep them open so
that he might witness her shortening breath, her spiraling
need. Daniel attempted to open them when the moist heat
of her mouth closed over his left nipple. He groaned, his
hips instinctively flexing, his arms tensing as his hands
found the curves of her feminine waist.

"Oh, God. Now that's entertaining, lass."

Nicole Beauvoire said nothing, moving her warm lips between the taut muscles of his chest. He could feel her soft breasts brushing his hips, but his mind was focused entirely upon her lips. She kissed him again where his chest gave way to the flatter, more defined muscles of his abdomen.

Her nose tickled his increasingly sensitive belly, and Daniel would have flinched had he not been so aroused. She kissed him again lower, choosing to follow the central line of his stomach. His right hand wandered to the back of her ebony head, which contrasted deliciously with the gold of his skin.

Daniel was breathing heavily by the time the lady sat up and pulled the pins from her long hair. The ebony strands fell about her shoulders and he found himself reaching up to remove her gown, aching to see her silky hair against her even softer skin.

Her garments were strewn across the floor and she stood before him, more beautiful than Botticelli's depiction of Venus. But this goddess was very real. Daniel reached for her, but she stepped away, not allowing herself to be captured.

She glanced at his buckskins and bent down to unfasten only the buttons necessary to pull them from his body. Nicole sat on her knees, pulling the trousers from his feet and then her hands were on his bare thighs. Daniel sat up on his elbows and looked at the woman as she whispered, "You have such beautiful legs," her heated breath enveloping his erection.

"Beautiful?" he asked, his voice strained.

"Aye." The lass nodded, meeting his eye as she felt her way up his thighs. Daniel stared, unable to move as Nicole crawled over him. "Very beautiful."

He swallowed, saying, "I'm glad you like . . ."

But his mind ceased to function when she pressed her lips to his left hip.

"I do." The lady lifted her head, her black hair skimming his sensitive length as she moved her head to kiss his right hip. "And do you know what else I find astonishingly alluring?"

"No," Daniel said, hoping that he did.

"Yes, I think that you do," she said, her lips hovering inches from the tip of his shaft.

She met his eyes then leaned forward and Daniel was torn between holding her gaze or staring at those moist lips.

"Show me," Daniel grated through clenched teeth.

The siren ran her tongue lightly round him and he groaned, forcing himself to keep his eyelids open so that he might witness her next caress. The lass smiled, knowing damn well the torture she was inflicting upon him. Daniel licked his lips, his mouth opening slightly in anticipation of her doing the same.

However, this time she stroked his shaft so gently that all Daniel felt was the tease of her excruciating caress. "You're killing me, lass."

Nicole ignored him, too lost in her own lust to satisfy his needs. And just when Daniel thought he would fall to his knees and beg the woman to end his torture, she took him fully in her mouth, stealing his breath and his mind.

She touched him only briefly before Daniel was lifting her to his lap lest he lose all control. The stunning creature was breathing heavily when she sat facing him, her bare backside settling onto his thighs. Daniel met her clouded eyes and kissed her deeply.

His right hand darted between them, but when he felt her wet, swollen sheath, Daniel grunted with anticipation. He leaned forward to capture her mouth, but stopped short when he felt her fingers wrap round his length.

"I want you like this." Nicole stared at him, her head falling back as she took him inside.

"All right." Daniel groaned his assent, lifting his hips to drive that much deeper.

She gave a soft moan of satisfaction then clung to his neck, lifting herself on her knees, which was almost as pleasurable as her sinking down again.

Daniel sat on the bed, grasping her backside, her breasts bouncing before his eyes as she rode him. He ignored the instinct to bury his lips between her breasts, concentrating his attention on their joining and the pleasure that she was giving . . . and taking.

It was that thought that was driving him wild, the obvious desire she had for him. He lifted his hips, matching her enthusiasm, driven by every cry of encouragement. The lass was so close to finding her pleasure that Daniel could sense her abandoning of all else. Sense her need to find enjoyment at this moment, at this time.

And he gave it to her, rolling his hips in one deep thrust as she cried out, shaking in his arms. Daniel watched her face for a moment longer and then closed his eyes, releasing himself and his mind of everything but the woman in his arms.

Nicole lay sprawled across Daniel's body, sated and spent. Just like, she was sure, every woman the man had ever made love to. Her forefinger twirled around the sprinkling of dark hairs on his muscular chest.

"How old were you when you first bedded a woman?" Nicole asked lightly, in keeping with the playful tone of the afternoon.

Daniel chuckled, the baritone rumble curling her toes. "A lady should not ask such things."

"Of course I shouldn't ask, but I am." Nicole positioned her chin on her arm so that she could see his striking eyes. "Perhaps I'm merely curious about the private lives of the British aristocracy."

Curious if other gentlemen of the *ton* were so gentle in their lovemaking, so affable in their demeanor.

"You're not penning an article for some lady's periodical, are you?"

Her heart skipped at the sight of his lopsided grin, making Nicole want to know all the more. "How old were you?"

"Guess."

"Nineteen."

"Fifteen," the rogue said impishly.

"Fifteen!" Nicole raised her head in shock.

"Aye, fifteen." Daniel absently ran his finger along her bare ribs.

"Who was the lady?" she asked, needing to know.

The viscount lifted his arm and placed it behind his head as he searched the canopy and his evidently countless conquests, for the name he sought.

"Mary."

"Lady Mary," Nicole said, thinking how much she disliked that name.

"Oh, Mary was no lady."

"Obviously not." Nicole mumbled.

The viscount grinned, ignoring her slight of his first paramour as he said, "I was rather large for my age, as you might imagine, and that fact did not escape the notice of our upstairs maid, Mary."

Nicole watched his alluring lips as he spoke, thinking this man incapable of escaping any woman's notice.

"A week before my sixteenth birthday I retired to my rooms, only to find Mary lying atop my bed as naked as the day she was born."

"You could have asked her to leave," Nicole pointed out with a raised brow.

"Aye, I could have, but Mary was a worldly woman of twenty-one who proceeded to share her knowledge for the next six weeks." Daniel sighed. " 'Twas the best birthday of my life."

The blackguard paused a bit too long in blissful remembrance of Mary the wanton maid, causing Nicole to elbow him in the ribs.

"Ow," the viscount complained.

Nicole rolled her eyes at the enormous man's low tolerance for pain. "What happened after six weeks?"

"My brother, Lackland, who was seven at the time, went to my mother's bedchamber and told her that he'd heard a ghost. A 'wailing woman.' "

Nicole giggled. "He did not!"

"He did," the viscount said, affronted. "Of course, my mother did not believe him, but she walked the lad back to his bedchamber, only to hear the 'wailing woman' with her own two ears."

"Oh, dear."

"She threw open my door, and there I was, bare arsed and banging away at Mary." His eyes sparkled at the retelling of the unfortunate scene.

"What on earth did you do?" Nicole asked, burning with curiosity.

"I ran like the coward that I am when confronted by my mother, but she cornered me before I reached the bedchamber door. So I stopped in front of her and she looked me straight in the eye," the viscount recalled, staring at the wall with affectionate respect, "and said, 'Just because you can rut with a woman does not mean that you should.'

"And then she told me to 'sleep in the barn with the rest of the animals.'" Daniel looked down at Nicole, rubbing her shoulder. "I slept there for a week, in the dead of a highland winter, mind you."

"As you deserved," she pronounced, laying her head on his solid chest. Nicole nestled against him, still smiling and wanting to stay there for the rest of the day.

The thought was disturbing.

Nicole planted her hand on his exquisite chest, pushing against his tempting strength.

"I'm afraid that I have things—"

"Don't." Daniel instinctively pulled her tighter against him, unwilling to let her go. "Just stay here with me awhile longer. The weather is miserable and we've nothing to do but snuggle."

"Snuggle?"

The lass said the word as if she'd no notion of its meaning, and Daniel leaned back to catch a glimpse of her expression.

"Aye, snuggle." He wrapped both arms around her waist, luxuriating in her soft heat as she leaned her head back down on his shoulder. "Like two rabbits in a burrow."

"Minus the dirt and smelly fur."

"'Tis a hard woman that does not like bunnies, Nicole Beauvoire, but I shall forgive you as you're very warm. I suppose you dislike children, too?"

"No, I adore children." Daniel smiled with surprise, pulling her tighter still. "Just not smelly ones." She laughed, adding, "I've always wanted . . ." The lady stiffened and Daniel's heart clenched. "I have always wanted four or five of my own."

I, a devastatingly singular word. "I'm so sorry you lost your husband before he could give—"

"I have to prepare for my meeting with Minister LeCoeur," she interrupted, getting out of bed. Daniel felt her loss against his side as he watched her bend down to grab her rumpled dress from the floor. "Are you still willing to help me prepare the meal?"

"I said I would."

"Yes, well . . ." Nicole disappeared beneath her dress and emerged, saying, "People say lots of things they don't mean."

"And I," Daniel said with such emphasis that the woman turned to meet his eye, "am not one of them."

"Forgive me, Viscount DunDonell," the lass said, distancing herself from him, and leaving Daniel bleeding on the ground he had just lost with her.

Twenty-seven

❦

Nicole stared through her carriage window at the drizzling rain that continued to blanket the capital. She adjusted her coverlet for the third time, finding it difficult to stay warm. She was cold from the inside out, and as the carriage rolled to a stop before the Ministry of Police, she wondered if she would ever be warm again.

As she had been today.

"We have arrived, Mademoiselle Beauvoire," her coachman said as he opened the carriage door.

Nicole glanced at the ornate building and looked down at her man, his black hat turning gray with a fine layer of mist.

"Please take this"—she handed him a missive—"to the office of Minister LeCoeur."

Nicole sat back and waited, positioning herself flatteringly in the corner of the squabs and trying desperately not to think of Daniel McCurren. She had never met a gentleman such as he, nor, she suspected, would she ever meet another.

The viscount was so large, so physically dominating, yet he never used his size, his pure masculine power, to threaten or intimidate her in any way. The gentleman seemed to have a true appreciation, no, more than that, he seemed to have a true affection for the fairer sex that Nicole had never witnessed before.

When he'd spoken today of his mother, there had been an underlying respect for the woman who had raised seven McCurren males. He had even admitted, exaggerated though it may be, his cowardice when dealing with the countess.

How many gentlemen of the *ton* would treat a woman not only as his equal but his better?

Nicole sighed, and the rain fell.

The viscount was too good to be true, and she reminded herself to be on her guard. She had known Daniel McCurren only a fortnight, and Nicole was sure he would disappoint her soon enough. It was far better for her not to give him the opportunity to do so.

She would rely upon herself as she always had done and perform the assassination as ordered. For men like Joseph LeCoeur never disappointed—they were bastards from the start. At least with the minister, she knew what to expect.

Joseph LeCoeur opened the door to his outer office and was surprised to see a liveried coachman speaking with his assistant, Major Rousseau. The two men looked toward him, and Joseph knew instantly that he was the subject being discussed.

"*Bonjour,* Minister LeCoeur," the coachman bowed. "I have a message . . ." He indicated the communiqué in Major Rousseau's suspicious hands. "My employer, Mademoiselle Beauvoire, has instructed me to await your reply."

His cynical assistant met his eye, and Joseph dampened his anticipation. He noted, with great amusement, the golden seal impressed with a single apple of the disruptive "Eris." Joseph read the brief missive and the suggestion therein before turning toward the lady's coachman.

"Inform Mademoiselle Beauvoire that I would be

delighted to join her for luncheon, and shall be down momentarily."

The coachman bowed, leaving him alone with the all-too-austere Evariste Rousseau.

"You know nothing of this woman, Minister LeCoeur," the major reminded him.

Irritation swelled and Joseph suppressed it, saying, "The lady is being investigated."

"Then you should avoid all contact with the woman until the investigation is complete."

Joseph raised a brow at his assistant's demanding tone. "Are you suggesting, Major Rousseau, that I remain celibate while you undertake an exhaustive investigation of the lady in question?"

"Of course not, Minister LeCoeur, I merely suggest that you find another woman, one who is known to us."

"Tell me, Evariste." The minister's smile was caustic. "Have you selected my bed partner, or am I allowed a choice?"

The major accepted the reprimand, lowering his black eyes. "There are many women on our list who—"

"Will do?" Joseph forgave the young man his ignorance. "A woman is more than a warm place to bury your cock, Evariste. When you are older, you will understand the enticement of quality rather than quantity of lovers."

His assistant shrugged in dutiful acceptance of his employer's assertion then moved on, saying, "You are to meet with Emperor Bonaparte at three o'clock this afternoon. It is now one o'clock."

Joseph chuckled at the man's final attempt to dissuade him. "Never fear, Evariste," he said, reaching for his greatcoat. "I shall return no later than half past two."

"Captain Turgeon," Major Rousseau called to the minister's bodyguard.

"No." Joseph waved his guard from the room. "I need no protection for this excursion."

"Minister LeCoeur, you are making yourself vulnerable unnecessarily."

Joseph laughed, his mind on the stunning woman waiting for him just downstairs. "Oh, being alone with Mademoiselle Beauvoire is very necessary, I assure you."

"If I am to be given the responsibility of seeing to your safety, then I must insist that Captain Turgeon sit with the lady's coachman so that he might be on hand—"

"You insist?" Minister LeCoeur felt his hackles rise, and he turned to meet his assistant's steady gaze.

However, much to his surprise, the major did not acquiesce. Evariste simply said, "*Oui,* Minister LeCoeur, if you refuse to take minimal precautions when venturing out in public, then I fear I can no longer be responsible for your safety."

"Are you offering me your resignation, Major Rousseau?"

"If you leave the protection of the Ministry of Police without Captain Turgeon then, *oui,* I shall be forced to resign my post."

Joseph smiled, appreciating the major's steely mettle.

"*Mon Dieu,* Evariste! You worry like a woman. Very well, the captain will sit in the rain with Mademoiselle Beauvoire's coachman."

His assistant bowed, obviously relieved, before calling, "Captain Turgeon." The fair guard opened the door and bowed for them both. "You will accompany Minister LeCoeur this afternoon and inform Mademoiselle Beauvoire's coachman that the minister is required back by half past two this afternoon."

The minister roared with laughter and glanced at the man who would protect Joseph's life with his own. "Let us depart, Captain Turgeon, as we appear to be on a very tight schedule."

The captain left the outer office and Joseph glanced at his assistant, making sure that the major knew his interference was being tolerated. "Have the documents ready for my meeting with Emperor Bonaparte."

Major Rousseau bowed deeply and with great respect. "All will be as you require, Minister LeCoeur."

The moment Joseph closed the office door, his mind was on Mademoiselle Beauvoire. He had not stopped thinking of those eyes, those exquisite breasts, since the theater four nights ago, and Joseph prayed that he, too, had occupied the forefront of the woman's mind.

The captain at his heels, Joseph rushed down the marble step of the Ministry of Police, eager to taste that quick tongue. However, Joseph slowed his pace as he approached her costly carriage, not wanting to appear too enthusiastic.

Her coachman bowed, holding the door wide as Joseph stepped into the interior of the carriage.

"You gave me ten minutes in which to join you," the minister said, closing the door against the soft rain and all unwelcome intrusions. "I make progress, no?"

"No, not particularly." The lady enticed him with her smile, and Joseph sat on the squabs next to her as the conveyance lurched forward. "I just thought allowances should be made for the inclement weather."

"Very kind of you, *ma chérie*." He shrugged out of his greatcoat and glanced at the silver trays set atop the opposite squabs. "I see we shall be dining in?"

"*Oui*." The striking woman sat up, looking pleased with her ingenuity. "I thought a picnic would be far more enjoyable than dining at some miserable café."

"And far more intimate?" Joseph glanced at her beautiful face, her ample décolletage, and savored the sight.

"I had not thought of that," the nymph teased, placing her gloved finger against those alluring lips.

Joseph stared at her mouth, the smells of the food mingling with his carnal appetite.

"What is on the menu, Mademoiselle Beauvoire?" he asked, anxious to feed.

"I have no idea what is to come, Minister LeCoeur." She smiled. "Shall we find out together?" The lady leaned forward, her breasts on full display as she lifted the silver cover. "It smells wonderful, if a bit pastoral."

The delicious image of Mademoiselle Beauvoire in a shepherdess costume flashed before his mind and Joseph grinned, saying, "Oh, I quite enjoy the pastoral." He reached for the wine in hopes of pouring as much of the intoxicating liquid down the girl as quickly as was possible. "Did I not tell you that I was raised on an estate in southern France?"

"Really?" The woman was truly astonished, causing Joseph to laugh.

"Not all ministers are hatched, Mademoiselle Beauvoire." He cut a piece of meat and speared it with his fork. "Some of us were reared," Joseph finished, placing the braised pork in his mouth while enjoying the melodious sound of her laughter.

"Why did you not stay on your pastoral estate in southern France?"

Joseph shifted his attention from his dish and met her eyes. "Revolution wreaks havoc on the countryside, and the capital's allure was far too powerful for a bucolic boy, such as myself."

"I don't believe you for a moment." The lady lifted the red wine to even redder lips. "You were never a 'bucolic boy.' You're far too ambitious." Joseph smiled at the lady's astute assessment. "No, it is far more likely that you were hatched in the basement of the Assemblée Nationale."

Their eyes held as Joseph's mind filled with sensual possibilities.

"What else do you have to offer me?" Joseph leaned across the enticing woman, placing his empty plate on the far side of the carriage.

"Grapes." Mademoiselle Beauvoire smiled, taunting him.

Joseph watched her pluck a grape from the vine and lift it to his mouth, asking nonchalantly, "Have you plans for this weekend, Minister LeCoeur?"

Merde!

Scorpion's political interference was intolerable, but to have the British assassin interfere with his seduction was more than he could abide.

"*Oui,* I'm afraid that I do." Joseph raised a brow, hiding his frustration as he leaned forward to take the tender morsel in his mouth. "Why do you ask?" he inquired, aching for her to admit her desire of him.

Mademoiselle Beauvoire shrugged her graceful shoulders, and his eyes dipped to her beautiful breasts. "I'm—"

"Amorous?"

"Uncommitted," she corrected.

"Ah." Joseph picked a plump grape and outlined her lips with glistening juice. "Now we make progress."

He watched, mesmerized, as her lips parted and the tip of her tongue gently caressed the smooth flesh of the grape. The woman took the fruit into her mouth, followed by the length of his finger, and a flash of lust scorched him when her tongue stroked his finger as if it were his rod.

"I shall be unavailable the entire weekend," Joseph said, his mind whispering of ways to fit her in—or rather, fit him in her. "I have been invited to Empress Bonaparte's Toussaint Feast."

"Pity," Mademoiselle Beauvoire purred in his ear as she arched her back in invitation.

He could do both, Joseph thought, burying his lips between the woman's spectacular breasts. Lord Cunningham had ordered Scorpion to perform the spurious assassination on Saturday at the Toussaint Feast. However, once the Englishman was captured, Joseph could treat himself to Mademoiselle Beauvoire.

She would be his reward.

Joseph smiled, liking the idea of Scorpion in Major Rousseau's vicious prison while he lived life to the fullest, savoring such a stunning woman as Nicole Beauvoire.

Unless the girl would have him now?

Joseph kissed her deeply, his life's goal to bury himself between her thighs. The minister wrapped his arms around her waist and pulled her against his aching cock, his right hand descending to the obstruction of silk skirts, only to be stopped by her gentle rebuff.

"I think not."

"You would leave me unsatisfied, Eris?" Joseph grinned seductively then leaned forward to kiss her lovely neck.

"Better you than me, Minister LeCoeur," the lady said, caressing the hair at the back of his head. "If I were to spend mere minutes draining you of your lust, I would most assuredly be the one left dissatisfied."

"What would satisfy you, Mademoiselle Beauvoire?" Joseph asked, wanting any glimpse into the mind of this incredible woman.

"Hours of unfettered exploration." The vixen ran her hand between his thighs, causing his jaw to clamp down on his self-control. "And days of carnal repetition."

"A weekend?" The minister smiled.

"At least." She smiled, their eyes holding.

"I am permitted"—Joseph leaned forward, kissing the plentiful swells of her breasts—"to invite a guest to the festivities."

His fingers swept the golden gown from her right shoulder, hoping that he had distracted her enough that he might bare her breast to his view.

"Is that an invitation, Minister LeCoeur?" Mademoiselle Beauvoire swept her gown to its rightful place, leaving him once again to speculate.

"*Oui.*" Joseph met her arresting eyes.

"Impossible."

"Why?" His dark brows furrowed and the woman looked at him as though he were mad.

"You are minister of police! You will be watched from the moment you arrive at Tuileries Palace."

"By my own men." Joseph was looking at her body again, dismissing her concern. "The list of guests is immense and I shall be one of several ministers in attendance. Once the feast begins and the wine flows, no one will take notice of who sleeps where."

"Ladies always take notice of eligible men, Minister LeCoeur." Mademoiselle Beauvoire was shaking her head. "Rest assured that your room will be observed by more than your guards. No, better we wait until—"

"I'll come to you." Joseph watched her entertain the idea and Joseph kissed her before she had an opportunity to reject him. "I'll come to your bedchamber and we can spend hours enjoying one another." He kissed her lovely neck. "Without fear of being watched." He kissed lower. "Without fear of being overheard," he finished, aching to make her scream.

"But how?"

"Shhh." Joseph kissed her one last time, making sure to have his fill. "Leave it to me, *ma chérie*. I am, after all, the minister of police."

Twenty-eight

❦

"Oh, look how clever you are, Jonathan. You've gotten the top to spin all on your own."

Falcon smiled at the delight in his daughter's voice as she looked at her adopted son. The boy grinned, his blue eyes wide with the surprise of his own success.

"Look, Granpa!"

"Well done," Falcon said, trying to muster an enthusiasm he did not feel as he reached down and tousled the boy's black curls.

"Now thank your grandfather for the gifts, then go with Mister White to your riding lesson."

The boy hopped up from the marble floor and squeezed Falcon around the neck, filling his old heart. "Tank you—"

"Thank you," his mother corrected the three-year-old.

The boy swallowed, his chubby cheeks bouncing on his face. "Thank you, Granpa."

"You're very welcome, Jonathan." Falcon patted the boy on the back and then the child ran to his mother, hugging her tightly. "I love you, Mummy."

His daughter's eyes filled with tears and she blinked them away. "I love you, too, darling. Have a wonderful riding lesson and Mummy will see you at dinner."

The lad ran in stuttered steps toward Mister White, who bowed to the baroness before taking Jonathan's hand and leading the child from the room.

They both stared at the closed door, and after a moment Falcon said, "He is doing remarkably well, Rose. I am very proud of you, and I cannot tell you how grateful—"

"Nonsense, Father, it is I who should be thanking you." She poured him a cup of tea, handing it to him. "When I lost . . ." His daughter dabbed at her eyes, ripping his heart in two. "When *we* lost Marcus, I thought I would shrivel up and die. And then you brought us Jonathan." Rose smiled the same little smile that had warmed his soul since she was a girl of three. "It is I who am grateful."

Falcon sipped his tea as they sat among the greenery and solitude of the isolated conservatory. He so enjoyed their weekly visit, but it often left them with nothing to say.

"Did she send the top?"

"Yes," Falcon said, tensing. "She is naturally concerned for the boy's well-being."

"Naturally," his daughter agreed, the brittle word softened by a sip of her tea.

"Rose." Falcon met his daughter's wary eye. "If she returns to England, she will not interfere with your rearing of Jonathan."

"If?" Her brown brows drew together with compassionate distress. "You are concerned for her safety."

Falcon nodded. "Very."

"Why?"

"There have been developments, but you know I am not at liberty to discuss them." Falcon sighed, the years of responsibility pressing down on him, and for one moment he longed to be nothing more than a child's grandpa.

"Oh, Father." Rose reached out and placed her hand on his. "How difficult your work must be for you."

"Thank you, my dear," he said, truly grateful for her

concern. "But I have come here to lighten my load, not add weight to it."

"Very well." His daughter's lips twitched with amusement. "What mundane aspects of country life shall we discuss?"

"Anything but horseflesh." Falcon chuckled. "That husband of yours will give me an earful about the topic over dinner."

"If only I had known of his fascination with horses when he asked me to marry him."

"You would have married him nonetheless."

"True." Rose blushed, embarrassed. "I was a bit besotted with the man."

"A bit?" Falcon snorted. "Your mother, rest her soul, dissuaded me from posting a guard at your door to insure that you would not run off to Gretna Green."

"We never would have eloped, Father! Alfred was too terrified of you to risk it."

"A bright young man, your Alfred," Falcon mused, grateful for this time together. He stared at the wooden top still lying motionless on the floor and purposely looked away, turning instead to his only daughter and thinking back to her beautiful wedding some twenty years before. "A very bright man."

Twenty-nine

❧⟡❧

"Don't go, Nicole," Daniel whispered over her right shoulder as she packed for the Toussaint Feast celebration. "You don't have to carry out this assassination." The viscount grasped her upper arm, his tone desperate as he spun her to face him. "Come back to London with me."

Nicole stared into his beautiful eyes, and tears filled her own when she realized what he was asking. She hesitated, longing to go to London and become his mistress, but knowing that Daniel McCurren deserved more . . . better.

"I can't go back." Nicole looked down, tears splashing onto her satin slippers.

"Sure you can, lass," Daniel persuaded, lifting her chin so that she would look at him. "Do you remember when you asked me why I had come to Paris?"

Nicole nodded, tears now streaming down her face.

"I came to France because of a woman." The words stabbed at her heart and Nicole squeezed her eyes shut in hopes of stopping the pain. "I wanted desperately to marry the lady."

She tried not to listen, but the viscount continued to speak.

"I had envisioned Lady Duhearst as my wife from the time we were children, but when Sarah came of age, she married one of my dearest friends, the Duke of Glenbroke."

Nicole sat down on the edge of her bed, but the viscount followed, placing his hands on either side of her hips and sinking to his haunches.

"Can you imagine the pain, the guilt of not only losing the woman you had chosen to be your bride, but of envying your friend his happiness? The pain of being invited to their happy home? The guilt of seeing Duchess Glenbroke with her children and thinking they should have been yours?"

"Stop it," Nicole murmured, unable to hear about his love for another woman.

"Can you picture the pain, lass?"

"Please, Daniel," Nicole breathed, her devastation clear.

"And then I met you," he whispered, caressing her cheek. "I came to Paris to forget the woman I fancied myself in love with, but then I met you, and all my childhood feelings paled in comparison." The viscount looked into her eyes, pleading, "Come to London with me."

Nicole was shaking her head, knowing that even if she went to London, she would still be an assassin and he would still be a viscount.

"I need you to come home with me."

You need a woman worthy of you.

"I can't."

"Why? I want—"

"It doesn't matter what you want!" Nicole shouted, bolting up from the bed and looking down at his wounded eyes. "I can't go back to England. I can *never* go back to England."

His mouth hung open in devastated shock; and Nicole knew that he could not form the words, the question he so desperately needed answering.

"The scars on my back," Nicole began, shaking, "were

not inflicted by French soldiers. They were inflicted by my British husband."

It took a moment for Nicole's admission to penetrate his confused mind. The viscount's eyes hardened and Nicole took a step back, frightened by the change in Daniel's demeanor as he rose to his feet, his jaw clenched more tightly than his enormous fists.

"Who is he?" Daniel demanded. "I'm going to kill the bloody bastard."

"You can't!"

"Just you watch me, lass," the viscount said with chilling resolve.

"You can't kill him, Daniel." Nicole swallowed her shame. "Because I already did."

Daniel's blue eyes focused on her face and not the distant task he had given himself. "What?"

"Sit down," Nicole said, pushing against his hard chest and moving the stunned man as if he were a feather. The viscount collapsed on the wing-backed chair, and she sat facing him on the tiny footstool between his feet.

"When I was eleven years of age, my mother died," she began, and Daniel nodded, still confused. "My father married shortly thereafter but he passed away when I had just turned seventeen, leaving my stepmother as my guardian." Nicole glanced up to see that the viscount was following her.

"My stepmother counted the days until she could be rid of me, and when her cousin of thirty-four years came to visit, the lady knew she had her chance."

Nicole bit her lower lip, finding it difficult to unearth the memories she had so thoroughly buried.

"You see, the gentleman was enamored of my charms." Daniel glanced at her décolletage and Nicole knew that he took her meaning. "Not to mention my robust fortune. So, my stepmother arranged, for a very large fee, that her cousin should marry me the day I came of age."

"Why did you agree to such a marriage?" the viscount asked with the naïveté of a man for a woman's world.

"I had no choice in the matter." Nicole snorted in disgust.

"My stepmother dragged me kicking and screaming before the local vicar, who was paid handsomely to turn a blind eye to my distress."

"I'm so sorry, lass." Daniel grabbed her hands, caressing the backs of them gently with his thumbs, and this time Nicole did cry.

"As to the scars . . ." She paused, finding it difficult to continue. "My husband enjoyed beating me before—"

"Shhh," the viscount breathed, his long arms wrapping around her as he pulled her to his chest. "It's all right, lass, you don't need to speak of it."

Nicole laid her head on his sturdy shoulder and let the strokes of his hand expel the relentless cold. And when she felt strong enough to endure his repulsion, Nicole sat back on the footstool and looked him in the eye. She stared into the blue depths so that he would know, so that Daniel would understand why she could not, and never would be able to, go to England . . . go with him.

"Daniel, my name is not Nicole Beauvoire." She let out her fear in one long breath. "My name is Nicole Stratton." Nicole watched the name bouncing around in his memory, and she was powerless to stop the inevitable realization. "Lady Nicole Stratton."

Clearly recalling the violent details of her husband's murder, the viscount jerked his hands from hers and Nicole forced her chin to stop quivering.

"I can't go with you, Daniel."

"You were hanged two years ago!" the viscount whispered to himself, his eyes looking at Nicole as if she were an apparition.

"Falcon needed a gently bred woman to infiltrate Parisian society." Her eyes dimmed with guilt. "He arranged for a substitute to be hanged in my place so that I might become that woman. A prostitute convicted of murder, sentenced to hang one week after my own execution. The woman had black hair and blue eyes, and needed only to be convincing on the short walk to the gallows."

"Why would she agree—"

Nicole stood, covering her face with her right hand to push the memories away. "The woman had a child, a one-year-old child. Falcon agreed to see to the boy, to his education, if she agreed to . . . take my place at the gallows," she managed to say.

"The gifts?" he said, staring down at her. "You send the lad gifts."

"Yes. His mother saved us both that day."

"Aye, she did." Daniel nodded, grabbing her gently about the shoulders. "So don't throw that gift away by getting yourself killed. Don't perform this assassination, Nicole! Come back to London."

Sobbing, Nicole shook her head with finality.

"I can't go back, Daniel." The light drained from his eyes, and Nicole realized that she had never experienced such pain. "If I return to London, I return to Newgate to be hanged."

They stared at one another, helpless, and then Nicole rose, walking toward the bed so that she might continue her packing.

"Do you care for me, Nicole?"

She closed her eyes, torn apart by the ache in his stilted voice, and knowing that she was about to add to his pain.

"An assassin does not have the luxury of caring," Nicole said, facing him.

"You did not answer my question."

They stared at one another, and Nicole broke the unbearable silence. "Go home, Daniel. You have responsibilities, a future, back in England."

"Now that I've found you, I can't picture my life without you, lass."

"Well, I can picture your life with me, a notorious murderess." Nicole nodded. "I'd ruin you, Viscount DunDonell, just before they hanged me." Nicole returned to her packing. "Nothing can come of this . . . us."

"I'm not leaving you, Nicole."

Neither of them could stand the hurt, but it was he who closed the distance between them to ease it. He bent his head and seized her in a desperate kiss while she pushed impatiently at his jacket.

The exquisite garment was flung to the floor, the sleeves turned inside out. His fingers fought the tiny buttons at the back of her gown until, frustrated, he yanked, sending the buttons cascading about the room like heavy drops of rain. They let go of one another, only to return the instant a new item of clothing went flying.

His shirt was tossed onto the carpet, and Nicole pulled her mind away from his mouth so that she could have a good, long look at his exquisite body. Nicole tugged at her gown and Daniel watched, his breathing heavy, as she reached round to untie her corset.

Her chemise went with it, and she danced on her skirts to disentangle her feet. Free, Nicole looked up and launched herself, naked, into his muscular arms, oversetting them both. They were kissing one another before they hit the mattress of the four-poster bed. Nicole closed her eyes, the unbearable heat of his chest on her breasts.

"Make love to me, Nicole," the viscount whispered in her ear.

"For the last time," she agreed.

Daniel looked down at her, the enormity of her words hitting them hard.

They became silent, words too inadequate a form of expression. Daniel's hands spoke for him, marking her as forever his, and they both gasped when he introduced one long finger into her wet heat. His mouth clamped over her nipple, and he suckled in rhythm with his gentle thrusts.

Every stroke seemed to linger longer than the last, seemed to torture her more. But it was his weight, the strength of his hands grasping her inner thighs, his sheer masculinity, that had her hips rising with approval.

Nicole nipped him on the shoulder, needing to taste him, and he countered by kissing her neck. She was close to finding her pleasure and Daniel knew it. Nicole could sense his excitement, feel his exhilaration as he pressed against her.

And then with one tender stroke, she shattered, crying

out with fulfillment. Daniel groaned in approval, suckling her breast, and then lifted himself to yank off his buckskins. He threw the duvet off the bed and crawled over her, pinning Nicole's wrists to the mattress.

Daniel was feral, driven solely by the primal need to mate. Nicole spread her thighs, offering herself to him and waiting to be filled by his power, but she was left wanting. Confused, she opened her eyes, only to see him staring at her wrists.

"I'm sorry." Daniel looked horrified and she'd no idea why. "I didn't think."

Nicole looked into his eyes and then, with a sharp intake of breath, she knew the source of his distress.

"You could never hurt me as my husband did." Nicole shook her head.

"'Tis why you don't like to be handled." Daniel rolled over on his back, propping himself against two pillows. "And I was tossing you about like a rag doll," the viscount said, torturing himself with guilt.

Nicole went to him, overwhelmed by the sheer decency of the man.

"I only like being handled when I wish to be." The viscount looked up, hopeful. "And a woman rather enjoys a man who is capable of tossing her about."

"If she wishes it?" he asked.

"If she wishes it," Nicole confirmed, but she could still see his hesitation.

She eased his concern by taking the lead, swinging her knee over his muscled thighs and settling in his lap. His eyes closed at the feel of her soft backside caressing his hard sex.

"Look at me, Daniel."

The viscount met her eyes, and Nicole felt his hands on her hips, guiding her as she took him in.

"Oh, lass," Daniel said, watching her as they joined. "I want you so much."

"Shh." Nicole knew he was not speaking of their lovemaking, but the alternative was too painful to contemplate, too painful to hear. She had him here and now, and Nicole intended to make the most of their last moments together.

For tomorrow she had a duty to perform and a debt to repay—but at present, all Nicole could think of was how to protect this noble man and how to keep him safe, not only from the French, but from himself.

Thirty

❧

The sunlight penetrated Daniel's eyelids, and he registered somewhere in the back of his mind that it was morning. However, it was not the bright sun but the banging at the front door of the apartment that roused him to some semblance of wakefulness.

He pulled on his tousers and a linen shirt with great reluctance, wondering where Nicole had wandered off to. They had much to do this morning, and Daniel smiled to himself as he walked to the door.

Last night they had made love, and although the lass had not said so, Daniel now knew that she had feelings for him. He could see it in her eyes, feel it in the way she touched him. They had been of one mind and one soul, just as he had always imagined love to be, to feel, and Daniel could not help grinning with contentment.

It was a great load off his mind, for he was not sure that his heart could have taken the blow if Nicole had rejected him. Oh, it had been a shock to learn who she was, who she had been, the infamous Lady Stratton. Yet after seeing the scars on her back, Daniel could not understand how any sane man could blame the lass for defending herself.

His stomach clenched when he thought of the pain she had endured at the hands of her husband, but it was tempered by a strange pride. Nicole Beauvoire was more than capable of defending herself, and she had no need of him to do it for her.

Perhaps that was what was so damned appealing. The lass had chosen him. Nicole was in no need of his money or his protection, but she was in want of him.

The pounding at the door persisted, cutting short his gratification. Daniel sighed with annoyance, calling, "Just a moment," as he shrugged into his jacket and slipped on his hideous shoes.

It had taken hours to convince Nicole to return to London with him, but in the end he had managed to persuade her. Daniel was sure that he would have no difficulty in gaining his father's influence to plead her case for a pardon. The lady had served the Crown faithfully and successfully for two long years, and Daniel had no doubt that her loyalty would be rewarded.

Grasping the brass knob of the entryway door, his mind was filled with the preparations that would need to be made for their return to England. They would need to secure a ship to Honfleur, where Nicole's British contact would be able to book passage to London. Then they would formulate their stratagem for presenting her case to the authorities.

Daniel opened the front door, and the moment the catch gave, he was rushed by three men before he had a chance to react to the ambush. His mind came instantly awake with the fear of Nicole's capture and he struck one of the assailants in the jaw, knocking the man to the wooden floor.

He spun round to face the French soldiers, but before he could pull back to unleash a second blow, his right arm was seized by two men. They used their combined weight to drive him to the carpet, knocking the breath from his chest, and before he could regain it, Daniel was being gagged, his arms and legs skillfully bound.

The three men stared down at him, breathing heavily from their scuffle, and to Daniel's great surprise, he saw that they were not French soldiers, but sailors. The men lifted him up and dragged him down the stairs, his bound feet useless.

He waited until they had reached the ground floor and was about to resist when they stopped. The oldest of the three men ordered, "Hold him still," as he opened the door.

Daniel glanced out the door to determine his fate, but was not prepared for the emotional kick to the gut when he saw Nicole Beauvoire sitting in her carriage. She nodded in confirmation to the sailor before meeting Daniel's eyes. Nicole stared at him and in the violet depths her intentions were clear.

Panic took hold of him.

He had to stop her from performing this assassination. If he could just talk with her, reason with her.

"Go," Nicole said to her driver, but more to him.

Her carriage inched forward, and Daniel butted one of the sailors in the head as he attempted to break free. The man staggered backward, blood dripping from his left eyebrow as he yanked painfully on the rope at Daniel's wrists.

Daniel watched helplessly as Nicole sat back in the carriage out of view, out of his reach. So he did not notice the downward thrust of a cosh as it came crashing down on the back of his head.

And then he saw nothing, slumping forward as the three men wrapped Daniel in cloth and carried him to a wagon waiting in the fashionable square of Place Vendôme.

Nicole stared at the morning sun, still numb from watching the deed being done. She took comfort in the knowledge that he was safe, that Daniel would be safe the moment he boarded the ship at Honfleur.

It was for the best, she knew, that the viscount return to London. Nicole reminded herself that she was an assassin with no use for the sentiments of love . . . or regret.

Swallowing her misery, Nicole thought of the assassination that would conclude Scorpion's grisly career. Tonight she would avenge Andre Tuchelles's murder, and earn the years of life the lady of Newgate had given her.

She sat envisioning what she would say, how the assassination, under such scrupulous security, would be managed. Nicole went through her script again and again, thoroughly, painstakingly, up until the very moment her conveyance rolled to a stop in front of the impressive Tuileries Palace.

Nicole shivered as she stepped from her carriage, amazed that the weather could turn so quickly. She glanced up at the dark clouds, her breath short puffs of smoke. Gravel crunched beneath her feet as Nicole wandered through the maze of landaus on her way to the front entrance, where she was quickly ushered inside.

Mademoiselle Beauvoire handed the butler her invitation and was shown to an enormous salon, where she was offered coffee and cakes while her luggage was carried to her assigned bedchamber.

"Coffee only, *merci,*" Nicole said to the footman, glancing about the roomful of guests and praying that she did not encounter Joseph LeCoeur before she was prepared to do so.

"Mademoiselle Beauvoire, was it not?" a masculine voice said from behind her.

"*Oui.*" Nicole stilled, smiling as she turned to find a strikingly handsome blond staring down at her, his hands clasped behind his back. "And with whom do I have the pleasure of acquainting myself?"

"Ah." The gentleman stepped forward, sweeping away the exquisitely tailored tails of his fawn jacket so that he might position himself on the settee adjacent to her delicate brocade chair. "But we are acquainted, Mademoiselle Beauvoire, and you wound me deeply to have forgotten the occasion."

The gentleman grinned rakishly as he reached out to capture her hand so that he might bestow a kiss. Nicole waited until the man lifted his head so that she might look him in the eye.

"Marquis La Roche!" Nicole purred. "How charming to see you again, but you must forgive me as I have never seen you in anything but a dressing gown."

Several mouths fell open and the marquis roared with laughter at her implied intimacy.

"*Oui.* However, I believe my costume of Zeus would more aptly be described as a toga," the marquis said loudly enough for others in the salon to hear.

"Oh, *oui,*" Nicole agreed as if searching her memory for the man's portrayal of the infamous god. "You made a rather charming Zeus."

"And you made quite the tempting goddess," Marquis La Roche whispered, a rake once again. "And if I recall, you were rather an accomplished artist."

"*Pardon?*" Nicole widened her eyes innocently. "Did I paint something for you?"

"*Oui.*" The marquis held her eyes. "Your invitation."

Nicole raised a brow and grinned. "You can hardly blame me, Marquis La Roche. I had heard from so many young ladies what delightful company you are."

"It is so nice to be appreciated." He smiled.

"Mmm." Nicole sipped her coffee.

"And are you here on your own, Mademoiselle Beauvoire, or have you managed to acquire a legitimate invitation to the Toussaint Feast?"

"What difference could it make now that I am here? Or perhaps you were more interested in the first question?"

The marquis smiled, glad for her understanding. "Are you here on your own, Mademoiselle Beauvoire?" His russet eyes shone with interest as the rogue awaited her answer.

"Alas, no." Nicole shook her head, her black curls bobbing. "I am merely accompanying a guest of Empress Bonaparte's."

"A gentleman guest, I presume?" The marquis nodded, confirming his own question.

Nicole lifted her shoulders and asked a question of her own. "Is there any other sort of guest?"

His heated gaze traveled from her head to her toe and

back again. "There are most definitely other sorts of guests, much more charming and entertaining sorts of guests."

Nicole glanced at the other ladies buzzing about the room . . . and the marquis. "And so very many choices."

His eyes darted to the other women and then back to her. "Who is this fortunate gentleman you accompany?"

Nicole saw no reason to lie, as she would be on the minister's arm very soon. "Minister LeCoeur."

"Ahh." Marquis La Roche lifted his head and sat back in his chair as if everything had been made clear to him. What had been made clear, she had not an inkling. "This explains everything."

"What explains everything?" Nicole's violet eyes were staring expectantly, and the marquis paused, clearly enjoying toying with her a moment longer.

"I was questioned by the Ministry of Police, and now I comprehend why."

Nicole's heart stopped, but she was too experienced to allow her tension to become visible. "Questioned?"

"Perhaps, I say too much?" The marquis shrugged. "But then again, I would be most pleased to have you annoyed with your escort. I was asked by Minister LeCoeur's men if I knew from where you hailed. I told them that I had not known you prior to the masquerade and I am afraid, *ma chérie,* that I informed them of your fallacious invitation."

Nicole went pale, her spine stiffening.

"You are annoyed with me." Marquis La Roche smiled and inclined his head toward her. "I beg your forgiveness, Mademoiselle Beauvoire, and am more than willing to atone for my indiscretion."

"Mademoiselle Beauvoire," a footman called, her room now ready for occupation.

Nicole rose and looked down at the amused marquis, saying, "You appear to be too late, Marquis La Roche," before walking out of the empress's salon with her head spinning.

Thirty-one

Evariste Rousseau examined his pistols before stepping down from the carriage that would carry the illustrious minister of police to the empress's Toussaint Feast.

"You two come with me." The major motioned to the most experienced guards. "The rest of you remain with the landau."

Major Rousseau and his men swept down the arcades of Place Vendôme, his eyes scanning the square as the sun descended behind the architectural balance of its buildings.

"Wait here," he said, posting the two guards at Minister LeCoeur's front door, wary of a frontal assault.

Evariste lifted the heavy brass and knocked. A footman opened the door and the major said not a word, looking through the man and toward his employer.

"Punctual as always, Major Rousseau."

Evariste ignored the compliment. It was his duty to arrive when ordered. "Your valet and luggage have been sent on to make ready your room."

"Excellent." The minister stepped from his home, the two guards at his heels. Joseph LeCoeur placed his beaver skin hat atop his head, then stopped when he caught sight of the carriage. "A bit much, do you not think?"

"Pardon?" Evariste asked, confused.

"Seven men, Major Rousseau?" The minister smiled. "Am I so very frail?"

"Scorpion—"

"Scorpion," Minister LeCoeur spat, stepping into the landau. "Is but a man and my horses have their limits. No more than four guards. You and I shall ride inside."

"As you wish, Minister LeCoeur, but might I remind you that Lord Cunningham was guarded by a mere five men?"

"Very true, Major Rousseau." The minister smiled, adding, "However, Cunningham was not guarded by you."

Evariste inclined his head, honored and deeply proud to have his talents acknowledged.

"There is another matter"—Major Rousseau began with caution, the carriage lurching forward—"which I feel must be discussed."

"Go on." Minister LeCoeur's eyes narrowed with interest.

"Mademoiselle Beauvoire—"

"God above!" Evariste was interrupted by an exasperated exhalation. "Have you nothing better with which to occupy your time?"

"The lady is—"

"The lady is my mistress!"

"The lady is a charlatan," Evariste said, crossing the line for the minister's own protection.

"You had better have proof of that accusation, Evariste, or our association is very much in danger."

Their eyes met, held.

"You lose your head with this woman," Major Rousseau said, disappointed by the minister's disloyalty. "So much so, that you would dismiss a man who has served you faithfully for six years?"

"Tell me what you have learned," Minister LeCoeur grated through clenched teeth.

"Mademoiselle Beauvoire leased her apartment—"

"I know all of this." The minister rolled his eyes. "You tell me nothing new."

"Were you aware that the woman has hired no servants bar a coachman?" Minister LeCoeur's eyes darted to his, and Evariste felt the vindication. "Were you aware that Mademoiselle Beauvoire forged her invitation to the masquerade ball at which you met?"

"How do you know this?"

"Marquis La Roche was most helpful."

The major watched his employer's mind sharpen. "Go on."

"A Parisian merchant sends packages to her sister in Honfleur. Yet no family of prominence is known by the name of Beauvoire in the entire city, nor in the region, for that matter."

"Did you inquire as to the family Damont?"

"None in Honfleur have ever heard of Daniel Damont."

"And in Paris?"

"I was able to locate the apartment of Monsieur Damont," Evariste said, pausing with smugness. "At the Place Vendôme." Shock stilled Minister LeCoeur, and Evariste continued the torrent of unpleasant information. "They have been residing together for—"

He was interrupted when Minister LeCoeur's fist came down atop his exquisite beaver skin chapeau, crushing it.

"Enough talk of Mademoiselle Beauvoire," Minister LeCoeur said, his nostrils flaring, his lips struggling to conceal his anger. "Tell me of your preparations for Scorpion," the minister ordered, turning his attention to where it should be.

Major Rousseau began his report of the exhaustive measures taken to capture this most elusive of English assassins.

"You will have but one room assigned to you, thus limiting the access Scorpion will have to your bedchamber.

I have two of my most trusted men guarding your bedchamber door, and in consideration of General Capette's assassination, I felt it prudent to position two men on your balcony."

The minister nodded in approval. "And you?"

"I will be at your side the entire evening, Minister LeCoeur."

"Bon."

"As you know"—Evariste reminded him of his cleverness—"I selected the Toussaint Feast as the site for your assassination, as the guests will all be searched upon arrival and the footmen are all imperial guards, highly trained to protect Empress Bonaparte.

"They have, naturally, been informed of the situation, leaving Scorpion to deal not only with our men but with hers as well."

"How many men have we?"

"Combined with those of the empress?" Evariste took a moment to calculate in his head. "Over one hundred."

The minister raised a brow, impressed. "The guards at my bedchamber door, Scorpion will anticipate. The other men are to be kept out of sight lest we send Scorpion scurrying beneath his rock."

"As you wish, Minister LeCoeur."

"I want him, Evariste." His employer smiled. "I want the British bastard badly."

"You will have him, Minister," Major Rousseau vowed. "On that I give you my word."

Thirty-two

❧

The road one mile south of Les Mureaux turned sharply to the left, and Daniel was slammed against a barrel in the back of a dilapidated wagon, waking him.

His eyes snapped open, but he was blinded by the pain throbbing at the back of his head. Daniel blinked, taking in the dim light that peeked through the sides of a dirty canvas tarp. Wooden crates piled with sacks of grain dominated the cramped space, and Daniel was left to ponder his whereabouts in a tiny corner of the wagon.

Nicole! He remembered.

She was going to carry out the assassination of Joseph LeCoeur as she had always planned. Daniel tried not to feel the sting of her betrayal, tried not to feel as though his coming to Paris had made no difference to her mission, to her. Nicole had not rejected him, Daniel told himself, but believed that she was shielding him from harm.

The viscount glanced at his bound wrists and ankles, not sure that this was what the lass had in mind.

"It grows dark," Daniel heard in French from somewhere toward the front of the wagon. "We had better make camp before we arrive at Les Mureaux. There is no need of our cargo bellowing in the background as we make our way through town."

A second man chuckled and Daniel knew that he had very little time. He pulled at the ropes tied around his wrists, but if there was one thing a sailor knew how to do, it was tie a sturdy knot. His ankles were similarly bound, and Daniel felt a wave of desperation as the wagon pulled off the main road and rambled to a halt.

Daniel lay back down and closed his eyes, planning as the first rope was being pulled through the canvas with an unsettling hiss. The light assaulted his eyelids in waves as the tarp billowed at each point where his captors concentrated their efforts.

"I die of hunger, Michel, and Les Mureaux is but a mile—"

"No, we shall eat at camp."

"The boy is correct," a third man said. "We shall be at sea soon and I myself could make use of a woman before—"

"Honfleur. You can eat and fornicate as much as you like in Honfleur." The tarp was pulled back with a snap, and Daniel had to concentrate not to flinch at the flood of light bombarding his eyelids. "We'll not be paid the remainder of our fee until this man is safely aboard. Now, get him out of the wagon."

"Damn, but the man is big," the younger man complained. "Can we not just leave him here?"

"It is November, and the sky gathers to snow," the sailor in command said as if the boy were an idiot. "He would freeze."

"We have woolen blankets that—"

"Stop your noise, Mathias," the third man growled. "You're just annoyed that the giant nearly broke your skull. Now, grab his ankles and we shall pull him to the edge then lift him together."

Daniel cracked his eyelids and waited patiently as the

lanky man planted his right knee on the edge of the wagon. The other sailors watched with little interest as the youngest of their crew reached for Daniel's ankles. But the moment he felt the man's fingers, Daniel struck, spreading his knees and grasping the young sailor in a headlock before the man knew what hit him.

Daniel looked up, ignoring the young man's blows on his thighs as he stared at the other more worldly men. The shorter sailor brandished a knife and took a step forward, but it was to the older man that Daniel addressed himself to when he said, "I'll break his neck if you do not release me."

Their weathered leader hesitated and Daniel twisted to the left. The lad screamed, his neck strained.

"You've been paid half of your fee." The tall sailor frowned at his own stupidity for revealing such information. "Take what you have been given, or this will end badly." The man stared, gauging his determination, so Daniel added, "My woman is in danger and I will not hesitate to kill all of you to save her," to make clear his desperation.

The man in command nodded. "Unbind him."

"Why?" the shorter sailor holding the blade asked in a huff. "There are three of us to his one!"

"The gentleman means what he says. I see it in his eyes. He will twist Mathias's head off and then fight us both tooth and nail. It is not worth the risk.

"We've been paid well to get the man to a place we were already headed. So count yourself fortunate and let us go find warm food and warmer companionship in Les Mureaux." The tall man jerked his head toward Daniel. "Unbind him," he ordered the man with the knife.

His disgruntled captor walked toward him and Daniel squeezed tighter on the lad's neck, causing him to moan in pain as he pushed against Daniel's knees.

"My hands first," Daniel ordered.

The stubborn subordinate obeyed, sickened by the loss of income. He leaned down and slit the ropes tied around Daniel's ankles and then stepped back to a safe distance, putting away his dagger.

Daniel eased his hold and the young sailor jerked backward, stumbling as he sucked in one, long breath. "Bastard," the lad mumbled, terrified.

Jumping to his feet, Daniel stared at the tall man. "I'll be needing a horse."

"No," the old sailor said simply, crossing his arms over his chest.

"The woman who hired you, the beautiful brunette in the carriage," Daniel began, his temper boiling to the surface. "That lady is my fiancée," Daniel lied, knowing in the deep recesses of his soul that he wanted it to be true. "And she is in grave danger."

The man shook his head. "Even if I believed you, *monsieur,* which I have not said that I do, the captain would have my hide for losing those horses."

Daniel assessed the sailors, determining their leader to be the most formidable of the three. But then he remembered, glancing at his own wrists.

"Here." Daniel unfastened his sapphire cuff links and tossed them to the old salty. "I'll purchase your horse and you can buy twenty before you arrive at Honfleur."

The tall man glanced at the jewels in his hands, and then his eyes darted to Daniel's. "The lady truly is in danger?"

"Oui." The viscount nodded adamantly.

"Pierre, saddle up the gray," their leader ordered before turning to Daniel, adding, "He is the fastest of the two horses, and if you take that road"—the man pointed down a path that seemed to follow the bank of the river—"it will lead you back to Paris."

"How long?"

"Six hours," the sailor said regretfully. Daniel grasped the saddle and swung himself onto the horse when the man asked, curious, "Why would your fiancée hire us to kidnap you, *monsieur?*"

Daniel smiled weakly, answering, "Because she cares for me."

But did she love him?

Daniel turned the horse and galloped down the road,

praying that he would make it to the feast in time to find the answer.

Nicole placed her hand on the door of her second-floor bedchamber and paused. She was stilled by the knowledge that Minister LeCoeur more than likely knew who she was and why she had come to the Toussaint Feast.

Why else would he have made inquiries of her?

She could think of no other explanation and was now faced with a choice. Leave now, assuming of course that she could—or carry out the assassination, knowing that she would most probably be arrested before she had the opportunity to finish it.

Neither choice was very appealing.

Nicole had known when she was given the order to kill the minister of police that her chances of survival were minimal. And when Daniel Damont had arrived at her doorstep informing her that the orders had been forged by the French, she was sure of it.

But flee . . .

Where would she go?

Nicole took a deep breath and became the person she loathed, the person she was so very good at becoming.

Scorpion.

She opened her door and strolled into the hall, noting the footman-lined egress as she smiled at the other society women. Nicole stared, fascinated, as the ladies flocked like migrating birds in the same direction, heading toward the first-floor grand entryway, where they would be joined by their gentlemen escorts.

Ambition abounded in the form of shimmering jewels and low-slung bodices that afforded the women of Paris the opportunity to find a protector, if not a husband.

The gentlemen, too, held ambitions. They had traveled to Tuileries Palace to be seen by society, by their empress, and then to end their Toussaint Feast by bedding the woman they desired so that they might feel alive even as they honored the dead.

Joseph LeCoeur had such ambitions, sending to Nicole's bedchamber a message informing her in flowery French of his arrival and of his eagerness to see her again.

But why? To arrest her or to bed her?

Finding herself at the top of the enormous staircase, Nicole looked out over the elite of France. She made one last adjustment to her plum-colored gown and placed her hand on the balustrade as she descended into the pit of hell.

Nicole scanned the throng for her prey, and then she found him. The minister was speaking with a group of elegant gentlemen to her left. One of the five men was speaking and then the group broke into muted laughter, with Minister LeCoeur snickering appropriately. But then the minister's eyes drifted to his right as if he had sensed her.

Their eyes met and held.

Without looking at his companions, his lips moved and the other men turned toward Nicole. Disconcerted by their scrutiny, she smiled and fidgeted with her diamond ear bobs. The man with whom the minister had been speaking raised a brow and whispered something, at which Joseph LeCoeur grinned, leaving their group and walking to the foot of the marble stairs.

"Mademoiselle Beauvoire," the minister said, bowing deeply when she reached the last step.

"Minister LeCoeur."

The minister held out his arm, saying as she took it, "You look stunning, *ma chérie*."

Nicole inclined her head toward him and then gave him a cursory assessment. His brown evening jacket was a credit to the subtlety of his tailor, exquisitely fitted to the minister's square shoulders and elegant in its simplicity. His cravat was elaborate, but not exceedingly so, adorned only by a blue sapphire pin that harmonized the blue of his all-too-astute eyes.

"And you look exceptionally handsome, Monsieur LeCoeur."

He smiled as if pleased, and they wandered into the

salon in which the empress's guests awaited their charming hostess.

"Champagne?"

"Oui, merci."

Joseph LeCoeur nodded imperceptibly to a passing footman, who rushed over, holding out his solid silver tray as the minister retrieved two crystal flutes filled with quality champagne. The footman bowed before leaving, and Minister LeCoeur handed Nicole a glass, lifting his in an intimate toast.

"May tonight bring us everything we desire." The minister gazed at her face, and then his eyes dipped lower to speculate before returning to her eyes and finally to her lips. "And more."

Joseph LeCoeur watched and Nicole taunted him as she set the champagne flute to her parched lips, swallowing before licking them of the excess and breathing, "To tonight."

His eyes flared and they stood staring at one another until the minister lifted his glass to drink for no other reason than to occupy his mind with other thoughts than taking her to bed.

"Mesdames et messieurs." The crowded salon became silent as conversation ceased, the guests brimming with anticipation. "May I present to you the emperor and empress of France."

Nicole stared, as everyone did, at the unexpected arrival of Emperor Bonaparte as he entered the salon with his elegant Austrian wife, Marie Louise, on his arm. The emperor nodded in warm welcome toward his guests while the aristocratic empress looked through them.

It was the first time Nicole had ever seen Empress Marie Louise, and she could not help staring at the strange couple. The girl was just that, a girl half the age of her darker, rougher husband. Her fair hair was not quite blond but not quite brown either. She was neither beautiful nor ugly, but was undoubtedly an aristocrat with the superiority of six generations of royal blood flowing through her veins.

The empress smiled elegantly as she walked past her guests, but her eyes held nothing of the warmth of her husband's welcome. Marie Louise stood to the right of her husband as the emperor greeted his guests with hands outstretched.

"It is so kind of you to partake in our celebration of Toussaint. It is fitting for us on this day to remember those loved ones whom we have lost, particularly during these troubled times." The emperor paused reverently before continuing. "However, it is also appropriate for those of us remaining to appreciate the lives which we have been given and to celebrate the glorious destiny of France."

Several gentlemen raised their glasses, shouting "Bravo, bravo," as Minister LeCoeur watched, clapping politely.

The emperor continued his inspirational speech, taking his wife's arm and patting her hand affectionately as he nodded toward his footmen, saying, "Therefore, *mes amis*, I introduce to you"—he stretched his right arm toward a set of side doors—"the King of Rome, Napoleon Bonaparte the Second."

The gilded double doors of the great salon parted as a governess entered carrying a small child of no more than six months, enveloped in a velvet robe with a miniature crown sitting atop his blond curls.

The ladies in the salon simpered and Nicole beamed suitably at the tiny babe, knowing that unless the British were able to stop Napoleon's forces, this child would surely inherit the continent, if not the world.

"Now let us adjourn into the dining hall so that the Toussaint Feast may begin."

The emperor's guests clapped enthusiastically, and the child was whisked from the room as the rich and influential citizens of France walked slowly toward their decadent feast.

"What did you think of our future emperor?" Minister LeCoeur bent his head to ask.

Nicole looked up, smiling, "I thought him very small."

The minister chuckled appreciatively, and they busied

themselves with finding their assigned places at the dinner table. Minister LeCoeur pulled out her chair so that Nicole might be seated before seating himself.

She repositioned her silk skirts then paused, the hair at the back of her neck standing on end. She was being watched—for what reason Nicole was not sure—but she had learned early on in her career to heed her intuition.

Wary, Nicole scanned the room, noting only the introductions being made up and down the long mahogany table. She glanced at Minister LeCoeur and saw that he had been observing her, anticipating something other than a late-night tryst.

Nicole feigned ignorance, making her introduction to the elderly gentleman to the left. All was made clear as the first course of their dinner was served.

"Tell me again of your family in Honfleur, Mademoiselle Beauvoire?"

The minister was watching her carefully and Nicole sighed with a frustration that belied her trepidation. "Do you inquire after my stepbrother again?"

"In part," the minister said, leaning forward to sip his asparagus soup thickened by fresh cream and topped with a paper-thin slice of hothouse cucumber.

Nicole looked down, lifting up her spoon and taking a mouthful of the delicious soup before she began in pleasant tones, "My mother married my stepfather when I was fourteen and Monsieur Damont, eighteen. My stepbrother left to study in Paris, and when he came home to Honfleur, I had grown to a girl of eighteen."

"Your stepbrother seduced you?" the minister asked in hushed tones, his eyes intently on hers.

Nicole tried not to feel the ache of loss as they spoke of Daniel McCurren. But Monsieur Damont was a fictitious character created by Falcon's assiduous mind.

"*Oui.*" Nicole nodded as if they were discussing nothing more than the miserable weather. "But often a man who is able to seduce a girl"—she met the minister's eye—"is unable to keep a woman. We have discussed Monsieur

Damont before and it tires me to speak of him again. My family is my own affair, and entirely separate from ours."

The minister waited until a plate of pâté was placed before them, a glass of sweet Sauternes to accompany. "And how do you envision our affair, Mademoiselle Beauvoire?" he whispered.

The man's tone was so curious that it caused Nicole to glance up. "As I wish it to be, Monsieur LeCoeur."

The minister held her eyes, his attention acutely on her features. "And how do you wish it to be, *mademoiselle*? Where do you see our liaison heading?"

Nicole sensed his irritation and her heart sped up as she smiled, soothing him by breathing, "To bed, of course, Minister LeCoeur. My bedchamber is—"

"You must come to me." Minister LeCoeur stared at her as if making a decision.

Nicole laughed nervously, praying to God that the minister was not deciding what was the most appropriate time to arrest her. "I'm afraid that is not possib—*Merci*," she said to the conspicuously large footman as he laid beef burgundy before her. "It is not possible," Nicole said beneath her breath, smiling for the benefit of the other guests. "I would be seen entering your bedchamber."

"I have made arrangements for this evening." The minister dismissed her concern. "You need only be ready in your bedchamber at midnight," he said, challenging her.

"To be taken to your bedchamber?" Nicole whispered, her heart pounding.

Minister LeCoeur smiled, saying, "Where else would I be taking you, Mademoiselle Beauvoire?"

The minister had some idea where else to take her; she could hear it in his voice.

Nicole hesitated, her leeriness visible as she stared at the other guests, their clamor increasing in proportion to the generous distribution of the emperor's wine. But they seemed unaware of the dangerous game taking place right before their eyes. The positioning of pieces before the battle ensued. Nicole would have to draw new plans for the assassination, but thankfully Scorpion was very good at adjusting her game.

"Midnight." Nicole raised her glass, picking up his gauntlet, sure that before the Day of the Dead was over, there would be one more to add to its ranks.

The only question was, which one of them would it be?

Daniel had to stop. He was half frozen and his horse near dead when he dismounted at a tiny tavern fifteen miles west of Paris.

He tossed the stable master his reins as he slid to the ground, panting heavily as he said, "I require a mount as soon as possible. You can have my gelding in exchange."

The man looked Daniel up and down, as well as his horse, and deciding both had some quality to them, offered, "You can have this bay. I'll fetch you when we've readied him."

"It is of utmost importance that I get to Paris tonight." Daniel met the man's eye. "Please, be as quick as you can."

The man heard the desperation in Daniel's voice and called to his stable boy to assist him as Daniel wandered inside the dingy tavern. The warmth of the fire washed over him, and he closed his eyes with relief. Daniel sat alone at a small table nearest the fire and held his head in his frozen hands, trying not to think.

Nicole had sent him away because she cared for him—but she did not trust him. She had never truly trusted him, and the ache of it hurt more than his throbbing head.

Hadn't he proven himself to her? Hadn't he shown her in every conceivable fashion that he could be trusted, that he would be there when she needed aid, when she needed love?

Damn it! He was not her husband.

Daniel swallowed his anger at the man who had done this to her. The lass had relied upon herself for far too long, and he had no notion if Nicole would ever be able to trust him, or any man, again.

He had to get to Paris. He had to show her that he would

be there for her when others were not, when others had sat by as the bastard beat the hell out of her.

"Monsieur," the stable hand called from the door just when Daniel was beginning to feel his fingers again.

He braced himself as he stepped into the snow, wishing to God that he had been wearing his greatcoat when they had abducted him from the apartment. The fresh-fallen snow crunched beneath his feet, and Daniel flipped up the soggy lapel of his jacket in the vain hope that the snow would stop finding its way down his back.

The stable master handed him the reins of the old bay, saying, "Here you are, *monsieur.*"

The man helped Daniel mount the elderly horse and then tossed him a wool blanket—the dirty blanket no doubt offered out of guilt for their one-sided bartering.

"Merci." Daniel wrapped the malodorous wool about himself then squeezed the reluctant bay insistently with his thighs to send the animal into the raging storm.

There was no moon in the sky, and the snow fell so heavily that Daniel could scarcely see where he was going. But he continued on, squinting against the onslaught of white flakes and pointing his mount toward the lack of trees, assuming that to be the road.

His teeth were chattering but Daniel tried not to think about the cold; he tried to remember his goal. Paris. He had to stop Nicole from performing the assassination and getting herself killed.

The thought of losing her spurred him on, and his urgency was bolstered by the increased frequency of cottages as he approached the outskirts of Paris. Daniel was exhausted, but as the snow let up, he sent the horse into a gallop, praying that they wouldn't encounter a patch of ice.

By the time Daniel reached the center of the city, the streets were empty and blanketed by a heavy snow that buried the constant stench of the city beneath it. A church bell tolled twelve in the distance, and he slowed his mount as the blazing torches surrounding Tuileries Palace came into view.

He was so close, but as Daniel stared at the well-protected walls of the palace, his stomach tightened. He had no notion how to get inside, no notion how to stop the woman who even now plotted to kill the guardian of Paris on its most fêted ground.

No notion if the woman he so desperately loved was even still alive.

Thirty-three

❦

Nicole started at the first of twelve chimes when the ornate clock in her bedchamber struck midnight. She rose, breathing deeply as she paced the room, all of her mind focusing on the task ahead of her.

She waited by the door dressed in her most provocative gown, which did not begin to compare with her scandalous chemise. The costly garments were the tools of her sordid trade. The weapons that had been so effective in keeping her alive while she made others dead.

Costumes all, allowing Nicole to perform the assassination as an actress would perform a play. Separating her from the inevitable guilt and despair she would inescapably feel afterward.

A soft knock at the door drew her attention, her eyes the only part of her not frozen by a peculiar foreboding. This, she knew, would be Scorpion's last performance, and Nicole waited for her inevitable capture with a morbid fascination.

She would have to have been blind not to see the guards surrounding the palace, which was undoubtedly why the clever Minister LeCoeur had chosen this location to spring his sinister trap.

But unfortunately for the intellectual minister, there was one thing that shifted the odds of this assassination decidedly in her favor.

Apathy.

While the ambitious minister of police valued his life immensely, Nicole could not say the same about her own. She had become irrevocably numb the moment she had sent Daniel McCurren back where he belonged. The armed guards surrounding the minister were merely obstacles to be overcome, not a fate to be feared.

Mademoiselle Beauvoire walked to the bedchamber door and cracked it open to the familiar footman standing before her.

"*Bonjour,* Mademoiselle Beauvoire." The young man bowed, his golden hair falling in front of his dark blue eyes. "Minister LeCoeur has sent me to escort you to his suite."

"This is unwise," she protested. "We shall be seen."

The guard lifted his chin, his confidence clear. "No, we shall not be detected, Mademoiselle Beauvoire."

Nicole nodded as the man glanced down the darkened corridor before gesturing her to move forward. She followed, but rather than turning left toward the staircase, the guard turned to his right.

They had taken only a few steps when the fictitious footman pushed open a discreet door that led to one of the many servants' stairwells at Tuileries Palace.

The guard rounded the spiral stairs as Nicole climbed after him, asking, "What did you think of the play?"

The footman paused on the step above, surprised that Nicole had recognized him as one of Joseph LeCoeur's personal guards. "I found the production as tender of heart as the men that perform in the theater."

"And are you not of a tender disposition?"

"Regretfully no, *mademoiselle.*" They stared at one another, their points made. "If you would remain close to me as we venture into the corridor." The guard shrugged. "The gentlemen of Paris have a tendency to stray from their beds."

They crossed the hall with no difficulty, seen only by the two guards flanking Minister LeCoeur's bedchamber door. The taller guard to the left opened the door, and Nicole's arrogant escort ushered her into the large room and then saluted the minister.

"*Merci,* Captain Turgeon, you may resume your post at the front entry."

"*Oui,* Minister LeCoeur." The fair captain gave Nicole one last glance before leaving the room.

Nicole watched the door close, surprised that she had been allowed to enter the minister's bedchamber without first having been searched.

"Mademoiselle Beauvoire," LeCoeur said, rising with refinement from one of two wing-backed chairs. The room was lit by a roaring fire, and she knew the minister was not alone by the black Hessian boots peeking from beneath the second chair.

The other man stood to make his introductions, and Nicole knew instantly that this was the man for whom Falcon had sent his warning. That he was the Frenchman who had murdered his own agent, Lord Cunningham, after having slaughtered five British soldiers.

However, what Nicole failed to understand was the hostility burning in the assassin's eyes.

"My assistant, Major Evariste Rousseau," the minister indicated with a sweep of his right hand.

"*Bonsoir, mademoiselle,*" the man sneered, making no attempt at civility.

"*Bonsoir,* Major Rousseau." Nicole was dismissive, turning her irritated gaze on her host. "I was led to believe that you wished to speak with me in private?"

"I do wish it." The minister met Nicole's eyes, and her

heart protested the intimacy by thumping sharply in her chest. "Please, have a seat."

Nicole glanced derisively toward the menacing major and said with raised brow, "Is your servant to remain, Joseph?" before sitting in the baroque chair nearest the fire.

"I told you she was delightful," Joseph LeCoeur chuckled. "*Oui, ma chérie.* I'm afraid Major Rousseau is rather involved in this discussion, as he is the man who discovered your identity."

Her eyes darted to the younger man, and the left side of his mouth lifted in satisfaction. Nicole had always known she would die, but until seeing this assassin's anticipation, she had never realized just how painfully.

"Or should we say the lack thereof?" Confused, Nicole turned to face her accuser. "I asked Major Rousseau to investigate the family Damont to see if you were worth marrying. Imagine my surprise when I learned that it was I who was the target of matrimonial ambitions."

"I have no idea of your meaning," Nicole said, eliciting a grunt of disgust from the minister's lethal lackey.

"Oh, do not be so humble, Mademoiselle Beauvoire. Your plan had merit. The coincidental renting of the apartment across the square was nicely done." The minister held her eyes. "I must admit that it was the exorbitant cost of the apartment which threw me from the track of your true path. You and your partner must have spent every penny you possess to meld into Parisian society."

"My partner?"

"Daniel Damont, if that is indeed his name, played the part of spurned lover to perfection. The man is handsome enough to be your former lover and appeared rich enough to be my rival."

"Daniel Damont is not—"

The minister held up his hand, interrupting her denial. "I am afraid that there is only one way for you to avoid a charge of fraud, Mademoiselle Beauvoire." Joseph LeCoeur crossed his legs and rested a pistol on his right knee, saying,

"You will become my lover, whenever I wish and for as long as I wish it."

Nicole had heard similar words on the night of her wedding, but she was no longer a frightened girl of eighteen. Her blood turned to ice as it always did before she killed, and she met the black eyes of Major Rousseau.

"It is required that I remove her clothing in order to search the woman properly." The comment was made to Minister LeCoeur, but the assassin smiled as he stared at Nicole.

"Leave that to me," the minister ordered. "In the meantime, Major, you are to wait outside my door in the event that our illustrious guest chooses to arrive."

Nicole smirked at the major's dismissal, and the assassin cut her a sidelong glance before turning to join the minister's guards, bringing their number to three.

"It is not wise to challenge Major Rousseau, *mademoiselle*." Joseph LeCoeur remained seated in his chair with the pistol in his right hand as he picked up a glass of champagne with his left.

"And you? I took you for a man who enjoyed a challenge."

"Oh, you were entirely correct, *mademoiselle*." The minister nodded. "Now, slowly take off your gown so that I might truly enjoy searching you."

Nicole complied, glancing at the balcony as she considered her alternatives.

"Don't bother, *ma chérie*." Minister LeCoeur laughed. "I have two guards posted on my balcony awaiting far more treacherous game than one ambitious woman."

Five.

Nicole let her gown drop to the floor, making sure that her petticoats went with it.

"I am a poor girl who seeks a rich husband." She shrugged her shoulders appealingly, standing in nothing more than a lace chemise and sheer stockings. "What is so wrong in that, Joseph?"

His eyes meandered down her body, and the minister

lifted the pistol saying, "Kick your gown over there." He jerked his head to the left, but his eyes remained on her form, unable to look away from his prize. "And then remove your exquisite chemise."

"Are you frightened of me, Joseph?" Nicole leaned her head to one side so that he could view the line of her neck as she removed her right ear bob and then the left, setting them on the small table between them.

"Frightened? No." The minister motioned with his pistol to hasten her. "Aroused, very much so. Slowly," He took another sip of champagne. "Remove the chemise, slowly."

Nicole peeled the lace garment from her arms and she could see the anticipation in Minister LeCoeur's eyes as she clutched it with her right forearm just above her nipples.

"And who is this other guest?"

"Stop talking," he said, examining every inch of naked flesh. Nicole smiled, performing for him by removing the pins from her hair and letting the soft curls fall around her shoulders. "Much better," Minister LeCoeur observed.

Nicole watched the minister's features carefully as she let the chemise slither over her large breasts before allowing it to fall to the floor. Minister LeCoeur's lips parted and his breathing increased, all thoughts of the danger he was in gone from his lecherous mind.

"Do I disappoint you, Joseph?" she asked seductively.

"No." The minister licked his lips. "You are everything that I had dreamed you would be."

Nicole smiled playfully and looked at the champagne bottle.

"Might I have some champagne, Joseph?" His gaze drifted to her eyes. "From the looks of you, I think you shall cause me to build quite a thirst."

Nicole poured herself a flute of champagne before carrying the bottle toward him, filling his glass as she said, "Do put the pistol down, darling. If you are to be my lover, you will most assuredly want the use of both hands."

The minister grinned, looking her over before placing the pistol on the side table, but still within his reach. Nude, Nicole kept to the fire, waiting for him to walk toward her before beginning their negotiations.

"As my new protector, what are you prepared to offer me?"

Joseph LeCoeur grasped her breast as if evaluating a new acquisition. "Your freedom." The minister raised a brow, meeting her eyes.

"Well, that is a bit less than I had hoped for, darling Joseph, but I suppose it is a start. To freedom then?" Nicole raised her glass in a sardonic toast.

"Perhaps you should earn your freedom before you begin to celebrate, Mademoiselle Beauvoire." It was not a question, and the minister tossed back the remainder of his champagne, setting his glass on the mantle so that he could grasp Nicole's left wrist.

Minister LeCoeur sat down again in the wing-backed chair, pulling her onto his lap. Nicole could feel his erection against her backside as his mouth fell to her breasts. She closed her eyes, repelled by his touch, and listened as his breathing became labored.

"Joseph," Nicole whispered in his ear.

"Oui." The minister's hands were shaking as he lifted his head to kiss her neck.

"Were you aware that many liquids form pretty crystals when they are dried?"

"What?" Minister LeCoeur's head fell back against the chair and he stared at her, his coloring off.

"It is true," she said, continuing his education. "Many substances crystallize when left to dry, and I have found that the crystals can be fashioned to resemble small diamonds."

The minister grabbed his stomach as the first tremors shook him, and being a man of intellect, Joseph LeCoeur glanced at the champagne, realizing who Nicole was and what she had just done.

But it was too late. His muscles were useless, paralyzed by the powerful poison, and Nicole knew that the man had but moments to live.

She rose to her feet and stared down at him, saying by way of explanation for his execution, "For all the men you have killed, the women you have destroyed, and the children you have allowed to starve in the streets, I execute you in the name of the Crown."

The minister fell back in his chair, dead, and Nicole felt . . . nothing. No hatred, no guilt, not even a flicker of patriotism. It was this that frightened her, this lack of feeling. After General Capette's murder she had felt despair, but now Nicole was nothing more than an empty shell.

She bent down and retrieved her garments, dressing slowly before dropping into the chair opposite Minister LeCoeur's lifeless body, thinking to enjoy her last hours of freedom. Nicole glanced at Minister LeCoeur's pistol, entertaining only briefly the thought of killing one of the balcony guards . . . but she had no pistol for the other.

What did it matter?

She was tired of killing and would be dead if she returned to England. Either by hanging at Newgate or by watching Daniel McCurren marry another woman. And he would. He was too passionate a man, and too fond of children, not to marry.

She only hoped that Daniel did not despise her for sending him home where he belonged, where he deserved to be, and that he would always hold a small place in his heart for her.

Nicole sipped her champagne and stared at the fire, waiting for dawn and regretting having poisoned the quality champagne still remaining in the tainted bottle. She glanced at the mantle clock, vaguely wondering if she would have time to sleep. No doubt Major Rousseau would interrogate her for hours when he discovered the minister's body, and Nicole wanted to be rested for the ordeal.

Major Rousseau. A chill went through her as Nicole recalled the sadistic major. The man enjoyed hurting people. One had only to look at him to know that it was true. Her husband had been cast from the same violent mold, and Nicole had never understood why.

Lord and Lady Stratton had been kind people. Had seemed to Nicole indulgent parents who refused to acknowledge their son's vicious nature. Only once had she thought Lady Stratton suspected her son of cruelty.

Shortly after their marriage, Lady Stratton had taken ill with a fever and Charles had left Nicole at his mother's bedside. In this state of delirium, the lady had told Nicole of the strange summer that three of their foxhounds had gone missing, only to be found dead days later.

It was then that Nicole began to suspect Charles, not a carriage accident, of killing his first wife. So Nicole endured the brutal beatings, waiting for their infrequent visits to Lord and Lady Stratton before divulging her husband's cruelty and begging their intervention.

Lord Stratton had called his son back into the room, demanding to know if Nicole's charges were true. Charles had denied the beatings, and his parents had chosen to believe what their son had told them. Charles had told his parents that an argument over pin money had led his young bride to accuse him of cruelty. Nicole had then received a lecture on greed from Lord Stratton and, later, the beating of her life from his son.

That was the night she killed him.

Unfortunately, Nicole had stabbed Charles so many times to ensure that he was indeed dead, that her argument of self-preservation was rather difficult to defend. Lord Stratton then testified to their "argument over her allowance," and the scars on Nicole's back were deemed a husband's disciplinary prerogative. However, the male members of the House of Lords were kind enough to judge that discipline "excessive"—prior to sentencing her to be hanged by the neck until she was dead.

And then she met Falcon.

He had come to Newgate to present his proposition a

week before her execution. He needed a woman of noble breeding to infiltrate the blue blood of Paris.

Initially, Nicole had been confused as to why the old man would choose her. She spoke French, of course, but so did every other society lady in London. This was not a sufficient enough reason, in her mind, to release a murderer from prison. And then he had explained.

Falcon needed a woman, a lady, capable of killing, and that was a far more difficult dearth of character to come by. A woman lacking a conscience was a rare and infinitely useful anomaly for the Foreign Office.

So Nicole had agreed, asking only that the men she assassinated be as deserving of death as her husband. And they had been, all nine horrible men who had, in various ways, abused their people and their power.

She stared at Joseph LeCoeur, and her conscience was clear. Nicole regretted only that she was capable of killing and that she had not met Daniel McCurren when she was an innocent girl of eighteen, before she had been hardened into this empty shell.

She drained her glass of the last drops of bubbly and savored the tart taste on her tongue. Her eyes drifted to the poisoned champagne and she smiled, thinking of the disappointment Major Rousseau would feel if she were to drink it.

She reached for the bottle, the hollow golden ear bob clanking against the glass as she filled her crystal flute to the rim. Nicole lifted her glass and stared at the tainted bubbles, amazed that there were no visible indications of the poison in the innocuous-looking libation.

The apothecary had been correct.

She glanced at the curtains covering the balcony doors and wondered how long she had before the soldiers would be relieved. The clock struck half past midnight and Nicole prayed that she would have until morning to rest.

Daniel would be sleeping.

A picture of him flashed into her mind. Daniel was well on his way to Honfleur, and from there would travel to England, to his home. Nicole smiled with contentment, knowing that her years as Scorpion would end with her saving a life rather than taking one.

Nicole blinked away gathering tears and then lifted her glass. She sniffed the champagne and, detecting no odor, tentatively took a sip.

Astonishingly, the champagne tasted no different from her first glass, and Nicole knew that she would have no difficulty in drinking the entire contents of the crystal flute.

She pressed the rim of the glass to her lips then heard a man on the balcony scream as if he were falling. Her head jerked toward the velvet drapes, which parted with a snap, and her eyes went wide when Daniel McCurren staggered into the room.

No!

Daniel glanced first at her then at Minister LeCoeur's lifeless body, and he knew he was too late. The viscount turned and his stunned eyes met hers, full of sorrow and pain.

"Daniel . . ." she began but stopped, wrapping her arms around her stomach as the cramps claimed her.

A crash at the bedchamber door drew Daniel's attention and he frantically swept the room with his eyes, looking, she prayed, for a place to conceal himself.

Why did he not leave?

A second, more ominous crack at the door rang out, and Daniel reached for the pistol on the table next to Joseph LeCoeur's body. But he would not be able to defend them. Major Rousseau had far too many men. *Run!* her mind screamed, but the word was stuck in her throat, pinned there by the fast-acting poison.

Daniel lifted the pistol to Minister LeCoeur's chest, and as the bedchamber door burst open, he fired, killing a dead man.

Time slowed to a painful crawl and Nicole watched, horrified, as the smoke cleared and the deafening bang dissipated.

"Long live King George!" Daniel shouted before being wrestled to the floor by the three French guards.

Nicole stared at Daniel, her eyes filling with tears. He had come back for the same reason she had sent him away.

He was in love with her. He was giving his life for her.

The room was rapidly dimming and Nicole knew she did not have much time. She reached for Major Rousseau's jacket to tell him that Daniel was not to blame, to tell the major that she was the assassin, that she was Scorpion. But the poison coursed through her, racking her body as she fell to the floor.

Her head rolled to the side and Nicole watched help-lessly as Daniel was being dragged from the room. Her view of the horrific scene was blocked by black shadows and Nicole blinked, her mind trying to make sense of the rounded lines that rolled above her. Nicole blinked again and her eyes settled on the face of Major Rousseau just before she sank into darkness.

Thirty-four

❧❧❧

Major Rousseau stared at the unconscious woman on the bedchamber floor then looked up at the man he had waited so long to meet.

Evariste sniffed, annoyed that the man epitomized the excesses of the British. He was altogether too large, too handsome, and too arrogant to be an assassin, and yet here he stood. However, the bastard would not be able to stand for long. "Take Scorpion to my cells at the Conciergerie."

"*Oui,* Major Rousseau," the more senior man offered, giving a very prudent and deferential bow.

"And if he escapes"—Major Rousseau met the older man's eyes—"I will kill you myself."

The guard saluted then rushed from the room to secure the prisoner, but Evariste's mind was once again on the odd scene set before him. He stepped over the prone woman and examined Minister LeCoeur's body.

He bent down and touched the minister's bluish lips and then examined the bullet wound. The blackened hole appeared to have very little blood seeping from the shot to the heart. Yet it was Evariste's experience that the heart tended to gush when pierced until it stopped beating.

The major looked at the woman on the floor, at her labored breathing, and his eyes darted to her nearly full glass of champagne. Evariste stepped over her again and called for the two guards still remaining in the corridor.

"Discreetly," Major Rousseau said to the smaller man, raising a finger to punctuate his point. "Find a physician and bring him here to me."

"*Oui, monsieur.*" The guard bowed before leaving on his mission.

"You, come with me," Evariste ordered the other man before returning to the minister's bedchamber. "Close the door."

Major Rousseau stepped over the girl and picked up the full glass of champagne, saying, "Drink this," to the larger guard, who was of the same approximate weight and height as the minister.

The man glanced at Minister LeCoeur's stiffening corpse and hesitated. Evariste thought about threatening him, but decided that a second round of gunfire echoing in the palace would be frowned upon by Emperor Bonaparte.

"Minister LeCoeur was shot," Evariste reminded the guard as if the man were an idiot. "And she"—Major Rousseau looked down at the girl—"has merely swooned."

"Then why—"

"Do you question me?" Evariste stared at the man.

"No, Major Rousseau, I would never—I merely wondered for what purpose—"

"You are the minister's approximate size," Evariste said as if this explained everything. "The minister did not resist his assassin and I would like to know how much champagne would be necessary . . ."

"I comprehend." The man nodded, satisfied by Evariste's convoluted logic before lifting the glass and consuming the entire contents of questionable champagne.

"Now, if you would place the girl on the bed," the major asked, waiting.

The guard lifted the small woman easily, carrying her across the room to the elaborately carved four-poster bed. He bent over and gently set the woman on the colorful duvet. However, when he rose, the guard staggered backward, his eyes widening in fear as he sank to his knees, pain drawing the veins from his neck before he fell over dead at Evariste's feet.

Major Rousseau's left brow rose, impressed with the alacrity at which the poison killed. He glanced at the bottle of costly champagne, thankful to have a portion left from which to ascertain its origins.

His eye returned to the beautiful woman on the bed. Mademoiselle Beauvoire could not have imbibed much of the poison or she, too, would surely be dead. Evariste watched the slow rise of her chest and he leaned over, placing his ear against the soft mounds of the lady's exquisite breasts.

Her heartbeat was steady, yet slow, and as Evariste listened, he stared at her cherry red lips, which were slightly parted to expel her silent breath. Evariste lifted his head and circled the unconscious woman's lips with the tip of his finger, envisioning what deeds he would have that pretty little mouth perform.

She was his to control, and he revelled in the knowledge. His finger descended over her chin and neck, and he smiled with anticipation as it continued toward her décolletage. His hand slid into the bodice of her gown, and Evariste grasped her right breast, his cock pulsing with need the moment he touched her softness.

Mademoiselle Beauvoire was indeed stunning, and he could understand Minister LeCoeur's obsession. However, now that the minister was dead, Evariste would have her in celebration of Scorpion's much-anticipated capture.

Once he delivered to Napoleon the notorious British assassin, he would no doubt be elevated to a new rank with even greater privileges of power.

"Au revoir, ma chérie." Major Rousseau leaned over and licked the woman's neck, whispering in her ear, "I

shall wait until you regain your strength so that I might enjoy taking it from you."

Evariste gave her breast one last, lingering squeeze and then released her just as the physician entered the minister's bedchamber accompanied by Captain Turgeon.

"You have captured him?" the captain asked.

"Oui." The major nodded and then pointed to the guard on the floor and addressed himself to the physician. "This man is dead, poisoned after drinking Minister LeCoeur's champagne." Evariste met Captain Turgeon's perceptive eye. "The woman is still alive. It appears as though she had little of the tainted liquid. The lady is your patient and your primary concern."

"Oui, Major Rousseau." The round physician bowed. "However, I will need a maid to assist me in undressing the young lady."

"Bon, you may ask Captain Turgeon for anything you may require, as he is now her personal guard." Major Rousseau was leaving the room when he stopped and looked at Captain Turgeon. "And if the woman wakes, notify me at once." Evariste's lips twitched ever so slightly. "I shall be at the Conciergerie."

And then Major Rousseau was striding down the corridor, thinking only of Scorpion and the meeting he had anticipated for so very long.

Daniel had been kneeling with his wrists hoisted behind his back for hours. His muscles strained to keep his sagging weight from pulling his shoulders from their sockets, but he was losing the battle.

He needed to adjust his weight, and the only way of doing that was damn near impossible—and most certainly would be excruciating. However, at this point Daniel did not much care. All he could think of was taking the strain from his neck and shoulders, no matter the cost.

He rose to his feet and reached back to grasp the chains above the iron shackles with his hands. The metal mandibles cut into the skin at his wrists, a prelude to what was to come. Daniel gritted his teeth and told himself it was just like all the trees he had flipped down from as a child, only this time there were no limbs, save his own.

Daniel tilted his head forward, his shoulders burning with the increased pressure, and then with one determined kick, he was tumbling over with his own restraints supporting him. He could feel his flesh ripping as his wrists spun in the shackles, but the moment his feet hit the cell floor Daniel knew the pain was worth it.

His arms, which had been pulled backward for God knew how long, now hung in front of him, and his body was grateful. He leaned back and stretched the knotted muscles between his shoulder blades as sweat poured down his temples and blood poured down his forearms.

Comfortable now, his mind returned to the harrowing events of the day. Daniel had spent the ride back to town thinking that the lass did not want him, that she had wanted to be rid of him.

But Daniel knew the moment he saw Nicole that he had been wrong.

He had seen it in her beautiful, violet eyes the moment Daniel had entered Minister LeCoeur's bedchamber. She had been terrified, not for herself but for him. Nicole had feared for his safety in the minister's bedchamber, and she had feared for his happiness when she had sent him home to England.

But what the lass did not realize was that now that he had experienced real love, there was no going back. He had wanted Sarah Duhearst for his wife, had pouted like a child when she married another man. But Daniel now knew that while he loved Sarah, his dear friend, he had never been in love with her.

Sarah Duhearst would have made a wonderful wife and mother to his children. But love was not so reasonable, so thoughtful, in her selection. No, he could not go back to London without Nicole Beauvoire, for if he did, he would go back half a man, his heart and soul forever in Paris. Daniel knew he could not survive without her.

Even if it meant dying.

Nicole had to be protected, and he was the only one able to do that at present. Daniel would give the lass time to escape the city, taking the blame for the assassination and enduring the inevitable interrogation for as long as he could.

He sighed, adjusting the shackles and reviewing the questions he might be asked and the answers that would spare her from suspicion.

Nicole's swooning had been a brilliant touch of drama. No one would ever suspect such a delicate flower of having done such terrible deeds.

What had Nicole said? She had killed nine men, at least one of them poisoned. LeCoeur would be Scorpion's tenth assassination. Where could Daniel have been living? At the hotel by the docks where he had been staying when they met. Andre Tuchelles had been his contact. The man had given his life to protect Nicole and could not now be refuted.

Yes, Daniel could pass as Scorpion. He was the sort of man one would imagine to be an assassin. Not Nicole.

He closed his eyes and rehearsed his fictitious life of the past two years. Daniel sat for hours; his body relaxed as he waited for the unavoidable—and then it came with the clanking of metal and the clicking of heels.

"The prisoner is in the first cell, Major Rousseau."

Daniel heard the two men before he saw them. The dark man from the minister's bedchamber was holding a file as he walked, but when the major looked up, he stilled.

"Why is this prisoner not restrained as I ordered?"

The question was asked with a calmness that appeared to chill the young guard to the bone.

"His arms were shackled behind his back, as ordered. I swear it, Major Rousseau."

The major looked through the bars at Daniel's bleeding wrists, and then he met Daniel's gaze, his black eyes illuminated by a glimmer of respect.

"Did it not occur to you, Sergeant, that a man of his obvious strength should have his legs restrained as well?"

"I . . . No one has ever—"

"He has." Major Rousseau's soft words averted the sergeant's eyes. "Get me a chair and a small table on which to write."

The young sergeant disappeared into the small office that Daniel had passed through when he was taken to his cell.

"Good evening, Scorpion," the major said, acknowledging Daniel for the first time. "I apologize for not being here sooner, but you left quite a mess in Minister LeCoeur's bedchamber, *vous comprenez*?"

Daniel said nothing, just continued to stare at the cold stone walls. The sergeant returned with the chair and Major Rousseau sat, pulling the small table between his thighs as he read the thick dossier the guard had been carrying.

"We have eight murders for which you have been credited." The major looked up. "Have we missed anyone?"

Daniel shrugged as if he did not understand a word the man was saying. *"Je ne comprends pas le français."*

At this the major chuckled, revealing crooked teeth.

"You wish me to believe that you have resided in Paris for two long years without learning a smattering of French?" Major Rousseau said in English. "Are there more than eight?"

"Do you count Minister LeCoeur?" Daniel asked in his most aristocratic French. "Or must the corpse be cold first?"

The major's eyes flashed but he showed no other signs of anger as he looked through Daniel, saying, "Oh, I prefer them warm."

"And defenseless?" Daniel rattled his chains.

"A necessary component of my work. Eight?" the major asked again, giving the illusion of a patient man.

"No." Daniel shook his head with satisfaction . . . and pride.

"More or less?"

Daniel smirked. "This is a stupid question."

"How many more?"

"Two," Daniel said truthfully, knowing that all murders would have been investigated by the office of the minister of police.

"Who are these two?"

Daniel smiled, having no idea what men Nicole had been sent to assassinate. "What kills have you documented in your little file?"

Major Rousseau's jaw clenched, but he otherwise ignored the insult.

"You poisoned Marcel Martin and you shot General Capette. But why was it necessary to poison then shoot Minister LeCoeur? That seems excessive, even for you."

Daniel had anticipated this question, and had his answer at the ready. "Poisons are unreliable. The woman survived—I made sure LeCoeur did not."

"Why did you not shoot the girl?"

Daniel's brow furrowed as if the man were an idiot. "The girl was not my target."

"Never fear, Scorpion, your poison might kill her yet."

"Pardon?" Daniel's heart stopped, the vibrations of his shock ringing in his voice.

The major's mouth lifted at one corner. "An innocent death pricks your conscience? This is amusing . . . and useful."

Daniel set his features, trying to hide the depth of his concern, but the man continued to assault him, all the while watching his reactions.

"The woman drank a portion of the poison and is even now precariously perched at death's door."

"Unfortunate." Daniel shrugged, terrified. "We are, however, at war."

"Oui." His captor nodded. "We are indeed at war, Monsieur Scorpion. Sergeant," the man shouted down the hall.

"Major Rousseau?"

The major looked over Daniel's naked torso, saying, "Bring me my tools," with a gleam in his black eyes.

Thirty-five

❧

Seamus McCurren stared into the fire with a brandy in one hand as he listened to the endless prattle trickling from the mouth of Christian St. John. Not, to be clear, that Seamus was unappreciative. Quite the contrary, Lord St. John could be very amusing at times, and Seamus appreciated the man's effort at keeping his mind occupied.

Unfortunately, every day that went by without news of Daniel seemed to drain his mind of the ability to concentrate on the world around him.

"I could not believe the lady's boldness. She just sat in my lap and propositioned me, knowing full well that the lady with whom I was sitting was my current mistress."

"What did you do?" Seamus asked, not really interested in Christian's never-ending exploits.

"What kind of cad do you take me for, Seamus?" His fair brows furrowed with indignation. "I thanked her for the kind offer and told her that I was not interested." Christian took a sip of brandy and grinned like the scoundrel he was, adding, "But I did keep her card."

Seamus chuckled and shook his head. "Has it never occurred to you, St. John, that these events do not merely 'happen,' as you so staunchly claim, but rather that you attract them like—"

"Bees to honey?" Christian's blue eyes sparkled.

"I was going to say like flies to manure."

"Are you calling me a pile of dung?" Lord St. John's left brow rose. "Wait, don't answer that. And no, I do not think I cause any of these things to—"

Christian was interrupted by a knock at the parlor door. Their eyes met and Seamus said, "Come," trying not to feel the fluttering in his belly, which turned to an absolute thunder when his butler announced, "The Duke of Glenbroke wishes an audience, my lord."

"Show him in."

Seamus set his snifter down and placed both hands on the arms of his chair, pushing himself to standing. He bowed as the powerful duke entered the room, followed by an elderly man whom the majority of the *ton* considered to be of no account at all.

"Good evening, gentlemen," Seamus said. "I take it you have received word of Viscount DunDonell, or you would not have ventured out on such a miserable evening."

The duke's countenance was grim, and Christian St. John cut the tension by offering, "I'll just get some drinks, shall I?" reminding Seamus of his lack of hospitality.

"Yes, thank you, Lord St. John. Gentlemen"—Seamus indicated the settee facing the fire—"do have a seat."

The enormous duke lowered himself onto the over-stuffed chartreuse settee and leaned back, crossing his legs before saying, "We believe we have information pertaining to your brother. Thank you." The duke looked up as Lord St. John handed him a snifter of brandy and the older Falcon picked up where the duke had left off.

"An operative working in Paris has just sent a missive with information which we believe refers to your brother." The old man held Seamus's eye while waiting for Christian St. John to resume his seat.

Seamus clenched his jaw to match his stomach. "Go on."

"Viscount DunDonell has been captured." The old man gave Seamus a moment to take the blow and then continued the barrage. "My agent mentions that a man meeting your brother's description was brought to the Conciergerie nearly three days ago."

"Has he been executed?" Seamus asked, swallowing the rather substantial lump in his throat.

The Duke of Glenbroke leaned forward, picking up the reins. "The missive was sent shortly after this man was taken to prison." His silver eyes sharpened. "We have no idea what has occurred over the last three days, nor can we confirm that this prisoner is even your brother."

Seamus nodded, staring at the floor. "Let us be honest with one another, gentlemen. How many six-foot-two, wide-as-a-barn-door, handsome-as-the-devil gentlemen with auburn hair are presently residing in Paris? Much less getting themselves arrested at the same instant my brother is delivering a message on behalf of the Crown?" Seamus took a large sip of brandy. "I calculate the odds to be exceedingly low."

"Yes, they are." Falcon spoke up and Seamus could see in the brown depths of the old man's eyes that this little visit was his way of preparing Seamus for the inevitable news that Daniel had been executed. "Exceedingly low."

"Is there nothing to be done?" Seamus asked, dreading having to inform his parents of this miserable development.

"No, I'm afraid not." Falcon shook his head. "The viscount is not only in enemy territory but in the capital, being held behind the walls of France's most impenetrable prison. Many of my agents have already returned to London and the few that remain are themselves in danger." The old man sat back, looking his age. "I am sorry."

The four men sat in silence and the duke eventually broke it. "I'm very sorry, Seamus." He began to rise, offering, "Please let me know if there is anything—"

"Let's go and get him."

All three men turned to look at Christian St. John, but it

was the elegant Duke of Glenbroke who recovered first. "Pardon me?"

Christian's bright eyes met his. "Let's go and get him." He pointed to Seamus and then himself. "The two of us."

"Lord St. John." Falcon felt it necessary to counsel the impulsive young man. "This is not a game. It is very likely that if you travel to Paris and attempt to rescue the viscount, you yourself will be killed."

"Damn it all." Christian looked at Falcon and then the duke. "I'm not a simpleton. I understand the risks. However, I am heir to nothing and will hardly be missed, and Mister McCurren here has enough brothers to form a battalion of heirs. Besides"—Christian winked at Seamus—"I think we have rather a sporting chance."

Seamus stared at Christian St. John, at his handsome features and amiable smile. He was the sort of man everyone liked. Charismatic, friendly, and very entertaining company, not to mention the rogue had the ability to talk the skirts off any lady he set his sights on.

"Do you speak French?"

"Fluently." Christian grinned.

"This is madness." The duke gave an exhalation of disbelief. "I will not send two gentlemen to Paris to retrieve one. All three of you could be killed."

"Fortunately," Christian St. John said, rising, "it is not up to you, Glenbroke. Right, McCurren, I'll secure our transportation. You search your musty old books for as much information on the prison . . . Conciergerie?" He turned to Falcon to confirm and the old man nodded. "Any underground pathways, entrances et cetera . . ."

"Christian, your brother and father will never allow you to go to France."

"There again." Christian's Nordic eyes turned to blue ice in a rare show of temper and unwavering stubbornness that many would never have suspected the impulsive lord of possessing. "My personal affairs are not determined by either the duke or the marquis."

And then the amiable Lord St. John smiled like a child

about to depart on some marvelous adventure. "Well, I had best go pack! I shall return later this evening and we can discuss our findings." Seamus nodded, still in shock from the news of his brother's capture.

"When do you think we can depart?" His mind was spinning with the work that needed to be done, and Seamus was thankful to have his thoughts occupied with something other than Daniel's impending execution.

"Tonight?" Christian looked at Falcon.

The old man rose to his feet, sighing as he said, "I shall make the arrangements. However, this evening is impossible. Better you leave tomorrow morning on a smaller vessel that will be traveling directly to Honfleur."

"Excellent," Christian St. John said as he accompanied Falcon out the parlor door, leaving Seamus alone with the concerned Duke of Glenbroke.

The door closed and Gilbert de Clare looked at Seamus, holding his eye. "You will both be killed, Seamus."

"Most likely." Seamus finished his brandy, setting the heavy crystal on a side table to the right of his chair.

"Daniel would not want you to do this."

"I want to do this."

"And St. John? Is Christian to give his life attempting a rescue that will very likely end with all three of you dead?"

"No." Seamus shook his head. "That is why you will ask Falcon to give Christian the wrong departure time. I will arrange to meet Lord St. John at the docks, but my ship will already have set sail for France."

"St. John will be furious."

"Yes, but he will be alive."

"Will you inform your parents?"

"No, I will pen a letter before I go. Would you be so kind, Your Grace, as to give it to them in the event that I do not return?"

"It will be difficult for them to lose you both."

Seamus nodded, looking at his old friend.

"You have no siblings, Your Grace, so perhaps this will be difficult for you to comprehend. I could not live with myself, knowing that I did not do everything in my power to save my brother's life."

The duke leaned forward, sympathy filling his steely eyes. "Daniel may already be dead, Seamus."

"But he may not," Seamus said resolutely as the duke stared into the fire. "I would like for you to be the one to inform my parents."

The duke cleared his throat and ran his fingers through his dark hair, nodding. "Of course."

The enormous Duke of Glenbroke rose as they shook hands, and in an unprecedented show of intimacy, Gilbert placed his left hand on Seamus's right shoulder.

"Be careful, Seamus." The duke gave his farewell with concerned eyes.

"I will," Seamus said, both of them knowing that the odds of his returning to England were negligible.

"Very well." The duke smiled, breaking eye contact. "I shall speak with Falcon about Christian."

"Thank you, Your Grace. And if you could have him send a note round with the correct departure time?"

The Duke of Glenbroke nodded and left, as there was nothing else to be said.

Alone once again, Seamus walked to his study and searched his extensive library for books on French architectural history, hoping to find some mention of the famed Parisian prison, the Conciergerie, and the obstacles that might await him there.

The owner of Dante's Inferno sat behind an elegant oak desk, tabulating the night's considerable earnings, when a knock sounded at the heavy door.

Enigma glanced up, meeting the eye of a man with a large scar across his left cheek, a scar given him by his employer. "Come."

One of the hell's whores entered the room then closed the door, saying, "Do you recall the gossip about the viscount that went missing two weeks past?"

Enigma nodded, saying nothing.

"I just had a patron from Whitehall. The gentleman said there were rumors that this viscount has been arrested in Paris and charged with the assassination of Minister LeCoeur."

"*Mon Dieu,* but Rousseau is a fool!" Both workers stared at their employer's uncharacteristic outburst. "You may go, Chloe."

The door closed and Enigma pulled out a piece of parchment, hastily informing Major Rousseau of his idiocy, clearly laying out for the dim major how his captive could not possibly be the assassin Scorpion, as Viscount DunDonell had been very much present and accounted for in London for the past two years.

"Take this to Paris on the next available ship." The bodyguard bowed and Enigma stopped him before he left the office. "And ask Major Rousseau if he needs me to come hold his hand while he tracks the true assassin?"

The man smirked, leaving Enigma to wonder how in God's name the emperor intended to win this war with men as stupid as these.

Thirty-six

❧❧

Nicole emerged from the darkness, opening her eyes.

Daniel!

She scanned the dim room, her head throbbing as she made out the figure of a robust gentleman sleeping in a chair by the fire. Nicole sat up, the movement splitting her head and rousing the elderly man.

"Oh, you're awake," the man said excitedly.

Nicole continued looking about Minister LeCoeur's bedchamber and saw neither the minister nor his vicious assistant, Major Rousseau.

"What happened to Minister LeCoeur?" she asked, feigning ignorance as the gentleman walked toward her.

"I'm afraid"—the man patted her hand—"that the minister was killed."

Nicole gasped. "He's . . . He's dead?"

"*Oui, ma petite,* and you very nearly died along with him. I am the physician who has been seeing after you."

"I don't understand," Nicole said, letting the old man talk.

"The champagne given you was poisoned." He leaned forward, titillated by the extraordinary events. "By an English assassin."

"No!" Her right hand went to her chest. "An assassin here? In the palace?"

"We never would have caught the Englishman if he had not returned to verify his success." The man's chins jiggled as he looked at the ceiling in contemplation. "I do not comprehend why he would do such a thing."

"What has happened to this wicked assassin?" Nicole asked, distracting the physician from his deliberations.

"Do not fear, *ma petite*." The gentleman smiled, misinterpreting the motivation for her inquiry. "The Englishman has been taken to the Conciergerie by Major Rousseau. Rest assured that the assassin will pay dearly for his crimes."

Nicole's heart dropped into the icy pit of her stomach. "How long have I been asleep?" she asked in desperation.

"Now, now." The gentleman patted her again and Nicole had to suppress the urge to scream. "You have been sleeping on and off for three days."

Three days!

Nicole forced herself to swallow her panic and think.

"Oh, but that is dreadful." She bit her lip, conveying concern. "My sister in Honfleur—"

"We have already sent a message to your sister. Or rather you dictated a letter the first night you were here. Do you not remember?"

"No," Nicole said truthfully and then she began recalling bits and pieces. "Was there a soldier present?"

The physician nodded, encouraging her memory. "*Oui*, that is correct. He delivered the message to your sister."

Nicole paused at the irony of having a French soldier deliver a message to her British contact in Honfleur.

"You said I 'dictated' the letter?" Nicole swallowed her trepidation. "What did I say?"

"Merely that 'you had been delayed and would travel to Honfleur the moment you retrieved your Scottish package.'" The physician smiled, adding, "I must confess

I thought you a bit delirious, so I gave you a large dose of laudanum in order that you might rest."

For three days! Nicole could kill the man.

"You are so very kind," Nicole grated, making a great show of falling against the pillows as if the effort of speaking had been too much for her. "And now, I believe I would like to resume resting."

The physician, however, remained, his bushy gray brows pulling together over dark blue eyes.

"Major Rousseau has requested that I stay with you, Mademoiselle Beauvoire."

"Nonsense," Nicole declared with feminine authority. "You shall work yourself to exhaustion, and then what good will you be to me?"

"Very little, I fear."

"Precisely! As you can see, I will be fast asleep the moment you leave this room in favor of your own." The physician appeared concerned and Nicole hastened to add, "And there is a guard outside the room?"

"Captain Turgeon." The gentleman nodded in confirmation.

"There! I can call Captain Turgeon to retrieve you from your bedchamber if I am in need of you."

Nicole saw the man longing for his own bed, but she saw fear there, too. "Major Rousseau—"

"Major Rousseau has left you to see to my well-being. And I would not be able to sleep a wink if I knew that you were at all uncomfortable." Nicole laughed. "You see? You must leave or you will be disregarding Major Rousseau's orders."

The old man laughed also, thankful for her consideration. "Well, we must not have that."

"No. Good night, *monsieur*." Nicole sighed, settling into Minister LeCoeur's bed. "I shall see you in the morning."

"First light."

"Agreed," Nicole conceded, then watched him hobble from the room on limbs shaped like cooked turkey legs.

Nicole waited five minutes to ensure that the doctor had

gone and that the captain remained in the corridor before throwing back the duvet and quietly stepping onto the carpet. She located her keys and her garments, which had been neatly folded and placed on a corner chair. Nicole dressed herself from memory, her mind numb with shock and fear for Daniel's safety. Her throat constricted and tears streamed down her cheeks as she recalled her last sight of Daniel being dragged from the bedchamber by French guards.

Three days!

Major Rousseau had had him for three days. Nicole pressed the tips of her fingers to her eyes, damming the flood of tears and all thoughts that Daniel might already be dead.

Fear hastened the lacing of her gown, and Nicole took a deep breath to calm herself, to remind herself that she also was an assassin. Her mind shifted from Daniel to the task at hand and Nicole pulled on her shoes, glancing at the door as she walked toward the balcony.

The latch of the balcony door gave with a click as she pressed down on the brass handle. She eased open the door, prepared with the excuse of needing air should the guard hear her.

The night air had turned the rain to snow and she tucked her hands beneath her bare arms, wishing she had something with which to cover herself. But she did not.

Nicole gritted her teeth and grasped the balustrade with both hands, ignoring the inch of snow that had accumulated atop the gray stones. She lifted her right leg over the railing, thankful for the underskirts that insulated her inner thighs, and then lifted her left.

She thrust her slippered feet between the sculpted stone slats of the balcony banister and looked down to the ground some ten feet below. The only way of getting down was to drop. So Nicole took a deep breath, knowing no matter how she prepared her body that the fall was going to cause her pain.

But nothing compared to the pain Daniel was sure to have endured for three days—and was enduring still.

She could only pray that he had survived it.

Nicole stepped into the void and tried to judge the distance to the white lawn, but the snow made the task all but impossible. She hit the ground hard, her knees buckling and sending her onto her back. Nicole scrambled to her feet, silently rushing to conceal herself against the palace walls. Glancing to her left, she brushed as much of the snow from her body as she could before it had the opportunity to soak through her gown.

This late at night, guards would be scarce and the snow would make their vision weak and their resolve even weaker. No, the difficulty would be exiting the palace grounds and hiring a conveyance before she froze to death.

But perhaps that would not be necessary.

Nicole kept to the shadows as she made for the carriage house, located a short distance from the palace. Her feet were numb by the time she reached the doors, and Nicole was thankful that they had not been locked.

The smell of horses and hay filled her frozen nose as she walked past the countless conveyances owned by the emperor's many guests. Nicole stopped at a particularly lavish landau and opened the small door, praying for a coverlet. She found two, and chose the one made of ermine.

Nicole wrapped the luxurious white fur around her arms and moaned at the warmth and feel of the makeshift shawl. She continued toward the adjoining stables, searching in the dim light for a horse small enough and placid enough to meet her needs.

Unsuccessful, she rounded a corner of the paddock to continue the search, only to find two soldiers sitting atop a pile of hay, playing cards. The young men jumped to their feet, as startled as she, and it took several moments for Nicole to react.

"Oh, thank the saints that you are on duty!" she said, berating herself for not having anticipated that the guards would have sought sanctuary from the snow. "I have just received word that my father has taken ill." Nicole began to cry and the soldiers glanced at one another in the helpless manner men have when confronted by the tears of a woman. "Major Rousseau said that I was welcome to make use of a horse."

The soldiers paled at the mention of the major, glancing at her ermine stole and diamond-studded slippers. The older of the two licked his lips, uncomfortable.

"We shall saddle a horse immediately, *mademoiselle*."

Nicole was on her way within a quarter of an hour. Nicole turned from the palace gates and sent the horse flying down the empty streets of Paris. She reached the apartment at Place Vendôme at half past three in the morning, her course of action decided.

The keys to the apartment slipped from her hand in a frantic attempt to open the door. She picked them up and tried again, the lock tumbling open. The moment she entered the foyer, her ruined slippers went flying and she ran barefoot to her bedchamber. It was now, in these still moments as she disrobed, that Nicole's fear clouded her mind and her judgment.

She took a calming breath, telling herself over and over again that she would do Daniel no good if she were unprepared. Nicole dressed in a midnight blue gown and matching pelisse, the collar lined with black mink. Her underskirts were light for freedom of movement, but Nicole compensated for the cold with thick stockings and heavy boots. Her mass of hair she secured into a chignon before pulling on black kid gloves.

Nicole stared at her reflection in the mirror, going over every aspect of her mission—the most important she would ever undertake. She pinched her cheeks and licked lips already made red from the biting cold. The woman who stood before her was impressive, screaming of income to anyone who looked.

But it was her behavior, the air of superiority, that would open the doors of the most ruthless prison in all of France.

The Conciergerie.

Daniel would be there, she knew. Nicole had heard horrible tales of Minister LeCoeur's obtaining offices at the notorious prison in order to interrogate political prisoners. However, now that she had met his assistant Major Rousseau, Nicole was certain that it was the major who had performed the cruel interrogations.

She only hoped that the major was not there now, prayed that Major Rousseau was tucked far away in the warmth of his own bed. He would no doubt be tired from the pain he had inflicted on Daniel's beautiful body. Nicole lifted her chin, not allowing the tears to fall, and reminded herself that the viscount was very strong.

As was she.

"I must confess, Monsieur Scorpion," Evariste Rousseau said, with a small knife in his right hand. "I have not done such fine work since Lord Cunningham was my guest."

Daniel's head hung forward, his sweat mingling with blood as it dripped down his chest to pool on the dirty floor in front of him.

"As a matter of fact, this is such good work that I believe I shall sign you."

Daniel's mind flinched, but his body was beyond all resistance. He gritted his teeth, knowing what was to come. The Frenchman went for his upper arm this time, the knife cutting in a downward motion.

"Who else have you killed?"

Daniel remained silent, as he had for the last three days. He tried to swallow, but the effort was too much. The knife made three short incisions for which he was unprepared, and then the sadistic man smiled, gazing at his rudimentary E.

"Who?" the major asked again as he scooped up a fist full of salt.

Daniel's head turned toward the grating sound of the granules as Major Rousseau bent over and whispered in his ear, "Who else have you murdered?" before rubbing salt into the fresh wound.

The excruciating sting of the salt caused Daniel to cry out. He clenched his fists to absorb the pain but it lingered, his entire mind centered on that fiery piece of burning flesh. The major waited until the initial pain had subsided and then made a second downward slice in Daniel's arm.

"This may hurt," the bastard warned before making a circular motion that gouged deep into Daniel's flesh, followed by a slashing cut. "There." Major Rousseau was breathing heavily. "An R."

The salt shifted for a second time and Daniel asked, "For what does the E stand?" hoping to delay the pain a moment longer.

"Evariste." The major smiled, "Evariste Rousseau is the name of the man that will kill you."

"Evariste?" Daniel chuckled, taking several deep breaths. "This is a woman's name."

"Tell me, Scorpion," Major Rousseau whispered so close to his ear that Daniel could feel the heat of the Frenchman's breath. "Is this a woman's sting?"

The major's black eyes hardened as he crushed the salt into Daniel's arm.

"No." Daniel licked his lips, panting. "But it is a device used by cowards."

Major Rousseau's left knee connected with Daniel's ribs, causing day-old wounds to reopen.

"Who have you been working with in Paris?" the small man asked, removing his jacket so that he might have the freedom to move.

"I work alone."

"You have a method of contacting London." Major Rousseau walked to the corner table and looked down, saying, "Describe it," as he slipped on a set of brass knuckles.

Daniel remained silent, his eyes little more than slits as the Frenchman walked toward him. He struck Daniel on his left side, a dull crack echoing in the small cell. Daniel doubled over, blinded by pain, and then his sight went completely as he faded into the God-given gift of unconsciousness.

Thirty-seven

Seamus McCurren stood on the docks with his arms crossed over his chest as he impatiently watched the final preparations for the ship that would carry him to Honfleur.

He reached into his waistcoat and pulled out a sterling silver watch and was glancing down to ascertain the hour when he heard "You bloody blackguard" from behind him.

"Morning, St. John." Seamus sighed and then turned to greet the man he was hoping to avoid.

"Don't fob me off, McCurren." Christian pointed at Seamus's chest, his eyes ablaze with consternation. "You intended to leave me here, didn't you?"

"Aye." Seamus nodded, seeing no reason to deny what was clearly irrefutable.

"Why?" Christian slammed his trunk to the ground. "Did you think me incapable?" Seamus opened his mouth to speak, but Christian was not finished with his rant. "Do you believe me 'the irresponsible spare' as does the majority of the *ton*?"

That gave Seamus pause. " 'The irresponsible spare'? What on earth are you talking about, St. John?"

"Don't you read?" Christian inquired of a man reputed to be a scholar of ancient literature. "I read the asinine designation in the *Gazette* last week. But I can hardly be blamed for Lady Graves pawing me throughout the entire opera, can I?"

Seamus laughed. "I thought that was the point of your taking Lady Graves to the opera."

"Yes," Christian said as if Seamus were a complete idiot, "to have the lady paw me *after* the opera." Seamus could not help laughing. "I thought Ian was going to kill me. My brother sat with Lady Appleton at the front of our box and glared at me throughout the entire production. You know how the marquis is when he is irritated."

"Aye. However, in this instance, I believe your brother had good reason to glare."

"Right. Where were we? Oh, yes." Christian's fair head popped up and he looked Seamus in the eye. "You bloody Scots bastard! You were going to leave me while you ran off to Paris alone."

"Aye."

"Why!"

Seamus looked at the angry Lord St. John, but he could see the hurt in Christian's light eyes. "I do not want you to get killed, Christian."

The tension drained from Lord St. John's shoulders and he smiled brightly, saying, "Oh, well, if that's all it was then, when do we leave?"

"When she's ready." Seamus pointed to their ship as a man with a gruesome scar across his cheek boarded her. "A half-hour, perhaps less."

"Excellent. Shall we pop round to an inn and have a pint before—"

Seamus grabbed Christian by the sleeve and pulled him toward the dock as a carriage rumbled past them. They looked at each other when the horses were pulled to an abrupt halt not ten feet from where they stood.

"Mister McCurren?" the driver asked reverently.

"Aye." Seamus stared warily at the coachman.

"My employer wishes a word." His eyes darted to the carriage and Seamus glanced at St. John.

"I'll go with you," Christian said, not asking.

A footman held the door open and Seamus peered into the dim conveyance.

"Do join me, Mister McCurren." The familiar voice of Falcon pierced the noise of the busy docks. "Ah, St. John. You as well."

The two men climbed into the conveyance and Seamus glanced at the footmen who were busily gathering their trunks and placing them on the back of Falcon's carriage.

"What has happened?" Seamus asked as he took a seat opposite the older man.

"We have had a second communiqué." Christian settled in next to Seamus and the door was closed, leaving a silence that twisted at Seamus's heart.

"Is he dead?"

"No, no, no. I'm sorry to have given that impression, Mister McCurren." Falcon tapped on the roof, and the carriage rolled away from the docks and the mission Seamus had set for himself. "My apologies."

"The letter?" Seamus asked impatiently.

"We have just received a communiqué from Paris. Scorpion is going after your brother."

Seamus stared at the black squabs, searching his mind for distant pieces of information. "Scorpion is the assassin my brother was sent to warn?"

"Yes."

"Is he capable—"

"Scorpion has successfully assassinated ten prominent members of the French government. There is no one more capable. If Scorpion cannot extract Viscount DunDonell, no one can, including you and Lord St. John."

Seamus met Falcon's brandy-colored eyes, not sure how to feel. "But I—"

"You have no chance in Paris, my boy. Scorpion does,"

Falcon said. "I will not lie to you. It is a slim chance at best that they will survive."

"But there is a chance?" Seamus could feel the hope swelling in his chest.

"Yes, ten dead men can attest to Scorpion's ingenuity."

"What do we do now?" Seamus asked, glancing at Christian St. John.

"Wait, Mister McCurren. You go home and wait, as the mission is already under way." Seamus closed his eyes and prayed for Scorpion to have the strength to bring his brother home. Falcon interrupted his appeal, promising, "I'll notify you the moment we receive word."

One way or the other. The words echoed in his head. *One way or the other*.

Thirty-eight

The dirty walls of the notorious prison were no match for the filthy scene she was about to witness.

Men and women from all over France had been gathered, for various reasons, behind the thick stones of the prison, their compliance demanded by the steel fist of France.

It was here that Daniel McCurren had been brought and here that Nicole would rescue him.

Or die in the attempt.

Nicole looked up at the dark stones, snow gathering on her lashes as she counted eight soldiers walking along the ramparts of the prison. Nicole glanced at the River Seine to her right and the Cour du Mai to her left, where the main gates of the Palais de Justice could plainly be seen.

A sudden gust blew flakes of snow onto her face, but it was the stench that accompanied the snow that caused Nicole to raise a glove to her cold nose. She lowered her head, inhaling the lavender-scented lining as she made for the front entrance to the famed prison.

"Good evening," Nicole said to the startled sentry. "My name is Madame Damont and I wish to speak with the commanding officer of the Conciergerie."

"I am sorry, *madame,* but the colonel is not here at the moment." The young man looked at her elegance in confusion. "It is three o'clock in the morning," he said as if Nicole were somehow unaware of the time.

"I am very aware of the hour," Nicole said with considerable irritation. "However, it is not often that my husband is taken to the Conciergerie for questioning, so please pardon the inconvenience. Now, open the door and take me to the man in charge or my father will hear of the treatment I have received here." The boy paused at the vague threat and Nicole added. "What is your name?"

"Right this way, *madame.*" The guard opened the small door cut to the right of the larger gate and pointed toward the main steps at the back of the cobblestone courtyard. "You may inquire with the sergeant on duty as to the status of your husband."

"Merci," Nicole said, already walking away.

She crossed the small enclosure unmolested, the cold keeping the soldiers huddled in the warmer corners against the oppressive prison walls. Nicole smiled to herself, adding human discomfort to the complex equation of their improbable escape.

Yanking the door wide, she swept into the tiny room the guard had indicated as if she were the empress herself.

"Who is in charge here?" Nicole demanded, lifting her chin.

The besieged sergeant ceased chewing his baguette and wiped the crumbs from his full mouth, saying, "Might I be of assistance, *mademoiselle*?"

"Madame Damont," Nicole corrected, looking down her nose. "And I very much doubt that you can. I have just arrived home from an extended trip abroad only to find my husband has been dragged to the Conciergerie for I know not what reason."

"Monsieur Damont, you say?"

"Oui." Her eyebrows pulled together with contempt. "Have you no idea whom you have taken into custody? My father, the count, will hear of this incompetence."

"Perhaps if you were to describe Monsieur Damont, I would be better able to locate him?" The beleaguered sergeant's helpfulness was no doubt an attempt to avoid political retributions.

"Tall, auburn hair. My husband is a very large man, and I find it difficult to believe that you have misplaced him."

The man's brown eyes widened, and Nicole could see from his shocked features that he had indeed seen Daniel.

"That man is your husband?" the sergeant asked with a note of fear that sent a chill down her spine.

"He is here, then?" Nicole held her breath, her heart racing.

"Oui." The sergeant sputtered and she could breathe.

"Take me to him, if you please."

"I'm afraid—"

"Now."

"I shall inform the men responsible for your husband that you have arrived, *madame*. If you would be so kind as to follow me?" The sergeant bowed, leading her into the belly of the beast.

Nicole paid careful attention to the way in which they walked, meandering through the endless halls of administration and finally descending to the dimly lit cells beneath.

She pushed out of her mind the desperate cries of prisoners beyond her help. She had to focus, had to concentrate all of her thoughts and energy on the mission at hand, freeing Daniel.

He was all that mattered now.

Nicole had long ago given up all hope for herself, but Daniel McCurren was worth saving. The viscount would lead a noble life of honor and dignity. Fighting for those he could help and offering compassion to those he could not. He would remember her, she was sure, and perhaps that memory would prompt him to introduce legislation to protect the vulnerable of British society.

But much like the ill-fated prisoners of the Conciergerie, Nicole was already far beyond saving.

Daniel stared through the rounded cell bars, wondering how much punishment his body could take before he simply died. Unfortunately for him, Major Rousseau appeared to have the same morbid curiosity.

"Place this in the fire," the major said, handing the young soldier one of the few clean blades before turning toward him. "I believe we were discussing Whitehall?"

"You were discussing Whitehall," Daniel said in English, his brogue slurred, his loss of blood causing him to drift in and out of awareness.

The major hit him in the gut, awakening both Daniel and his cracked ribs.

"Whitehall?" Major Rousseau stared down at him, and Daniel could see in his black eyes that the major was losing patience.

"Quite an impressive street, Whitehall. Very wide, very pretty in the spr—"

Daniel was struck this time across the left cheek, but he no longer felt the blows.

"I want the names of the men who sent you."

"I'm certain that you do." Daniel breathed, very near delirium. "But I'll not be giving you any names."

"You British are so smug," the little man said in heavily accented English. "So sure of yourselves that—"

A knock at the door drew Major Rousseau's attention and his anger.

"*Pardon,* Major Rousseau. Captain Turgeon has just arrived."

"Send him in."

The fair-haired captain he had seen at the theater came into view, looking at the major when he said, "Major Rousseau, the woman has awakened and is ready to be questioned." Daniel closed his eyes in relief. "But as far as I can detect, Mademoiselle Beauvoire knows noth"—the captain glanced at Daniel—"ing. Why have you arrested Daniel Damont?"

"Daniel Damont?" Major Rousseau stared at the captain, shaking his head. "No, this is the assassin, Scorpion."

The captain smiled, amused as he stared through the bars at Daniel. "Well, the man may very well be Scorpion, but he is also the gentleman Minister LeCoeur had under observation. Monsieur Daniel Damont."

The major went rigid, the knuckles of his clenched fists turning white. "Go to Tuileries Palace and bring that lying bitch to me."

Daniel's heart stopped, knowing there was nothing more he could do to protect her.

Captain Turgeon clicked his heels and bowed before leaving Daniel alone with the man who would kill him . . . and then Nicole.

"Daniel Damont? I have heard much about you from the minister. He would be pleased to know that you were executed." The major grinned. "And that you died so painfully."

A second knock sounded and the sergeant appeared before Major Rousseau.

"What now?"

"A lady has just arrived claiming to be this man's wife."

Daniel's head jerked up, his eyes widened by fear. Major Rousseau noted his distress, his lip curling with anticipation as the man looked into his eyes, saying, "Search this woman and then bring her to me."

The guard left and Daniel tried to appear unconcerned as his mind focused on the muffled proceedings in the other room.

"Is your wife as beautiful as Mademoiselle Beauvoire?" The Frenchman's ominous inquiry sent a jolt of fear through Daniel, tightening his stomach. "I most sincerely do hope so."

"I don't have a wife," Daniel said, adopting an air of indifference.

"Intriguing, then, that a woman would claim to be your bride, *monsieur.*" Rousseau leaned forward, whispering for effect, "Why would a woman claim to be the wife of a man so precariously close to being executed?"

"I have no idea." Daniel shrugged as if bored by the entire affair but the malicious man was not deceived.

"Then let us ask the lady, shall we?"

Major Rousseau rose, walking through the cell door and into the corridor separating the three small cells from the cold stone wall. Daniel turned his head, waiting and praying that it would not be Nicole. He could feel his blood rushing through him, pushed by panic as the guard searched the woman in the small office just out of his line of sight.

His ears strained, acutely aware of every brush of silk, every clank of metal, and then, finally the lady claiming to be his wife came into view.

Nicole.

Their eyes met and Daniel sank heavily against his restraints, despair shredding what remained of his heart. He had endured the hours, the days of torture at Major Rousseau's skillful hands because he knew that Nicole was safe. That she had once again deceived the very men she sought to destroy.

"Ah, Mademoiselle Beauvoire." Daniel glanced toward the anger he had learned, through painful experience, to detect in Major Rousseau's silken voice. The major stiffened, Rousseau's throbbing jaw confirming the dark man's darker rage. "Or should I address you as Madame Damont?"

"No," Daniel hastened to say, and the Frenchman turned his wrath on him. "I have no wife."

"Has this woman been searched?"

"*Oui.*"

"Wait outside," Major Rousseau ordered his guard as he continued to stare at Daniel with malevolence.

But Daniel ignored him, his eyes fixed on Nicole. She waited to hear the click of the door before lifting her delicate chin, saying, "I have come—"

"Hold your tongue, Mademoiselle Beauvoire." The major's black eyes and his fury trained on Nicole. "Or I shall make sure that you are unable to use it."

"I have never met this woman before tonight," Daniel said, his injured flesh prickling with fear.

"But of course you have, Monsieur Damont. Captain Turgeon has observed you living together in an apartment on Place Vendôme." The major yanked Nicole to him by roughly grasping her upper arm and shoving her toward the bars of the cell. "You hired Mademoiselle Beauvoire to seduce Minister LeCoeur so that you might then kill him. Do you not recall it?"

"No." Daniel shook his head, knowing that denying Nicole was her only hope of survival. "The lady might have been in the minister's bedchamber, but I had never seen her before this evening. Captain Turgeon is mistaken."

"Then the lady was merely Minister LeCoeur's whore?" Daniel glanced at Nicole's calm face, her violet eyes unreadable as the major continued, saying, "You were unconscious this morning, *ma chérie*." Major Rousseau then whispered in her right ear, loud enough for Daniel to hear, "It is so gratifying to see that you are now well enough to resume your duties."

The major's cold eyes met Daniel's and he smiled, grasping Nicole's breast from behind. Daniel flinched, his hands forming fists, his jaw setting.

"A pity you have never known this woman, never seen her before." Evariste Rousseau smirked, pressing his lips to Nicole's elegant neck, his eyes still locked on Daniel. "She tastes delicious. Shall we see how she looks?"

"Don't," Daniel shouted hoarsely, remembering the abuse she had suffered at the hands of her husband.

"Don't what?" The major smiled, sliding the sleeves of her pelisse from her arms. "Don't touch your woman?"

Daniel watched Nicole's lovely eyes close as Major Rousseau unfastened the tiny buttons at the back of her gown. The cobalt silk slithered to the floor and Nicole shivered, standing only in her corset and thin chemise.

"Mmm." Major Rousseau gazed at Nicole's body in lustful anticipation. "The woman is stunning, but Minister LeCoeur made a momentous mistake when dealing with Mademoiselle Beauvoire." He grasped Nicole's breast and placed his other hand on her hip, pulling Nicole's backside more firmly against him. "The minister treated her like a lady, when he should have been treating her like a whore. I will not make such a mistake."

"Don't touch her." Daniel used all of his weight to pull against his metal shackles, but Major Rousseau ignored him, slowly removing Nicole's corset until Daniel blurted out in desperation, "My name is Daniel McCurren, Viscount DunDonell, heir to the Earl of DunDonell. I assumed the identity of Scorpion two years ago and have performed ten assassinations of prominent French military leaders under orders from His Majesty, King George."

"Three days of torture and not a useful word." The callous man ripped Nicole's chemise. "But now . . ."

Major Rousseau's words trailed off as his mind took in the thick scars traversing Nicole's back. His eyes widened, impressed. "Is this the work of France, Mademoiselle Beauvoire?" Nicole refused to answer, forcing the man to speculate. "You aid this assassin for revenge, no?" The major carefully observed her pristine features.

"No." Nicole looked up, her eyes serene and clear.

"For love then?" The major chuckled, truly amused, and then leaned toward her, whispering as he met Daniel's eye, "The viscount will be dead soon."

"I think not."

Major Rousseau grinned, enjoying her defiance, and Daniel's blood ran cold. "Did you hope to buy his freedom, *ma petite*?" the Frenchman asked, running the backs of his fingers across her cheek. "Did you pray that I would not be here?"

"Yes." Nicole nodded, her gathering tears more damaging to Daniel's soul than anything Major Rousseau had inflicted upon his body.

"But I *am* here, *ma chérie*." The major stared at her.

"So offer me something in exchange for the viscount's freedom."

"Very well, I shall pay you—"

"No."

"Name your terms."

"I will have you, here and now, Mademoiselle Beauvoire. And there shall be no negotiations."

"Don't touch her," Daniel growled, yanking at the chains with all of his strength. The mounts loosened with a dusty scrape of metal on stone, but not enough to free him, not enough to save Nicole.

"This will torture you more than my knife, *Oui*?" The major kissed Nicole's neck leisurely, taunting Daniel with each caress. "Tell me, Viscount DunDonell, shall I have her against the wall so that you might see her face, or shall I have her against the bars so that I might see yours?"

Daniel closed his eyes, aiding the Frenchman in his decision.

"*Oui,* more difficult for you to witness her pain, I think."

The Frenchman shoved Nicole against the wall and Daniel saw her grimace at the painful impact with the uneven stones. Major Rousseau pulled down her gaping chemise, exposing her breasts to his lecherous eyes.

"You're a pretty little whore, and if you please me, I shall take you as my mistress." The man spoke so that Daniel would hear. "What do you think of that, Scorpion?"

"You should address yourself to mc," Nicole said, removing the comb from her beautiful black hair.

"Why would I bother asking you?" The major smirked.

"Because," she whispered in his ear, "I'm Scorpion."

Her hand swung downward and Daniel saw a flash of silver before Nicole plunged the makeshift dagger into the Frenchman's cold heart. His black eyes went wide and she twisted, eliciting a low groan before she pulled the knife from his side, aided by a rush of blood.

The major fell to his knees, irony twisting his lips.

"A woman after my own heart." Major Rousseau chuckled at his double entendre. "I wish I could live long enough to see you die. Guard!" the Frenchman shouted as best he could then fell to the floor, dead.

Daniel heard the squeak of the outer door and Nicole's head snapped up. She pulled up her chemise and hid the knife behind her back, blood still dripping over the diamond-studded hilt that had been fashioned into the shape of an ordinary hair comb.

Helpless, Daniel watched Nicole run toward the office door, her long black her flowing after her.

"Quickly," she begged, sounding hysterical. "He has killed the major."

Boots pounded in the stone corridor and the young guard came into sight. He looked at Major Rousseau's bloody corpse and then at Daniel still shackled in his prison cell.

His chestnut brows were pulled down in confusion and he turned to Nicole, saying, "I don't understand . . ."

But then he did, and his body went rigid the moment he was illuminated by the major's pistol in Nicole's left hand.

"One sound and I will kill you as I did him, *vous comprenez*?"

"*Oui.*" The guard nodded, his eyes darting to his dead superior.

"You will unlock the cell door and shackles, quickly and quietly." She cocked the pistol, adding, "If you move suddenly, I will not hesitate to kill you."

The young sergeant lifted his key ring and inserted the appropriate key in the lock. His hands were shaking, and Daniel could see the fear in his eyes as the sergeant twisted the key to the right and the lock gave with a welcome click.

"Excellent, now all you need do is unchain Monsieur Damont and then we will leave you alive and well in this very cell," Nicole said softly, soothingly, sensing the guard's panic as he swung the door open into the cell. "Do you understand what I wish you to do?"

"*Oui,*" the sergeant said, lifting a smaller key.

"I will gag you." Nicole bent over and began untying Major Rousseau's silk cravat with one hand, while holding the pistol in the other. "And we will place you in the shackles so that you will not be blamed for anything that has taken place here."

Nicole spoke as if they were allies. The sergeant lifted the key but hesitated, and Daniel could see that the man was weighing his options.

Nicole saw it, too, and she responded by rising and looking the young guard in the eye. "Do you know of Major Rousseau's reputation?"

The sergeant nodded, unsure of where she was going with her inquiry. *"Oui."*

"I just killed him. I stabbed him in the heart with a knife. Do you sincerely believe you have any chance against me with a pistol? Do you really think that threatening your prisoner will somehow save you? If you harm Monsieur Damont, I will kill you. If you don't comply, I will kill you. My goal is his release." Nicole shook her head. "There is no need for you to die."

She bent down again and finished gathering the cravat from the major's neck. "I will gag you and shackle you so that you will not be blamed. You may even tell the soldiers who discover you that Major Rousseau was killed after you were placed in the cell," Nicole plotted, allies again. "Now, release the prisoner."

The sergeant followed her logic, seeing that he had no choice and that compliance gave him a better chance of survival. The man unlocked one of Daniel's wrists and then the other.

Daniel fell to the floor, his arms long since useless. The impact with the floor was excruciating and he rolled on his right elbow, ignoring the shiny smudges of his blood left by the wounds on his back.

"Good," Nicole said, disregarding Daniel and focusing totally on the young guard. "Now lock yourself in the shackles."

The man complied, and once he was finished, Nicole gently stuffed the cravat in his mouth, taking his keys and asking, "Can you breathe?"

The guard nodded. Nicole tossed the keys into the hall and reached for her clothes.

"Aren't we going to need those keys, lass?"

Nicole wiggled into her gown, buttoning herself as best as she could. "We've no time to sort through keys. Do you have a jacket?"

"No," Daniel said, his fingers being pricked by pins and needles.

"Right. You will just have to concentrate on not bleeding." She bent down and Daniel draped his arm over her shoulder while Nicole slid her hand around his waist. "On your feet, McCurren."

Daniel staggered to his feet, wondering if his euphoria was the beginning of his own demise. "Get me the hell out of here, Nicole."

They stumbled to the small office and Nicole turned him, ordering, "Sit on the desk."

She slipped from beneath his arm and Daniel watched her through his heavy pants of exertion as Nicole slid on her pelisse, placing her clever knife in one pocket and concealing Major Rousseau's pistol in the other.

"I like your knife." Daniel grinned, more to himself than to her.

"I rather thought you would. Now be quiet." Nicole opened the door and glanced down the hall. "Come on," she said, dipping beneath his arm once again and pulling him to his clumsy feet.

They stepped into the hall and Nicole turned to the right as if she knew which direction they were headed. Daniel followed, his mind dimming as he stumbled forward.

Her hand tightened on his waist and she pulled him against her, saying, "You must stay awake, Daniel. Can you do that, darling?"

Daniel heard fear in her voice for the first time, but it was not for herself, but for him.

"Aye," he said, hoping it was true.

They walked for several minutes down the dark corridors, which seemed never to end. His breathing was becoming increasingly labored, and then they heard the shouts. Soldiers scrambled in the distant corner of his mind and Daniel stopped.

"They're coming, lass. Go on."

Nicole looked him in the eye and said with finality, "I'm not leaving you, Daniel," giving him no room for argument. "This way."

She turned to the right, pulling him down a small corridor, which ended abruptly at three ancient wooden doors. Nicole reached into her pocket and pulled out her brass ring of picks and ordered, "You must not bleed on anything, Daniel," as she slipped from beneath him to unlock the middle door.

"Right." Daniel licked his lips, swaying unsteadily as he wondered how one went about not bleeding.

"And don't fall," Nicole whispered. And just as they heard the soldiers turning in their direction, the door opened.

Unfortunately, the center door opened into a small storage cupboard with shelving that made it impossible for one to hide.

"They're getting closer, Nicole," Daniel said, truly alarmed and wondering how he could protect her. He turned to face the multitude of oncoming guards and opened his heart, saying, "I love you, lass."

Nicole yanked on his arm, and then a door was closing. He stumbled and Daniel could feel something pressing him to the wall before the dark room dimmed completely and he slipped into unconsciousness.

Thirty-nine

❧❦❧

Nicole could see that he had lost awareness, but her only concern now was lowering him quietly to the floor. She pressed harder against his bare chest, bracing her legs as she eased his immense weight down the wall. His backside landed with a soft thud and Nicole steadied him, trying not to remember that the cold wetness on her hands was Daniel's blood.

She heard two soldiers enter their tiny hall, and her head snapped round to the unlocked door. Frantically, Nicole let go of the injured viscount and turned the brass lock just as a soldier opened what she thought to be the closet door.

Daniel began to slide to the left, leaving streaks of blood on the white plastered walls. She reached out, catching him just before his head hit the stone floor. The doorknob rattled and Nicole held her breath, her heart pounding as she watched the handle twisting to its right.

"The other doors are locked," she heard one of the soldiers say, and then Nicole heard them running down the hall.

She breathed deeply her relief and then she looked at Daniel, tears filling her eyes. She reached with a shaky hand to touch his tortured body to assure herself that Daniel was still breathing, still alive.

"I'm so sorry," she said, knowing it was her fault, knowing that he had endured so much pain to protect her, a woman not even worthy of his notice, much less his love. "I'm so sorry, Daniel."

Nicole removed her pelisse and pressed it to the oozing wounds, comforting herself in the knowledge that he could not feel the sting. Her brows narrowed as she tended his injured arm, making out the letters E and R. Her jaw set, and Nicole would have happily killed Evariste Rousseau again.

But for now, her primary concern was getting Daniel warm and getting him medical attention as soon as was possible. She wrapped him in her pelisse as best she could and then searched the small office for any items that would be of use to her.

The desk was stocked with parchment, matches, ink and blotter, cheroots, quills, sealing wax, and two bottles of gin. Nicole stuffed several of the items in her pocket and retrieved her knife, cutting two stripes of muslin from the bottom of her underskirt.

She lit a cheroot with a match and drew the aromatic smoke into her mouth, quietly coughing as she placed it on the desk with the lit end hanging off the battered edge.

"Daniel," she whispered, not willing to contemplate the possibility that he was dying. "Daniel." His eyes flickered, so Nicole continued to speak to him. "Daniel, darling, we must get out of here. Our transportation is waiting with a warm blanket just outside. Do you think you can stand, *mon amour*?"

He nodded slightly, his eyes still closed, and Nicole swallowed her relief.

"We'll stand together, and you will lean on me. It is not far. Daniel," she said firmly. "Stand up. Daniel!"

He responded to her command, rolling over and pushing himself from the floor with his large hands. Nicole slipped beneath him, lifting him the rest of the way, knowing that if she could just get him moving, they did not have far to go.

She unlocked the door and stretched for the lit cheroot sitting atop the desk, making sure not to burn him as they staggered into the empty corridor. Drops of blood fell steadily from his fingertips dangling over her shoulder, but Nicole ignored the trail that would direct the guards to their location.

"Daniel, I need you to hold this." Nicole placed the cheroot in his right hand and he glanced down at it.

She could see confusion in his turquoise eyes, but ever the gentleman, Daniel took it, saying, "Thank you," and then placed it between his swollen lips.

Nicole lowered her head and continued on the route she had meticulously planned, leading them deeper into the ancient depths of the Conciergerie. But the guards were getting closer and Daniel was resting more heavily against her shoulders.

Something had to be done.

Nicole stopped and leaned Daniel against the wall as she thought. "Stay here, darling," she whispered, reaching into her pocket for a bottle of gin.

She uncorked the bottle and stuffed a portion of a muslin strip into the clear liquid. When she had finished, Nicole reached up and took the cheroot from Daniel's mouth and kissed him on the lips, saying, "I'll return in just a moment, darling."

Nicole ran toward a storage room she had seen down one of the main corridors. She was panting now, reversing her mental map of the prison in her mind.

She reached the storage area, which was merely a darkened corner with sacks and barrels of supplies stacked one upon the other. Rushes had been tossed around the room to absorb any of the liquids that might leak during transportation.

Nicole fell to her knees, shoving the straw to the base of the wooden barrels, but she froze when she heard a solitary soldier round the corner and run into the supply area. She ducked behind a barrel and removed her knife from her pocket as the guard stopped, scanning the corridors as he searched for the escaped prisoner.

The lone guard disappeared around the far corner and Nicole breathed, rising. She hurried a safe distance down the hall and removed the gin bottle from the folds of her expensive gown. The glowing tip of the cheroot was hovering in her right hand when the solitary soldier returned.

Startled, the guard looked her in the eye as he stood at the other end of the wide corridor.

"Don't!" He held up his hand, terrified as he realized her intentions. "The barrels contain gunpowder."

"Then you had better run," Nicole said, lighting the muslin strip and tossing the bottle of gin into the volatile storage area.

The soldier's eyes grew wide as the gin ignited, but Nicole was already running toward Daniel. Right, left, the corridors narrowed and she was almost there. Nicole rounded the last corner when the gunpowder exploded, throwing her against the wall. Dust and rubble rained down from the ancient ceiling of the forgotten corridors and she coughed, struggling to breathe.

Nicole looked up and could see Daniel lying on the floor. She had to get to him; they were mere yards from the small outer door that overlooked the River Seine. She reached into her pocket and staggered past Daniel with her picks in hand. The smoke billowing down the corridor was becoming thick, blinding, as she wrestled with the rusty lock.

She was crying, needing Daniel's strength to open the door. They were so close. Just on the other side of the door, a small boat was waiting to take Daniel to the ship that would carry him to Honfleur.

Desperate, Nicole lifted her foot and planted it to the right of the door. She pulled with both hands, leaning back with all of her strength, and the door gave with a gritty groan. She wiped her hands on the bodice of her gown and took a firmer grip, pulling again, and the door flew open.

Nicole fell backward and she was greeted by a blast of snow. She closed her eyes with relief and then stood, poking her head out the door to glance down the street. It was mercifully empty, but Nicole knew that they would need to cross quickly to the stairs leading down to the river.

"Daniel." She patted him on the cheek. "Get up!" His eyes opened at the sound of her harsh tone and he rose on shaky legs. "It is not far," Nicole said, stepping onto the street.

She could hear the sounds of confusion at the front of the famed prison as the stunned soldiers learned that they were vulnerable to attack. However, it was her trade, and had been for the past two years, to find vulnerability, to use the assumptions of the powerful men of France against them.

As she had tonight—but this time Nicole worked not for the Crown or her political convictions of right and wrong. Tonight, at the Conciergerie, she had used her acquired knowledge to save rather than to kill.

"We must be quick, *mon amour*," she whispered, starting across the street.

Nicole looked up and gave a prayer of thanks for the heavy snowfall that obscured them from view. The only thing to betray their location was their footprints, and a crimson trail of blood that was rapidly being covered by the purity of white snow.

They hurried across the street unseen and started down the stairs, but Daniel slipped on the icy steps. Nicole helped him up, her goal in sight. "See, dearest, the boat is just there," she said as she helped him to his feet.

They managed to get to the waiting dingy and the Dutch sailors helped them aboard.

"Go," Nicole ordered, settling Daniel against her as the men launched the boat into the Seine.

Nicole reached for a woolen blanket and covered Daniel, knowing that with each stroke of the oars he was that much closer to receiving the attention of the ship physician.

"Daniel," she said, her heart stopping when he did not answer. "Daniel!" Nicole touched his cheek, but he did not respond. "Please, hurry," she said, her words strangled.

The boat ride to the ship felt like an eternity, and Nicole was standing before the dingy had fully docked. She jumped out of the vessel barking orders.

"Retrieve the physician and several blankets. Handle him with care. The poor man has been robbed," she lied.

Two men lifted Daniel's long body and a third came down to help with his bulk as the others were heading up the gangplank. Nicole followed anxiously, knowing that a cabin had been prepared for Monsieur Damont's impending arrival.

A cabin boy opened the small door and the sailors gently placed Daniel's motionless body atop the wooden bunk. The men left and the physician squeezed past the last of them, placing a bag atop the small table that had been secured to the wall.

The doctor, a lanky Dutchman, fair in coloring and clear of mind, looked at Nicole skeptically and said, "I was told that this man had been ambushed."

"*Oui,*" Nicole said evenly, both of them knowing that Daniel's injuries could not have been acquired in one isolated attack.

"Are there similar wounds on his back?"

"*Oui.*" She nodded once.

The man rubbed his hand over his face and said in choppy French, "He is very bad. These wounds are old but have been treated with—"

"Salt," Daniel interrupted, his voice raspy.

Nicole turned to the table and retrieved a glass of water, ignoring the physician's pale color and the tears welling in her own eyes.

"Here, my darling," she whispered, sitting on the side of the bed and lifting the water to Daniel's parched lips.

"First, we must bandage his injuries." The physician looked over Daniel's body in a cursory examination. "The fresh wounds I will sew with very little scarring. But these . . ." He pointed to the older of Daniel's incisions. "The salt." The Dutchman closed his eyes. "The salt will help to prevent festering, but I have never seen wounds such as these."

"What are his chances of survival?" Nicole held her breath, her heart on her sleeve.

"The poisoning of his blood is of greatest concern, but he is alert. If we see to him straight away, I think he will live."

Nicole covered her face and wept openly, crying harder when she felt Daniel's hand on her back.

"It's all right, lass. I shall be fine."

Daniel's voice was weak, reminding her that he needed to be treated. Nicole tilted her head to the left and removed her diamond and sapphire ear bobs, pressing them into the physician's hand.

"Anything you need." She held the man's gaze, unable to say more.

"I'll do my best, *mademoiselle*."

The physician's kind eyes comforted Nicole, and she took a breath to gather her strength so that she could leave Daniel in his capable hands. She leaned down and kissed him for the last time, whispering, "I love you, Daniel McCurren." Then she turned and walked out of the cabin door.

"Wait, Nicole!" She heard Daniel shouting, breaking her heart. "Where are you—"

"You must remain still, Monsieur McCurren," the physician said firmly. Then Nicole heard a tremendous thud, causing her to run back to the cabin. She saw Daniel leaning against the wall, his face white, his breathing shallow.

"Daniel, you must get back in bed, dearest," Nicole coaxed in English.

She helped him to the bunk and Daniel lay down saying, "Where were you going, Nicole?"

"To speak with the captain."

"Do not lie to me, lass." He blinked, licking his lips in preparation to speak. "If you leave this room, I'll not let this man touch me."

"Go home, Daniel," Nicole begged, her eyes filled with tears as she stared into his turquoise depths.

"Not without you, lass."

The captain stepped into the cabin and looked at Nicole, saying, "We are ready to set sail, Mademoiselle Beauvoire. The dingy is waiting to take you ashore."

The viscount sat up in bed and the physician put his hand on Daniel's shoulder to stop him from moving further. "This agitation is not advisable, Monsieur McCurren."

"I'm not leaving Paris." Nicole could hear the pain, the resolve, in Daniel's voice as he met her eyes. "Not without you, lass."

So Nicole made her choice. His life for hers.

"I shall be sailing with you to London," Nicole said to the sea captain as she reached into the pocket of her pelisse and pulled out her bejeweled dagger. "Please accept this as payment for my passage. You may depart immediately."

The captain's eyes widened, whether from the blood-stained blade or the magnificent jewels, Nicole had not an inkling. He reached out, accepting the costly instrument of assassination. And as the weight of the blade lifted from her hand, so, too, did its burden.

At peace, Nicole smiled down at Daniel, saying, "Please bandage his wounds."

Daniel relaxed against his pillow, holding tightly to her hand. "I'm just going to close my eyes, lass, so don't you let go of my hand."

Nicole caressed his forearm as the ship swayed into deeper waters.

"I'll not leave you, Daniel," she promised and felt his grip tighten as his beautiful eyes drifted closed.

Forty

Daniel awoke, his eyes opening as his empty hand clenched at the lack of warmth.

"Nicole!" he shouted, glancing down at his bandages, his breathing increased by alarm.

The physician entered the cabin and held up his hand. "Calm yourself, Monsieur McCurren. Mademoiselle Beauvoire has been in this room for an entire day and merely needed a bit of fresh air."

Relieved, Daniel settled back on the tiny bed and turned to the physician, asking, "How far to Honfleur?"

The young doctor laughed, his blond brows rising as he leaned over Daniel to examine his wounds. "We are not sailing to Honfleur."

"What?" Daniel exhaled the question along with his surprise. "Where the bloody hell are we going?"

"London." The doctor rose, reaching for a pot of balm. "Mademoiselle Beauvoire paid a fortune to have the captain sail directly to London," the Dutchman said, rubbing a portion of the aromatic concoction across the deep wounds on Daniel's upper arm. "We should arrive sometime this evening."

"I'm going on deck." Daniel sat up in bed and the cabin began to spin, forcing him to lie back on his bunk.

"Do take care, Monsieur Damont. I bled you yesterday to stop a fever from taking hold." Daniel glanced at the bandage that covered the crook of his left arm. "You will need time to recover your strength."

"I'll be all right." Daniel tried again, slowly this time, but it was no good. He could feel his wounds pulling open as he strained against them. He stared at the blurry wick of a lit candle, panting as he said, "Perhaps—"

"I shall summon Mademoiselle Beauvoire."

The fair physician disappeared through his cabin door. Daniel listened as the man's steady footfall faded only to be replaced moments later by the lighter, infinitely more elegant footsteps of Mademoiselle Beauvoire.

"What on earth are you doing, Daniel?" he heard from the cabin door and turned his head, smiling at the woman who had saved him. "You must remain in bed."

Nicole swept black strands of hair from her beautiful face, and he could see the concern in her violet eyes, warming him more than a roaring fire on the most punishing of winter days.

"I'm fine, lass." Daniel held out his hand and smiled when she took it. "I just needed to speak with you."

Nicole sat on the small wooden chair that had been pulled to the side of his bed, and they stared at each other for a very long while before she lifted her head, saying, "We will arrive in London this evening."

"Aye." He nodded. "The physician informed me, and I cannot wait to sleep in my own bed."

"Promise me that you will sleep for an entire week when you arrive home, Daniel."

Her beautiful eyes were stern and he comforted her, saying, "Oh, getting me in bed is never the problem, lass." He winked. "It's getting us out of bed that will be the difficulty."

Nicole turned away from him, and his heart dropped

somewhere near the desolate pit of his stomach. "Daniel, when we return to London—"

"Why did you do it, lass?" he interrupted, unable to hear what she was about to say.

"Send you away?" Her delicate forehead pulled together, and she searched his eyes as if he were feverish. "You were in danger. You could have been killed, Daniel."

"No, that was not my meaning." He sighed. "Why did you . . ." He stared into her eyes and could not ask the question. "Never mind," he said, shaking his head, not willing to expose his heart further.

"Daniel." Wounded, he dragged his eyes to hers. "I sent you away because . . ." Tears filled her eyes. "The thought of your being killed, your being injured . . . I could not bear it." Daniel pulled her toward him so that he could feel her breath as she whispered, "I'm in love with you, Daniel McCur—"

His lips covered hers and he drank in the words, the elation of being loved by such a woman. His right hand speared into her beautiful hair and he desperately wanted to make love to her, but he was feeling light-headed, weak.

He sagged against his pillow, and Nicole gazed down, settling him in bed for an entirely different reason then he had intended.

"Sleep, Daniel." She pulled the woolen coverlet over him and he let her. "You will recover more quick—"

"Is that why you drank the poison?" He felt the fear of losing her again, the memory unbearable. "Because you thought that you had lost me?"

"Oh, Daniel. I love you so much." Nicole sat on the bed and rubbed her fingers over his cheek. "But honestly, darling, if I were inclined to take my own life, I would have done so years ago."

Daniel glanced up in surprise.

"I told you when we met that I was very good at my profession. I have spent hours with the apothecary discussing the potency of various poisons."

"Have you?" Daniel could not help smiling.

"Yes," she confessed. "We discussed, in great length, the dosage needed to kill a man and the dosage needed to make a person merely ill." Nicole shrugged. "I thought it highly unlikely that a woman herself poisoned would then be suspected of poisoning her victim."

"No, I suppose that is true—and very, very clever."

"It is not particularly clever, simply practical. People, men in particular, see what they wish to see."

"And women?" Daniel could not help asking, amused.

"Women see what needs to be done."

"And that is why you killed your husband?"

"Yes." Nicole stilled, laying her head against his chest, and Daniel rolled on his side to make room for her on the narrow bunk. "I didn't want to kill him, but it was him—"

"Or you." Daniel stroked her forehead, hoping someday that she would be able to forgive herself. "Like the highwaymen that attacked me."

"Yes, just like them." Nicole sat up and looked him in the eye. "But, Daniel, the men that I was ordered to kill . . . They were horrible men."

"Aye, they were."

"And even though I did not want to kill them, I am still unsure if I truly believe it was wrong." Her violet eyes begged him to understand.

"I don't know either, Nicole," he said in all honesty.

Tears spilled in rapid succession over her black lashes, and Daniel kissed her forehead, pulling to his injured chest the woman who was far more wounded than he.

Seamus McCurren reclined in his sitting room sipping coffee, unable to countenance food until he received word of his brother's fate.

His mistress embraced him from behind, delving her hand between the lapels of his burgundy silk dressing gown to his nude body beneath. She caressed his chest, pressing her bare breasts against his back.

"Are you all right?" she whispered in his ear, the question ridiculous.

His brother was either being held in a French prison, having God only knew what being done to him, or he was dead. How on earth could he possibly be all right?

"Yes."

"Good." She kissed him on the cheek, Daniel's fate obviously dismissed from her paltry mind.

Irritated, he pulled her hand from his chest, kissing her inner wrist before releasing her. Seamus leaned forward and reached for the *Gazette,* pretending to read with great interest so that he would not have to talk about his brother.

Seamus had always thought that he would know if something were to befall one of his brothers. When they were children, he had always known. It was the reason his father had blamed him, in part, for what had happened to Daniel.

If he had seen his brother more often, perhaps Seamus would have sensed the inevitable danger of this mission. Perhaps he could have talked Daniel out of going to Paris altogether.

But he had not. He had not talked him out of going, had not known the extent of his brother's drinking, and he had not been available to the Foreign Office to receive this assignment.

It should have been him in Paris.

"Seamus?" He looked up at his mistress, now in her own dressing gown as she sat on the settee opposite him. "I know you don't wish to discuss . . ." She met his eyes meaningfully, brushing her fair hair from her forehead. "What might . . . transpire."

Seamus went numb and he stared at the woman who had been his lover for the past nine months.

"Yes."

"But if something were to happen to Viscount Dun-Donell." He stared at the woman whose company he had chosen over that of his family. "If the viscount were never to . . . return?" Guilt overwhelmed him. "How long a period of time would you be required to wait before assuming, unfortunately, of course, the title?"

His jaw was dropped by the ambition sparkling in her speculative eyes.

The lady was a widow, respectable by the standards of the *ton,* had been his lover for quite some time. It was only natural that she would harbor hopes of marriage—marriage to the future Earl of DunDonell, if Daniel, his brother, did not survive his ordeal.

"We're finished," Seamus said coolly, fighting to suppress his rage.

"What?" His paramour laughed uncomfortably.

"You heard me." Seamus held her eyes. "Gather your clothes and get out of my house. We're finished."

"Seamus?" He rose, turning his back on his mistress as he walked to the velvet bell pull. "You're distraught. The viscount's disappearance will eventually have to be dealt with. Do not unleash your frustration on me, when you know that I am correct."

"I will deal with my brother's death, if and *when* it happens." Seamus gathered her garments and dumped them into her reluctant arms. "But rest assured, Fiona, you will not be there to scoop up your winnings."

"Seamus!" He guided her toward his bedchamber door. "You are being preposterous. You're overreacting, darling," she purred.

"Am I?" Seamus asked, herding her into the corridor and slamming the door in her exquisite face. "I don't think so."

His callous lover knocked on the door and Seamus stopped, rolling his eyes as he turned to open it.

"I'll not . . ." Seamus began but his eyes narrowed in confusion as he stared at his butler. "Yes."

"The Duke of Glenbroke is waiting in your study, my lord."

Seamus stood, paralyzed by trepidation.

"Thank you," he managed. "And I would very much appreciate if you would assist me in dressing?" Seamus asked rather than ordered as he walked hurriedly to his wardrobe, both of them understanding the importance of the duke's early-morning call.

"Yes, my lord," his man said, eager to be of assistance.

Seamus opened his study door eight minutes later and saw the enormous back of the Duke of Glenbroke as the man warmed himself in front of the fire, which had yet to expel the autumn chill from the room.

"Glenbroke?" Seamus said, wanting to see the duke's face, wanting to see the fate of his brother in the man's features, in the man's eyes. "You have news of the viscount?"

"Yes." The duke turned and they were both standing before the fire when Glenbroke smiled, saying, "Daniel has just been taken to your parents' home."

Thank God.

Seamus turned and placed both palms on the mantle, allowing the mahogany wood to support his sagging weight. His eyes saw through the dancing flames as he stared at the huge fire blazing beneath him.

"Is Daniel all right?"

"He is injured." The Duke of Glenbroke smiled again. "But he will survive."

Clutching at the carved mantle, Seamus closed his eyes in an attempt to absorb the relief, which came in waves that seemed to do nothing more than constrict his throat.

When the lengthy silence became uncomfortable, Gilbert de Clare, Duke of Glenbroke, gathered his hat and greatcoat. "Falcon is with him now, but when he has concluded his inquiries, you may see your brother if you wish."

"Of course I want to see Daniel. The bloody bastard." Seamus laughed with relief. "I had every matchmaking mama in London sizing me up for a wedding suit." The duke laughed. "Bloody inconvenient. Their matrimonial ambitions got right in the way of my research."

They smiled, neither one believing a word of his irritation.

"Sounds bloody awful." The duke's silver eyes held his, and they both knew Gilbert's true meaning.

"Aye," Seamus said, swallowing the enormous lump in his throat. "It was, bloody awful."

Forty-one

❧

Mademoiselle Nicole Beauvoire, as she had come to think of herself, sat in the Earl of DunDonell's second-floor drawing room sipping tea and waiting.

What she waited for, she was not sure. But she waited nonetheless, longing to be at Daniel's side, and going over in her mind the inevitable questions that would be posed by the Earl and Countess of DunDonell.

The difficulty was in the answering, in looking the earl and countess in the eye and telling them that she was the reason for Daniel's decision to go to Paris, that she was the cause of their son's pain.

It would be unpleasant, she knew, but Nicole would be forever grateful that she was explaining to his parents how Daniel had come to be injured rather than explaining how he had come to be dead.

Nicole continued to sip her tea, content that she had been able to save the man she so desperately loved, that she was able to give this noble man a chance at a happy life before she would pay for her many sins.

But the thought of her execution was no longer frightening to her. For so very long her existence had seemed utterly pointless, utterly selfish. Nicole had become an assassin to save her own life, justifying the murders of corrupt men in the name of their countless victims. People she had never met and people she would never know.

But perhaps she was wrong.

Perhaps the past three years of her life, the abuse inflicted by her husband, her year in prison, the numerous assassinations—perhaps all of these events had occurred so that she would be prepared, both mentally and physically, for that one moment, that one night where all of her skills had been used to save one deserving man.

Daniel.

Nicole leaned forward and placed her empty teacup on the mahogany table in front of her then reached down for her reticule so that she might retrieve a handkerchief from her purse.

"Mademoiselle Beauvoire?" she heard in melodious French, causing her heart to stop beating.

"Oui." Nicole lifted her head and turned to Countess of DunDonell and simply stared. Nicole blinked away the tears that were forming in her eyes when she saw the woman who had been so kind to her so long ago. "I am Mademoiselle Beauvoire."

Nicole curtsied for both the countess and the earl, who stood like an immovable mountain over his wife's fatigued shoulder.

"The earl and I cannot express our appreciation for your having brought our son home to us." The countess smiled and the earl continued to stare, making Nicole decidedly uneasy. "We are told that the ship's physician did an excellent job in caring for the viscount, and that we have you to thank for his safe return."

"I merely booked passage for Viscount DunDonell," Nicole said, too ashamed to admit any further involvement. "His health should be credited entirely to the ship's physician."

The countess smiled pleasantly and a thunderous voice said, "We would very much like for you to stay for supper, Mademoiselle Beauvoire," from beneath a bushy brown beard.

"How kind of you to offer." Nicole looked up at the Earl of DunDonell and blinked, unable to hold the intensity of his hazel eyes. "However, I regret that I have a previous engagement at Whitehall that cannot be missed."

The fair countess looked up at her husband and asked, "The gentleman with Daniel is from Whitehall, is he not?"

"Aye." The earl nodded once.

"Perhaps," the countess said, smiling, "you would be able to speak with this gentleman and save yourself a trip across town?"

"I . . ." Nicole began, hardly able to explain to the Earl and Countess of DunDonell that she was going to Whitehall to turn herself in for the murder of her husband.

"I'll just take you to him, shall I?" The countess swept forward and guided Nicole toward the drawing room doors before she had a chance to protest.

Nicole followed politely, eager to see Daniel before she was escorted back to Newgate, eager to see with her own eyes his convalescence. Every step down the elegantly decorated corridors of the Earl of DunDonell's home confirmed her belief that Daniel was destined for more than she could provide. The viscount had been raised to marry a lady of prominence, a woman with an impeccable reputation and a perfect pedigree—not an ex-assassin with a scandalous first marriage and an even uglier future.

"Here we are." The countess opened the door, sweeping in. Nicole searched the bedchamber for Daniel, verifying that he was well as he sat in the enormous canopy bed.

"Viscount DunDonell." She curtsied to show her respect. Then Nicole turned to greet the man from Whitehall and was stunned to meet the old man's eye. "Good afternoon . . . my lord."

"Mademoiselle Beauvoire," Falcon said. "It has been so very long since last we met."

Nicole's chin quivered, but she held it with considerable effort. "Yes, it has been a very long time. Two years, if I recall correctly."

"Yes, two years." Falcon nodded.

They stared at one another, but Nicole refused to shed a tear or feel a moment of regret. "As you are a representative of the Foreign Office, I believe it is my duty to inform you of my return—"

"I'm afraid, Mademoiselle Beauvoire, that I am not on duty this afternoon." The old man's brandy-colored eyes warmed, and he spoke to the room in general as he continued to convey his thoughts. "You see, I have come to the home of the Earl of DunDonell as a guest." He glanced at the earl. "A very close friend, if you will, of the McCurren family."

"Oh." Nicole turned to Daniel, tears blurring her vision.

"If you will excuse us, Mademoiselle Beauvoire," the earl said, walking out of the room with the countess and leaving Nicole in utter confusion.

Falcon waited, choosing his words with care. "When I commissioned the viscount to bring Scorpion home," he began, his ambiguity a force of habit, "I had hoped to send a pardon along with him."

Hoped. Her despair was crushing, even though she had never thought to be forgiven.

"Unfortunately, the members of the Foreign Office who approved of Scorpion's recruitment also pointed to the violence with which Lord Stratton was killed as well as the subsequent assassinations as proof of Scorpion's inability to reform."

Nicole swallowed her tears and nodded. "I understand, my lord, and I thank you so much for—"

"However, with the retrieval of Viscount DunDonell from the Conciergerie, Scorpion showed not only exceptional bravery, but the ability to value life, even at risk to Scorpion's own. This contradiction, combined with two years of service and appeals from both the Earl of Dun-Donell and the Duke of Glenbroke, forced the Foreign

Office to reevaluate Lady Stratton's sentence of death."

Nicole could not move, could not breathe as she stared at Falcon's amber eyes.

"The Foreign Office has since declared Lady Stratton to have been hanged two years ago and . . ." Falcon held up several documents. "Has provided official documentation of the arrival in London of the French noblewoman, Mademoiselle Nicole Beauvoire." Nicole stood in shock, so Falcon prodded her, saying, "They've pardoned you, Nicole."

Thank you.

"Thank you." Nicole ran to embrace him. "Thank you," she whispered.

The old man cleared his throat, uncomfortable with her gratitude. "It is I who am grateful, my dear. I have never been able to forgive myself for what you have been through these past two years, but it was the only way in which to save you."

Nicole's brows furrowed and she looked at Daniel, who was equally confused.

"In my position, I know . . . things, I investigate rumors." Falcon's eyes hardened. "I investigated the death of the first Lady Stratton and was unable to find evidence to prove Lord Stratton a murderer, and then he married a girl of eighteen who was brave enough to fight back. Your conviction made me quite angry."

"So you did something about it?" Nicole grinned. "And saved a young boy along with me?"

Falcon held her eyes and nodded. "Well, I have work to do." He paused at the door. "Welcome to England, Mademoiselle Beauvoire." The old man laughed, adding as he left, "Although I suspect that will not be your name for very long."

Daniel sat up as the door closed, wincing at the pain in his side.

"Come here, lass," he said, his turquoise eyes holding hers firmly as she sat on his bed.

Nicole leaned against him, giving in to her relief. Daniel stroked her hair, permitting her a moment to cry before she felt him turning away from her. Nicole sniffled as she lifted her head, only to find a large box sitting next to him.

"Nicole Beauvoire?"

"Yes." She swiped at her eyes, confused.

"Would you do me the honor of becoming my wife?"

Nicole's heart shattered and she reached out for perhaps the last time, caressing his cheek. "Daniel, you know I can't possibly—"

"Open it," he interrupted.

Nicole looked down at the rectangular box and lifted the lid. She stared for a moment and then reached out to touch the pearls that shimmered on the bodice of the most beautiful wedding gown that she had ever seen.

"Do you like it, lass?"

Her tears fell freely as she looked at the enchanting gown, noting that the bodice had been fashioned with a high collar to cover the horrible scars on her back.

"It's perfect," Nicole whispered, unable to say more.

"Excellent!" Daniel was grinning from ear to ear, pleased with himself. "We'll be married—"

"Daniel, you can't marry an assassin."

"Why not?" He stared. "No one need know who you are." Daniel shook his head, correcting himself. "Who you were."

"Your parents would know." She lifted her head to look at him. "You don't sincerely believe that the earl will approve of this union?"

"Is that all that troubles you, lass?" Daniel laughed as he stroked her cheek, lifting the gown as he said, "Who do you think gave me the wedding gown?"

Nicole's mouth fell open and Daniel laughed harder. "It was your mother's?"

"I've already spoken with my parents. The earl and countess remembered you as a child and have always thought . . ." Daniel shook his head. "It was not right, what happened to you, lass."

"No." Nicole laughed through her tears. "It was not

right," she mimicked his glorious brogue, but was unable to capture the rich tones of the man that spoke them.

"So, Mademoiselle Beauvoire." He winked. "Will you marry me?"

The question was asked with humor, but Nicole could see the anxiety in his stunning eyes. "*Oui,* Daniel McCurren," she teased in French. "I would be honored to be your lucky bride."

Daniel smiled then pulled her toward him for a searing kiss.

"It was my kiss, wasn't it?" he teased. "You could not resist my kiss."

"Yes, Daniel." Nicole rolled her eyes. "I married you because you kiss so well." Her fiancé nodded with a bit too much masculine pride, so Nicole lied. "'Tis your lovemaking that needs improving."

"Well, get to teaching, lass." Daniel flipped the counterpane down so that she might lie next to him, both of them knowing that he was too weak to make love.

Nicole lay in his arms, avoiding his injuries, saying, "How about we just lie here for the rest of the afternoon and 'snuggle'?"

Daniel laughed, wrapping his arms tightly around her so that she would not leave the instant he fell asleep.

"Very well, lass, I shall give in to your constant demands to snuggle, for after the wedding . . ." Her future husband grinned. "You'll be the most exhausted woman in all of Scotland."

Epilogue

The wedding banquet was everything Nicole had ever dreamed of, and she took a moment to appreciate every winter rose and every chord of music pulled in unison across the strings of the twenty-piece orchestra.

Nicole could not stop herself from smiling as she stood at the edge of the ballroom floor gawking at her stunningly handsome husband as he spun his mother about the room. Daniel caught her staring and winked like the rake that he was, and Nicole pretended to ignore him, sipping her champagne.

However, the moment the Austrian crystal touched her lips, she felt a tiny tug on the voluminous silk skirts of her elaborate wedding gown.

Nicole smiled as she looked down at an ebony-haired child with bright blue eyes.

"Hello, Jonathan." Nicole grinned as an elegant woman of middle years scooped him up so that they could speak eye to eye. "I was so pleased that you could come to my wedding. I don't think that I could have gotten married without you here."

"Because I holded the rings?"

The two women grinned at one another, and the baroness corrected, "Held the rings, darling."

"Held the rings."

"Exactly so."

"Oh," the cherub said, his little red lips forming an adorable circle.

"And because I was a friend of your mother's." The baroness stiffened and Nicole hastened to add, "Your mother is a very kind woman and I do so hope that we shall always be friends."

The baroness held Nicole's eyes, her chin quivering before she recovered, saying, "What do you think, shall we invite Lady DunDonell to visit us, Jonathan?" The boy nodded. "Now, give her the letter, darling."

The child held out his little arm. "Granpa gived this to you."

"Gave, darling."

"Gave."

"Thank you, Jonathan."

"Welcome." The child turned his dark head toward the banquet table. "Mummy, I want to eat more cake."

Nicole laughed, as did the boy's mother. "Well, you had better hurry, Jonathan. The McCurren clan is rather large."

"Congratulations, Lady DunDonell."

"Thank you." Nicole paused, meaningfully. "For everything."

The baroness squeezed her hand, nodding, and then went to claim a cake for her adorable son.

"He's a bonnie lad," Nicole heard as her husband joined her.

"Aye, Jonathan is quite a 'bonnie' lad."

"Are you mocking me, lass?" His turquoise eyes shone with feigned indignation. "I don't think it very kind to mock a man. Particularly the man you just married."

Nicole laughed and then turned her attention to the note in her hand.

"Who's that from, then?"

"The old man." Daniel scanned the room and she aided him, adding as she broke the seal to the correspondence, "He is in the corner speaking to Seamus."

> *Lady DunDonell,*
>   *I was so pleased to hear of your impending*
> *nuptials, and I wanted to offer my most sincere*
> *congratulations. I know now what you suffered and*
> *offer my deepest apologies for choosing to remain*
> *blind. There is no one more deserving of happiness*
> *than you, and it brings me great peace to know that*
> *you have found it.*
>
>   *Sincerely,*
>   *Lord Stratton*

Nicole was so shocked that she looked toward Falcon with tears in her eyes. The old man had been watching her and lifted his champagne glass in her direction.

"What's the matter?"

Nicole smiled at the concern in her husband's voice, and she turned toward Daniel, saying in all honesty as she looked into his beautiful eyes, "Nothing, darling. Everything is absolutely perfect."

Turn the page for a special preview of
Samantha Saxon's next novel

The Lady's Code

Coming soon from Berkley Sensation!

Seamus McCurren dragged himself into the Foreign Office at ten o'clock having never gone to bed.

He had spent the entire evening gaming at Dante's Inferno and in the end he had still come out losing. Not much blunt, but it was vexing nonetheless. He had wandered home at sunup to be shaved and to change his attire, but his external appearance was merely a palatable façade covering deep fatigue.

"Morning, James," he mumbled to his assistant.

"Good morning, Mister McCurren." The man eyed him suspiciously, prompting Seamus to raise his brows.

"What?"

"Are you feeling well?"

"Why?" Seamus asked evasively.

"Your eyes?" His secretary pointed toward Seamus's face, making small circles with his index finger as he said,

"Are all . . . They look as though a sheet of glass is covering them."

"Just get me some coffee, will you?" Seamus's brogue was extracted by his irritation. But the man's brows were drawn together in concern and Seamus thought to ease his anxiety. "I'm just tired, James. I had a very late night last night."

The married father of five smiled, envying Seamus's bachelor lifestyle.

"I see." What his assistant saw, he had no notion, but the man must have thought Seamus needed reviving because he dashed out the door, saying, "I shall just go and retrieve a strong cup of coffee for you." His secretary was half way out the door when he stopped and turned, saying, "Oh, you've just received a report, and I've left it on your desk."

Seamus nodded, too tired to respond, and then opened the door to his large office and settled in his comfortable desk chair. He sighed heavily and reached for the report, leaning his chair back and propping his feet on the corner of his desk as he read.

The report was from the Naval Office, giving a detailed account of the sinking of a British supply frigate just west of Bordeaux. However, it was not the loss of the ship that landed this report upon his desk, but the manner in which the ship had been sunk.

The vessel had been ambushed, by all accounts, by three French ships which appeared to have been lying in wait in the port city of La Rochelle. And while this information could easily be disputed as a coincidental encounter, it was the attack within the two week time frame of the E anomaly appearing in the *Gazette* that made the attack suspect.

"Damn."

Seamus was rereading the report when James knocked on the inner office door.

"Yes," Seamus said, continuing to read.

However, when no coffee was produced his brows furrowed and he was just going to look up after finishing this last paragraph when Falcon said from the doorway, "Good morning."

Seamus dropped the front two legs of his chair to the floor as his head snapped round to meet the astute eyes of his employer.

"Morning," he greeted politely, but upon seeing a woman at the old man's side, Seamus dragged his boots off the abused desk and rose to his feet. "Good morning," he said to the lady and bowed with as much elegance as he had remaining, before he focused his attention on the small woman's face.

"May I introduce to you, Lady Pervill," Falcon offered.

"That is not necessary, my lord." The girl's astonishingly blue eyes met his as she held out her hand in his direction, adding, "Mister McCurren introduced himself three nights ago at the Spencer ball."

Seamus kissed the back of her hand, taking her bait . . . and a bit more. "Aye, but I'm astonished that you remember, Lady Pervill, as I recall you to be rather occupied at the time."

"Oh, no, speaking with my father never requires more than half of my mind," the lady said, calling him out.

Seamus hid his amusement behind a polite smile and offered to his guests, "Please, do have a seat."

The lady sat in Seamus's leather chair while the old man found a wooden chair tucked in the corner of the spacious office.

Falcon looked up at Seamus who remained standing and said, "Lady Pervill will be assisting the Foreign Office with our inquiries, and I have determined the best use of her skills would be in this department."

The thought of a woman running underfoot stiffened his smile, and Seamus stared at Falcon and then glanced at Lady Pervill. A knock at the door broke the awkward moment, and when James Habernathy entered with his coffee, Seamus could have embraced the man.

"That is a very generous offer, Lady Pervill. However, I already have a secretary. Thank you, James," Seamus said, overly appreciative as he took his warm cup of coffee from the man's dutiful hands.

Seamus took a long sip to prove his assistant's usefulness and Lady Pervill raised a brow and then turned, irritated, toward Falcon.

The old man rose, saying, "You may go, Mister Habernathy." When the door closed, Falcon's brandy colored eyes met his. "I'm afraid you are misunderstanding the situation entirely, Mister McCurren. Lady Pervill will not be your subordinate. She will be your colleague."

Seamus waited for the end of the jest, and when none came he laughed, saying in a thick brogue, "Pardon me?"

"I will be moving a second desk into this office and you will be working hand in hand with Lady Pervill to decipher French communiqués intercepted in Britain."

Seamus glanced at the woman glaring back at him and then turned to Falcon, "Perhaps, my lord, it might be more appropriate if we discuss this matter at another time."

"This matter is not up for discussion, Mister McCurren. You have done excellent work thus far, but you need help, and Lady Pervill is eminently qualified to provide you that much needed assistance."

"Or guidance." The lady smiled caustically, eliciting a turn of the head from the old man as he looked directly at her.

"Or guidance"—Falcon nodded—"in untangling this latest code. Lady Pervill has been briefed and her clearance is of equal status as your own."

It was a slap in the face and Seamus was set back on his heels. The petite woman made a great show of evaluating him from the tips of his boots to the top of his less than academically adequate head.

"Well," she said to Falcon as if Seamus was not standing in the middle of the bloody room. "It appears as though it will take a day or two for the man to adjust. I can certainly see why his intransigence of thinking might prove ineffectual in decoding French communications."

"Thankfully, we were fortunate enough to acquire your services, Lady Pervill," Falcon said with a nod of respect. "I shall have your desk ready by tomorrow morning and all pertinent papers will be awaiting you."

"Thank you, my lord." Lady Pervill rose and the two small people walked around Seamus as if he were a lamppost. "I shall look forward to working with you."

Falcon opened the door and the woman left without once glancing in Seamus's direction. No sooner had the door to his office closed than did he voice his protest.

"My lord, you can not be serious?"

"Oh, but I am, my boy. Lady Pervill will be working with you as of tomorrow."

"The lady is unqualified, not to mention impolite."

"The woman is brilliant, and you deserved every barb

she gave you." Falcon gave him the full force of his author-ity, saying, "My decision is final."

"Then at least put her in her own office."

"It is more beneficial for the Foreign Office if two scholarly heads are put together." Falcon opened the door and smiled, his yellowing teeth hidden by what Seamus thought to be amusement. "Beside, I don't have another of-fice to put the lady in. Good day, Mister McCurren."

Seamus McCurren arrived in his office at precisely half passed eight the following morning.

He had come at such an ungodly hour to ensure that the location of the desk provided the inconvenient Lady Juliet Pervill was placed where he wished it to be.

Well, that was not entirely accurate, for he wished it to be located in the corridor. But if he was to be shackled with the woman then he would damn well position her desk as far away from him as was possible.

"Good morning, James." His secretary glanced up from his desk, clearly stunned to see Seamus arriving so early in the morning. Seamus ignored the man's surprise, opening the inner office door as he asked, "A cup of coffee if you ple—"

His request was cut off by the sight of Juliet Pervill sit-ting behind a small desk which had been placed in front of the office window. Her chestnut hair was twisted in a se-vere chignon at the back of her neck and she wore a gown that made her skin turn as drab as the gray color.

The lass glanced up and nodded politely toward Seamus while speaking to James Habernathy. "Have you located the documents I requested?"

"Uh." Mister Habernathy looked toward Seamus for as-sistance. "No, ma'am. I was just on my way to prepare Mister McCurren's morning coffee."

Seamus raised a triumphant brow and acknowledged the woman's presence. "Good morning, Lady Pervill." Then making clear that James was his secretary, said, "Black would be fine."

The lady's light blue eyes flashed and she set her gaze on Seamus. "Surely, this late in the day Mister McCurren is in no need of refreshing?" Then her eyes pierced his discomfited secretary. "And do you not think it more urgent, Mister Habernathy, that our office deals with the security of this country before the comforts of its occupants?"

James paled and Seamus took pity on the poor man. "You may retrieve my coffee when you have finished gathering the documents so"—he turned his head and met the woman's unflinching gaze—"*urgently* needed by Lady Pervill."

"Yes, my lord," James said, leaving before the lady had an opportunity to take a second bite.

Seamus took a step toward his desk which faced the wall opposite hers when the lass asked with a raised brow, "My lord?" She pretended to mull the title over in her mind. "I'd no idea that you held a title," she said, knowing full well that he was the DunDonell spare.

Annoyed, Seamus sat in his chair and turned to face the bothersome woman.

"It is a courtesy title." She smiled and he added, "Rather like yours, *Lady* Pervill," before politely turning his back on the lady that behaved otherwise.

"Would you be so kind as to tell me, *Mister* McCurren," she began, having caught his slight. "The details of the discovery of this code?"

Hackles raised, Seamus lifted his head and spoke over his right shoulder. "As his lordship has no doubt told you, the anomaly appeared in three publications which—"

"Means the mathematical probability of a consistent printing error is highly unlikely," she finished, reading his mind. "Yes, I agree."

"I am so pleased our conclusions meet with your approval," he said, picking up a new report in need of analysis.

Seamus had not even read half the page when he saw the tiny woman standing beside his overcrowded desk. "And you have found no pattern in these articles?"

Seamus sighed and looked up at the lass, her dusting of freckles more visible as she stared down at him.

"No."

"And you have found four anomalies printed in three publications over the past two months?"

"Yes."

"May I see them?" the lady asked, failing to take the hint.

Unaccustomed to having his findings questioned, Seamus looked into her clear eyes, holding her gaze. "There is no pattern in those articles, Lady Pervill."

"Nevertheless." The girl smiled. "I would like to read them."

Seamus handed her the clippings, knowing that she would find nothing.

"Do let me know your conclusions," he said, smiling before returning to the document on his desk and completely ignoring her.

The woman eventually wandered off and he heard not a peep from the opposite side of the room until James Habernathy returned to the office with a stack of newspapers and a laden luncheon tray, both of which he set on the lady's small desk.

"Lady Appleton sends luncheon with regards."

"Oh, how thoughtful of Lady Appleton," Lady Pervill said as though she had just been invited to tea. "Thank you so much for bringing it to me, Mister Habernathy."

"Not at all," James said with considerable pleasure, adding an overly reverent inclination of his head.

Annoyed at his secretary's lack of loyalty, Seamus continued to read while ignoring the subtle clanking of bone china. However, what he could not ignore were the delicious aromas wafting in his direction from the opposite side of the all too small room.

"Well"—he rose, his stomach suddenly very empty— "I'll just leave you to dine."

Seamus walked from the room and he could feel Lady Pervill's hostile gaze ushering him out of the office.

He closed the door, thinking that summarized the problem with the entire arrangement. How was he to concentrate on his work with Lady Pervill watching his every movement? The lass had not been there half a day and she was already distracting him from the critical work that needed to be done.

Seamus ate his midday meal alone at his club, all the while trying to decide how long he would wait before informing the old man that this forced partnership was unacceptable. A week? Yes, that would be enough time for him to assert that he had truly made an effort to work with Lady Pervill.

A week! God in heaven.

Seamus rolled his eyes as he wandered back to his office, his steps increasingly languid. He eventually opened the outer office door but James was no where to be found. He placed his hand on the knob of the inner office door and took a deep breath, opening it. However, he was startled to find Lady Pervill not at her desk, but on her hands and knees with multiple newspapers spread across the dingy wooden floor.

The woman looked up excitedly and opened her mouth to speak. But upon seeing Seamus, she closed it and looked down at the papers again. He watched her glancing from one page to another, her large blue eyes growing wider as she read.

Then he heard the office door opening and the old man stepped passed Seamus with James Habernathy at his heels.

"Well?" Falcon asked.

Lady Pervill jumped up and smiled like a child bursting with a newly discovered secret. "I've found something."

SAMANTHA SAXON

The Lady Lies

Lady Celeste Rivenhall lives a double life;
she's a British agent posing as a French spy.
The Lord Aiden Duhearst is delivered into her
hands as a prisoner of war—and she will risk
anything to save him. Anything but the truth.

0-425-20358-1

"A riveting must-read. brimming
with vibrant characters.
Saxon's talent is amazing!"
—Virginia Henley

Available wherever books are sold or at
penguin.com

B094